BOOKS BY TIM MCBAIN & L.T. VARGUS

The Violet Darger series

The Victor Loshak series

The Charlotte Winters series

The Scattered and the Dead series

Casting Shadows Everywhere

The Clowns

COUPLE KILLER

a Violet Darger novel

L.T. VARGUS & TIM MCBAIN

SMARMY PRESS

COUPLE KILLER

PROLOGUE

The blood gleams on the sidewalk. A patch of red wetness about the size of a silver dollar.

Brian stops and stares at it. Head angled so that his chin almost touches his chest. Shallow breaths billowing in and out of his nostrils.

Blood?

Even partially lit in the streetlight's glow, the pool looks dark on the concrete — like a puddle of chocolate syrup — but it glints red where the light reflects from it.

Definitely blood.

Could be fake, but... looks real enough.

He surveys the empty street around him. Scans up and down the block for any sign of life. Not sure if he wants someone else to be there or not.

There's no one. It's late. Coming up on 2 A.M., he thinks.

Brian is drunk. Shitfaced drunk. Vision blurry. Legs a little wobbly.

It's rush week. Brian has just left an Asig party where he'd been forced to humiliate himself. Dropping on the ground and pretending to sizzle like bacon anytime one of the brothers shouted "oink." Anything to make the cut.

He'd guzzled down more than a dozen Bud Lights to try to dull the indignity — a hell of a lot of alcohol by his standards.

The walk home has been a bumpy affair to this point. His legs rickety beneath him. He had been about halfway back to the dorms, having just made a left onto Winchell, when he came upon the blood on the sidewalk and stopped in his tracks.

And now here he is. Standing still. Alone on an empty street.

He looks at the blood again. Really looks. Concentrating this time to make the drunk juddering of his vision smooth out.

He starts to trace his eyes down the cement path leading on from here, and a cold feeling creeps over him as he does.

There's more blood. Drops and smears and patches forming a dotted line over the sidewalk. The wet places sheening faintly under the orange of the streetlight.

A trail.

A trail of blood stretching out in both directions from where he stands.

Fresh.

A voice speaks just behind Brian's neck and makes him pogo straight up. His head cranks around to see who it is before he can process the words being spoken.

"What's crackin', preppie?"

The figure behind him — his roommate, Cody — recoils a little himself as Brian jumps. Staggers back a step and a half on drunken sea legs. Teeters.

"Whoa," Cody says. "Calm down, weirdo. Jesus Christ."

Cody extends his arms. Clutches Brian's shoulders to steady himself. His stupid sandals scuffing at the concrete. Spiked hair bouncing. Frosted tips glittering under the streetlight.

"Damn, preppie. You're jumpy as hell tonight. Even more spastic than usual."

He calls Brian "preppie." Makes no sense to Brian. Cody himself couldn't be preppier.

Cody is a business major, and like all business majors Brian has met, he's a total bro. Polo shirt. Puka shell necklace. Tribal tattoos. Basketball shorts year-round.

And those goddamn flip-flops always snapping against the

bottoms of his dumb feet.

The bro fishes a pack of Marlboros out of his pocket. Lights one up. His face glows a deep orange as the lighter's flame flickers beneath it.

Cody goes to Color Me Tan pretty much every weekend. Sprawls in a tanning bed. Bakes his skin to a deep hot dog shade somewhere between bronze and burgundy. He's always asking Brian to go.

But all of Cody's primping seems alien to Brian's sense of style — strictly casual. T-shirts. Jeans. An English major.

"Seriously, though. Why are you standing here like a lobotomy case, homie?"

Cody refers to them as "friends." "Homies." Sometimes "boys." A couple times he even called Brian his "main dawg."

Brian strictly uses the term "roommates" to describe the relationship.

Now that they're both rushing Alpha Sig, though, maybe they could be allies, Brian thinks. Maybe.

"There's blood," Brian says, regretting it even as the words leave his mouth. Stupid.

"There's… blood?" Cody says.

"On the ground."

Cody stumbles forward. Looks at the spot on the sidewalk. Bends at the waist to get a closer look. Head leaned forward, eyes squinted to slits.

Finally, he gets down on hands and knees. Practically sticks the tip of his nose into the red pool. Then he jerks himself up onto his knees. Twirls to look at Brian. Points two copper-toned index fingers at the bloodstain.

"Dude! This right here! Do you *know* what this is?"

Brian blinks before he answers.

"Uh… blood."

"No shit. But it's gotta be part of the hazing thing, man! You know it is. They knew a bunch of us would have to walk this way to get from the Asig house back to the dorms tonight, dude. Perfect setup."

When Brian doesn't say anything, Cody goes on.

"It's like a scavenger hunt. We've gotta follow this blood trail. See where it takes us, right?"

Brian blinks again. Tries to process this.

"Mm… I don't know."

"It's like a test of courage, kinda. If we bitch out, it's… like… bad."

"It's just… Shit looks pretty real to me."

"Don't be a pussy, Brian. We've talked about that, haven't we? How you're a giant gaping vag all the time, and no one likes it?" Cody says, getting to his feet. "Come on."

To Brian's chagrin, this actually *is* something Cody has talked about numerous times. His roommate offers up a kind of bro wisdom, always telling Brian that being a coward is what drags him down, especially with girls. Maybe the tan idiot is even right about that last part — Cody certainly has more luck with the ladies than Brian does.

Still, no one would believe how many times the term "giant gaping vag" has come up between them in the time they've lived together. It's been… excessive.

Brian thinks about asking which way they should follow the trail, since it leads both ways from where they stand. Instead he falls in behind Cody, who has already begun tracking the blood splotches heading toward campus and their dorm room — that's probably for the best, anyway. Get this over with and go to bed.

They walk in silence. Both sets of eyes angling down toward the sidewalk.

Maybe Cody is right. Maybe it really is a hazing stunt. Still, Brian can't help but feel slightly queasy as they draw closer to... wherever this leads.

He stumbles after Cody, and it occurs to him that the hazing rituals *have* gotten more creative of late. Ever since that freshman died during rush week a few years back, the frats have been forced to veer away from the strictly drinking-based antics.

The local news outlets plastered the kid's face everywhere for weeks in the wake of his death. Brian can still see the picture in his head even now.

A sad-looking kid. Bony. Something lonely in his eyes. Poor bastard.

The name pops into Brian's mind, unbidden. Devin Tait.

The guys in the TKE house had forced Tait to chug a fifth of Jim Beam in a half-hour or some shit. Acute alcohol poisoning. They said his face was black as a raven's wing when they found him dead in the arboretum the next morning. Face down in one of the gazebos.

These days the various fraternities seem to compete with one another to see who can concoct the most elaborate — and sometimes bizarre — initiation challenges. No more simple chug-a-lug. Wild rumors spread over campus, hinting at details to the outlandish rituals, but it's all technically "top secret."

The more Brian thinks about it, the more he has to admit that this whole blood trail scavenger hunt thing is plausible. Asig would do something like this.

Some poor kid dies, and now we gotta jump through all these crazy hoops and shit to get in.

Kinda fun, though.

It hits Brian that he feels drunker now. Spotting that first blood smear had shot adrenaline through his system, momentarily sobered him up a little. As the shock fades, he's back to staggering along.

Shit. That's no good. Especially with his roommate here to peer pressure him into bad ideas.

Cody mutters something that shakes Brian out of his introspection. Maybe a word. Maybe just a grunted syllable.

Brian follows his roommate's gaze to the lump in the distance. Lets his eyes refocus.

Swallows when he sees it.

The blood trail leads to a car. A Toyota Corolla with its trunk hanging wide open.

"See?" Cody says. "What'd I tell you? Does this not have Asig written all over it?"

"Maybe."

Brian still isn't sure. But he remembers seeing a few horror posters in some of the bedrooms at the Asig house, now that he thinks about it. A horror scavenger hunt could make sense. It wouldn't be a bad idea. Less degrading than some of the stuff he'd already done.

Cody picks up speed and Brian struggles to keep pace. They rush for the yawning trunk. Lean over the shadowy space.

More blood puddles on the scratchy black upholstery inside. Dark and thick. Looks like pools of hot fudge in the poor light.

Brian's breath catches in his throat. Head going light. He thinks he might faint.

"OK. I think I get it," Cody says. "This trunk is the starting point. Now we gotta see what's at the other end of the trail."

Brian cringes inside. Wants to go home already. Cody keeps talking.

"We can race back the way we came. Jog and shit. If we hustle, maybe we can still beat Simmons and his man servant."

Ted Simmons is another kid from their dorm rushing for Asig. One of those precocious rich kids who gets pretty much whatever he wants.

Brian doesn't often find common ground with Cody, but this is one thing they do agree on: Ted Simmons sucks ass. And Brian desperately wants to get into the frat over Ted and his minion, Tucker.

He shakes his head. Can't believe he's going to do this.

When Cody takes off running, Brian follows.

By the time they get back to that first blood swatch, Brian is sucking wind. Booze always kills his stamina. Not that he's into cardio in sober times.

They slow to a walk and trace along the red trail again. Moving away from campus and back toward town.

The businesses here have all gone dark for the night. Shadowy and vacant and still.

It's quiet. Eerie. Brian can't help but feel like they shouldn't be here. Almost feels like walking through a graveyard.

"Dude," Cody says.

He points a deeply tanned finger that looks like a wet cigar in the dark.

The blood veers off to the left of the sidewalk. An arcing angle of red dribbles that leads over a strip of grass and moves into a mini-mall parking lot.

They look at each other. Cody grinning. Brian terrified.

The blood looks glossy and black on the blacktop — viscous like patches of fresh motor oil. Brian traces the splotches to the middle of the empty lot. There's a bigger puddle of blood there. About the size of a dinner plate.

Without speaking, they rush to it. Kneel. Examine the sheening spot in silence — an imperfect bloody circle.

"Think this means anything?" Cody says.

Brian shrugs.

"That someone bled here. A lot."

But Cody is standing and pointing again. Not listening to Brian, which is actually pretty normal.

The trail leads away from the lamps over this shared parking lot. Tracks into a shadowed place.

And there's something dark lying on the front stoop of the Auto Zone.

An inert bulk. Dark.

It's a body, Brian thinks. Lying still.

Cody wheezes laughter between his teeth. Squishes it out of his nose.

"Oh shit. This is it. We got here first."

Brian feels his face flush. Molars grinding together.

"What if it's real?" he says, his voice low now. "Like just a, you know, badly injured guy. Mixed up in something… something dangerous. There are dudes running meth out here and shit, man. Bikers and shit. This is Michigan. I mean, Jesus, Cody. Everything here is meth-related."

Cody laughs again.

"It's not meth biker-related. That Toyota back there look like a Harley to you? It's a hazing prank, man."

Cody holds up his hands before he goes on.

"Think about it. If something actually, like, violent happened, there would have been noise. Screaming. Gunshots. Someone would have called the police. But there wasn't any of that, because it isn't real. This is a setup, man. It couldn't be more obvious. I bet you, like, a thousand dollars that when we walk over to that dude, he's gonna jump up and try to scare the shit out of us. It's *classic* Asig."

Brian shifts his weight from foot to foot, wishing he'd never spotted that blood on the sidewalk. If he'd just kept walking, he would be back in his room by now, passed out in his bed. Instead, he's stuck here with Cody. Feels like no matter what he chooses to do, he's going to end up looking like a dumbass or a pussy.

Cody keeps talking, which is also pretty normal.

"Shit, if we play this thing right, it could score major points with Trevor, man. All the Asig dudes, they'd know we're cool under pressure and shit. The unprankable lords of Brimley Hall."

"What?"

"Nothing. Just stay cool, Bri. Trust me. We go through with this, our acceptance is a slam dunk."

"OK, but what if it *is* real? Just, like… what if it's that two-percent chance or whatever. We're unarmed. I've never been in a fight in my life, and you have arms like two floppy tubes of Go-Gurt."

An annoyed snarl flashes over Cody's face.

"For the record, I bench like 150." His features soften slightly. "But I take your point. Better to be prepared."

Cody turns and scans the area. Walks over to a big tree on the edge of the lot. Grabs a thick branch from beneath it.

"This should do the trick." He does a practice swing. Makes a noise with his mouth like a hammered fastball. "If anyone tries to get froggy with us, I'll give 'em the Bryce Harper treatment."

They stand there a moment. Still some forty feet shy of the slumped body in the shadows.

Cody puts his finger in front of his lips and nose to shush Brian despite the fact that he hasn't made a peep this whole time. Brian glares at him.

They start forward — Cody, then Brian. Approaching slowly, quietly. Crossing the line into the murky area.

Warped versions of their silhouettes reflect in the dark glass at the front of the Auto Zone. Blurry copies of everything they do — even Cody's sick grin is visible in his mirror image. Makes Brian uncomfortable.

At about ten feet out, that smile falters some. Tan skin slowly closing over the bleach-white teeth.

Cody swallows hard, a lump bobbing visibly in his neck. He stops, and Brian stops alongside him.

Again, they wait. Listen. Brian's pulse thunders in his ears.

Cody points to Brian, then points at the body. Wags the tree branch and then rests it on his shoulder.

The implication is clear. *You check him. I'll cover you.*

Brian takes a breath. Closes his eyes. The fluorescent bulbs buzz behind them at the other end of the lot, glowing orbs which now seem miles away.

He stands there for several seconds. Thinking. Half trying to psych himself up. Half wondering why he's going to do this.

This was all Cody's dumb idea. If anyone should get close to this guy, it should be Cody.

But no. If Cody's right — if this *is* an Asig prank — he has to do this. He can't puss out now.

Finally he opens his eyes. Slides forward. Inches closer to the body.

His feet scuff, the soles of his shoes grinding against the blacktop. Sounds impossibly loud in the quiet. Each little piece of grit screeching out its own high-pitched scream.

The body is curled in a semi-fetal position, facing away from them. Head practically wedged against the bottom of the glass door. Even at five feet out, Brian can't see the facial features. Can't tell if it's someone he might recognize from Asig.

He watches for signs of breathing. Any expansion of the

ribcage. The vaguest twitch of the muscles there.

Nothing.

Shit.

And his vision zooms in on that fallen figure as he draws closer and closer. Details coming clear as he closes in.

Something in the body's shape tells him it's a man. The slightly scrawny build visible beneath the polo shirt. The hard angles of bone and muscle.

The body looks scrawny, more boyish than manly. Definitely doesn't look like any kind of meth biker.

When he's less than a foot away, he stoops. Reaches out a hand in slow motion. Fingers moving toward the neck.

To what? Check for a pulse?

No. He needs to see first.

His hand settles on that ball of muscle on the side of the shoulder. He rolls the boy — *is it a boy?* — onto his back. The body slumps over. A slack thing slapping against the concrete stoop, head coming down too hard and making that dull melon thud that always sounds wrong.

Dead weight.

Brian shuffles back a step like the thing might lurch at him. Feet scuffling again. Body rocking into some involuntary karate stance. Legs set all wide.

He takes several heaving breaths. Fists raised and shaking before him.

The kid doesn't move. His face looks as slack as the rest of him. Young. Maybe Brian's age or a couple years younger. Almost pretty-looking, like one of those boy band types. Mouth hanging open. A little blood visible on the teeth.

Is it…?

It's real. This has to be real.

After a second, a wavery voice whispers behind him.

"Is he… Is he dead?"

Brian doesn't look back. Shrugs.

His voice comes out flat and distant.

"I don't know."

He shuffles closer again. Kneels. Kneecaps digging into the gritty sand, into the cold asphalt.

He brings his hands to the neck at last. Fingers feeling along cold flesh. Finding the spot along the throat.

Nothing.

Wait.

There *is* something, he thinks.

The faintest tremor there?

Or is it his own adrenaline? His own blood knocking through him, confusing the issue.

He leans closer. Brings his face right down to the boy's mouth. Listens for any faint breathing sounds.

Nothing.

At first.

Then the boy gags and coughs.

A wet cough.

Neck bucking. Lips parting wider.

Blood flings out of his mouth. A quarter cup of viscous fluid shooting into the night.

A sheet of red slapping Brian's face.

CHAPTER 1

"Married?" Violet Darger repeated the word, not sure she'd heard Owen correctly the first time.

Owen's voice crackled out from the speaker on her phone. "That's what I said."

She let it sink in. Pictured the long white dress. The veil flowing down. The church pews packed with friends and family.

"Well, good for her," Darger said finally, nodding to herself.

"Good? My mother has barely known this guy for six months," Owen said. "Shoot. I only met him two days ago."

Darger put on her blinker and changed lanes to pass a semitruck with "Keep on Truckin'" mudflaps. She was about ninety minutes outside of Detroit, headed to the college town of Remington Hills to assist on a case.

"But you said Claude seemed like a good guy," she said, easing back into the right lane.

"That was before I knew he was planning on marrying my mother. I mean, don't you think six months is awfully fast to up and get hitched?"

"Maybe. But your mom isn't some naive 22-year-old. She's a smart lady."

Owen grunted something unintelligible and then went on. "I just don't see what the rush is. They already set a date for Christ's sake."

A large insect splatted onto the windshield, and Darger turned on the wipers. It took a deluge of wiper fluid to get rid of the smear, but after a few seconds, she'd cleared most of it.

"It's alright, though," Owen went on. "I have a plan."

"What's that?"

"I'm going to give him the Owen Baxter Special."

"I thought I was the only one that got the Owen Baxter Special."

"Ha. I'm talking about a background check. The full deep dive. I can guarantee you there's dirt on this guy, and I'm gonna find it. Once I show my mother who he really is, she'll have no choice but to call the whole thing off."

Darger caught a glimpse of herself wincing in the rearview mirror. She knew Constance Baxter well enough to know the woman wouldn't appreciate having her son meddling in her love life.

"Are you sure that's a good idea?" she asked.

"What do you mean?"

Darger chewed her lip, trying to figure out how to tell Owen to chill out without getting him more worked up.

"Your mom is a grown woman. She's more than capable of making decisions in her own life. And on some level, her love life isn't any of your business."

"Come on, Violet. Don't tell me you wouldn't do the same thing if it was your mother shacking up with some strange man."

She sighed.

"That might be true." She held up a finger even though Owen couldn't see her. "But I'd hope you'd be there to talk some sense into me."

"This guy obviously doesn't have good intentions," Owen said with a snort. "Otherwise he wouldn't be so hot to trot down the aisle. Piece of trash is probably after her money."

Darger frowned.

"I thought you said he was rich."

"That could just be part of the scam. He pretends he's some hotshot millionaire with a penthouse in Palm Beach, but in reality, he's in deep debt and looking for a sugar mama. I've seen it a hundred times."

It was Darger's turn to snort this time.

"Now you're just being ridiculous."

"Why is it ridiculous?" Owen asked. "For all I know, he's got a whole scheme mapped out. As soon as the ink on the marriage certificate is dry, he'll take out a life insurance policy in my mother's name. They'll fly down to Jamaica or somewhere for the honeymoon, and there'll be a tragic scuba diving accident."

"Oh boy," Darger said. "Owen — and I say this with all the love in the world — you're talking crazy right now."

"How am I crazy? You admitted yourself that this is all happening too fast."

"That's not exactly what I said."

Darger realized her current approach wasn't working. She remembered a technique one of her college psych instructors had taught her for dealing with patients in a clinical setting.

"Logic and rationale don't always work," Dr. Mazar had explained. "Especially not with a patient in crisis. It is sometimes better to take a practical angle. Show the patient how your suggestions will benefit them."

Darger listened as Owen continued on his rant against his mother's new fiancé.

"You can't expect me to just sit on my hands and allow this to happen. Not when my gut is telling me this whole thing smells bad enough to gag a maggot."

"I get it," she said. "And I'm not saying you shouldn't do anything. But might I suggest you try to be discreet about it? If either your mother or her fiancé find out you're poking around in his affairs, they're not going to be happy."

"So what?"

"If he's as evil as you suspect he is, don't you think you'd benefit from the element of surprise?"

"I guess so." There was a pause on the line. "But I'm always discreet. That's part of the job."

"I'm only suggesting you do this quietly. And thoroughly. Get the full picture before you go running to your mother with his tax returns and whatever else you dig up."

"Tax returns. Good idea," Owen said.

Darger rolled her eyes. She could only hope that this irrational suspicion would fade over time. The news of his mother's engagement had obviously given him a shock. Maybe he'd cool off once he had a chance to get used to the idea.

"Anyway, I'm gonna let you go so I can get to work on this. The clock's a-tickin'."

"OK," Darger said. "Just… remember what I said?"

"Sure, sure. Tax returns. Oh… and discretion." She could hear the impatience in Owen's voice. "We'll talk later?"

"Yeah. Bye now."

Darger ended the call, shaking her head. Owen's fervor was somewhat unexpected. He was usually so laid back and nonjudgmental.

Then again, his mother was really the only family he had left. He was estranged from his father, and his twin brother had been killed a few years ago. It made sense that he'd be protective of the sole survivor of his immediate family, but there was such a thing as being overprotective.

Darger spotted the sign for Remington Hills and SMU. A moment later, the robotic voice of the GPS system on her phone told her to take the next exit.

She inhaled deeply through her nose and then heaved the

air from her lungs. She could worry more about Owen and his mother later. She was almost to her destination, and that meant it was time to get her head in the game.

She ran through what she knew about the case so far. Three dead couples. The first had occurred in the neighboring town of Delphi. The two most recent attacks happened practically on campus, less than a week apart.

The killer targeted couples in cars, not unlike David Berkowitz or the Zodiac Killer. With no witnesses, they had to piece together exactly what happened based on the gory crime scenes. The working theory — he incapacitated the male victim first, binding his hands and forcing him into the trunk. Then he'd sexually assault the female victim. The killer's final act was to shoot both victims in the head, first the woman and then the man.

The male victim in the most recent case had lived long enough to crawl away from the scene. A couple of freshman students found him draped over the front walk of an Auto Zone, barely clinging to life. He'd died before the paramedics arrived, not even twelve hours ago.

Darger steered her rental car down the exit ramp and took a right turn, passing by a gas station and a McDonald's. Those two types of buildings had been the only ones she'd seen for the past half an hour. Dense woods periodically interrupted by the glow of the golden arches or a truck stop sign advertising fuel prices.

And the trees only seemed to thicken now that she was off the interstate. Clusters of overgrown sumac and sassafras crowded the shoulder, and huge oaken boughs stretched over the road as if reaching for the cars down below. Even in broad daylight, the woods seemed somehow threatening.

She'd read once that human beings had a primordial

distaste for such spaces. The species much preferred flatlands and prairies dating all the way back to the time of the Neanderthals. The woods closed off one's field of view. Something claustrophobic in it. Humans universally found joy in having a clear view of the horizon in all directions, soothed by some ancient desire to be able to identify potential threats from a distance.

Staring out at the twisting ivy and clumps of ferns clogging the places between the trees, at the perpetual twilight beneath the canopy, Darger could understand it. Who knew what dangers might lurk in the dark of the forest?

But the real danger here in Remington Hills hadn't come crawling out of the dark, dark woods. Forget lions and tigers and bears, oh my. This was a predator that walked upright, stalking its prey on two legs.

Ten minutes down the road, Darger spotted the first signs that she had entered SMU country. The first was a billboard for the SMU football team that said, "Beat The Ravens? Nevermore!" A few seconds later, she spied a flag on someone's porch that read "Go SMU!" in the school colors of purple and green.

She rounded a bend and the seemingly impenetrable woodland suddenly opened up to reveal the small town of Remington Hills. A looming Wal-Mart sign marked the beginning of the urban sprawl, followed by a hospital that faced off with a row of strip mall standards: a nail salon, a Chinese restaurant, Biggby Coffee, Pizza Hut.

The GPS instructed her to turn left at the next intersection. She did so, rolling by a bowling alley and movie theater. Every fast-food joint imaginable thrust its glowing sign out over the streetside. Lots of yellow and red signage offering everything the people in a small Midwestern town might want.

The car juddered as the tires rumbled over a bridge, where a sign marked the waterway below as the Muktypoke River. Up ahead, the steeple and bell tower of a church rose above the buildings and trees, a white lance jabbing its point into the sky.

As Darger traveled closer to the university district, the foot traffic grew heavier. Bodies dotting the sidewalk in thicker and thicker blobs. By the time she reached the first of the residence halls, fresh-faced coeds streamed everywhere. Flowing. Milling. Clogging the sidewalks and rectangles of lawn in front of the buildings.

Darger glanced out at them through the windshield. Backpacks slung over shoulders. Books clutched to chests. They all looked impossibly young to her.

She remembered returning to her alma mater just after she'd turned thirty and thinking that all the kids looked about sixteen years old. Now she swore they all looked about twelve.

Children, she thought. *They all look like children.*

And now a killer stalked them night after night. Taking them down in twos.

CHAPTER 2

Darger drove through one of the student residential areas on her way to the most recent crime scene. Oaks and maples bordered the asphalt, and beyond them, the street was lined with large older houses that had been sliced and diced into apartment units to accommodate the ever-growing student body. Her first apartment had been on a street not unlike these.

If Darger squinted hard enough, she could almost see these homes as they once were — stately and impressive. Back in the late 1800s and early 1900s, they would have been marvels of craftsmanship, every ornate detail executed with precision and care.

But most had fallen into various states of disrepair as the decades rolled on. Peeling paint. Moss-covered shingles on the roofs. Missing shutters. Crumbling front steps. One house had some sort of hydraulic jack supporting the roof over the front porch to keep it from caving in.

The houses thinned as she rolled closer to a part of town that seemed to be a mix of industrial and commercial. She passed a convenience store, a Little Caesar's, a sports bar, and a warehouse with a "For Sale" sign out front. Across the street, a place offered payday loans via big black letters on its red awning.

The flap of the yellow crime scene tape caught Darger's eye as soon as she turned onto Vine Street. At the center of the cordoned-off area, a bunny-suited crime scene tech circled a newer model Corolla with a camera, snapping photos.

Darger parked behind a row of law enforcement vehicles

and climbed out, studying her surroundings for a few seconds as a breeze tossed strands of her hair around her face.

The street felt more like an alleyway, with all the backs of the surrounding businesses facing this way — brickwork and dumpsters and hulking air conditioner units set like chess pieces atop pocked asphalt. No houses sat in the immediate vicinity, and a significant portion of the block was surrounded by a chain-link fence that isolated an active construction site — grooved concrete walls rose from the ground in what looked like the early stages of a parking garage to Darger.

Late at night, when the attack occurred, this section of street would likely have been completely deserted even though it was technically part of the school's grounds — only a mile or two from the heart of campus. No wonder they hadn't found any eyewitnesses.

Darger spotted Loshak up ahead, talking to two men in SMU Police uniforms. One of the men sported the standard-issue crew cut and cop mustache. The other was clean-shaven and wore glasses. Both men looked fresh-faced. Almost as young as the coeds she'd seen crawling all over campus.

Loshak turned as she approached.

"Agent Darger," he said by way of greeting. "Fine weather to investigate a heinous crime, no?"

She could see a smile flitting around the corner of his eyes. He always seemed like something very clever was occurring to him.

Loshak introduced Darger to the two officers standing with him.

Crew Cut's name was Kirby, and his handshake was obnoxiously forceful, as though he thought he was proving something by trying to crush her metacarpals. The officer wearing glasses — Dixon — had a more gentle handshake, thankfully.

Kirby's jaw moved up and down at a near-constant pace, working diligently on a piece of gum. Darger could smell the artificial watermelon flavor from several feet away, and the scent took her straight back to seventh grade. Probably the last time she'd chewed something as cloying as that. She wondered how Kirby could stand it.

"It's pretty wild to have the FBI here," Kirby said. "Me and Dicks-n-balls here were just tellin' your partner the same. Feels like something out of a movie."

The chatter continued, but Darger's attention was drawn to the scene. Just a few yards away, one of the CSIs squatted in the road, dusting the rear door handle on the Corolla for fingerprints.

"You guys are free to look around," Dixon said. "But if you want to go inside the taped-off areas, you'll have to suit up."

"I'm fine staying outside the tape," Darger said.

She could see well enough from outside the barrier. Plus, the techs occupied most of the space inside the cordoned-off zone, and the last thing she wanted to do was get in their way.

She crept closer to the trunk of the Corolla, which still hung open like a gaping mouth. It was empty and clean except for a dark puddle on one side. Blood. It had begun to coagulate, with a mottled brown skin forming on top that reminded Darger of some kind of soup.

The men gathered around the trunk with her, and the four of them stared down at the gummy stain for several seconds without speaking.

"We recovered a nine-millimeter casing from the trunk," Dixon said, finally breaking the silence. "Probably the bullet that killed Kyle Herbert, though not instantly, obviously. All of the five other victims were shot twice in the head. Herbert only took one bullet. We're thinking that something spooked the killer — passing traffic or something — and he ran off after the first shot."

Darger nodded silently, watching the tech pull a set of prints from the door handle. The woman mounted the lifting tape to a white card and handed it off to another tech, who logged and labeled the prints. The first tech swung the rear door open, raised her brush, and began swiping bichromatic powder over the inside of the door, focusing much of her attention on the window and latch areas.

Darger moved around to the side of the car to get a look inside now that the door was open. Her stomach turned at what she saw. The far end of the bench seat was spattered with blood droplets and flecks of gloopy tissue — brain matter?

Darger knew from the crime scene photos that this was where Layla Perlman had been shot. Dark smears of the girl's blood marred the cream-colored synthetic leather upholstery. The stains appeared nearly black where they had soaked into the floor mat.

Aside from the bloodstains, little else occupied the backseat. No clutter. No mess. No stray French fries or crumpled Starbucks receipts like the floor of her own car. Inside and out, the car was very clean. Like new, despite being several years old.

She squinted into the front seat and saw it was the same. Not a speck of dust. No smears on the windows or windshield. Darger's defroster was on the fritz, and she was forever clearing away fog with her hands, leaving smudges on the glass. The only foreign object in this car was an orange SMU parking pass stuck to the bottom corner of the windshield and a cell phone mount jutting out of the dash.

"Do we know anything about what the victims were doing

last night before the attack?" Darger asked.

Dixon nodded.

"Earlier in the evening — around 1900 hours — they went bowling across town with another couple. From the bowling alley, they came over here to hang out at Macbeth's pub. That was at approximately 2100 hours."

He gestured down the street to one of the squat brick buildings Darger had seen on her drive in.

"I guess it's a regular thing for them, and they stayed almost until last call at 2 A.M., according to the friends they were with. The other people in their group parked a few streets over, so they parted ways outside the bar."

Darger tried to imagine this spot late at night. Dark and isolated. She swiveled her head to face the construction area, noticing how the fence came within two feet of the next building. If the killer had tucked himself back in that gap, he could have lain in wait for a pair of victims to wander along, completely out of sight of anyone on the street.

She imagined him nestled there. The dark shrouding him. Watching as the unlucky couple approached their car. Marking them for death without them ever knowing until it was too late.

"Do we know anything about how he approaches his victims? Does he wait until they're in the car, or does he approach them when they're still outside?"

"Good question. Keys were in the ignition when we arrived on the scene, so I'd think the victims were in the car."

Darger noticed a trail of yellow evidence markers extending away from the car and down the street, forming a crooked path that eventually veered into a parking lot just barely visible from where she stood.

"This is the path Kyle Herbert took after he escaped from the trunk?" she asked.

Kirby nodded.

"Yeah. There's a pretty clear blood trail from the trunk over to where he was found."

He adjusted the aviators over his eyes.

"From the looks of it, the guy was just gushing blood the whole way."

Darger followed the string of tent-shaped markers, the big bold numbers printed on them growing higher as she moved away from the car. Kirby was right about the amount of blood. Herbert must have been hemorrhaging as he ran from the car. Darger wondered if he'd even been fully cognizant or if he'd been in some kind of shocked survival mode, his legs moving of their own volition in a desperate attempt to seek help.

She and Loshak reached the parking lot in front of the strip mall, which had also been blocked off with tape. There were no techs here at the moment, which made sense. The killer was most likely to have left evidence in and around the car.

Another sticky-looking patch of blood stained the concrete just in front of the Auto Zone. Darger had seen the photos and knew this was where the two students had found Herbert.

Even half-conscious, Kyle Herbert must have been terrified as he lay there bleeding out, knowing that Layla Perlman was already dead and that he would likely soon join her.

Darger ran through the file in her head again. No fingerprints aside from those of the victims. No semen found on the female victims. But there *had* been trace amounts of spermicide and condom lubricant on the first two. She assumed the same would be true for this third woman.

Her heel scraped against the cement as she whirled to face Loshak.

"Have you heard about this forensic chemist at the University of Central Florida? The one who's creating a database of the chemical makeup of condom residues for use in processing rape cases," Darger said. "We should get in touch with her."

Loshak pointed at her.

"That's a good idea. Figuring out what type of condom he's using doesn't quite narrow the suspect list down the way a DNA profile would, but it's better than nothing."

The two policemen had caught up with them by then, and Kirby lifted the sunglasses from his eyes to peer at them.

"You mean you haven't heard?" Kirby smacked the side of his head. "Shit, that's right. It's not in the report on account of the Chief wanting to keep a tight lid on it for now."

"What's not in the report?" Darger asked.

Kirby licked his lips.

"Well… not to get all technical with my forensic jargon, but we got a *shitload* of trace evidence this time around," the big cop explained. "A water bottle, a cigarette butt, and a chewed-up piece of gum in a foil wrapper. All of it strewn about the backseat. Right where we think the rape took place."

"What makes you think these items didn't belong to the victims?" Loshak asked.

"You saw the car, right? It was immaculate. Kyle Herbert was a bit of a neat freak according to his friends. A germophobe and all that. Also, neither victim smoked, so we know for a fact the cig ain't from either of them. The other thing the vic's friends told us was that there's no way he'd let someone smoke in his car. So… who else but the killer?"

Kirby hiked up his pants and nodded. Smiled a funny smile for just a second. Then he went on.

"Dude blew it. We're thinkin' that one way or another, something interrupted the killer while he was at work, and he not only failed to put the second bullet in Herbert's head, but he also left all this stuff behind. Stuff he would normally clean up, you know? Big mistake. Could be the big break in the case. I mean, hopefully."

"The crime lab up in Lansing is expediting all the DNA evidence," Dixon added, crossing his thin arms over his chest. "We should have something as soon as tonight."

Darger blinked, almost not believing what she was hearing. Three pieces of evidence that should yield DNA? They rarely got this lucky.

"That's excellent," Loshak said.

"Yeah," she agreed.

Her heart thudded over the prospect of having a DNA profile on the killer so soon. Hard evidence for once.

The overly practical part of her brain reminded her not to get too excited. Even if they did get a profile, they still had to match it to someone. If their guy didn't have a profile already on file, seeking him out would still be like searching for a needle in a haystack.

Still… it was something.

CHAPTER 3

Darger stepped away from the crime scene. Away from the puddle of congealed blood.

Somewhere in the distance, she smelled burning leaves. People must still do that here. It made her think of fall when she was a kid. Corn mazes and hayrides and bobbing for apples.

Flitting white blotches drew her eyes back down the street, where the techs still hovered around the Corolla like ghosts in their pale jumpsuits. But she barely saw them. Her mind wriggled inside the file once more, flipping pages and recalling photos of the crime scenes.

She pictured Layla Perlman sprawled in the backseat, naked from the waist down, an exit wound on the back of her head the size of a grapefruit. Blood everywhere. Her mouth still frozen in a grimace.

It had been the same with the other two female victims. Found dead of gunshot wounds in the backseat of the vehicle. Sexually assaulted.

The attacks had been almost identical to one another, all the little details lining up just so. She supposed it was possible that he was reenacting how the first one had gone, but her gut said this had all been calculated from the beginning. Forcing the man into the trunk at gunpoint. Assaulting the woman. Extending the suffering. Then killing them both. He'd thought this out. Done it this way on purpose. It was too precise. Too… mechanical.

So far, Kyle Herbert nearly escaping was the only outlier in the three cases. The only deviation from the agenda.

And the fact that the killer had apparently left behind multiple pieces of trace evidence in his rush to flee the scene. She wondered what had caused him to stray from his carefully crafted procedure.

Darger heard the scuff of feet on the cement and turned to find her partner approaching.

"Have you seen much of campus yet?" Loshak asked.

"Only what I saw on the drive in."

"It's got that midsized Midwestern college town vibe," he said.

Darger tried to suppress a smirk at the word "vibe," lest Loshak think she was making fun of him.

"Feels smaller than it is, you know?" he went on. "Of course, that's probably in part because the population is what you might call 'artificially inflated' by the student population. Remington Hills is a town of about 75,000 during the fall and winter semesters, but that dwindles down to under 50,000 in the summers. Bet it's pretty quiet from May to September. If it weren't for the college, this would be just a dot on the map in the middle of South Michigan."

"It is interesting how much a college town feels like a college town," Darger said, nodding. "This place reminds me a lot like where I went to school."

She snuck a peek at the two officers standing a few yards away.

"What kind of impression did you get from the locals?" she asked, her voice low. "Friend or foe?"

"Well, Chief Fleming was quick to admit that they were in over their heads. So I think *friend*. Though you know as well as I do that it always tends to be somewhat of a mixed bag."

A half-snort escaped Darger's nose.

"That's for sure."

Loshak gasped then, swiveling to face her more directly.

"Did you see Merle?"

"Who?"

"Merle the Mastodon! A few years back they found an almost fully intact mastodon fossil just outside of town. Some farmer was breaking ground for a new silo and dug up a tusk. Can you imagine that?" Loshak's eyes twinkled. "The actual bones are on display at the Smithsonian now, but there's a statue of Merle outside the university library. He's considered a good luck charm by the locals. There's a spot on his trunk where all the patina is rubbed off from people trying to soak up some of the good fortune."

"So you're saying we should go collect our allotment of good luck from this woolly mammoth in hopes it'll help us solve this case?" Darger asked.

"Merle is a mastodon, Darger. Not a woolly mammoth."

"What's the difference?"

"Mastodons are smaller, and their tusks are straighter. They were also wood browsers, whereas the mammoths ate grass. So the teeth of the two beasts are radically different."

Darger almost asked what the hell a wood browser was before deciding she didn't really need to know.

"I didn't realize you were such an archeology buff."

"I'm not." He shrugged. "Not really. But I always look into the local history of a new place. You never know what might end up being relevant to the case."

"Oh sure. No doubt all those mastodon and mammoth facts will prove invaluable to our investigation," Darger said.

Loshak narrowed his eyes.

"If you're going to take that kind of scornful tone, then I'm not sure I'll be sharing the juiciest nugget of local culture with you."

Darger rolled her eyes.

"Oh come on. I was only teasing."

Pressing his mouth into a thin line, Loshak crossed his arms.

"I don't know. Your attitude in regards to local lore has thus far been very poor."

"I'm sorry. Really."

Loshak unpursed his lips and leaned in, too excited to withhold the information any longer.

"Aliens!"

Darger blinked.

"Aliens?"

"Back in the 80s, there was a whole slew of UFO sightings. There's a documentary about it. Three separate families all have the same story about seeing these lights in the sky, and then waking up somewhere else, with several hours unaccounted for. All in the same night, right around the same time. Their accounts are remarkably consistent."

"Which in our field is often a sign of it being rehearsed," Darger pointed out.

Loshak waved her off.

"It's fine. You can act cool and smug with your doubt all you want. I know at least *one* person who will appreciate it."

"Who?"

"Spinks."

"Ah yes. Spinks and his conspiracy theories."

"Hey, the federal government has now confirmed the existence of UFOs. It's not really a conspiracy theory at this point."

Loshak glanced around the scene. Adjusted his aviators.

"Anyway, I think I'm all set here. How about you?"

Darger's gaze wandered to the orange cones surrounding the place where Kyle Herbert had taken his last breaths.

"Yeah, I'm good. What do you think about talking to the kids that stumbled upon this scene last night?"

Loshak slipped his sunglasses on, a smirk dancing around the corners of his mouth.

"One step ahead of you. I've already set up the interview."

CHAPTER 4

Officer Dixon offered to escort Darger and Loshak over to the residence hall in question, and the agents accepted, tailing his cruiser through winding campus streets choked with pedestrians.

Dixon bypassed the small parking lot next to the residence hall, pulling instead into the fire lane directly outside the front door. Darger and Loshak followed suit. Darger was just pulling the key from the ignition when Dixon appeared at her window.

She opened the door and he handed her a laminated parking pass stamped with the SMU PD logo and large block letters that read, "OFFICIAL USE ONLY — DO NOT TOW."

"Parking is a real bitch on campus, so in the event you have to illegally park somewhere, just stick this on your windshield, and hopefully you won't get towed."

"Hopefully?" Loshak said.

Dixon shrugged.

"If you *do* get towed, you'll end up in our impound lot, so just come by the station, and we'll straighten it out."

Darger studied the front of the building as they approached the doors out front. It wasn't much to look at. A massive cube of concrete and brick.

Dixon held the door open for them, and they passed inside. The dimly lit lobby smelled like lime-flavored Skittles. Darger paused, allowing her eyes to adjust to the shady interior.

Institutional beige lacquered every flat surface inside the building. Smeared on the walls. Varnished into the floors and countertops. Even upholstered in a rough weave on the waiting-room-style furniture huddled before a TV off in one corner.

To Darger's right, a large bulletin board covered much of the wall. Posters and leaflets papered the corkboard. A request for a ride to Columbus, Ohio, the weekend of October 12th. Information on a student film festival. A cautionary warning about date rape drugs. The colorful plastic nubs of pushpins protruded from all of the pages.

A table underneath the board held yet more stacks of pamphlets. Loshak snatched one titled, "The Sinister Truth About Plastics."

Dixon led them down a corridor to an elevator door. A sign posted on the flat aluminum surface of the door said, "OUT OF ORDER."

"Well shit. It's six flights of stairs up to the room," Dixon said, pointing to a stairwell just off the lobby. "Or we can call up to the room and have them come down here to talk."

Loshak slapped the pamphlet he'd picked up against his open palm.

"Better we talk to them on their own turf. The more comfortable they are, the more malleable."

They began the hike up the stairs, pausing on the third floor to catch their breaths. A girl breezed past them with a full laundry basket, feet bounding off the risers, seemingly unbothered by the endless climb. Darger tried to remember what it was like to have that kind of stamina.

"Jesus Christ!" Loshak said, his nose stuck in the pamphlet. "Listen to this: 'You may have heard of microplastics, which the U.S. NOAA defines as any piece of plastic less than five millimeters in length. But what you might not know is that the average American unknowingly ingests approximately 2,000 microplastic particles per week in their food and drink. That adds up to about five grams of microscopic plastic bits entering your system, the equivalent of the plastic needed to make a credit card, every week.'"

"Yum," Darger said as they took the next flight of stairs.

Loshak continued reading.

"'The numbers are worse for those who drink bottled water instead of tap. The average bottled-water drinker consumes an additional 90,000 microplastic particles per year compared to their tap-drinking counterparts.' Christ. I wonder what that is in credit cards. Like forty-five or something, right?"

They paused again when they reached the apex of their climb. Darger glanced out the sixth-floor windows and spied clusters of students on the lawn below. Some sitting in groups, others alone, with textbooks spread open in their laps.

Dixon pushed open a door off the stairwell, revealing a long, straight hallway with a series of doors on either side. As they entered the corridor, the radio clipped to his shoulder crackled and squawked. He reached up to adjust the volume down.

A kid with a shaved head peeked out into the hallway, sneering when he caught sight of them before disappearing back inside. A few moments later, "Dead Cops" by MDC blared out from the room. Darger noticed that a large anarchy symbol sticker had been pasted to the door.

When Darger realized what the song was screaming over and over, she blinked and turned to Dixon.

"That seems awfully hostile."

Dixon winced.

"Yeah, we get a lot of that on campus. Mostly 'cause of Kirby."

"What do you mean?"

Dixon stopped and put his hands on his hips.

"Well, there was a bit of an incident a while back. It was before I joined the department, so I don't have all the details, but Kirby was breaking up a party in the student ghetto — cheap housing in the Ivy Neighborhood just off campus — and got a little… overzealous with his nightstick."

"How overzealous?"

"Knocked out a kid's teeth."

Darger recoiled and placed a hand over her mouth in some empathetic pain response.

"Yikes."

"Yeah."

"And Kirby didn't get fired over that?"

Dixon shrugged.

"I guess the kid started it. Kirby had his back turned, and the kid came up behind him and gave him a good shove. Not that I'm justifying knocking a kid's teeth out, mind you. I think it took Kirby by surprise, and then he overreacted."

"Just a little," Loshak said.

"Anyway, there's a video that went sort of viral, at least locally. So even though the department cleared Kirby of any wrongdoing, the video has made the rounds, and the student population all know about the cop that fixed Jesse Horner's teeth. So he's not super popular around here."

Dixon shook his head. Pointed off toward another part of campus.

"Last fall, we were on duty for the annual SMU—CMU rivalry game. I was partnered with Kirby, and we had our car parked on fraternity row while we did some foot patrol. Someone spray painted a huge dick on the side of our patrol car. Kirby denied that it had anything to do with him, but there were four other cars out that night and none of *them* got tagged."

Dixon inclined his head toward one of the dorm room doors. There was a dry-erase board attached to the flat steel surface on which someone had scrawled, "Chicken noodle soup for the soul, buttrash!"

"This is it," he said and stepped back from the door. "It might be better for me to wait out here. They'll probably be more comfortable without a uniform in the room."

Considering what Dixon had just told them, Darger thought that was probably a good idea.

Loshak lifted his fist and rapped it against the door. Darger could hear music playing from inside, and when the door opened a crack it grew louder.

The gap widened further, revealing a scrawny nineteen-year-old in an SMU hoodie.

"Are you the, like, FBI people?" he asked, his eyebrows trying to crawl up his forehead to hide in his hair.

"I'm Agent Loshak, and this is my partner, Agent Darger."

"I'm Brian," he said. "It's, um, nice to meet you. Do you want to, like, come in?"

They entered the small room, and Darger took stock of her surroundings.

Two beds, both raised off the floor. One had a futon underneath, the other had two small desks arranged side by side.

Another boy, around the same age as Brian, sprawled on the futon. He wore a t-shirt with the words "BUY THE DIP" written across the chest in block letters, and he was fiddling with his phone. His skin was deeply tan as though he lived on the beach somewhere instead of rural Michigan.

"Cody, can you turn the music down?" Brian asked. "They're here."

Instead the music seemed to increase in volume. A hip hop

song with nakedly pornographic lyrics oozing out of the speakers. Brian whipped his head around.

"Cody!"

The kid affected a look of exaggerated ignorance.

"Huh?"

"Turn it down!" Brian repeated.

Cody grinned and pointed at his ears.

"I can't hear you."

Brian snatched the phone from Cody's hands and turned the music off completely.

Cody's grin faded.

"Hey!"

"I told you I don't like that song. It's not…" Brian glanced at Darger, "… appropriate… for mixed company, I mean. It's vulgar. Like… really vulgar."

Cody cackled.

"Whatever you say, Ben Shapiro. We're all adults here. We're all perfectly comfortable hearing a song talk about dripping wet pussies. Except for you. Now, why do you think that is?"

He stood and patted his friend's shoulder.

Brian's face went red. Lips curling at the corners. Eyelids opened all the way, quivering around the whites in a way that made him look like a frightened Pomeranian.

Darger stared at Cody's smug expression, remembering vaguely what it was like to be this age. To think she knew everything. To believe that every adult over the age of thirty was dim, uptight, and oblivious.

"We're all adults. That's right," Darger said with a nod. "Now, my partner and I would like to ask the two of you a few questions. If you're done discussing dripping wet pussy, that is."

Cody inhaled sharply and then shrieked with laughter.

Darger realized Loshak was staring at her, mouth agape. She shrugged at her partner and waited for Cody to compose himself.

When he had, Darger asked the boys to explain what they'd seen the previous night. Cody took the lead on answering.

"OK. We basically, like, followed this blood trail on the ground. We thought it was a frat… thing. Like a prank, kinda. Maybe. Anyway, the blood splotches led to a car — a Toyota, I think — with the trunk hanging open."

Darger nodded slowly.

"And did you look inside the car?"

"Just in the trunk, which was empty. 'Cept for some blood pools or whatever. We were preoccupied, right? I wanted to find out where the blood trail went, you know? I mean, we thought it was fake. The blood, you know," Cody said.

"We're both rushing for Alpha Sig," Brian explained. "Cody was convinced it was part of the haz— er… the like… uh… initiation, or whatever?"

"Jesus, bro. Just call it hazing. You think they care?"

Cody aimed a thumb at the two agents.

"The FBI's got bigger fish to fry than some frat in a tiny college town engaging in a little light hazing. They're trying to catch a vicious murderer."

"OK, but it's like… the initiation stuff is supposed to be top secret. Trevor was very clear about that," Brian whispered.

"I told you to quit taking everything so literally," Cody said, giving Brian a light shove. He then lipped some words that Darger couldn't make out possibly ending with "badge." Seemed more like a taunt than anything.

"What about the area around the car?" Loshak asked. "Did you see anyone else out on the street? Any cars idling nearby or anything like that?"

"Nothing like that," Cody said. "The street was pretty empty. I mean, it was late. I stay out late on the big party nights. Working."

"Working?"

Brian elbowed Cody and gave him a warning look.

"Will you fuckin' relax? I told you, they don't care about this small-time shit." Cody turned to face them again. "I sell cigarettes at parties. Loosies, you know? Dollar a piece. I net about thirteen bucks a pack, and I can usually sell at least two packs in a night. Four or five on a good night. That's almost a 200% ROI, by the way. Anyway, I always like to stay as late as possible to maximize profits. The later it is, the drunker my clientele. And the drunker they are, the more they buy. They just can't resist. It's the perfect product, really."

"How enterprising of you," Darger said.

"I'm a business major." Cody crossed his arms, looking smug. "All in all, it worked out pretty good for us."

"What did?"

"This whole thing. I mean, we're basically celebrities on campus. We'll get into Asig for sure now."

"Cody, God! Why would you…" Brian rubbed a hand over his forehead. "That's not cool, man."

"What?"

Brian's hands balled into fists at his sides.

"Two people are dead."

"No shit. But us *not* getting into Asig isn't going to bring them back, so…"

Cody quirked his shoulders into a shrug. Flashed another smile.

"It's not like I'm saying I'm glad they're dead. I'm just saying that if some good can come from this tragedy…"

Brian shook his head.

"Now what?" Cody asked.

"You're just… you're a real jackass sometimes, you know that?"

Cody only grinned.

"Did Kyle Herbert say anything when you found him? Was he conscious at all?"

The gleefulness drained from Cody's face finally, and he turned serious.

"No. Dude just coughed blood all over my man here," he said, aiming a thumb at his friend. "A significant amount of blood right in the face. Like *a lot* of blood."

Brian gave a solemn nod.

"I… I think I might have swallowed some of it."

Cody threw his head back and guffawed.

"Oh my god, dude! Why would you swallow it?"

"It was an accident," Brian said. "I didn't mean to."

"Well now you definitely need to get like three AIDS tests. For sure. You don't know where that guy has been. I mean, face down on concrete at the Auto Zone, you know that, but it doesn't exactly bode well for what else he was up to, does it?"

"Shut up," Brian said, scowling.

Cody blinked.

"No, I'm serious, dude. Like, I know I said it as a joke before, but think about it… I don't know how any of that shit works. There's no telling how many STDs you might catch from slurping down some random guy's blood."

Brian glared at Cody.

"Why do you always have to be such a dick?"

Hand to his chest, Cody blinked innocently.

"Wow. That's the kind of thanks I get for expressing concern over the well-being of my main dawg?"

"You're just constantly—"

The second half of Brian's sentence was interrupted by a sudden shout in the hallway.

All heads turned toward the open door.

CHAPTER 5

It was a female voice, raspy and accusatory.

"One, two, three, four! We won't take it anymore!"

Half a dozen other voices joined the first now.

"Two, four, six, eight! No more violence! No more rape!"

Darger could hear the rhythmic stomp of feet as the clamor drew closer. She stepped into the hallway and found Officer Dixon surrounded by a group of students shouting in unison. They were mostly female, but Darger spotted at least two young men among them.

"Yes means Yes! No means No! However we dress! Wherever we go!"

Dixon had his hands up in a placating gesture, and he raised his voice to be heard above the chanting.

"I understand you're upset, but this is not—"

A girl with short blue hair stuck her finger in Dixon's face.

"Enough with the doublespeak, Barney Fife. We want answers, and we want them now!"

Darger recognized her voice as the one that had led the chanting. She wore an olive drab military jacket and combat boots. The latter gave her a slight height advantage over Officer Dixon.

To his credit, he didn't shy back from the snarling blue-haired girl towering over him.

Darger and Loshak drew up on the group just as Dixon spoke up again.

"Obviously I can't discuss an ongoing investigation with you, but I assure you, we're doing all we can."

"Well, I'm sorry if that doesn't exactly reassure us when the SMU police force seems more interested in committing violence against their own students than catching rapists."

The girl raised her fist in the air and began another round of chanting.

"Hey hey! Ho ho! Sexual assault has got to go!"

The blue-haired girl stamped one booted foot in time with the cadence of the voices.

"Hey hey! Ho ho! Sexual assault has got to go!"

Again Dixon put his hands up.

"OK, I'm going to need you folks to calm down."

He sighed. Lowered his voice as he spoke to the blue-haired girl directly.

"Tobi, a dorm hallway really isn't the place for one of your impromptu rallies. Take it outside, will you?"

"Or what?" Tobi demanded, inching closer so that her face was less than half a foot from Dixon's. "What are you gonna do, huh? Knock my teeth out?"

Worried things were about to take an ugly turn, Darger stepped forward.

"What's going on here?" she asked.

Tobi's eyes locked on hers.

"Who are you?"

"My name is Violet Darger." She pulled her badge from her pocket. Unfolded it and held it up. "FBI."

"Oh thank Christ. The FBI will put a stop to this."

This comment came from a petite girl with a nose stud and cat-eye glasses standing to the right of Tobi.

Tobi scoffed.

"We'll see about that." She zeroed in on Darger. "Tell me, are you going to look into the fact that SMU has been actively covering up rapes on campus?"

Darger glanced at Dixon, who only offered a shrug.

"We're here to assist the local police in investigating the murders and associated crimes. Anything beyond that would be outside of our domain."

Tobi snapped her fingers and someone in the back of the crowd passed up a stack of papers. She shoved one of the fliers at Darger.

"It's all related. Before he was the Couple Killer, he was the Ski Mask Rapist. And before that, he was the Campus Flasher."

Darger's eye scanned the flier, which had dates and locations of the various crimes, as well as physical descriptions of the Ski Mask Rapist and the Campus Flasher.

"What makes you think it was the same perpetrator?"

"A tall guy with stooped shoulders committed all of the crimes, and the timeline matches up perfectly. A month after the last flashing incident, the string of ski mask rapes began, and just under three weeks after those stopped, the first of the car murders took place. Just look at the behavior. The evolution of his crimes is practically textbook."

The girl's eyes flicked up and down's Darger's face. Searching for something there.

She's trying to read me, my reaction.

Whatever she saw, Tobi crossed her arms over her chest before she went on.

"These murders didn't have to happen. Never should have happened. If the school had done their due diligence in the first place, he would have been caught long ago. Instead, the administration decided that preserving the school's reputation was more important. They've got their goon squad out to ensure it — campus cops performing amateur dentistry by way of nightstick. They're even censoring the student newspaper to keep a lid on the story."

"Now hold on, that wasn't about censorship," Dixon said. "It was a student safety concern. You were going to publish information that was critical to the investigation."

Tobi let out a laugh devoid of humor. Her eyes went hard in a way that reminded Darger of a snapping turtle.

"There was no investigation! This guy was spotted over a dozen times, detailed descriptions given, and yet where were the police sketches? Were they circulated among the student population? Posted online? Published in the newspapers? Shared with the local news stations? No. None of those things."

She narrowed her eyes. Set her jaw. Stared at Dixon like a boxer during the prefight handshake just waiting to pummel the other guy's face in.

The cop blinked and looked to the floor.

Then Tobi shifted her gaze back to Darger.

"Safety issue. Please. It's obvious where this school's priorities lie, and it's not on keeping its female population safe from predators. Instead, we're told that *we're* the problem. *Don't drink too much. Don't stay out too late. Don't walk alone at night.* How about this for a change? Instead of telling women how *not* to get raped, why don't you start telling men to *stop raping*?"

The girl lifted her chin and stared Darger in the eye.

"So tell me, Miss FBI. When it comes time to uncover everything the university has been hiding, everything they've swept under the rug these past few years, whose side will you be on?"

"I'm on the side of justice," Darger said. "Always."

Tobi blinked.

"We'll see."

With that, Tobi turned on her heel and marched back down the hallway. The rest of the crowd followed like a brood of baby ducklings.

Darger watched them go before turning to Dixon and holding the flier up.

"Do you know anything about these other cases?"

"I've heard a little about it, but like I said before, I'm a newbie, really."

He squinted at the flier. Made a little clicking noise somewhere deep in his mouth.

"Most of this stuff would have taken place before I got here. But I'm sure we have the files back at the station if you'd like to take a look."

Darger glanced over at Loshak, who gave a nod.

"Let's go."

As they proceeded back to the stairwell, Darger heard a new song blasting out from the room with the anarchy sticker on the door. This time it was NWA's "Fuck Tha Police."

CHAPTER 6

A quick drive across campus deposited Darger and Loshak in front of the Campus Police Department — a small, pale brick building with a glass entryway that reflected the glaring sun. The structure reminded Darger of a mom-and-pop sandwich shop she frequented in high school, the kind of place where you could get one of those huge meat-stuffed subs wrapped in wax paper. Didn't look like a cop shop much at all.

"This shoebox is where we're having the task force meetings?" she muttered on the walk up to the building. "I passed the Sheriff's Department on the way in. Probably three times this size. Maybe more."

Loshak shrugged.

"I think we're going to find that the university has a lot of clout here. A lot of sway over everything that happens in this town. Maybe that means the girl with the blue hair was onto something in her semi-coherent ranting, or maybe it doesn't. Either way, my gut tells me that the school wants to keep all of this close. Under its thumb, if it can."

Darger wanted to say something to that, but they pushed through the gleaming glass doors, and the conversation was quickly forgotten.

After some introductory chitchat with a desk sergeant who was comprised of equal parts beef and mustache, they'd been led through a pair of swinging batwing doors into the belly of the campus police beast — as small a belly as it was.

Now they huddled in front of a tiny desk in a back room, poring over the older case files. Apparently, the SMU police force had been attempting to go digital for the past few months, but since most of the stuff was still hard copies in file boxes, she printed off the remaining files just to have everything in one pile.

It was a little confusing, but after an hour or so of shuffling folders and skimming files, Darger thought she'd created a rough timeline of the attacks, starting with the man dubbed "The Campus Flasher."

The first such incident happened in early October, nearly two years ago.

Just after dark, a sophomore engineering major was at a computer in the library when she heard a faint tapping sound. She looked around. Discovered a man standing just outside the window she sat next to. He wore a ski mask and a long coat.

Once he knew he had her attention, he grasped the flaps of his coat and pulled it open, exposing his genitals, which he then stroked and pressed to the glass. When the girl jumped up to call for help, the man ran off into the night.

Two weeks later, there was another incident, which played out in almost the exact same way. Same time of day, same window. Again the man disappeared as soon as the victim tried to alert someone to what was happening.

The campus newspaper originally referred to him as the "Library Flasher," and two campus police officers were stationed at the library in the evenings for several weeks — one inside and one outside. Perhaps the flasher had noticed their presence, or maybe he'd known he'd be pushing his luck to return to the same place a third time.

Instead of striking the library again, he branched out over the following weeks, reenacting the incident at half a dozen other locations around campus: outside one of the chemistry labs, in a dorm parking garage, behind a Subway.

The final reported flashing occurred inside the campus bookstore, where he exposed himself to a female patron among the floor-to-ceiling shelves of books. Right on the face of it, this was his most bold offense so far. Face-to-face. No protective wall of glass between him and his victim.

There's the first escalation.

Darger cued up the security video from the bookstore. Grainy footage showed the victim entering the building. Some twenty seconds later, a man entered. He wore a long coat and wore what appeared to be a knit beanie on his head, but Darger suspected it was probably the ski mask. She leaned in, trying to get a look at his face, but his features were almost completely concealed by a large pair of sunglasses and a scarf wrapped around the lower half of his face. Slightly above average height and stoop-shouldered. That fit what Tobi had said. Beyond that, the most Darger could tell about the man was that he had light skin.

The man trailed his prey around the bookstore, waiting until she was alone in one of the aisles before approaching her. This time, he took the attack one step further. When he opened his jacket, the woman instinctively recoiled. Stepping backward, she found herself pinned against a bookshelf. The man advanced forward, fondling himself and then pressing his naked body against the woman. By the time she found her voice and let out a shriek, he'd already escaped through an emergency exit at the back of the store.

OK. Major escalation.

Darger couldn't help but notice that the official police report seemed to soften what had happened. The final line of the report, *The perpetrator then leaned into the victim*, seemed quite the euphemism for what Darger had watched on the screen.

Searching the local news sites added another layer to the story. The footage of the bookstore attack had never been circulated to the local media. Darger gritted her teeth. So far the blue-haired girl had been right about the school trying to do damage control.

Less than a month after the bookstore attack, the first rape was reported. Again, just like Tobi had said.

The victim was a young single mother, living in on-campus housing for students with families. She occupied half of a small duplex located near the soccer practice fields on a quiet corner of campus. It was late spring, and the weather that week had been unseasonably warm. The AC units hadn't been installed yet, so the woman had left a window open. At 3 A.M., she awoke to a man standing over her, pressing one hand to her mouth and holding another to his lips, indicating that she should be quiet. He was naked except for a ski mask. He did not carry a weapon.

He spoke softly. Not even unkindly, per the woman's description. He did not threaten her or her one-year-old daughter who slept at the far side of the room.

The second attack was very similar to the first. The victim in this case was a resident adviser who was staying on through the summer to facilitate Freshman orientation. She was in-between orientation groups, so the floor was completely empty except for her. Again the rapist gained entry through an open window. Again the woman awoke to a hand held over her mouth. Again he wore nothing but a ski mask.

There were two more attacks — both of which took place off-campus in the student housing area and within two blocks of one another. The third case began as almost a carbon copy of the first two, except that the attack was interrupted when the victim's male roommate came home unexpectedly.

Seizing the moment of surprise, the victim punched her would-be rapist in the throat. As he fell to the floor, she began screaming for help. Her roommate burst into the room and spied a naked man in a ski mask scrambling out the window. He grabbed a makeup brush from the dresser and stabbed it into the rapist's left buttock with such force that the end broke off in his flesh.

While the victim dialed 911, the roommate ran outside to give chase but found no trace except for the snapped twigs on the bushes outside the bedroom window. When the police arrived, they searched for a blood trail from the stab wound inflicted by the victim's roommate but came up empty. Again, the rapist had escaped without leaving much evidence behind.

The fourth and final Ski Mask Rapist attack gave the first sign that the rapist was becoming more violent. Again the victim awoke to a naked man in a ski mask standing over her. But this time, he had a knife.

He gestured with the weapon as he told the woman to be quiet, and then he set the knife on a bedside table. The attack proceeded much as the previous after that. He talked to the woman as if she were a willing participant, calling her "his good girl."

When a pair of headlights shined into the bedroom from outside, the rapist grabbed the knife from the nightstand and pressed the blade to his victim's throat, demanding to know who it was.

"Are you two-timing me?" he asked, and then he threatened to kill the victim if he found out she was cheating on him.

A moment later, the lights receded, as it was apparently someone only using the victim's driveway to turn around. The rapist turned apologetic then, putting the knife down and stroking the victim's face, promising he didn't mean it. "I just love you so much," he said. "You can't blame me for getting a little jealous sometimes."

Unlike the Campus Flasher, there were almost no news reports about the Ski Mask Rapist. The first attack got a single paragraph under the headline *Home Invasion on Campus*. It mentioned "an assault" but did not hint at the sexual nature of the crime. All the rest of the cases went unreported in the local news.

Maybe there really was something to what the girl with blue hair had said about a university-driven cover-up. It certainly wouldn't have been the first time.

With the likes of Jerry Sandusky and Larry Nassar being protected by their respective universities for years after reports of their misconduct came to light, it wasn't hard to imagine something similar happening here at SMU. Hell, she'd recently read about a case where one man had been accused of sexual assault by six women at three different Louisiana universities, and not a single one of the schools or local law enforcement agencies had taken action.

Darger tore her eyes from the screen and stared up at the ceiling tiles. If the Campus Flasher, Ski Mask Rapist, and Couple Killer really were one and the same, that meant a predator had been allowed to stalk the SMU campus for two years. His crimes progressing. The darkness growing.

The idea made her feel slightly ill. Claws curling against the walls of her belly.

Why had no one stopped him? Or even tried?

She glanced around the station. It was small. Really small. One of the fluorescent lights overhead flickered, which gave the place an overly shabby feel.

Darger had a feeling the campus police had a lot more

experience writing traffic tickets and responding to noise violations than with homicide, let alone a serial case like this one. They'd been in over their heads from the start.

It was Loshak who finally broke the silence.

"So? What do you think?"

Darger blinked.

"You can almost see the progression here in these files, assuming this is the same perpetrator. He starts out exposing himself to women in semi-isolated public spaces. He gets bolder, with the flashing incidents happening more and more frequently, and that eventually escalates to actually making physical contact at the bookstore."

She tugged one of the manila folders from the stack and pointed at the date on the incident report.

"Notice that the first rape is barely a month after that. Maybe the fact that he successfully made physical contact with the woman in the bookstore is what gave him the confidence to take it to the next level."

Loshak nodded along with her.

"I also see a progression in the rapes themselves," he said. "He starts out as a classic Power Reassurance or Gentleman Rapist type. Talking to his victims as if they're a couple."

Loshak held up a finger. Paged through one of the files.

"Listen to this. 'Victim states the perpetrator then stroked her hair and asked if it was good for her.' When he left, he kissed the girl's hand and said he'd call her soon. She said he didn't have a weapon. Didn't threaten her at all."

"No, that doesn't happen until the fourth attack," Darger said. "After the third rape, which was interrupted when the victim's roommate came home, and the two of them managed to fight the rapist off and send him running for the hills."

Loshak drummed his fingers against the table.

"I bet that spooked him. He decided he better start carrying a weapon, just in case."

"I think it made him angry, too. You can see that coming out in the fourth attack. When he sees the headlights in the driveway."

Darger found the line in the report and read it aloud.

"'Perpetrator then pressed the knife to the complainant's throat and demanded to know who was outside, telling her, 'If I ever find out you've been with another man, I'll kill you both.' He incorporated the third victim's male roommate into his fantasy. He's not just imagining himself and the victim as a couple anymore. He's seeing any male she's close to as someone she might be having an affair with."

Loshak quirked his head to the side.

"It's an interesting theory," he said. "The question I have now is why he changed from attacking women home alone to attacking couples on the street. That's a pretty massive escalation in a very short period of time."

Darger chewed her lip.

"Well, we know he stalks his victims, right?"

"Do we?"

Darger flicked through a few of the computer files until she came upon the one she wanted. She tapped a knuckle against the screen.

"Right here. During the second rape, he made the victim put on a specific dress. 'That yellow one you wore on Wednesday,' he said. 'You look so lovely in it.'"

Loshak rubbed his hands together.

"Good catch, Darger. I must have skimmed right past that."

"OK, so he spends some time getting to know his victims. He pays attention to what they wear. Whether they live alone. Etcetera. So what if, in the course of following what he intends to be his fifth rape victim, he sees her with a man? Watches her touching, kissing, hugging him? It's the exact thing he's been imagining in part of his new fantasy, except this time it's not just in his head. It's for real."

"Yeah." Loshak slowly bobbed his head up and down. "I could see that."

"It explains why he went from his standard surprise attack style to more of a blitz attack. Neutralizing the male victim first by locking him in the trunk. He assaults the female victim, but he's still so angry at the perceived infidelity that he kills both victims, just like he told the fourth rape victim he would."

"And then, once he gets a taste of murder, there's no going back," Loshak said. "Like John Wayne Gacy. He assaulted young men for years and never killed. Not until he picked up a 16-year-old boy named Timothy McCoy from a bus station and brought him home. Gacy plied the boy with alcohol and initiated sexual contact. The next morning, McCoy got up and made breakfast. When he went to wake up Gacy, the kid was still holding the knife he'd used to prepare the food. Gacy misinterpreted this as a threat. He took the knife from McCoy and stabbed him repeatedly. He said murdering the boy gave him a quote, 'mind-numbing orgasm.' And just like that, he'd established a new modus operandi, going from what I believe to be a Power Reassurance or Gentleman Rapist type to the Anger Excitation or Sadistic type in a single act."

Darger squinted.

"You think Gacy was a Power Reassurance type?" she asked, shaking her head. "I've read the reports on his 1968 sodomy charge — the one he got years before he killed Timothy McCoy. One of the boys he attacked said that when he resisted, Gacy tried to strangle him. And then more recently a man came forward and said that Gacy assaulted him when they were both just boys, and Gacy threatened to kill him if he told anyone. That's classic Power Assertive."

Loshak gave her a wry smile.

"Well, look who's been doing her homework."

"Also, it wasn't a single act," Darger said, smirking back at him. "There was an attack between McCoy and his next known murder victim. Gacy murdered McCoy in January 1972. The same month, he assaulted a nine-year-old boy in a department store bathroom. He used a knife to frighten him into submission and again threatened to kill him if he told anyone."

"Alright, so it wasn't as instantaneous as I first suggested," Loshak admitted. "It makes sense that he'd try to go back to his standard M.O. before deciding it wasn't doing the trick anymore. Not the way murdering Timothy McCoy had. It still shows a progression similar to what we're seeing here. According to a Ray Hazelwood study, only about a quarter of serial rapists escalate their violence over time, but those who do commit about twice as many rapes as those who don't. Basically, we're probably looking at the worst possible type of offender here on campus. Not good."

Darger heard a loud crunching sound and then footsteps. She turned to find Kirby approaching.

"Hey there, Agents," he said.

He held a Big Gulp cup in his hand, with the drink lid pulled off and dangling from the straw on one side.

"Officer Kirby," Loshak said.

Kirby leaned back his head and shook the cup over his gaping maw, depositing a few ice cubes into his mouth.

"If you're about done here, meeting's about to start."

The grating sound of Kirby chewing ice punctuated his words. Darger watched his jaw move in little up and down motions, something squirrel-like in the way his mustache quivered.

"Great. We'll finish up and see you in there, then," Loshak said.

Kirby, still chomping away on the ice, gave a singular nod and went back the way he'd come.

Darger watched him go. When she was sure he was out of earshot, she turned to her partner.

"You think those students we met in the dorm were right? Did the university really try to cover up the rapes?"

Loshak frowned and gazed up at the ceiling.

"I don't know. But we should tread lightly on that front. Throwing out an accusation like that won't do anything but make our job harder."

Darger scoffed.

"Please. You think I'd do something so reckless?"

Loshak's eyes rolled dramatically over to hers.

"You?" he said, his voice deadpan. "Never."

CHAPTER 7

Given the size of the station as a whole, Darger probably shouldn't have been surprised at how few people were taking part in the task force meeting. As she entered the conference room, she tallied a total of twelve people aside from her and Loshak: the SMU Chief of Police, Sheriff Kittle and one of his deputies, plus a handful of SMU officers, mostly uniformed with two detectives wearing black suits among them.

Chief Fleming was at the head of the table, fiddling with a tablet on a stand. He stepped back with his hands on his hips.

"Dixon, what the hell is it doing now?"

The young officer leaned across the table, angling his head to see the screen.

"Just hit the 'Start Meeting' button."

The Chief jabbed a thumb at the screen. After a few moments, a woman's face appeared. She was probably in her late fifties or early sixties, with a feathery bob favored by female politicians.

"Ah, there we are," the woman said, her voice surprisingly crisp over the tiny tablet speakers. "Are we ready to get started?"

"Absolutely. The, uh, president — uh — President Whitman of the university," Chief Fleming stammered out, not facing the others in the room as he said it. "She'll be sitting in on the task force meeting on the tablet here. Being that there are so many students potentially at risk, we just think it makes sense to keep the administration abreast of what we're doing and what they might do to keep the kids safe. Work closely with 'em and whatnot. Uh… yeah. That's all."

The Chief didn't mention aloud that the university technically employed him and funded the department, that in a very real sense he answered to President Whitman, but Darger thought his bumbling explanation got the notion across louder than screaming it.

"Why don't I start by introducing the two agents the FBI so graciously sent out to assist on this," he went on. "Agent Darger and Agent Loshak."

"We're so pleased that you're here," Whitman said. "Welcome to SMU. I hope you'll have a chance to walk around our beautiful campus while you're here and enjoy the charm of our little school."

Darger was tempted to mention that they were here to catch a man who'd already killed six people, not take a tour of the grounds like a couple of highly sought-after athletes, but she kept her mouth shut.

"It's good to be here," Loshak said. "And nice to see you're taking such an interest in the investigation."

Darger bit her cheek. So she wasn't the only one intrigued by the fact that the university president would be attending the task force meeting. Only Loshak had come up with a way to put a positive spin on it.

"And why wouldn't I? I've been charged with taking care of all 27,000 people here — students, faculty, and the school itself. Anything that happens here is my business."

Darger thought her tone seemed slightly huffy.

"Of course I deeply regret that I can't be there in person, but my duties require me to be elsewhere for the time being. Soon enough. Thankfully the wonders of technology make it possible for me to participate virtually, which is nearly as good.

Now… Chief Fleming. Bring me up to speed in terms of the investigation."

Darger's eyes went from the tablet screen to the chief.

"Well, like we talked about earlier in the week, we've beefed up security on campus," the chief said. "We're doing regular street patrols around the clock."

"And I assume Sheriff Kittle is doing the same around town?" Whitman asked.

Darger expected the man to bristle at being quizzed by this academic bureaucrat, behaving as though she were the one running the show.

To his credit, perhaps, Sheriff Kittle seemed wholly unbothered. Darger was starting to wonder just how much influence the university president had around here.

"That's correct, ma'am. Half of my men that usually do traffic duty have been pulled over to the patrol detail."

"I just talked to the crime lab," Fleming went on. "It'll be another few hours on the DNA results, but they're still promising that we'll have them by the end of the day."

Whitman nodded solemnly and appeared to jot something down with a pen. Her steely gaze flicked back up to the camera on her end of the video call.

"I'd like to hear from our two FBI agents now."

Loshak turned and waggled his eyebrows at Darger. They were up.

CHAPTER 8

Because of the tablet and the small size of the room, Darger and Loshak stayed in their seats to present their profile. Loshak went first.

"Since there's a sexual component to these crimes, I think it would benefit us all to talk a bit about the different rapist typologies. Now, before I begin, I want to make one thing crystal clear. To a layman, rape may seem to be about sex. But it's not. Rape is about rage. It's about power. It's about control. It's about violence."

Loshak counted these items off on his fingers.

"Some combination of these things has been fetishized by the rapist, so that the sex itself has become a weapon of sorts."

Loshak began the slideshow he'd prepared for the meeting.

"Now, there are several different ways to categorize rapists, but I think we're best served by Groth's Typology in this case. Groth broke offenders into four categories. Power Reassurance, Power Assertive, Anger Retaliatory, and Anger Excitation. The Power Reassurance type is also known as the 'Gentleman Rapist,' because he is often 'polite' to his victims. Gentle, even. The name really says it all. Power Reassurance is the psychological motive. He's highly insecure, and the forced sexual contact is a way of reassuring himself.

"His underlying fear is that he is somehow not normal or not worthy of having a relationship. This type of rapist often coerces his victims into saying they had a good time. In his mind, the act guarantees the victim's acceptance of him. He's playing out a fantasy version of a normal relationship. He is specifically not interested in violence and rarely carries a weapon. I like to think of these perpetrators as being insecure above all, fearful inside and out. Their only interest is assuaging that fear."

Loshak clicked to the next slide.

"One step up the scale in terms of violence and cruelty is the Power Assertive type. This type is similarly insecure, but he more or less blames women for those feelings and thus needs to exert power over them to resolve his inadequacy. You might say that this is the Power Reassurance type turned inside out. All that fear and doubt and insecurity is turned outward, converted into anger. The doubt makes him want to prove his superiority — or *assert* it, thus the name. Again, this is all about serving a fantasy version of reality, an internal version of the world he is trying to make external, trying to make real. He cares little about his victims. They are a means to an end within his own psychology. He also isn't particularly interested in harming his victims, though he has no qualms about resorting to violence as a way to control them. Women are quite literally objects to him. Controlling them is the only way he feels a sense of power."

The slideshow advanced again.

"Next is the Anger Retaliatory rapist. Here we move from power as the fetishized element to a full bore emphasis on fury — the expressions of rage themselves are what bring him pleasure. The anger is the point, so to speak. This type of perpetrator is out to do harm. Brutality. Overkill. His attacks often occur after some sort of negative interaction with a female in his life, thus the use of 'retaliatory' in the name."

Loshak held up a finger.

"It's important, I think, to note that he rarely retaliates against the person who made him feel that way in the first place. Instead, he uses his victims as proxies. Another thing that separates this type — his attacks represent a complete loss of control. They are often sudden, impulsive, and less likely to involve much forethought. He will beat and strangle his victims, or otherwise inflict violence far beyond the level of force necessary to keep a victim compliant. Like I said, rage itself is the actual fetish.

"This type of offender will project overtly masculine traits in most every phase of their life. They will seem almost cartoonishly macho in how they dress — camo, sports gear, and muscle tees. In what car they drive — sports cars, muscle cars, Jeeps, etcetera. In what line of work they pursue — military, law enforcement, or associated jobs."

Loshak reached the final slide now.

"And at the very far end of the spectrum, we have the Anger Excitation type. Here the driving desire shifts again, from a rage fetish to a fixation on the psychological suffering of the victim. Now it is the victim's experience that brings pleasure, the victim's fear and pain that is the point. These are your Ted Bundys, your Robert Ben Rhoadeses, your Lawrence Bittakers.

"They are even more violent, even more full of rage than the Anger Retaliatory type, but they are more 'in control,' so to speak. They are careful planners, and their crimes often have a highly ritualistic pattern. The violence and the rape at this point are almost secondary in nature, mere tools to elicit the fear of their victims, which is why we also call this group the 'Sadistic' type. Many people incorrectly interpret sadism as the enjoyment of inflicting pain. While some might consider it splitting hairs, a sadist's gratification usually comes from the victim's *reaction* to the pain. The sense of fear and terror in the victim is what gives the perpetrator a sense of absolute power.

"This type of offender may have much in common with the overtly macho appearance of the Anger Retaliatory rapist... or not. The distinguishing characteristic in terms of their life apart from the crimes themselves, I think, is how the fantasy has become their primary focus in life. Total obsession. They often have extensive pornography collections, usually quite specific and linked thematically to their crimes. Their rituals are often the most detailed and specific of the four types, and they are the most likely to keep souvenirs or record the crimes in some way."

There was a brief silence, then. Darger knew that Loshak was preparing himself for what he would say next, unsure of how it would go over with the group.

"Knowing what we know, it's not uncommon for this type of perpetrator to have a prior history of sexually deviant behavior, perhaps less severe in scale. Peeping, flashing, breaking into homes to steal ladies' undergarments, etc. We took a look at some of your unsolved cases over the last few years and identified two previous repeat offenders that might be related. Your so-called Campus Flasher, and later, the Ski Mask Rapist."

Chief Fleming shifted in his seat. Was he uncomfortable with this line of discussion or trying to keep his leg from falling asleep? Darger couldn't be sure.

"But the Ski Mask Rapist never tried to kill anyone," Sheriff Kittle said, his brow furrowed. "He didn't even bring a weapon to most of the scenes. Why would a perpetrator go from committing rape to rape *and* murder?"

"A significant portion of serial offenders — thankfully a minority — seem to gravitate to higher and higher levels of violence, their fantasy arcing toward sadism. They want more. More stimulation. More savagery. More suffering. Like a junkie upping their doses, chasing a bigger high."

Loshak held up the sheet of paper he'd used to jot notes on as they'd pored over the files.

"If you look at the four Ski Mask Rapist attacks, there's already a clear progression. He starts as a classic Power Reassurance or Gentleman Rapist. But the altercation with the third victim's roommate seems to push him into Power Assertive Territory. I don't think it's an accident that the fourth attack was the last one. If this is the same man, I believe he realized the old pattern wasn't going to do it for him anymore."

Loshak held up his finger again to avoid more debate. Darger knew what he was about to do, because it was exactly what she would do. Not wanting to get bogged down in a debate about the local history and handling of past cases, he changed the subject.

"The bottom line is this: We are looking for a criminal who I believe is currently escalating from Anger-Retaliatory into that Anger-Excitation mode. His progression may not be over. Bad as it's already been, I would look for further escalation sooner than later — mutilation or some other means of physically injuring the victims. More brutality. His ritual is sharpening now, and he's more confident and knowledgeable than ever before. Emboldened, I'd say. More driven."

He paused to take a breath.

"And much more dangerous."

CHAPTER 9

The room held quiet for a beat after Loshak's warning. Taut. Eyes twitching all around the oval of the table, looking at each other and then glancing back to the glossy tabletop. Darger could hear someone's breath whistling in their nostrils.

President Whitman cleared her throat on the tablet screen, and though she didn't say anything, it seemed to break up the silence. Others followed suit. Daring to adjust their positions and check their phones.

Darger sat up straighter in her seat. Shuffled the pages before her. Now it was her turn.

"So let me start with the basic profile. It's likely we're looking for a white male. Probably mid-to-late 20s. Possibly into his early 30s. Older than his victims, perhaps, but not by much. This type of perpetrator generally prefers victims in his own peer group. He would find it unsatisfactory to prey on victims he considers weak, like children or the elderly. Based on the component of the male victims involved, I think we're looking for someone who'd fall into that overtly macho category Agent Loshak mentioned before."

Darger took a sip of water before she continued.

"So hes probably in good shape. Muscular build. Masculine dress type and line of work — could be something blue-collar, like a construction worker or a lumberjack, or it could be something with authority. Security, law enforcement, or maybe fire and rescue. Military history likely but not guaranteed. Almost certainly into sports and possibly a former athlete.

"For these reasons, I would theorize that the stooped

shoulders described in the earlier crimes may be an affectation — something to change his appearance and throw the investigation off. Based on the crimes, our unsub would have perfect posture or close to it.

"There are signs of sophistication in the crimes. Binding and controlling two people at once, even at gunpoint, shows some competence, and even more, it shows extreme confidence. I think the odds are that we're looking at someone with at least average intelligence and probably above. Even with the threat of the gun, he's talking his way through parts of these crimes, getting people to comply. That suggests his social skills are at least adequate. He may have even had lasting relationships with women — we've seen that with criminals of this type — but he wouldn't have been loyal to any of them."

Darger flipped a page.

"The car could end up being a good angle, especially given the nature of the crimes. He undoubtedly drives something flashy. A sports car or muscle car. Something that projects that over-the-top so-called manliness. We can certainly be on the lookout for vehicles that match the profile, and it might be wise to go back through all the witness statements with that detail in mind. But let me take a step back and talk again about the core motivations at play here."

Another page flip.

"As my partner highlighted with the various typologies, these crimes are an expression of a fantasy arising from intense feelings of inadequacy in the perpetrator. The fantasy becomes an escape from a reality he can't cope with. Above all, he wants to identify with strength. He wants to see himself as powerful," Darger said. "This is a person who deeply, deeply hates women. Expressing rage is a way to see himself as powerful.

"This compulsion probably dominates his life. A massive

porn collection depicting violence against women is very common in this type of perpetrator, as are elaborate collections of the more bizarre types of bondage gear. We're talking about stuff that would make the author of *Fifty Shades of Grey* blush. Even when they aren't committing crimes, this type of unsub is partaking in the obsession, one way or another.

"The inadequacy driving this fantasy, this obsession, was probably imprinted at a young age."

Darger brought up a photo of Ed Kemper.

"Ed Kemper, the so-called Co-Ed Killer, had an abusive mother who literally locked him in the basement as a young child. There's some room for interpretation on Ted Bundy, but the oft-repeated motive in the standard telling of the Bundy myth was the rejection of his rich, beautiful girlfriend in college. Even though he went on to law school, worked his way up in local politics, and even had chances to win this old girlfriend back directly, he couldn't get over that imprinted sense of rejection, of inferior feelings and rage that he directed at women. He couldn't rid himself of the mark it had left on his psyche."

With a flick of her finger, Darger moved on to the next set of photos she'd put together.

"There are three notable serial killers who targeted couples: the Zodiac Killer, the Son of Sam, and the Golden State Killer. Now, neither Zodiac nor Son of Sam sexually assaulted their victims, but the motivation in both cases most certainly arose from a deep insecurity centered around their relationship — or lack thereof — with members of the opposite sex."

The next screen in Darger's presentation showed a series of composite drawings.

"But perhaps the killer whose crimes most clearly echo what we're seeing here is Joseph James DeAngelo Jr., the

Golden State Killer. His earliest crimes were a series of burglaries in the Visalia area that began in 1973. That spree culminated in an attempted kidnapping, which was thwarted by the girl's father. Not long after, DeAngelo committed the first of approximately fifty rapes. The original attacks were on women and girls who were home alone. But after the media reported this fact, it seemed he took it as a personal challenge and began attacking couples.

"He'd force the female victim to bind her partner before taking her to another part of the house where the assault would take place. His attacks were carried out in this same methodical fashion until October 1979, when the couple he was attacking managed to escape their bonds. DeAngelo fled the scene, and the couple survived. The remainder of his victims wouldn't be so lucky."

Darger paused for another sip of water.

"DeAngelo committed the first of his rape-murder series in December of 1979. In this case, he appears to have shot both victims after the male victim managed to free himself from his bindings. Whatever happened that night, it marked another progression in DeAngelo's crimes. He not only murdered his final eight victims but changed the method of killing from shooting to bludgeoning."

Leaning back in her chair, Darger crossed her arms.

"This is notable because bludgeoning is much more savage than shooting. A shot to the head is quick. Some might even say it's merciful, comparatively. But beating someone to death with a blunt object requires not only time and immense effort, but a certain lust for violence and brutality. He wanted to inflict damage and pain. He wanted to prolong that feeling of power. To expel his rage in a very visceral way.

"Like Agent Loshak said, we have seen this type of sadistic

offender progress from less to more violence over time. Seeking more excitement. More arousal. More cruelty. But those feelings of rage and inadequacy are never quelled, and the hunger inside only seems to grow with each crime."

Here, Loshak raised a hand and jumped in.

"One interesting thing I'd like to note about the Golden State Killer was the fact that in the initial series of rapes, he seemed to be almost reenacting a specific episode from his life. After she broke off their engagement, DeAngelo went to his ex-fiancée's house in the middle of the night and attempted to kidnap her at gunpoint so they could elope. Thankfully, her father ran DeAngelo off, but he would go on to choose homes very similar to his ex-fiancée's for many of his attacks. He also said her name during multiple attacks, alternately apologizing to her and saying he hated her. It's quite possible that incorporating men into his attacks was a way of fighting back against the humiliation he'd felt after being chased away by his ex-fiancée's father."

Darger nodded along as Loshak spoke.

"Just as the psychology is often an imprinted trauma, these crimes themselves become rituals. The key psychological components are repeated, sometimes in exacting detail. The perpetrators are acting out a fantasy, and there is an ideal version of that fantasy that they are trying to create. That's why some of the oddest details get replayed over and over. DeAngelo almost always turned the TV on and put a blanket over it during his attacks, as if even the lighting had to be perfect. The M.O. can change dramatically, such as switching from a gunshot to bludgeoning, but ultimately the details of the ritual will be repeated, one way or another, always refining toward a more perfect version of the fantasy driving it all."

The next screen was a crash course in some of the finer

points of profiling.

"So let me elaborate on that," Darger said. "This driving fantasy is also called a criminal's signature, which often gets confused with the modus operandi. I like to think of the modus operandi as the practical aspects of the crime. The how, the when, the where. The signature, on the other hand, fulfills some emotional need of the killer. I like to use Dennis Rader, the BTK Killer, as an example.

"Many killers might bind their victims as part of their modus operandi. The act of binding serves a practical purpose only in those cases. They might tie the victim at one scene, use duct tape at the next, and perhaps eventually start using handcuffs because they're faster and more secure.

"For Rader, however — BTK — the act of binding his victims was part of his signature. He'd been obsessed with knot-tying and bondage from a very young age and spent hours practicing elaborate knot configurations. He'd taken photographs of himself in bondage, wearing items he'd stolen from his victims. Binding his victims went well beyond the practical in this case. It was part of his fantasy, part of what drove him to commit these acts, part of what brought him pleasure. Rader's M.O. changed over time, but his signature never did."

This was Darger's cue to show a lineup of photos illustrating a few of the knots found at the BTK crime scenes.

"So, going back to the Golden State Killer, his M.O. was initiating surprise attacks, late at night, by sneaking into the victim's home," she said. "From a purely practical standpoint, it would make more sense to only attack women who were home alone. Less chance of getting caught. Less work to incapacitate only one victim, versus two. We know DeAngelo thoroughly stalked the neighborhoods where he committed his crimes, so he easily could have chosen to *only* attack isolated victims. So why didn't he?

"I believe attacking couples became a part of his signature. He *enjoyed* forcing the woman to bind and incapacitate her partner. He *enjoyed* knowing this man had to lie there, powerless to stop the rape of his wife or girlfriend. He *enjoyed* humiliating not just the female victim, but also her partner. It gave him an enormous sense of power, which superseded the practical reality that attacking a single, lone victim is inherently less risky."

Darger licked her lips.

"I think we're seeing something similar with the Couple Killer case. Attacking couples is part of this killer's signature, a key part of his fantasy. The act of binding the man and putting him in the trunk, knowing he's just a few feet away while he's assaulting the female victim… this serves a psychological need in our killer. He wants to humiliate the man. Wants to make him a cuckold. Wants to revel in his fear and suffering just as much as with the female victim. It's a distinctly macho desire, I think. A way of declaring himself superior to the other man. And that need drives him just as much as any other part of his crimes."

The Chief spoke up with a question.

"So does that mean he'll only attack couples? We've been telling people not to go out at night alone, but maybe we should be telling people not to be out in pairs."

It was Loshak who answered.

"Not necessarily. There's a tendency to take the notion that the signature doesn't change very literally. To use Golden State as an example again, he clearly came to prefer attacking couples, but in his final spree, he did attack two lone women. There's some evidence to suggest he believed the spouse of at least one woman would be there during the attack. The fact that the women turned out to be alone didn't change his mind, however. He carried out the crimes anyway. He could still serve that signature need of prolonging the terror and suffering." Loshak stroked his chin. "If my partner is right, and I believe she is, this killer won't hesitate to attack lone victims if that's what happens to be available."

Loshak rapped his knuckles against the table.

"Something else I'd like to address, and that's the manner of death. I don't believe shooting the victims is part of his signature. This is just a means to an end, not crucial to his desires. The fact that the shooting of the male victim last time went awry speaks to that. He got sloppy, and this type of killer rarely gets sloppy when it comes to the critical parts of the fantasy. As I said before, I predict that we'll see an increase in the level of violence. Just like we saw in the Golden State case."

The room was quiet for several seconds after that, until Loshak spoke again.

"Like I said. Mutilation. Increased brutality. Acceleration. Intensification. These are what the scenes suggest to me. I know that's not what anyone wants to hear, but the simple fact is that this type of offender rarely stops on their own. Almost never. It's going to get worse. And worse. And worse. Until we find him and put an end to it."

That tense quiet settled over them again like a blanket. Those whistling nostrils rising up to fill the emptiness.

"Just one more question," Sheriff Kittle said, his voice small. "This Golden State Killer, DeAngelo or whatever, what line of work was he in?"

Darger held his gaze a moment before she answered.

"He was a cop."

CHAPTER 10

Whitman's lips were sucked into a little pout.

"Well," she said, blinking. "That was… interesting. And we thank you both for your input. Isn't that right, Chief Fleming?"

The man sat forward in his chair. An abrupt motion like a kid caught napping in Social Studies.

"Yeah. Yes. Quite informative. Thank you. So as far as implementing a strategy going forward—"

Whitman interrupted, her head bobbing on the screen.

"Yes, what are we doing, exactly, to try to ensure he can't attack again?"

Loshak raised a hand.

"I have a suggestion, if I may."

Whitman nodded her head.

"I'd suggest organizing some sort of citywide neighborhood watch effort," Loshak said. "People in groups of, say, four or five people, patrolling their own neighborhoods. Given that this guy has a very specific ritual he's playing out, one that takes time, you'd be greatly reducing his opportunity to carry out an attack."

Whitman was vigorously shaking her head.

"Wouldn't it be wiser to impose a curfew instead? It seems to me that encouraging people to be on the streets at night is a recipe for disaster. We'd be quite literally putting them in harm's way. Keeping the kids safe is my number one priority. Chief?"

"I mean, yeah," Fleming said. "Yeah, a curfew would keep the kids out of trouble, I'd think."

Darger couldn't help but wonder where that 'number one priority' had been when the Ski Mask Rapist had been terrorizing her campus, but she kept the comment to herself.

"You'll never keep everyone inside," Loshak said. "Generally speaking, it's better to play offense than defense with this kind of perpetrator. A curfew isn't proactive. And we'd have to enforce it. It uses our resources to police the student body instead of putting our people in position to arrest this guy."

"I'm sorry," Whitman said. "I just don't see the neighborhood watch concept being conducive for the community. Do you, Chief Fleming?"

Darger was a little surprised that Fleming didn't ask how high he should jump. The Chief fingered the brim of his service cap on the table in front of him as he spoke.

"I think we'll table the neighborhood watch concept for the time being. With the DNA results en route, it might not be necessary."

"Exactly. Perhaps we'll circle back at some other juncture. But I have another question," Whitman said. "I have yet to see any sort of sketch or description of this man. Is that something we're working on, or...?"

Fleming cleared his throat.

"Ah... well, we'd need an eye-witness for that, Dr. Whitman. And right now the six people who would have seen the killer are... well, dead."

With a click of her tongue, Whitman rolled her eyes.

"But surely *someone* else must have seen him. He can't be invisible. What about security cameras?"

"So far all of his attacks have been in somewhat isolated areas. Alleyways. Dead-end streets. Next to construction zones," Fleming said. "No cameras."

Whitman frowned.

"That's really suboptimal."

Tell me about it, Darger thought, willing herself to not roll her eyes. Why was it that bureaucrats always acted as though they were personally inconvenienced by crimes like this? Six people were dead, and this woman was using terms like "suboptimal."

"And tell me, Chief Fleming, did the crime lab give you a reason for the delay on the DNA? Why exactly are they moving so slowly?"

The chief grimaced.

"With all due respect, Dr. Whitman, this is lightning fast compared to the processing speed for most trace evidence. It's all but unheard of. The lab is doing us a huge favor in promising such a fast turnaround. Normally we'd have to wait weeks or even months on something like this."

Fleming shook his head as he tacked on a final thought.

"We should count ourselves lucky they were willing to put everything else on hold for us."

Whitman raised an eyebrow, clearly still not satisfied.

"Months? That seems — I'm sorry — terribly inefficient."

"The sad fact is, the crime lab is facing the same limitations as everyone else. They only have so many people, so much time, so much money. And the criminal world… well, they don't have to take factors like manpower and budgets into consideration."

Whitman held up a hand.

"I hope this isn't going to segue into another request for an increase in overtime pay. I can't imagine a more inappropriate time or place."

"Of course not," Fleming said, his cheeks coloring at the reprimand.

Darger piped up then, eager to get things back on track.

"While we're on the subject of trace evidence… Agent Loshak and I were discussing earlier that there's a chemist at the University of Central Florida who's compiling a database for condom identification. We could not only potentially figure out the exact type of condom he uses, but we might also be able to link the previous rapes to the current spree."

There was a notable silence from the rest of the group.

"I thought we had actual DNA evidence from the car," Whitman said.

"That's correct," Fleming said.

"Why would we waste time on the condoms when we can get a full DNA profile?" Whitman asked. "Surely the profile is far more useful in terms of the specificity of the evidence."

Darger shrugged.

"A DNA profile is *one* piece of evidence. And *if* we get lucky, our guy is already in the system. But in our experience that isn't often the case. That means we'd have to wait to find a suspect before we could even hope for a match. There's no saying how long that might take."

Darger jabbed a finger into the tabletop. Fingernail clicking against the wood.

"But if we had a brand of condom, there's a chance it could be something scarce. Something that only one convenience store in the whole area stocks… that would give us a place to focus our investigation."

"That seems like a shot in the dark to me," Whitman said. "I just don't see how it's any more likely to work out than a DNA profile."

"It's not about more likely or less likely. It's about each additional piece of information giving us more to work with."

Two deep wrinkles formed between the president's

eyebrows.

"You said we'd have the DNA profile by the end of the day?" Whitman asked.

"That's what the lab promised."

Whitman clasped her hands in front of her.

"I think we should wait and see how that turns out before we go off on these tangents."

"I'm inclined to agree," Chief Fleming said. "We've got a solid lead with this DNA evidence. That's what we should focus on at the moment."

Darger sighed and glanced over at her partner, who gave a telling quirk of the eyebrows.

She'd wondered before if the university had actively made an effort to cover up the Ski Mask Rapist case, and she thought she had her answer now.

CHAPTER 11

As the meeting wound down, Darger's irritation at President Whitman only grew. The woman thought she was protecting the reputation of her university, but that meant she was also protecting a serial rapist. How could she not see that?

The moment the meeting concluded, Darger was up and out of her chair, heading through the door. She needed to be away from here, lest she say something she couldn't take back.

Outside, she paced the sidewalk. The fresh air helped calm her some.

Six people brutally murdered, and the powers-that-be were still focused on damage control. That rankled.

Still, this was SMU PD's jurisdiction, and she was here as a consultant. She could scream about it until she was blue in the face, and they could simply ignore her.

She heard the door open behind her, and then Loshak was there. Grim lines creased his face, and she steeled herself for a reprimand.

"I know we agreed not to push them on the Ski Mask Rapist stuff," Darger said. "But I think they're being shortsighted, not pursuing all of the evidence."

"Oh, it's beyond shortsighted. They're being fucking morons."

Darger's eyes widened. She stared at Loshak, who shrugged.

"Even if we're not dealing with the same perpetrator, it was ludicrous — not to mention dangerous and irresponsible — to think they could ignore the Ski Mask Rapist in hopes that he'd just… go away. And if it *is* the same perpetrator?" He shook his head. "They're dreaming if they think they'll be able to keep that under wraps. It'll all come out eventually, and the press will eat those two for lunch."

Darger let out a small sigh of relief.

"I thought you were going to lecture me."

"I don't lecture," Loshak said with a haughty flutter of his eyelids. "I dispense pearls of wisdom."

Darger scoffed.

"Anyway, I was thinking about taking a walk around campus," Loshak went on. "I wanted to take a look at some of the places the Campus Flasher and Ski Mask Rapist were seen. Care to join me?"

"Let's go."

☾

They came to the library first, where the original Campus Flasher incidents had taken place.

"The file said it was a window on the southwest corner of the building," Darger said, consulting her GPS to find the correct location.

Walking under a line of Japanese maples and past the massive monument to Merle the Mastodon, they found the place, noting that the ground floor window in question was almost completely concealed by a row of hedges.

"He could have hidden there for some time, waiting for the right person to sit near that window," Loshak said.

Darger pointed across a narrow strip of lawn.

"And there's a parking lot right over there. He could have either parked there or just hidden out among the cars once the alarm was raised."

They moved onto the bookstore, the site of the final

Campus Flasher report. The building sat at one end of a bustling quad. Some sort of fair bustled on the lawn, with a few dozen small tents set up, a crowd brimming before each.

Darger searched the internet and found it was Language Day. Each booth was run by one of the foreign language clubs on campus. She also found an event listing for the quad and discovered that there was something happening in the space almost every day this time of year.

"Looks like a busy spot," Darger said.

"Yeah. A good place to get lost in the crowd."

They stood for a moment, observing people entering and leaving the bookstore. Darger imagined the man lying in wait until a suitable victim entered the store. Loitering in plain sight and then using the throngs of people in the quad to disappear after the attack.

"Seems likely that he's familiar with the campus," she said. "And someone who wouldn't look out of place here."

Loshak nodded.

A group of girls filed out of the student center, each of them clutching a bag branded with a different fast-food logo: Taco Bell, Chick-fil-A, Pizza Hut. Darger heard a snippet of their conversation as they filed past.

"I was so excited to get a single this semester," one of the girls said, thumbing open a miniature pizza box. "I thought having a room to myself would be so fucking great."

"No roommate that smells like feet and eats all your snacks?" the girl with the Taco Bell bag asked.

"Exactly. But now… with everything going on… I *wish* I had a stinky roommate. I hate being alone in that room at night."

☾

Kelly plopped down against the trunk of the catalpa tree they often ate lunch under. She dabbed at the oil on top of her pizza with a napkin, sopping up a shocking amount of orangey ooze.

"Jesus, will you look at all of this grease?" She wadded up the dripping napkin and tossed it aside. "Anyway, I lined up all of my crystals in front of the window, just in case."

"What, to like… ward off evil?" Jess asked, wiggling her fingers like a witch casting a spell.

Kelly knew Jess thought her crystals were stupid, but she didn't care. She mostly collected them because they were pretty. She only kinda-sorta believed in the magic stuff.

"No. Because they're sharp. If someone tries to climb in through the window, they'll end up getting jabbed by a bunch of pointy rocks. Also the crystals will make a lot of noise if they got knocked over."

"Yeah, well, try living off campus alone," Christina said as she unwrapped her chicken sandwich. "You have someone like literally five feet away at all times in the dorms. When I got to my house last night, the street was completely deserted. Just walking the twenty feet from my car to the door was terrifying. And it was barely any better once I got inside my apartment. I've been sleeping with the lights on. And I put a pair of knitting needles under my pillow."

That gave Kelly an idea.

"Maybe we should team up," she said. "Buddy system, right? I'll sleep at your house one week, and you can stay in my room the next week."

Jess peeled back the paper wrapper on her burrito.

"I don't know what you're worried about, Kelly. He's only attacking couples." She snorted. "You'd have to actually, like, go on a *date* first."

Kelly picked up the grease-stained napkin and tossed it at

Jess's face.

"Fuck you."

Jess only smirked.

"Besides, if anyone we know was going to get raped, it'd be Melissa since she has the biggest boobs."

"Jesus, Jess!" Kelly hissed. "That's not funny."

Jess rolled her eyes.

"You know, that's the worst part about this whole thing. No one has a sense of humor anymore."

"Oh that's the worst part?" Christina said. "And here all this time, I'd been thinking it was the *raping* and *killing*."

Kelly swallowed a mouthful of pizza, which landed like a rock in her stomach. The whole conversation was making her feel slightly ill.

"How can you joke about it? Aren't you scared?"

"I mean, not any more than usual. You think there's just one guy out there raping? If the cops catch him, are you just going to magically stop being worried about walking alone at night?"

Kelly stared at her.

"What do you mean, *if* they catch him?"

"Do you know anything about crime statistics in this country? Michigan has a 38% clearance rate on homicides for the past ten years. That means more than half of them go unsolved."

"That can't be right."

"OK, it's 38.5%, if you're going to be a stickler about it. I wrote a paper on it for my criminal justice class last semester. If you think that's bad, there are jurisdictions in Illinois with clearance rates around 15%."

"Shut up," Christina said. "That's insane."

Jess shook her head and squirted hot sauce onto her

burrito.

"It's not like the TV shows, you know. In real life, the bad-guy-of-the-week doesn't always get caught."

Kelly found she had suddenly lost her appetite. The idea that there was a homicidal maniac prowling their streets was bad enough. The notion that he might never be caught was too much to bear.

She dropped her half-eaten slice of pizza back into the box and shut the lid.

"Can we... talk about something else?"

Jess shrugged.

"Whatever. You guys watch *The Bachelorette* last night?"

She took a bite of burrito and then washed it down with a gulp of Baja Blast.

"That Angelo dude is mega-cringe."

☾

As Darger and Loshak neared a cluster of residence halls, her mind drifted back to the girls she'd overheard in the quad. She'd sensed the fear in their voices. The dread. Even the one who'd kept joking around the whole time hadn't been exempt — she just covered it a little better than the others.

Darger thought she'd been a little like that when she was younger. When she was scared of something, she'd go to great lengths to conceal it from everyone.

Memories flitted on the movie screen in her skull. Going to a haunted house for Halloween one year. Pumpkin heads and skull faces lurching in the dark. Her pretending to think the whole thing was laughable, even though she'd been just as startled by the jump-scares as everyone else. Even admitting to that kind of mostly pretend fear made her feel too vulnerable.

She'd been tempted to stop in front of the girls eating lunch under the tree. To tell them, no, your friend isn't wrong about crime statistics. But also, this was different. The FBI was involved now. And they wouldn't rest until the Couple Killer was caught.

But could she really promise that? Just a few months ago, one of the more egregious killers she'd come up against had slipped through their fingers. Still at large, even now.

The girl had been right. In real life, the villain-of-the-week sometimes got away.

Darger clenched her hands into fists as she walked. She wouldn't let that happen here. Couldn't.

They passed through an archway between two buildings and then shuffled down a wide set of concrete steps. Students sat in clusters on the steps. Reading, talking, fiddling with their phones.

Loshak pointed at a squat brick building up ahead. It looked almost identical to the residence hall they'd visited earlier in the day.

"This is where the second Ski Mask Rapist attack took place," he said. "Corwin Hall. The perpetrator climbed into a ground floor window on this side of the building."

Again they discovered that the attacker had chosen a secluded area, nestled in the space between two buildings, concealed by trees and bushes, out of sight of any passersby. Darger gazed at the foliage there, wondered which bush he'd crouched behind.

"Yeah, I'd definitely say he's familiar with campus," Loshak said. "It's doubtful he'd just happen upon this spot otherwise."

They rounded the front of the building then. Kids sprawled on blankets on the lawn, propped up on their elbows. A group of four girls at the far end of the rectangle of grass practiced some kind of dance routine. The level of activity here stood in stark contrast to the quiet, shaded spot they'd just come from.

As they zigzagged through the crowd, Darger picked out snippets of individual voices from the composite murmur. Most seemed cheerful. Bright. She caught a few fragments of laughter.

And then a different tone of voice distinguished itself as they skirted around a cluster of young men. One of them cracked open a can of Red Bull, the metallic click ringing out over the yard. The skinny can looked dinky in his big mitt.

"Pisses me off thinking that this sick fuck is out there somewhere right now. Living his life. Free to go around raping and killing."

☾

Tony tipped the Red Bull to his lips and chugged half the can on the first drink, throat opening wide, tongue zinging with that bright acidity. His eyes looked out over the clusters of kids occupying the courtyard, talking and vaping and tinkering with their phones, but he wasn't really seeing them now — his camera had turned inward.

He couldn't stop thinking about his little sisters. His mom. What the hell kind of world were they living in, that they let this shit happen to women and no one did anything?

"I'm an atheist, so I don't believe in Hell, but I wish there was one just so this piece of garbage could eventually burn in it."

His lip curled in a sneer.

"And the fucking cops… everyone knows the campus police are a joke. If they end up catching him, it'll be dumb luck."

"Maybe Kirby the Curbstomper will do us all a favor and knock his teeth out, right?" Josh said. The tall, skinny kid looked like Ichabod Crane next to his squat, muscular friend.

Tony scoffed.

"I'd like to get my hands on him myself, I swear to God."

He lifted his arms and squeezed his hands as if strangling the air in front of him. Kept talking through gritted teeth.

"I'd rip his goddamn head off."

"They've gotta catch him, man. And soon," Beau said. The smallest of the three smirked, preemptively amused with himself. "I mean, it's totally destroying the vibe at parties. And good luck getting any girls to put out during this, right? They're so scared, their cooches are clamped shut tighter than a… uh… what's something tight? A… clamshell? No wait, a bank vault."

Tony dropped his arms to his side and took a step toward his diminutive friend. Was this fucking idiot for real? Sometimes he didn't know why he let Beau hang out with them. The guy basically gave everyone perma-douche chills. Constantly running his stupid mouth.

Tony's voice came out in a low growl.

"What the fuck is wrong with you? You think this is funny?"

Beau took an unsteady step backward, hands raised defensively.

"Tony, chill." His eyelids fluttered. "I was *kidding*, man."

Tony's nostrils flared.

"I know that, dumbfuck. What I don't know is why you'd think it's funny."

Beau maintained eye contact for a few more seconds before looking away.

His voice shook when he spoke again. Sounded like he might cry.

"I'm sorry, OK? I shouldn't joke about it, you're right."

Jesus, was this shitheel going to cry now? Tony almost wanted to laugh. God, he was so predictable. He always talked big, but the second anyone challenged him, it was like he couldn't backpedal fast enough. The pussy.

Tony backed down and took another sip from the skinny can in his hand. Slower now. Needed to make it last.

"Goddamn right."

☾

Darger pushed through the edge of the mob into the open. Moved away from the angry students turning on each other, their voices swallowed up in the cacophony.

Witnessing this heated interaction only served to confirm something she had been thinking about since the group of students confronted Officer Dixon in the dorm hallway: tensions were running high here on campus. Protests. Blasting angry music. Disagreements boiling over in private.

Student life here might appear to have been largely unaffected by the murder spree thus far, but a closer look revealed hairline fractures running throughout. Pressure building beneath the surface. Ready to blow.

Darger caught a whiff of pot smoke as they made their way around one of the soccer practice fields. Through the branches of a stand of pine trees, she spied a group of students huddled in a small circle. She watched as one of them passed the joint to one of the others.

"Here. I can't even enjoy this, man."

"Enjoy it? I'm just trying to calm myself the fuck down."

☾

Jay paused as he inhaled and held the smoke in his lungs, finally letting it out in a plume of bluish haze. His voice came out kind of hoarse.

"That girl who got killed last night? She's in my Sociology class. Or… *was*, anyway."

Eyebrows went up on the three faces circling around him.

"Holy shit, dude."

"Yeah. She was real quiet. But she seemed nice."

He shook his head. Took another puff. Talked in a weird strained voice as he held the smoke in.

"This shit is crazy. It's like, you see it on the news, but you don't think it's gonna happen to anyone you know."

Lorne sniffed and smeared the back of his hand over his nose. Took the joint and hit it. His face somehow morphed from a Shaggy-looking stoner type to that of a weird chinless hick whenever he clenched his lips around the doob, everything puckering funny.

"Well I heard it's the same guy that was showing people his dick in the library a while back. The, uh, flasher or whatever, you know?"

Phillip snatched the joint from the fingers of Lorne's non-smearing hand and rested it between his lips. His eyes looked half-squinted and glassy, like he was already baked, but Jay was pretty sure the kid just looked that way permanently now.

"Was it big?" Phillip said.

"What?"

"The flasher's dick."

"How the hell should I know?" Lorne said. "I never saw it. What the hell kind of question is that, anyway?"

"It's just that, I always kinda figure, like, if a guy has to resort to showing it to people in public, like really lean into the shock value or whatever, then it probably ain't real big, you know? Like if a guy's packin' a big ol' kielbasa, he don't need to resort to pulling shit like this to impress anyone. Is all I'm sayin'."

Phillip paused to scratch his chin. A thoughtful look occupying his face. He shrugged and finished his thought.

"It's like he's compensating, you know? Like driving a sports car, except slightly *less* desperate than driving a sports car."

Jay raised an eyebrow.

"You seem to have a lot of insight into the inner workings of the mind of a man with a small dong."

"Yeah well…" Phillip's lip curled. "Wait. What?"

Jay only chuckled.

"Hey, fuck you. I don't have a small, uh, dong. I just, like, have some keen insights into psychology. That's all."

"Sure," Lorne said, nodding dubiously.

"My dick is well above average, asswipe." Phillip gave him a shove. "Just ask your mom."

A hiss of laughter escaped through Lorne's grinning teeth.

"I did. She said she had to get out a magnifying glass to even find the damn thing. She was pretty nonplussed about the whole encounter."

Phillip stuck both middle fingers in the air.

CHAPTER 12

The site of the first Ski Mask Rapist attack sat among a row of identical duplexes tucked away in an area of campus that didn't get much foot traffic. These homes were specifically designated for students with families, Darger remembered.

They approached the house from the side, which offered a view of both the front and back of the building. The front yard looked bright and sunny. A few children's toys littered the patchy grass. The backyard was nearly nonexistent, with the rear of the house backing up to those wild, tangled woods Darger had passed through on her drive in. Again, it was clear the perpetrator had chosen a place where he could lie in wait.

As Darger and Loshak stood in the driveway, studying the scene, the door of one of the units opened. A young woman, no more than 25 years old, came outside. She balanced a toddler on one hip.

"Can I help you?"

Darger recognized her instantly from the police files. This was Lucy Seagal. The first of the Ski Mask Rapist victims.

"We didn't mean to bother you," Darger said. "We're just looking around."

The toddler in Lucy's arms began to squirm.

"You're here about the murders, aren't you?" she asked, setting the little girl down in the grass.

"That's right."

Lucy wrapped her arms around herself.

"Does this mean… you think it's the same guy?"

"We can't say that for certain."

Tears rimmed the woman's eyelids. Not quite enough to spill over.

"You know, I spent the whole last year beating myself up. For going along with it. For not trying to fight the guy off. That's what everyone thinks when they hear about it. They don't say it, but I know they think it."

She let out a bitter laugh. Rubbed a knuckle at one of her eyes.

"It's what *I* think, for Christ's sake. Why would I allow that to happen to myself?"

Her gaze strayed down to the small child ripping handfuls of grass from the ground.

"If it wasn't for Ava, maybe I would have fought. But I was just so scared she'd wake up and start crying, and he'd hurt her. I just wanted him to get it over with and leave."

"No one blames you for what happened," Darger said. "No one expects you to have done anything any different."

Lucy shook her head.

"You don't understand. These are tears of relief. If this is the same man, then maybe I was right not to fight. Because maybe then he would have killed me. Or hurt Ava. We're *alive*. That's all that matters now."

"Could we ask you a few questions about that night?" Darger asked. "It's OK if you're not comfortable with that—"

"No, I want to help."

"Did he threaten you or Ava?"

"No. But I didn't give him any reason to. I just nodded and did everything he told me to. I didn't even cry. Wouldn't let myself. I was just so terrified he'd hurt her. I knew I had to keep it together for her sake. Stay calm."

Lucy swallowed. Eyes swiveling in her head, studying the ground again.

"Once he left, that's when I lost it. I grabbed Ava up out of her crib, and I ran next door to the Watsons' — they're the couple that live on the other side of our unit — and I was just hysterical. I couldn't *stop* crying then."

There was a pause, but Darger could tell Lucy had more to say. She waited out the silence.

"You know, I go to this support group for sexual assault survivors sometimes, and the women there all talk about the violation of the actual rape itself. But for me, the thing I couldn't get over, that I still can't get over, is that I truly thought I was going to die. I thought he was going to rape me and then kill me, and then he'd kill Ava. The notion that my life could end like that, that her life could end like that… so unexpectedly… it crawled under my skin, I guess. Crawled under and stayed there. But then I guess most deaths are unexpected in one way or another."

She blinked a couple of times.

"When he was done, and he just left, I couldn't believe it. He didn't threaten me or anything. I think, in his mind, it was like we were on a date. We had a nice time, and that was all. He even said he'd call me later."

"Did he?"

Lucy nodded.

"He left a voicemail saying he had a wonderful time the other night. Can you believe it?"

"Did the police trace the call?"

"They told me the phone was a burner. Used for that call and then disconnected from service."

They asked Lucy a few more questions and then thanked her for her time. She scooped up her daughter and carried her back into the house.

As she and Loshak turned away and started back to the

station, Darger couldn't help but think about how the system had failed Lucy Seagal. Had failed all the victims of the Ski Mask Rapist.

And heat crawled up over Darger's shoulders and settled in her cheeks. Pins and needles pricking in her arms and legs.

Something about the cover-up was more real now. Something about looking Lucy and Ava in the face made it that way. Having Lucy tell her she was thankful to be alive, how that wasn't so for some of those who came after her.

Rage gripped Darger's chest so tightly it was hard to breathe.

CHAPTER 13

They walked in silence, back through the throngs of burbling student voices. The rage faded, at least a little, but Darger's thoughts remained fixed on Lucy and the other three victims of the Ski Mask Rapist. She couldn't stop wondering what might have happened had the case been more thoroughly pursued. If it was the same perpetrator, maybe they could have prevented what was happening now.

When they reached the campus police station, Darger spotted Dixon and Kirby standing in the parking lot. Kirby sucked at his Big Gulp cup, having apparently refilled it at some point.

"How's it going, my federale amigos?" Kirby said, grinning like a fox. "Stylin' and Profilin'?"

"I'm thinking we'll head back to our hotel for the night," Loshak said. "But first, can you guys recommend somewhere to eat?"

"Chile Toreado," both men said in unison.

The corners of Loshak's eyes crinkled.

"That good?"

"It's not the fanciest joint ever, but they've got the best tacos and burritos I've ever had," Kirby said. "Decent Polish dogs, too, if that's your thing."

"Make sure you ask for extra green sauce, and if you like heat, add some of the blistered jalapeno they give you," Dixon added.

They thanked the men for their recommendation, climbed into the rental car, and drove off.

The sky bled to purple as they drove. Dusk settling over the small town.

Loshak pulled the car into a bare gravel lot, and the red food trailer that was Chile Toreado took shape before them. Anthropomorphic chili peppers featuring large sparkling eyes adorned the sides of the truck in bright flourishes of paint.

A long line of patrons stretched outward from the window, but it moved quickly. When their turn arrived, Loshak ordered the carnitas tacos and Darger the chicken con limon burrito.

Five minutes later, they had their foil-wrapped orders in hand. A cluster of small tables with umbrellas sat next to the trailer, but with the sun down, the air had turned brisk, and Darger swore she smelled rain coming. They both agreed they'd rather eat in the car. Warmer. Drier.

Inside, they unwrapped the food and got to work. They'd each been given two small cups of salsa — one red and one green. Darger added both to her burrito while Loshak opted for just the green on his tacos.

"Smells good," he said. "Bright."

Darger took a bite and instantly understood why the place had come so highly recommended. It was delicious. Hot and fresh and perfectly seasoned, with the slightest bit of char from everything cooking on the plancha.

Her mouth tingled, and she got that sense of euphoria that came with eating spicy food.

"I haven't had tacos this good since I was in New Mexico with Jan," Loshak said, already having mowed through two of his tacos. "Can't believe a place like this exists in this dinky town in Michigan."

"How is Jan?" Darger asked.

"She's good. Got a new dog. A mutt we think is half Pug, half Yorkie, maybe."

Loshak ate another bite of taco and chuckled to himself.

"Wanna hear what a profiling genius I am? I took the little guy for a walk the last time I was there, and we were heading back to Jan's place. Keys in one hand, bag of dog crap in the other. She's got a small garbage bin in the garage for all the poop bags. I was thinking about how I need to remember to change her furnace filter while I'm there, you know, totally on autopilot and not thinking at all about what I'm doing. So I walk up to the bin and instead of tossing in the bag of crap, I chuck my keys in. I watch them get sucked down into all those little bags of dog shit. Just sinking into them like quicksand. So then, of course, I had to fish them out. I'm kneeling there, elbow-deep in bags of shit. Didn't smell *great*. And I'm thinking, yep, the FBI's best and brightest. That's me."

Darger started to laugh, almost choked on a grain of rice stuck in the back of her throat.

Loshak's phone jangled, and he glanced at the screen.

"SMU police," he said.

Darger's laugh cut out. She remembered exactly why they were here. What they were dealing with.

And then the images came to her again: the mental picture she had of the naked man in a ski mask climbing into the rooms of sleeping coeds.

The crime scene photos of the dead bodies crumpled on their sides — one in the backseat of the car, the other lying outside the Auto Zone.

And then the scared and angry and confused voices of the students milling around outside the school.

Loshak answered the call and put it on speaker.

"Loshak."

"Hello Agent, this is Officer Kirby. Chief asked me to give you a call. We just got the DNA results from the crime lab."

Darger could tell from his tone of voice that it wasn't good news. But how could that be? What had they found in the car again? A water bottle, a cigarette butt, and some chewed gum. Each one of those, if reasonably fresh, should be rife with epithelial cells or saliva.

"Are you telling me they couldn't get a profile?" she asked.

"Oh no," Kirby said. "No. That's not the problem."

Darger could hear him grinning as if he found the whole scenario amusing.

"They got a profile alright. Three of them, to be exact."

Three? Darger squinted. Stared at the phone between her and Loshak like it was malfunctioning, somehow spitting out false information.

Three profiles didn't make sense. Unless…

"Multiple perpetrators?" Loshak asked before she could get the words out.

"Doubtful. See… all the profiles are female," Kirby explained. "We got a Caucasian female on the gum, an African American female on the water bottle, and a different Caucasian female on the cigarette. None of them are in CODIS, so they remain unidentified."

Darger tried to make sense of this. How could the DNA profiles of three separate women end up inside the car like that?

And then it hit her. She felt her legs go numb and sucked in a breath.

"He's pulling a Green River Killer," she said.

"A what?" Kirby asked.

"Gary Ridgway, the Green River Killer, contaminated his own crime scenes by scattering a bunch of random trash in the area where he dumped a body. Cigarette butts and such."

Not only did this obscure the real perpetrator, Darger

thought, it also wasted the investigation's time and resources. Led them on all sorts of wild goose chases. They'd gotten very lucky that all the profiles were female. If any of the profiles had been male, Darger wondered how much time they might have spent attempting to track down the wrong guy.

After the call ended, she and Loshak just looked at each other for several seconds. Finally, Loshak broke the silence and summed up the moment with three words.

"Well. That sucks."

CHAPTER 14

Darger had been right about the weather. By the time they reached their hotel, a light mist had begun to fall.

They checked in at the front desk and then took the elevator up to their rooms. She and Loshak parted ways in the dim hallway of the third floor, agreeing to reconvene at 7 am the following morning.

The first thing Darger did was peel off her rain-moistened jacket. The hangers in the closet were all of the anti-theft variety, permanently attached to the rod, so she hung the jacket over the back of a chair and scooted it as close to the heater as she could, hoping that would be enough to dry it out by morning.

The rain must have picked up, because she could hear it now. A patter against the window that sounded like the faintest tapping of fingers. Droplets dappled the glass. Smearing the glow of the fast-food lights outside.

Darger kicked her boots off and paced around on the carpet for a while. She couldn't stop thinking about the planted evidence.

Why had he started leaving false evidence now, at the third of the double-murder scenes? Could he have made a mistake during one of the previous attacks and wanted a way to muddy the waters if that mistake led police back to him? Or was he just getting more clever?

That thought left her squirming.

This guy might be smarter than they'd given him credit for. The old way of thinking about these kinds of crimes had been the more elaborate the ritual, the more elaborate the fantasy, and therefore perhaps the more intelligent the perpetrator. There was a logic to it that held, even if the original theories had evolved through the years.

In some ways, Darger thought the lower-IQ perpetrators were more difficult to find. The more erratic the mind, the more erratic the behavior. It was harder to distinguish patterns when an unsub was all over the place, mentally.

And sometimes, even the dumb perps got clever. Gary Ridgway was a prime example. For despite having the cunning to contaminate his own crime scenes and elude the police for years, the Green River Killer scored well below average on intelligence tests.

Darger flung herself onto the bed and turned the TV on. One of those trashy reality shows flickered saturated colors on the screen. Deep oranges and greens. Two middle-aged Barbie women screamed at each other while a handful of other middle-aged Barbie women looked on with faux shock.

Darger thought it was funny that they called these "reality" shows when it was so clear that the scenarios were scripted. Someone always just so happened to flip a table or throw a glass of wine in someone's face in the season finale.

Bored of the mock squabbling, she changed the channel and landed on an infomercial for some sort of body hair removal device that claimed to "painlessly and efficiently burn the hair away." Darger couldn't help but imagine the smell of burning pubes.

She flipped through a dozen more channels before turning the TV off.

Her phone lay a few feet away on the bed. She picked it up and dialed Owen.

"What's up?" he asked.

"Oh, just settling in for the night. Thought I'd check in."

"Well, I already found some sketchy details on ol' Claude."

Darger wrinkled her nose, a bit disappointed that Owen was apparently still obsessing over his mother's fiancé.

"Oh yeah?"

"Turns out Claude isn't even his real name. His birth name is Fabio."

"So maybe Claude is his middle name."

"Nope. His full name is Fabio Balthazar Lombard."

Darger chuckled.

"Well I'd probably go by Claude too if my name was Fabio Balthazar."

"The guy isn't even an American citizen. Born in Toronto."

"Whoa," Darger said. "Hold on, let me get the Department of Homeland Security on the line. A *Canadian*? Sounds much more dangerous than an American, eh?"

"Be serious. He could be marrying my mother to get a green card."

Darger snorted.

"Right. To escape the poverty and famine of Toronto."

"Are you mocking me?"

"I mean… a little."

Owen let out an annoyed grunt and changed the subject.

"How's your investigation going?" he asked.

Darger sighed.

"Not great. We thought we had some solid DNA evidence, but now it looks like the killer planted garbage at the scene to throw us off."

"Hmm," Owen said.

"And there's a chance that before this guy started murdering people that he was a serial rapist who wasn't caught because the university covered it up."

Owen didn't respond, and Darger could hear the click-clack of his laptop keyboard.

"No reaction?" Darger asked.

"Sorry, what was it?"

"I think the school covered up the fact that there was a serial rapist on campus. It might be the same guy."

Again, Owen didn't reply.

"Also, there's a mastodon on the loose," Darger said, testing him. "Gored a bunch of people with its tusks."

"Tusks?" Owen repeated, his voice sounding distracted. "Oh, I get it. I'm not being a very good listener, am I? I'm sorry. It's just that I'm kinda down a rabbit hole here."

"I noticed."

"Look, I'll call you tomorrow, OK? I promise I'll have my head out of my ass by then."

"OK," Darger said, not sure if she believed him.

They said good night to each other and hung up.

Darger started typing up some of her case notes, but after staring at her screen for an hour, her eyelids started to droop. It was a little early, but it'd been a long day. She closed the curtains over the window, blotting out the glare of the streetlights and muffling the sound of the rain.

She climbed into bed, legs knifing under the covers, thinking again about the clear escalation of the crimes. From indecent exposure to rape to rape and murder. What would be next?

As she drifted off to sleep, Loshak's words from the task force meeting echoed in her mind.

This type of offender rarely stops on their own... It's going to get worse. And worse. And worse. Until we find him and put an end to it.

She only hoped they did.

CHAPTER 15

The headlights push into the night. Poke twin holes in the darkness. Open just enough space in the murk for the little Volvo to speed into.

Carrie's eyes flick from the glowing yellow lines on the road over to Silas in the driver's seat. He looks funny with the green glow of the dash lighting him from below the chin, tinting his chiseled jaw the pale shade of a lima bean.

She turns to gaze out the passenger window. Sees dark splotches out there. Trees and houses rendered in charcoal tones. The occasional floodlight hung up over a garage and driveway, a lone bulb that beats back the shadows and shows a pop of color, be it the red of brick or the muted yellows and blues of vinyl siding.

"Where are we going?" she asks, breath congealing as moisture on the glass before her and then disappearing almost at once.

"Don't know," Silas says. "Just felt like driving around, I guess."

She nods. No real surprise there. He always seems to drive them around for a bit after they've gone to a movie, even if they've gone to the midnight showing like tonight. With both of their living spaces perpetually overrun with roommates, going back to either of their rooms isn't a good option, so here they are.

This late, sometime after 2 A.M., the roads are empty. Dead. And as they hurtle into the rural nothingness outside of Remington Hills, even the lights die back. No more glowing signs. No more streetlights. Those periodic floodlights are the only thing outside of their own headlights.

A mist starts to fall. Not rain. Just that hanging wetness that always seems to occupy the sky out here in the swampy backwoods. Droplets that hover in midair, undulating, ribbons of them curling over each other in the breeze.

"The movie kinda sucked," she says, breaking up a long stretch of silence.

He smiles a little.

"That it did."

Images flash through her head. Memories of the horror as it flickered on the big screen. Blood. Knives. Violence. Gore.

The windshield wipers squeak against the glass. Squeegee away the mist dappling the surface.

"Here's my question," she says. "Most horror movies suck. Like probably over sixty percent of them are ultimately unsatisfying. That's conservative, I think. Could be much higher than sixty."

"Uh-huh. But that's not a question."

She rolls her eyes. More amused than annoyed.

"I'm getting to it, if you'll frickin' let me," Carrie says. "Why do we go see so many of 'em? *That's* the question. If most of 'em blow ass, why do we go see 'em all?"

He shrugs. Blinks in the dark.

"The good ones make it worth it, you know?"

She's about to respond to that when he puts up a finger between them and goes on.

"Plus, it's almost October. What else are we gonna do?"

"It's the second week of September."

"Exactly. And Halloween season starts in mid-to-late August and runs up to Thanksgiving Day. Everyone knows that."

She laughs a little.

"Oh, does it?"

He smiles in the greenish light. His hard features softening into something boyish but just for a moment. That severe brow and jaw retaking control of his face as the smile fades, making him look not of this era, like maybe he should be tilling a field somewhere or overseeing soldiers fighting in the Civil War.

And Carrie realizes that in a way it's this that she has always liked about him. He's a throwback. Masculine in a way that seems to have faded from the halls of society in recent years. A touch formal in the way he speaks, though mostly in a dry way that she finds endlessly hilarious. Always saying things like "Holy mackerel!" or "Man alive!" or "Good God!" in that deep voice of his. Even his name, Silas, seems old-timey to the point of foreignness — the name almost sounds exotic in an era rife with Ashtons and Logans and Jacksons.

He's a man, an actual man, even at twenty years old. And she likes that.

She watches his face transform again, awash in that pale green glow. His lips part. His eyes open wider.

"Oh," he says. "I almost forgot about these."

He digs in his jacket pocket, keeping his eyes on the road. A small cardboard box emerges from the shadows between them, the top half of the box folded over. The little package glides into the circumference of the dash light.

"Rest of your gummy bears," he says, handing them over.

She unfurls the top of the box. Dumps a few bears into her mouth. Then she peers down into the cardboard flaps. Picks out an orange one and hands it over to Silas.

He doesn't eat much candy — "I'm not into sweets," he often says — but he likes the orange gummy bears from the movie theater concession stand, so she likes sharing them with him. Somehow the shared experience enhances the whole thing, brings her more joy than any other aspect of going to the movies. When she hands over the orange bears, it feels all the more like they're doing this together.

His jaw works up and down. Hollow cheeks flexing, lacerated by shifting shadows that seem to open and close on the angular contours of his face.

"Up here…" he says, voice going softer. "Up here is where it happened."

She turns. Her attention drifts outside the car for the first time in a while, and she realizes that they've curved back toward town. In the dark, she doesn't recognize the buildings around them right away. The bricks and glass all look alien. Mysterious.

The police tape brings her right back. Four yellow lines flapping in the wind. Boxing off the area where the police found the car. The closest of the strands of yellow tape has been strung around a telephone pole on one end and knotted around a skeletal traffic sign stand on the other.

This is where the couple was killed, just two nights ago. The male victim had crawled away from the scene. Leaving a trail of blood. Making it to the front door of a nearby business before he bled out.

Silas slows the car, just a little, as they pass the scene of the crime. Both of them crane their necks. Look out at the empty area within the yellow tape like it might offer up some explanation or other.

Goosebumps ripple over Carrie's arms. Her skin going clammy. The cold and the mist outside seeming to cinch tighter around the car all at once.

Suddenly she finds herself dreading going home. Settling into the tiny first-floor bedroom. Alone in the dark.

And for just a second she thinks about what her parents would think of her being out this late, what her mom would say. They were so strict. Engulfing. Domineering. Obsessed with obedience and punishment to the point of total suffocation.

Carrie was the only one of her friends who couldn't be out past ten on weekends, even as a senior in high school. The only one not allowed to have a boyfriend or go on the senior trip to Cedar Point. Her mom had even forbidden her to shave her legs, so she had to do it in secret, like a drug user setting up with a razor in the bathroom, working in silence, oddly shamed and thrilled simultaneously to be disobeying, for having this one tiny glimmer of agency over her body, over her life.

Even now, in her second year away from home, she feels the tyranny of her mother eyeballing her, scrutinizing her, judging her. Always there in the back of her mind. Like one of those paintings with eyes that follow a person around the room.

"I don't want to go home yet," she says, her voice coming out huskier than she meant for it to.

"Good. Me neither."

She fumbles for the box of candy again. Digs out another orange bear and hovers it in the dark space between them. Silas holds up his palm. The bear sticks to Carrie's fingers before it plummets into the cupped part of his hand. And somehow that exchange calms her a little, a deep breath entering her quickly and rolling out slowly.

"Want to keep on driving?" Silas asks, his eyes flicking up and down her, trying to interpret something there.

She nods with gusto. Feeling better and better.

Neither one of them notices the car following along behind them with the headlights off.

CHAPTER 16

He drives. Follows in the dark. Creeps along at a distance.

It feels strange to drive with the lights off. Plunging into nothingness. Only those red taillights ahead pricking out of the gloom to guide him.

Exhilarating.

Cold blooms inside the car. The heat is off. Always off.

He likes that chilly feeling around his body. Crisp. Bracing.

The steering wheel slides its iciness against his palms and fingers. That faint twinge of numbness just brushing at his cheeks, at the tip of his nose.

Shivery. Calming. And even so, the cold can't touch the fire inside.

He can still picture her. The girl.

Walking out of the theater. Curves somehow showing through the jacket, through the dark in the parking lot. One streetlamp above lighting her from an angle, glinting on the feminine contours of her. A swaying silhouette that leaves him in rapture.

He licks his lips.

He only saw her for a couple seconds. A glimmer. A slice. A glimpse that makes her all the more tempting.

Two seconds. She'd appeared there for two seconds. And it had changed the course of both of their lives.

And later, in just a little while, two seconds will change them again. When he reaches for her. Touches her.

Two seconds.

Two seconds that will pull them into a shared moment.

Transfer them fully into the here and now together.

Grave intensity. Pain and pleasure. Life and death.

All the way real. All the way alive. If only for two seconds.

Eyes opened wide. Hearts thrumming like hummingbird wings. Knocking against the walls of their chests.

Tonight will be special. Singular. The main event that all their lives have built to. Every movement, every second, bringing them here. Placing them right here, right now. Together.

Awake. Eager. Writhing with it.

His tongue juts out to wet his lips. Dragging over cracked skin. His eyelids flutter involuntarily. Some jolt of chemical pleasure erupting in his brain just thinking about what will be.

Already it all feels fleeting. Passing him by. Ticking down to nothing. Almost over.

But for those two seconds?

He shifts his hands against the wheel. Cold and smooth assailing his chapped palms, resaturating them with the chill settled deep in the cabin of this vehicle.

And he has a plan. Something to make tonight even more special. Something that excites him.

The darkest adventure yet.

New depths. He's driven to seek new depths. Some compulsion to dig deeper, go further. Push. Push. Push himself and others to new depravities.

He doesn't understand it. He's just drawn to it. A moth flying into a porch light over and over, circling to it, some part of its instinctual architecture convinced this incandescent bulb really is the moon.

What's that term? Cutting edge. He smiles when he thinks of it.

His right hand sinks to his waistband. Feels the bulk there.

The hilt of the blade.

Yeah, he's got something special for tonight.

Something permanent. Something for keeps.

He doesn't quite know what it is yet. Doesn't know what he'll do until he gets there. Until he sees her up close. Until he feels it.

Anything is possible. A prospect that excites him all the more.

Flushes his face. Beads sweat on his brow. Makes him chew involuntarily on his bottom lip.

The red taillights sink behind a hill up ahead. The dark swallows them. And his throat tightens as he loses sight of the car. Her car.

His own vehicle drifts in the dark. Feels untethered from reality now. Floating in the emptiness.

He feels gravity shift into a lean as he crests the hill. Tilting him back in his seat.

Those two red eyes reappear before him. Glowering over the back bumper of the Volvo. Puddling scarlet on the asphalt.

And a fresh wave of excitement enters his bloodstream. New pictures opening in his head. Of him and her and the knife tucked down in his pants even now.

The guy could be a problem. One of those farmer-looking types. Stout and thick-limbed.

But that was OK. The gun, he could still use it on the boyfriend. Take him out fast.

And her too, maybe.

Maybe the special moment could come when they were both gone. Evicted from their bodies. Dispatched.

Then the blade could come out and play. Press itself into action.

Something to take. Something to keep. Forever.

Yes.
Yes.
It feels right.

CHAPTER 17

A BIC lighter rasps and flares. Casts orange light on jaws and chins and white paper tubes stuffed with tobacco. Beats back the encroaching night for a fraction of a second.

Three cigarettes smolder. Sending miniature smoke signals to no one.

While her friends hug close to the brickwork of this little alcove they're standing in, Tobi keeps her shoulders square to the building across the street. Lets the icy breeze push tufts of crinkled blue hair back from her forehead. The cold air makes her eyes water, just a bit.

When the wind dies back, Jade braves a peek at the building. Eyes squinted to slits. Body language exaggerated.

"This is it," she says, adjusting the frames of her cat-eye glasses. A statement, not a question.

Tobi nods once. Her eyes crawling over the glass doors, the yellow light, the cruisers parked at acute angles from the facade. This is where they're going tonight. A clandestine journey into the campus police department.

The third member of their trio, Andre, doesn't look over at the building. He sighs and pulls his hands up into his hoodie sleeves. Leaves the cigarette dangling out of the side of his mouth, smoke twirling into his eye.

A frigid gust rips into the small brick recess. Whistles against the grout lines.

And then the mist seems to appear around them all at once. Tiny flecks of water suspended in the air. Descending at an imperceptible rate.

The others pull their hoods up over their heads. Huddle as though hunching their shoulders might keep them an nth of a degree drier.

Tobi leaves her hood where it is. Stares at the building. Unmoving.

"Perfect. Jesus Christ," Andre says, holding his sleeved hands up into the wet and shaking his head. "Are you, like, sure we should do this?"

Tobi breathes smoke into her lungs. Holds it for a second. Lets it out before she answers in a deadpan.

"Yeah."

The downward curve of Andre's mouth bends harder. The expression reminds Tobi of one of those perpetually grumpy-looking fish.

"I mean, if we get caught, we'll get kicked out of school, won't we? Like for real? Permanently and shit?"

Tobi shrugs. Doesn't break eye contact with the door of the police station across the street.

"We won't get caught."

Jade chimes in again.

"Stop pissing your pants about it, Andre. We're not talking about sneaking into the J. Edgar Hoover building or Scotland Yard or something. These are campus police. They won't catch on."

Tobi smirks at the slow nod from the scaredy-cat, visible just out of the corner of her eye.

"Yeah," Andre says to himself as much as them. "Yeah, I guess so."

They smoke again in silence for a bit. Churning clouds streaming up through puffs of blue hair and billowing around the bare light bulb above.

The wind rips into the alcove again. Moans against the

facade. Freezes them all in place.

Still Tobi can't take her eyes from the shiny little building. Watching and waiting.

Scratch the surface. See what lies beneath.

Words pound in her head. Sometimes, when her passion blooms, like now, she starts writing the drafts for her blog in her mind.

Peel back the college town facade. The ideal. An image packaged and presented by those who stand to gain.

Words hammering in her skull almost involuntarily. Sentences. Paragraphs. Fully formed pieces of writing thundering out of the nowhere of her right brain. Feels like someone else is putting them there, transmitting them into her thoughts, though these words are quite clearly her own.

Maybe all images are constructs. Manipulations. Figments of sales and marketing. Skin-deep creations made to serve those who mediate them.

Here in Remington Hills, those in power have made a mask for the town, for the school. A way to hide a harrowing truth.

Sexual misconduct that escalated while they hid it. Indecent exposure turned to rapes. Rapes turned to murders. All carefully concealed behind the archetypal veil of the small-town college campus.

And while they worked to cover it up in private, publicly they served up distractions. Appealed to outdated sets of values and standards.

They served up football and the 4th of July and Apple Pie and, "Gee Wally. That's swell." while a rapist and murderer stalked campus night after night.

But sometimes it only takes the slightest touch to make even the biggest lie fold in on itself.

Fingernails brought to the shell. Slid over the skin. The

darkness seeping out of the slashed places. The truth laid bare.

Scratch the surface.

Words that she will recall later verbatim and type on her laptop, perhaps choosing to sharpen a line here and there, though for the most part these involuntary words need no editing. Their energy pulses on the page. Turns of phrase that cut like diamonds. These are the best passages she writes, the ones that appear in her head without warning.

Her eyes swivel over the glowing glass of the campus police department. Scanning endlessly. Set hard. Unblinking.

Yes. Tonight is the night.

CHAPTER 18

"Now where are we going?"

Carrie chews a gummy bear while she asks, that rubbery bit of candy squishing between her molars. An acidic lime flavor spills free from the gelatin blob. Green. Her least favorite.

They are heading out of town again. Out past the hospital and the super Wal-Mart. Trees and cornfields rising up on the sides of the road, flickering mostly indistinct shapes against the windows. The darkness pooling over everything.

"I know a place," Silas says, smiling to himself.

Carrie's heart beats a little faster at the implication. She sits forward in her seat.

"We're parking somewhere?"

Her voice comes out kind of squeaky, surprising her. Jesus. Is she that scared?

"Why? You think the killer's gonna find us?"

Carrie feels her shoulders hunch involuntarily. Vulnerability physically contorting her.

"That's not funny, Silas. People died. Brutally killed. It's not a joke."

His smile recedes and hard lines form on his forehead. Deep wrinkles creasing there like the folds on a pug's face.

"Quite right. There's no excuse for it. But this is a spot where no one will find us, OK?"

Carrie blinks a few times. She tries to straighten her spine, but her shoulders seem to have locked themselves into a stoop.

"Yeah? And where's that?"

"There are roads out here between some of the fields.

They're mostly for tractors, yeah? Not official roads or anything. Just worn grooves between the corn and soy beans. If you know where to look."

He waggles his eyebrows up and down before he goes on.

"And I do."

Carrie smiles to herself. While she had moved here from the suburbs surrounding Detroit, Silas had lived just outside of Remington Hills all his life. Worked the fields, even as a kid, detasseling corn and such.

"You used to come out here a lot, huh? On these little farmer's tracks?"

"Man alive," Silas said. "All the time."

"Probably took your farm skanks out into the soy beans. Gave 'em the ol' corncob treatment until they said e-i-e-i-o, right?"

Silas chuckles.

"Used to come out here and set off fireworks with my friends. Drink like two Bud Lights apiece and be totally shitfaced off it somehow. Felt weird, you know? Exciting and scary. To be on another man's land. Trespassing."

The tires judder over divots in the road. Makes the whole car shake a few seconds before it relents. Then Silas continues.

"This was in middle school and high school. Most of it would have been after Chip got his license, I guess. My dad had sold our own acreage by then, but I wouldn't have gone out in our fields like that anyway. It feels kinda dangerous to go out trespassing and all, but my dad? Boy, he would have skinned me alive if he caught me at that kind of foolishness on his land."

Carrie's voice stops shy of her lips, hesitates to respond. Silas's dad had only died about ten months earlier, and Silas seems to subconsciously wind all conversations in that direction now.

"You must miss him," she says after a lull. "Your dad, I mean. You must miss your dad."

"Yeah. I mean… yeah."

Silas holds quiet for a beat before he goes on.

"He was really funny, you know. Had this way of talking that was unlike anyone else I've known. Somehow incredibly blunt and indirect at the same time. Witty. But he was older. He was almost fifty when I was born, so it was just a different thing than what most kids experience, I expect. That extra generation between us. More like a grandpa in a way."

"A stern, funny grandpa," Carrie says.

"Yeah, basically. Oh, here we go."

A gap appears in the field to the right. Almost too small to be seen unless one is looking for it. Partially hidden by the few trees just along the road.

The car slows. Veers into the cleft. Crunches over the gravel on the shoulder.

The headlights swing over a sprawling field of crops. Beams finding the parted place in the cornstalks. Piercing the darkness there.

Silas steps on the gas, and they plunge into the field.

There's a big dip as soon as they're off the road, and Carrie's stomach lifts in her abdomen. Feels weightless and strangely queasy, like that first big hill on a roller coaster.

Silas sits up higher in his seat. Strangles the steering wheel. Tries to wrestle the car back under control.

Carrie wraps both hands around her seat belt and squeezes them into fists.

The car shimmies beneath them. Thudding and jostling, the rear end fishtailing over the wet greenery.

Then the tires find two muddy grooves slashed into the

ground, and the ride smooths out some.

The darkness thickens around them. The opening among the spiky plants is only about the width of the vehicle.

Bent-over tassels bat at the sides of the Volvo. Leaves brush and scrape at the windows. All those stalks crowding around, huddling over them.

Silas chuckles again, a deep sound emitting from that pale green glow lighting the driver's seat.

"Kind of fun, right?" he says, head turning, eyes swiveling everywhere until they find hers.

A little laugh snorts out of her, surprising her. She realizes that, despite the fact she's crushing the seat belt with both hands, she *is* having fun. That cold surge of excitement thrumming through her.

Out so late. Free and uninhibited.

"Yeah. Kind of freaked me out, going down that damn mudslide. I thought we might end up stuck in the ditch for a second there. But yeah. This is fun."

"See? *That's* why I like horror movies. Danger and fun are inextricable, ultimately. Excitement is born out of a sense of peril. And the more real the danger, the more intense the excitement. Anyone who says otherwise is lily-livered, I say."

Carrie hisses out a laugh.

"Lily-livered? I think you're officially the last person still saying that one."

"There are control freaks, you know, who hate horror. They think, 'Why would anyone want to watch a scary movie or go to a haunted house and feel out of control?' I've thought about that a lot. Tumbled it around in the ol' dome to try to make some sense of it. I think it's like this: they feel like they're giving up some kind of command over themselves or something by subjecting themselves to horror, right? But that's the thing. You don't have any control! Not in this life. You never did. Not really. No one does. Horror gives us a safe way to explore that. A way to get a heaping helping of excitement even though the danger ain't real."

Carrie nods.

"My mom is like that. Hates horror. Anything dark. And she is definitely a control freak. Just hovering over me, trying to oversee my life in a weird way. I had to fight for the tiniest bit of breathing room, like a bug she kept in a jar or something. Like I didn't tell her when I started my period. She finally figured it out a couple years later."

"Are you serious?"

Carrie shrugs in the dark.

"It was like we were having this war over my body in a way. I knew that my growing up was like a grave threat to her, or something. It terrified her. So I couldn't tell her."

"Damn... that's... I don't even know what to say."

"Eh. It's over now. I got out of there."

The car tracks around a tight curve to the left, and the land slopes upward beneath them. At the top of the rise, they find a small clearing.

Silvery moonlight shimmers down on a shelf of dewy grass, the foliage sounding crunchy and somehow wet against the undercarriage. In the distance, the land eventually gives way to woods.

"Here we go," Silas says, nearly under his breath. "This is a little turnaround for the tractors. The perimeter of the field, you know?"

He pulls the car up to the edge of the woods, where the shadows are thickest. Carrie swivels around in her seat. Gazes out the back windshield where she can just make out the path in the field behind them, lit up in a dull red by the taillights.

She watches the gap in the crops as though she expects something or someone to come bounding out of there. Nothing does.

"Pretty private, right?" Silas says, waggling his eyebrows again.

She shrugs at first. Then she nods.

He kills the engine, and the quiet swells around them. Night sounds suddenly huge outside the car. Bugs chirping. The wind rattling faintly through the cornstalks. All of the noises muffled by the windows. Muted and hollow-sounding.

"Killer sure as shit ain't gonna find us way out here, am I right?"

He dumps the car keys into the cup holder as he says it. The crashing metal jarring in the stillness. Sharp.

Again her shoulders hunch without her telling them to. Her skin goes tight with gooseflesh. She wishes he wouldn't keep bringing the murders up, joking around about them.

He turns on the radio at a low volume. Flips around until some oldies song is coming through clearly enough. Then his eyes flick up and down her face, and his smile dies back.

"Ah, I'm sorry. I know I shouldn't keep joking about it. I guess it's just on my mind, you know? I mean, I ain't scared, personally. Like I ain't scared for me or you, I guess. But it *is* scary to know he's out there. Right now. Tonight. He's out there. Somewhere in our town. Shoot."

He leans over to her. His face close to hers. And he's whispering now.

"You know I'm sorry, don't you?"

She feels his eyelashes fluttering against her cheek. Lips tickling along her jaw as he keeps whispering.

"And you know I won't let anything happen to you. Not tonight. Not ever."

She wants to turn her head away. At least wait until the creeping feelings on her skin recede. But that tickling on her cheek persists, and she can't defy him any longer.

She leans forward. Into him. His head dips and tilts as well.

His lips find hers. Brushing. Meshing. Cool to the touch.

They slide close together, torsos bumping then settling against each other. His arms cinching around her shoulders, gently squeezing her closer still.

She nuzzles against his chest. Firm and strong. And she feels warm here. Safe here.

She loses herself in their kissing. Heat creeps into her cheeks. Vaguely she is aware of the soft murmur of the radio, of the steam slowly building on the windows around them.

Time passes. And then more time passes. Drifting.

His torso goes rigid in her arms. He sits up straight, pulls free of her grip, and their lips disengage.

"Did you hear that?" he says. His voice is low. Stern. Serious.

She watches him. His eyes wide. Swiveling everywhere, swiveling everywhere.

"No," she answers, finally. "Just the radio."

His teeth gnaw at his bottom lip, and he blinks a few times. Weighing what to say next, she thinks.

"It sounded like a car door closing," he says. "And it sounded close."

They both turn to look out the back windshield, but the steam clouds over that pane of glass the same as all the rest. Their eyes meet again.

She almost wants to laugh at how scared he looks. Almost.

"We would have heard a car coming up the trail, wouldn't we?" she says, though as soon as it's out loud, she's not so sure.

"I don't know. I mean, I would think so. But we were kind

of distracted."

They're quiet for a few seconds. A Del Shannon song plays softly on the oldies station.

Silas swipes the fog off his window with the sleeve of his shirt. Peers out at the darkness. It doesn't seem to reveal much — just moonlit grass and a slice of the woods up ahead of them — and it starts fogging back up almost instantly. Still, there's nothing out there now, that much seems plain.

He turns back. Shrugs.

"Maybe it was nothing," he says. "We haven't heard anything else, right?"

His face relaxes, and he settles back into his seat.

She finds herself relieved that he's no longer quite so scared, and yet it also concerns her in a new way. If he's not watching and listening as closely, it falls back on her to be the vigilant one, doesn't it?

Within a couple of minutes, they're kissing again. Bodies pressed close, pressed tight.

The world seems to ease into a soft focus for Carrie, not unlike the smear of mist coating the windows. Soon she loses touch with everything but Silas, drops the rest of reality from her consciousness.

She only partially even sees him through half-opened eyes. His face close and dark. All angles and shadows. Muscles dimpled and carved and curved.

And in a way it feels like floating. Drifting. Unchained from the ground, from the car seat. Ethereal.

A dark shape moves outside the car. Broad shoulders shifting in the mist.

And Carrie screams.

She pulls away from Silas. Shoulders shaking. Diaphragm flexing to make her ribcage buck.

She tucks her hands up against her chest in a Tyrannosaurus Rex pose.

Silas's eyes go wide again. He cranes his head around. Eyes scanning everywhere.

"What?" he says, his voice hard and sharp. "What is it?"

Carrie struggles to get the words to rise from her trembling torso.

"I saw something… outside the car. A… a… a shape. Moving."

Now his eyebrows crush together.

"A shape?"

"A silhouette. Shoulders. Moving along the… the…"

She points. Sweeps her finger across the driver's side window behind his back.

"You're sure?"

She nods, but she can hear the doubt in his voice now. That sharpness changed to something else, some hint of blame or disgust for her, like his fear is somehow her fault.

"The windows are pretty steamed up," he says.

He won't even look at her anymore.

"I saw it," she says, but her voice is growing smaller, weaker. "Right over there."

He leans back. Smears his sleeve on the driver's side window again. This time he does a better job. Clears the whole thing and then goes over it again.

He leans up close to the wet glass. Stares out into the darkness for a long moment.

"It was probably just a deer or something. Anyway… I don't see anything there now."

He turns back and tries to smile at her. Shrugs his shoulders ever so slightly.

"This dark, how can you even tell?" she says.

He huffs. Turns on the flashlight of his phone. Shines it around out there. The swinging beam of light reveals only mist and wet tree branches that look almost black.

"See? Nothing."

He looks back at her again. Does that thing where his eyes swivel up and down her face. Whatever he's reading there, he can see she's not satisfied.

"Here. Maybe this'll give you some peace of mind."

He leans forward. Shoves his arm under the driver's seat and roots around under there a while. When he pulls his arm out of the dark space, there's a ratty-looking beach towel clutched in his hand.

He starts wiping off the windshield. Little squeaky sounds emitting from where the towel rubs at the condensation.

When the front slab of glass is clear, he leans over her lap to wipe off the passenger side window.

She looks out in front of the car. Sees a slice of dark woods framed by the rectangular sheet of the windshield. Nothing there.

Just as he finishes up the passenger side window, they both jump back.

The shape shifts in the shadows there next to her door.

Something big.

Something yanking on the door handle.

CHAPTER 19

Jade makes a show of smearing both hands over the glass door of the SMU Campus Police Headquarters. Her palms squeak over the cool glazing.

She imagines herself looking like a zombie in a George Romero movie. A corpse pressed to the glass like a suckerfish, throbbing and wobbling.

With the makeup Tobi pancaked on her face, she does look just about dead. Pale cheeks. The faintest blue hue to the lips. Purpled pockets of flesh deepening the shadows beneath her brow, exaggerating the depths of each orbital cavity so her eyes look sunken in her skull.

After what feels like an appropriately dramatic smear session, she pushes the door open and stumbles into the lobby. Chatters her teeth. Stoops her upper back. Hopes the dumb cop on the other side of the counter notices the soaking wet hoodie drooping and dripping off of her.

She stumbles up to the counter. Leans her forearms on the Formica ledge.

The desk sergeant, a gray-haired man with a mustache that looks sort of withered on one side, puts down his phone. His eyes go comically wide, and a surprised breath scrapes into his throat.

"Oh, gosh. Are you OK, miss?"

"I just… I just…"

She can barely get the words out through her chattering teeth. She wonders, for just a second, whether or not the makeup looks realistic under the harsh fluorescent bulbs in here — the long tubes overhead have a faintly visible flicker, giving everything in the room a stop-motion quality.

The desk sergeant rolls away from the desk in his office chair, the wheels grating against thin carpet. He hurls himself to his feet. Rushes through the batwing doors that divide the area behind the desk from the front.

He stops just shy of touching Jade. Some caution overtaking him now, like maybe he is overreacting. His crooked mustache seems to bulge as he presses his lips together.

"Are you… OK… miss?"

Jade just stares at him for a few seconds, letting her eyes drift out of focus. Looking through him.

She senses that a dramatic pause here will work wonders. Sink the hook all the way in. Once she's got him on the line, she's all set.

All the improv drills she's done over the past three years in her theater classes have given her an innate sense for what should come next in a scene. What will have the most impact. What will get a good gasp or chuckle out of the crowd.

She moves her lips as though trying to speak, tiny tremors in the corners of her mouth.

"Miss?" he says.

His voice has gone airy. Soft like someone talking to a sleeping baby.

Jade gives it a couple more seconds. Really wants to stretch this out.

She slow blinks. Lets her eyelashes stick together just a bit before she peels them apart again. The effect looks a little like a milk drunk kitten, she thinks, having watched videos of herself practicing it.

"Hey… hey, Anderson," the desk sergeant yells, glancing

back over his shoulder. He waits a second, eyes swiveling back and forth. When he gets no response, he yells louder, a sharp edge in his voice now. "Get your hiney out here, Anderson. We've got a, uh… a situation… out here, man."

She waits until his eyes are fully locked on her again. Takes one more shuddering breath.

Show time.

She lets out a faint moan. A soft tone emitting from deep in her throat, exhaled as much as spoken. The sound lifts in pitch at the end, bent upward like the sound of a question, like the sound of fear.

She lets her shoulders slacken. Upper body swaying faintly as though gravity is wrestling her for control now and getting the upper hand. Neck bobbing her head around like a buoy in a rough sea.

Finally she rolls her eyes back until only the whites are visible. Eyelids spasming over those blank orbs in a way she thought looked especially dramatic in her practice video — it reminded her somehow of a spinning slot machine reel whirring too fast to see.

She then makes a big show of her torso and head spiraling. Body language screaming clear as day, "I'm losing my balance." She takes her time with this, hopes it's long enough that this idiot will overcome his shock and catch her.

When it feels right, she pitches forward. Straightening her back to give off the full "timber" effect of a felled tree. Tilting. Bending.

She lays herself out in a freefall for the ground. Arms as limp as soggy noodles.

And she waits for his hands to come to her.

CHAPTER 20

Silas can't stop staring at the gun. A black bulk thrust into the open passenger door.

The weapon just sits there in the man's hand. Gleaming black under the yellow dome light. Oiled and glistening.

Shadows still shroud the man wielding the pistol. He stands in the wedge of the open door. His face jutting up into the darkness.

A black hoodie and black jeans adorn the body. Big aviator sunglasses over his eyes, even in the dark. The hood is cinched tight to obscure the bottom half of his face, all bunched up in a way that distorts his proportions.

The gun moves then. Lifts with a jerk of the wrist. Leaps up like that twice in a row. The man seems to be gesturing with it.

Silas lurches for him. Some delayed reaction. Instinct kicking in at last. Fight over flight.

He kicks his legs. Pushes off the floor. Thrusts for the dark shape. Diving over Carrie.

The creeper clubs him in the nose with the butt of the gun. Swings it straight down like a hammer blow.

Motes flare inside Silas's head. Like sparks bursting out of a log in a campfire. Exploding bits of brightness.

He feels the cartilage in his nose splinter. All the flesh collapsing around that shard of bone, like a rotten peach squelched against the pit.

And then the dark gets bigger. Deeper. Sucks him under. The dimmer switch in his skull cranked all the way down.

Dark.

Quiet.

Nothing else is real. Just the dark and the wet of the blood draining down from his nostrils like a faucet. Warm thickness adhering to his top lip, spilling down over his chin.

He bobs back toward the surface.

Blinks a few times before he can get his eyelids to stay open. Stares up from his slumped position. Eyes adjusting.

The night comes back first. Stars. The moon. Pinpricks in the slice of darkness he can see above.

And then the shape reappears just after that. That dark silhouette filling the doorway, blotting out an angular slab of the stars. Broad shoulders that taper to a thin waist.

The dome light fades back in above him only after he's scrabbling back. Sickly yellow light filming over the interior of the car.

He blinks again. Finds himself splayed over Carrie's lap. Lying on his side. Hands already bound in front of him by twine. Carrie's fingers tightening the knot while the shape in the doorway watches.

Tears flood his eyes. Blurring everything.

The blood gushes from both nostrils. The spigot jetting full blast. Cascading over Carrie's legs. Pooling on her lap. Steaming a little where the cool night air touches it.

The shape moves. Shifts in the doorway. Flicks the gun again.

Silas squirms on his girlfriend's legs. Bleeds on her. Tries to push himself up, but his bound arms skitter out from under him like the legs of a newborn deer. No strength there.

His top half tips down toward the floor. Gravity pulls him. Wedges his head and shoulders between the dash and Carrie's legs.

It's only after a second that the words come to him. The

shape is speaking to them. Telling them what to do.

"You'll stay here," he says. His voice is deep and hollow. The faintest rasp to it like dead leaves scraping together.

He faces Carrie as he says this, the tiniest smile on his lips. He turns her upper body. A rough touch that spins her around, yanking her arms behind her.

He tucks the gun in his belt, and then a length of twine loops around her hands. Pulls taut both the rope and her posture.

He works quickly. Hands sure. Knotting. Cinching.

"Into the backseat," the shape says, getting the gun back out.

She obeys. Moves to climb over the seat, though with her hands bound behind her back, it's more leaning than climbing.

Silas spills deeper toward the floorboard as her legs slither out from beneath him. His shoulder touches down to the rough car carpeting.

He tries to push himself up. Arms quivering from the strain but not collapsing this time. He manages to lift himself back onto the seat on hands and knees.

The dark man shoves Carrie over the hump of the headrest, and she rolls as she falls into the backseat. Winds up on her back, balled into a loose somersault position. She looks a little like a box turtle trapped on its back, wet eyes blinking hard.

The killer turns back to Silas. Gestures with the gun again.

"You. Come with me. Exit through the passenger door. And bring the keys."

Numb spreads through his body as he plucks the keys from the cup holder. The metallic bits jangle against each other for a second and then float upward in silence.

This can't be real. This can't be happening.

And then he's moving out of the car. The mist swirling

around him. Wetting his forehead, the bridge of his nose.

He squints. Eyes blind in this darker stuff. For a second he can't see the man before him, and then he does.

The dark shape seems to form out of the blackness as he steps closer. A jagged thing off to his left. All hard edges under the curved dome of the hood. Feet scuffing over the dewy ground.

Silas follows the directive of the gesturing pistol. Turns toward the rear of the car.

The gun jabs him in the lower back. Cold and hard. Prodding into the taut muscles there just above the hip.

They walk to the back of the vehicle. Slow steps.

"Go on and pop the trunk. Then give me the keys."

He uses the fob to unlock the car. A collective clack sounding through the vehicle.

Then Silas's fingers feel for the release button. Digging in the wet shadowed place. Smearing in the crevice just above the license plate.

He finds the jutting disc of plastic. Pushes it. Opens the trunk.

The killer rips the keys out of his hands. A jerky motion that catches Silas off guard.

"In you go," he says.

His knee comes up. Jams its stony point into Silas's spine just above the tailbone.

Silas bends at the waist. Leans into the dark opening. Falling as much as anything. His hands come down on the rough synthetic fiber coating the cargo space like AstroTurf, twine biting at his wrists.

He takes a sharp breath and climbs in. One part of him not sure why he's obeying these orders. Another part not sure what else he could do.

He crawls into the dark. Tries to keep his back and butt low to fit. Awkward motions, arms and shins scrabbling like crab legs. His upper back scrapes the lip where the metal forms the top edge of the trunk.

He sinks lower. Deeper. Climbs forward until the shadows swallow him, until he feels the front barrier of the trunk. More of the rough, dry carpet-like material grating at his fingers there.

The sounds fade out as he finagles the rest of the way into this box. The metal enclosure muffles everything. Dampens the sounds of the night outside — the mist sizzling against the leaves in the distance, the faint whispers of the wind touching the wet places. It leaves only a strange echo of his own scuffing about in the trunk, little sounds that are somehow right on top of him.

Nestled into the hollow, he turns. Faces that rectangular opening where the moon and stars still shine above, where the mist wafts around the killer's silhouette — a black shape in the night.

The trunk door comes ripping down. Slams home. Latches with a click.

And then all that's left is the dark.

CHAPTER 21

Tobi shifts her feet over the wet asphalt. The soles of her shoes slurping and scratching.

She squats with Andre between police cruisers in the parking lot outside the campus police building. They've found a shadowy place just twenty or so feet from the front door, and it's even semi-sheltered from the wet.

Waiting. Waiting for Jade to play out her hypothermic pantomime. Waiting for their cue.

She pokes her head up over the hood of the car to watch the gleaming glass front of the building again. Andre follows her lead, his head bobbing up a second later, accompanied by a mournful moan that almost sounds like a whistling tea kettle.

Inside, Jade has just started wobbling around. Looks like a punch-drunk boxer. Out on her feet but somehow still standing.

The beefy cop from behind the desk stands before her. Looks like his eyes are about to leap out of his head like ping pong balls.

"Jesus, she's taking forever," Andre says. "Isn't she?"

"She's good," Tobi says. "Look at that cop's fucking face. He's buying it. He's making eight weird faces per second. Like the full range of human emotion is being expressed through his eyes and mustache."

Andre mulls this over for a second.

"Yeah. Looks like a tick about to pop."

They fall quiet for a second. Watching Jade stretch it out.

Andre sighs again. Ducks back down behind the fender,

tucked in the shadows once more. When he speaks, his voice sounds shaky.

"Are you sure we should, like, actually do this?"

Tobi doesn't say anything. Just stares at that cop's twitching lips, swiveling eyes.

"I mean… I just…"

It sounds like he's about to cry now. Voice getting heavy and breathy.

Tobi grits her teeth. Says nothing. Doesn't want to acknowledge Andre's fear in any way. To utter a word now would only feed it, only allow him to dig his heels in like a stubborn toddler.

"Oh shit," she whispers. "She's going down."

Andre bobs back up. They watch together as Jade flings herself forward. Tipping. Her back stiff. Almost looks like a mannequin toppling over.

The beefy cop steps forward. Knifes both his arms under her armpits just in time. Tobi swears she can see his eyeballs actually quivering.

He hesitates there a second. Holding her at an awkward angle about three feet off the ground.

Then he lowers her to the carpet. Turns her onto her back. Brushes the dark hair out of her face, away from those cat-eye glasses.

"She did it," Andre says. "It worked."

Two other cops come bustling out from behind the counter. Pausing just beyond the swinging half-doors. Then rushing to Jade.

They look frazzled. Rigid. Pacing and fidgeting. Deeply uncomfortable.

"You think they'll do it?" Andre says. "Take her back to the first aid area?"

Tobi chews her lip as she answers.

"Just wait."

The cops all pivot their heads around. Hands moving nervously from their belts to their chins and back again.

The beefy guy from the front desk stands up from where he's been squatting by Jade's fallen figure. He seems taller than before. Shoulders set wide. Chest thrust out. Mouth biting off words. Face going red.

The others hold motionless as he yells at them, and then everyone is still for a beat. Looking at the floor.

Finally, they team up. Squat to lift her by the arms and legs and carry her back behind the counter.

An eel thrashes in Tobi's gut. Sends bright voltage through all of her body. Makes her smile so hard her cheeks hurt.

"Go time," she says. "Masks on."

They both pull ski masks down over their faces. Push themselves to their feet. Tobi's thighs feel faintly numb from the squatting and the cold.

The lights over the parking lot touch their windbreakers for the first time. Gleaming on the purple and green of the school colors. They wear SMU gear, windbreaker jackets and tearaway pants of the same shiny polyester, all bought at the University Bookstore earlier with cash.

They look like tourists. Dorks. Missing only the bulging fanny packs at their hips. But they will be unrecognizable on the security videos.

Disguises. Nondescript. As generic as possible. It had been Andre's idea, oddly enough.

They run across the wet blacktop of the parking lot, the whole thing rendered a shallow mud puddle now. Strands of water kick up from their shoes and spray both forward and back.

Tobi hears a gibbering sound that makes the hair on the back of her neck stand up. An uneven burble. Yukking and hissing.

She looks over at Andre. Sees his wet teeth exposed, his tongue rippling within that circular mouth hole in the ribbed fabric of his mask. Realizes that the sound is coming from him.

He's laughing like some kind of maniac.

And it occurs to her that Andre seems to have suddenly grown more brazen now that his face is covered, now that he's anonymous. Something about that makes her chill go even colder.

He races out in front of her. Rips open the door. Crosses into the bright light of the lobby.

His feet stutter slightly as he nears the front desk. Still spritzing water, now on the thin layer of industrial carpet, the pale gray of it going darker as the wet seeps in.

Tobi pushes harder. Forearms the door. Catches up to him.

Together they sidle through the batwing doors. Move behind the counter.

Tobi obeys some instinct to get low, and Andre follows her lead. Crouch-running now behind the cover of the cubicle dividers.

Soundless. Bobbing as they walk from heel to toe.

She eyes the top of the doorway in the distance, the one she believes they've taken Jade to. Voices carry from there. Cops freaking out about the fainting girl on their hands.

"Hell, could she be hypothermic? Should we call a fucking ambulance?"

"I don't… I don't… know."

"Shit. Miss, can you hear me? Hey, did her eyes just move? Sarge, I think her eyes just moved. Look. Wait. I swear they did. They moved a second ago. They, like, moved."

The cops sound so close it makes Tobi's jaw flex in pulses. Teeth gritting in spasms. Her own breath sounding loud, sounding right on top of her.

The cubicle dividers form a barrier between them and the doorway, though. They'd have time to get hidden should anyone pop out just now, and she doesn't think they will anyway.

They move toward the back of the room. Staying low and quiet.

At one of the back desks, Tobi rocks up higher for a second, almost standing. She grabs a big ring of keys — almost looks like a janitor's keyring. She assumes it belongs to one of the officers with Jade, judging by the brimming mug of coffee just next to it, still warm enough to be coiling steam.

They keep moving. Traverse the rest of the big room. Feet mostly dry now, light on the carpet.

At the back hall, they veer left. Moving away from the voices.

Doors line the back hall. Left and right. Placards above label the rooms — Interrogation Room 1, Interrogation Room 2, and so on. That makes things easy enough.

Based on what they'd overheard, the task force was headquartered in Conference Room 2. It ends up being the last door on the left.

They scuttle up to the door. Tobi reaches out a hand for the knob. Expects it to be locked.

She can already picture having to work through the thousand keys. Trying to find the right one.

Her fingers find the cool steel. She twists. Braces for it to deny her.

The door opens. A wedge of darkness exposed as the panel of wood glides inward.

Andre and Tobi look at each other. Shake their heads in unison.

An unlocked door. Of course. The campus police at their finest.

They rush into the shadowy room and close the door behind them.

CHAPTER 22

Carrie squirms in the backseat. Twine digging at her wrists.

She gets herself upright, and her eyes lock on the nearer of the two rear doors. The indicator shows her it's unlocked.

She takes a big breath. Feels her lungs shake with it.

Then she lunges for the door. Legs thrusting. Waist flexing. Torso lurching. She feels like a jumping frog.

But she doesn't get far. More of a hop than a leap.

She changes tactics. Slides her back over the seat. Turns herself and leans toward the door.

She tries to wrench her arms that way. Stretches. Feels the twine gnawing at her wrists. Feels her shoulder muscles strain against her commands.

Her arms won't budge. Locked behind her. Tied so tightly it stings even when she doesn't move.

The dome light clicks off. Plunges the inside of the car into darkness.

It makes a lump rise in her throat. A dimpled golf ball lodged there, bobbing upward.

She needs to hurry. Needs to hurry.

She throws herself backward this time. Jumping and diving and falling all at once. Shoulder blades propping her against the point where the door and window meet.

Her fingers stretch, fumbling over rubbery upholstery. Her teeth grit so hard it makes her jaw quiver.

It's not working. She can't see the door handle. Can't reach.

She stops. Hears something. Listens.

Muffled voices burble somewhere behind the car. An

unintelligible stream of deep sounds. All the consonants swallowed so it sounds like cooing in strange, choppy bursts. All *oo*s and *aa*s.

She rolls her shoulder into the plushness of the backseat. Needs to get onto her back. She might be able to kick out the window that way. Bash both heels into it like twin sledgehammers.

She can already picture the glass shattering. The arched passageway clearing there. She could wriggle out of it. Spill onto the dewy ground like a worm.

Her torso slides down the back of the seat, but the point of her shoulder keeps bunching up the upholstery and getting caught. Slowing her descent.

She wiggles. Tries to lie back. Heart thumping. Chest heaving. Arms and legs prickling with icy needle pokes.

She hears the trunk door slam shut. The resonant thump vibrating through the car. The seat bobbing once beneath her.

She freezes. Cranes her head to look out the front of the car. Sees only the dark of the woods through the windshield. The tree branches glint the faintest dappling of pale from the moonlight. Nothing moves there.

She listens. Hears footsteps chopping at the dewy grass. Crunching stalks and stems.

He's coming.

Little wheezy sounds come out with her breath now. The wind whistling against the edges of her teeth.

His silhouette slides over the driver's side window, and she shrinks back. Pumps her legs to scoot her to the opposite side of the backseat.

He seems to hesitate there. His shadow bobbing just on the other side of the door.

Then the door handle clicks. The arched piece of metal

slides open. Slowly, slowly.

The dome light clicks on once the door is a few inches open. Blinding yellow light pierces her eyes. Stabbing. Stinging.

She blinks hard. Fights to open her eyes to slits.

And he's there. He's there now. Perched on the front seat. Facing the back. Hands looped over the headrest. Knees folded in front of him.

He is naked.

Stripped from head to toe.

Tan skin slicked with sweat. Gleaming under the dome light. Something rigid in the carriage of the riveted musculature. All jagged angles like his face. Taut.

He adjusts his squatted position. Leaning back so he can close the door behind him.

Heavy breath blows between his lips. Sounds wet. Strained. Charged with some dark energy.

He holds still there a second. Hands gripping the headrest. Chest heaving with rapid breaths.

His face seems angled into shadow somehow. Darkness stretching down from his brow, leaving only his forehead-well lit, the dome of dark hair above it.

Even so, she can see the shiny eyes there. Opened psychotically wide. The faintest smile visible in the lines radiating around them like spokes.

He moves. Lurches forward. Coming for her now.

The dome light snaps off as he straddles the front seat. And then he's a dark shape again, climbing into the back.

The shape moves closer. Closer. Stark lines of dark muscle. Angular. Lean and hard.

His weight lowers onto her. Rough hands clutching at her.

She closes her eyes.

CHAPTER 23

The cardboard file box makes a faint *thump* as Tobi overturns it. Pages flopping and spreading over the glossy conference room tabletop. A puddle of paper, thinning as it disperses like a wave crawling up to lap at the beach.

"Photos first. We can read everything later," Tobi says, as much to herself as Andre.

She bites her lip. Resists the urge to let her eyes creep over these pages and soak up all the information as fast as she can.

Instead she runs her hand over the pool of paper. Flips a page. Snaps a photo with her phone. Shoves it back into the box. Moves on to the next one. And the next.

Andre grimaces. Eyes blinking hard in the ski mask holes.

"We have to get everything?"

Tobi watches him out of the corner of her eye. Surprised at how much she can read his whiny expression even through the ribbed acrylic of the ski mask.

"Everything," she says.

He huffs. Shoulders sloping down.

He goes to dump another of the file boxes on the table, but Tobi shakes her head at him.

"One box at a time to stay organized," she whispers. "Divide up the stack. Make sure we get photos of everything."

Andre nods. Peels some of the pages off and slides them to his side of the table. Now he's snapping as fast as she is, clearing the photographed pages into the box just the same, paper kind of flung into the cardboard chamber as though it were a basketball hoop.

They work. Their phones click out artificial camera sounds in staccato bursts. Pages flapping like papery wings. Paper scuffing against paper and scraping against the edges of the cardboard boxes. Their pace ramps up and up.

Andre stops once. Pads across the room on light feet. Takes a second to listen at the door.

"What is it?" Tobi asks.

"Nothing," he says after a moment. "Thought I heard something."

A few seconds later, a deep click emits from somewhere in the room. They both freeze. Eyes swiveling to meet each other, then frantically scanning high and low.

After a pregnant pause, hot air hisses out of a vent in the corner. A seemingly endless exhale.

"Just the furnace," Andre says, whisper-giggling to himself.

The work goes quickly after that. Some of the boxes are less than half full, and with the two of them being quick about it, they're down to the last box in less than ten minutes.

"This is it?" Andre whispers.

"Yeah. Not so bad after all, huh?"

"Hell yeah. I mean, we've still gotta get out of here, but…"

Andre tears the lid away. The last box is the least full yet. Less than a quarter occupied by bleach-white documents, the rest a gaping expanse exposing pale brown walls.

He lifts the cardboard cube over the table, turns it over, and the pages plop onto the glossy plank of wood. Fanning there as Tobi runs her fingers over the short stack.

They fall into their rhythm again. Cameras clicking. Paper flapping. Raspy cardboard scraping as the pages flutter back down into their file box cell.

Tobi snaps a photo of the last page. Some part of her grows nervous, thinks maybe some of the photos will be blurry due to their speed. But swiping through the last few on her phone eases the anxiety. Crystal clear. The black text stark on the white pages. Not just legible. Strikingly sharp.

She crams the last page atop the haphazard stack littering the bottom of the box. Nestles the lid on top. Puts it back in the corner with the others.

"Holy shit. We did it," Andre says, looking even giddier than the last time he spoke.

"We fucking did it," Tobi agrees.

They grin at each other. Teeth shining in the holes of their ski masks.

"Wait," Andre says, his smile cutting out. "Listen."

Tobi's breath catches in her throat. She quiets herself. Listens over the buzz of the furnace vent.

Footsteps thump in the hallway. Growing louder. Coming this way.

"Can't find my fucking keys," a voice says just outside the door.

Someone is coming.

CHAPTER 24

Pain.

A bright flash of pain that disorients her. Pulls her out into the dark, into the abyss.

Until all that's left is the vaguest of contours. Physical forms undulating in the dark. Too murky to be understood, to mean anything at all.

No more context.

No more reason.

No more self.

Pain.

Whatever and whoever she is, it's not here anymore. Not in this time and space, where all that exists is thrashing shadow without purpose, without sense. Violence beyond comprehension.

Her eyelids flutter. The shapes jerk and writhe around. Dark puppets pulled about on their strings.

And the numbness deepens within her. A yawning emptiness.

Faintly, she can still feel the pressure of his weight. All else seems far away.

He mutters nonsense words. Some indecipherable dirty talk tilted toward control.

Slow talker. Deep voice with a touch of gravel to it.

Soon she can't even hear this. Pulled further and further into herself. A vacuum in the back of her skull sucking her deeper into the shell.

Empty.

Drifting in the peace of the void, of the abyss.

A nowhere self. A nothingness.

She doesn't notice right away when the weight relents. Pulls away.

The shape rises over her. The chiseled edges of its v-shape stark against the window.

He wrenches her head upward. A rough touch. Shoves her skull until it's leaned semi-upright against the car door.

The shadow's other arm lifts. Points something at her. Another angular bit protruding from the hand.

The torso goes taut. Arm flexing. Hand squeezing.

The muzzle flare lights the inside of the car in fiery orange. A flash that exposes the soft upholstered ceiling. Casts its glow over his dead-eyed face fully for the first time, just for a second.

He's plain. Thin-lipped. Pointy-nosed. Hollow-cheeked. Crop of dark hair.

Utterly ordinary. Just another face on the street that she might pass anywhere, any day.

A nobody.

And then a searing blaze tears across her scalp. Scrapes right along the part line of her hair, or so it feels to her. Draws a crease of agony into her head.

Open. Burning. Wet.

She feels the blood sluice down. Hot liquid leaking over her forehead. Rushing over her brow.

And somehow she knows that it's a graze. A flesh wound.

She closes her eyes and plays dead.

CHAPTER 25

Dressed now, he strides to the back of the car. The gun still dangles from his arm. Ready to finish this job.

But he's not quite finished, is he? Even after he bores fresh holes in this poor sap's head, he's not done.

Not tonight. Not this time.

The blade itches where it rests in his waistband. Ready now to partake in tonight's games.

He licks his lips. Presses the wrist of his free hand against the hilt of the knife. Feels the metal press into his waist, against that knotty muscle just along the pelvic bone.

He can already feel the way the knife's tip will enter her. A delicate touch that parts her flesh, peels skin away from bone.

His heart beats faster just imagining the tactile experience of pressing that sliver of metal through her. Working it under the edge of skin.

Peeling her.

The words echo in his head. *Peeling her.* Goddamn.

And this will only be the practice run. The walkthrough. A rehearsal.

The next time he takes his knife to a girl, she'll be awake and alert and moaning in ecstasy and suffering, that inextricable blend of pleasure and pain. The most intense and sensitive horizon possible in the human experience.

A higher plane. Sprawling vistas of euphoria the average dolt will never experience.

He thinks of all the people out there. Their quiet lives of desperation. Trapped in some suburban nightmare.

They'd never dare to dream so darkly as this.

But not his girl. She will get a taste.

She will gasp and whimper and cry. And her boyfriend will listen in from the trunk, experience his own muted version of terror in the dark.

He will carve her. Slice her. Cut her open.

Amputate.

He smiles to himself. Thinks he already knows what piece he wants to keep.

Then he wheels around the back fender of the car. Fumbles for the keys with his left hand. Gun still wobbling before him.

The tip of the key finds the keyhole. Plunges home with a clatter. He gives it a twist and hears the soft click of the latch disengaging.

Muffled yells spill out of the trunk's chamber before he even opens the door. Sounds like the boyfriend is crying now. Moaning and carrying on in a wavering voice.

About to die in the soggy mess of his own tears.

Pretty funny.

He flings the trunk lid wide. Raises his gun. Waits for the dark innards of the cargo space to come into focus.

The human form congeals there. Emerges from the shadows. The moonlight revealing him in the fetal position.

No hesitation. He squeezes the trigger.

BANG.

BANG.

CHAPTER 26

Carrie throws herself through the gap between the two front seats. Bumps her rump on the roof of the car.

She lands on her side. Her top half nestled into the cupped bottom of the driver's seat. Her legs draped over the center console.

She wriggles there. Works her way upright. Moving with urgency now. Teeth clenched. Something primal pushing her.

A fire inside.

A voice whispers inside her head. Urgent sibilance.

Live through this.

Find a way.

Using the steering wheel to support her shoulder, she manages to squirm backward until she can fish her fingers against the small square panel housing the door handle.

Bound hands reaching. Outstretched fingers finding that cold metal bit. Wrapping around it.

The door handle feels slick against her sweaty palms. Glossy chrome.

She starts to pull the handle, but something stops her.

Sound carries from the trunk. Muffled cries.

Silas.

He moans and whimpers. Soft sounds. Muted in such a way that they remind her of a pigeon.

She hesitates. Swallows. Blinks a few times. Tears itch behind her eyes.

She's shaking now. Her torso quivering. Her jaw rattling. Her fingers trembling against the door handle.

She tries to listen over the sound of her own respiration, over the thunder of her pulse in her ears.

Her breaths come and go in shuddering gasps. She fights to keep them quiet, but she's powerless to stop her chest from convulsing, her whole body tremoring against the seat, against the wheel.

The car shifts beneath her just a little. Bounces once on its shocks. And then the gunshots come.

The muzzle flares strobe over everything in the car. Two quick bursts of orange light. Glinting over the upholstery and dash. Flashing in the mirror.

CRACK.

CRACK.

She winces with each blast. Shoulders progressively arching. Hunching. Making her smaller and smaller. Like something compressing her.

Her ears ring. And she knows. She knows.

Silas is dead. Gone.

Jesus fucking goddamn Christ.

The itch behind her eyes wins out and the tears come spilling. Hot water fleeing the corners of her eyelids, tracing over her cheekbones.

The fear isn't real. You can't touch it, and it can't touch you.

Only action. Only survival.

She jerks the door handle. Shoves her weight back into the door. Shoulder blades hitting first.

She feels the strange suction of the door in its frame. A pull. Resistance. Like it wants to stay there. Clamped in place against the rubber weather stripping that forms a seal.

She rams it again. Crashes through.

The door gives. Flung out of the way all at once. Chrome handle ripped from her grip.

She falls backward into the empty space left by the door. An odd sensation.

Nothingness. Sinking.

She lands hard on the dewy ground. Jolts of pain shoot through both shoulders as her bodyweight crumples her arms beneath her. Joints wrenched. Something popping along her collarbone on one side.

The impact bashes the wind out of her lungs. All those muscles around her ribcage constricting. Sucking emptiness roiling in her chest.

Footsteps scuff somewhere behind the car.

She works to sit up, even with her ribcage frozen and the flickers of pain still rolling up and down her limbs.

Rolls her arms out to her left side as far as she can. Worms her torso to get upright. First rising onto one elbow. Then shifting her legs and steadying her feet underneath her.

Up she goes. Leaning a hip and shoulder into the side of the car when her balance gets wobbly.

More footsteps behind her. Wet plants gritting and popping against the earth with more urgency than before.

She bites her bottom lip.

This is it.

She pushes herself away from the car and runs for the darkness beneath the trees. Willing the woods to swallow her up.

CHAPTER 27

Tobi stares out from under the table. Squatting in the shaded place at the far end of the plank. Motionless like a frightened squirrel.

She can feel Andre quivering behind her. His face tucked down between her shoulder blades as if he can't bear to look.

The door swings open. And the officer's taupe pants come into view from about mid-thigh down.

He scoffs.

"You dipsticks left the lights on back here," the officer's reedy voice says. "Again."

After a beat of silence, a dopey yell in the distance responds to his call.

"What?"

The cop in the doorway sighs.

"Nothing."

Another pregnant pause.

"Did you say something, Anderson?"

Anderson yells this time, frustration crackling in his voice.

"It's nothing!"

Then he mutters to himself.

"Can't hear for shit and can't turn the lights off. Flippin' morons."

At last the taupe pants stride over the threshold and into the conference room, revealing a yellow stripe running down the side. Plodding steps advance toward the table.

Anderson sighs. Whispers something to himself that Tobi can't make out.

His feet are heavy. Two sledgehammer heads thumping the carpet. Scuffing faintly as he picks them up.

Andre lifts his head from her back. The sudden absence of his warmth makes her feel chilly and vulnerable.

He leans over Tobi's shoulder. She realizes that, now that it's happening, he can't bear to *not* look.

She glances back and sees a lump shifting in Andre's throat. His Adam's apple bobbing up and down. For a second she thinks he's going to vomit. She can just imagine the adrenaline-induced nausea spraying every which way, cascading over her shoulder like a waterfall tumbling over jagged rocks.

The taupe pants stroll all the way across the room. Walking along the edge of the table. Coming closer and closer to their position underneath.

When he's finally parallel to their hiding spot, he squares himself toward the table and stands right in front of them.

Shallow breath.

His feet set themselves a little more than shoulder-width apart, a ridiculous stance adopted only by superheroes and cops, in Tobi's experience.

Shallow breath.

He holds still there. Goes dead silent. Motionless. What the hell is he doing?

Shallow breath.

The furnace vent cuts out, and the quiet blooms in the conference room. Swelling bigger and bigger until its tension fills the space.

Shallow breath.

The silence gives her goosebumps. Now she thinks that *she* might vomit.

Tobi's chest constricts. No longer able to inhale.

The cop knows. Senses them, somehow. Why else just stand

there?

Her heart knocks against her breastbone. Blood roaring in her ears.

She doesn't move. Doesn't blink. Doesn't dare look at Andre next to her, though she can feel his body gone rigid against her shoulder. Taut like a stretched rubber band about to snap.

The stillness persists past what seems like its breaking point. A screaming awful silence. Tobi feels like she's going to explode.

Nothing.

Nothing.

"Found them!" the cop yells loud enough to be heard out at the front desk.

Both Andre and Tobi shudder under the table. Startled by the sudden yell. Shoulders shaking around loosey-goosey.

The keys clink on the table. Partially hidden there in a few loose papers, where Tobi had quickly stowed them before diving under the table.

Anderson plucks them from their hiding spot. Slides them over the table. Clips them to his utility belt with the tiniest snick like fingernail clippers.

The cop takes a few steps away from the table at last. Stops himself. Grumbles something inaudible, a sound not unlike a bear snuffling around a campsite, Tobi thinks.

The plastic of a chip bag crinkles in the corner of the room.

"Well, well, well. Looks like someone left Officer Anderson a snack," Anderson mutters to himself. "Don't mind if I doozy."

Anderson saunters back toward the door. Crunching loudly. He flips off the lights. Exits the room. Clangs the door shut behind him.

Tobi and Andre sit there in the dark. Silent. Still too scared to move, Tobi thinks.

Her skin crawls. Rippling and twitching. An itchy tickle spreading over her arms and chest and neck and cheeks.

Then, as if on cue, they both breathe. Throats sucking in deep gusts. Chests heaving.

"Jesus fuck, I'm going to be sick," Andre says. "I'm going to piss, shit, and be sick. Like right here."

"Go for it," Tobi says.

Whispery giggles explode from Andre first and then Tobi, chittering laughs like squirrel sounds, and then they both shush each other. Fumbling to touch each other a little in the dark. Hands finding bony shoulders. Squeezing like it may help squelch the giggles. Nervous and trembling and lightheaded with a strange shared euphoria.

The same carbonation fizzes in both of their skulls. Tobi is somehow sure of it.

She tries to fight the giddiness. Tries to shove it down. But it's hard to stop laughing.

Andre turns on the flashlight of his phone. The beam lights up a swath of carpet, cuts a tunnel in the darkness, and they crawl out from under the slab of oak and into the light.

"Did we get a look at everything?" Andre asks, pulling himself together.

"I think so."

Tobi wipes a tear from her eye. Scans the area again. Spots something shoved way back in the corner, under what appears to be a small snack bar.

"Wait. One more box," she says, eyeing the brown and white stippling of the cardboard file box. It looks older than the others, and that excites her.

She staggers over to it on wobbly legs. Leans under the

countertop and slides the box out. Sets it on the table. Peels it open and starts photographing.

The camera clicks. The pages shuffle.

The adrenaline rush still surges in her blood as she works. It's unlike any Tobi has felt before. Almost overwhelming.

The jolt turns her arms and legs rubbery. Makes it feel like something sharp pricks behind her eyes — an ice pick prodding, probing.

Current coursing through flesh and bone alike, the voltage cranked up so high it stings a little everywhere. Makes her brain feel kind of fried and frantic and euphoric at the same time.

And she kind of loves it.

CHAPTER 28

He hears something. A thud. Close. He can't identify it.

An icy prickle spreads over him. Constricting his skin. Goosebumps.

Instinct pedals his feet backward. Almost stumbling. Then he stops himself.

Listens. Ears still ringing funny from the gunshots.

Is someone there? A witness happening upon the scene? Out here in a dark field in the middle of nowhere?

He doubts it. He hasn't heard any vehicles approaching. Hasn't seen the glint of any headlights shining over the rows of corn and soybeans, wheeling down the muddy path they'd taken out here.

But the sound was real. He does not doubt his senses.

He mops the back of his hand over his mouth. Listens again. Mind whirring to try to make sense of it.

Another thud near the front of the car. Then soft scuffing sounds.

The dome light blooms over the ground around the car, its glow partially blocked from his vision by the trunk lid obscuring the rear windshield.

A louder thump accompanies the light. Heavy. Undeniable.

There's something there. Someone there. Somehow.

Slowly he steps toward the car. Wheels around the back bumper. Heart punching in his chest.

She leans against the car. His girl. Faced away from him. Standing on two legs.

Not dead.

Blood wets her hair. Coats much of her neck and shoulders and back. Looks shiny and black in the moonlight.

His breath catches in his throat. Feet stopping beneath him. Eyelids fluttering.

Holy shit.

She takes off as though she'd heard his thought out loud. Spooked like something wild. Fast.

A bloody ball shot out of a cannon. Zipping through the foliage with her arms still pinned behind her.

Blurring. Shiny from the wetness. A bolt headed into the woods.

Holy shit. Impossible.

His throat clicks. Hitches. Still can't draw a breath.

The memories montage in his skull. Vivid images cut together in a flitting gallop.

He'd shot her in the head. In the brain. Point blank range or close e-goddamn-nough.

Felt the gun buck in his hand. Saw the flare light everything in flickers of red and yellow, bright and dark.

He'd watched the blood weep down her forehead, down her face. A sheet of red covering over her all at once. Blotting her out.

He'd made sure. Had to, after that last one.

How the fuck?

The back of his hand smudges over his mouth again. His own appendage somehow made foreign by shock. Dry skin wiping cold lips. All of it a little distant. Outside of him.

Jesus.

He takes a breath and gives chase.

CHAPTER 29

She runs into the black nothing. Squints. Just able to make out the darker columns where the tree trunks jut into her vision as she gets close enough. Seeming to bloom from the ground. Black streaks that reach up for the heavens.

She runs through outstretched stalks and branches — all those arms reaching out, brushing against her, snagging at her clothes, trying to ensnare her.

She fights through the thicket. Sprints until her lungs burn. A stinging heat that crawls up into her neck.

Breath heaves in and out of her. Sucks over wet lips, wet teeth. An autumn breeze that's cold and harsh in her hot throat, chest, mouth.

The dark seems to lurch around her. All those dark shades swelling and receding. The night itself breathing.

She rips through some thick creeping vine. Strands of it tangle everything here. Wrapping around her head and neck. Clinging to her hair. They smell green and bright and sharp.

Her torso wrenches. Turns her sideways. She shoulders her way through, tearing free of the twining strands. Moving beyond the cluster of vines.

And then she sees it.

A light. A blemish in the blackness somewhere ahead of her. Not so far off.

More than one. Glowing rectangles faintly penetrating the darkness under the trees. Houses. Windows alight.

A big breath shudders into her. Makes her chest quake.

She might actually make it.

The toe of her shoe catches a jutting tree root. Thumps out a heavy sound.

She trips. Sprawls. The ground a strange shadow trying to swallow her.

She tries to put out her arms, catch the fall, but they're pinned behind her. Caterpillaring against her back. Useless.

She slams down face-first. Bangs another knotty tree root on her head. Skids to a stop among a cluster of ferns.

Wooziness seems to lurch up from the shadows to grab her. Spiral its confusion into her head. Tighten its grip.

She breathes. Smells the rich black soil in her nostrils. Feels the cold earth reach through her shirt to clutch at her chest and belly.

The chill and the smell get through. All else seems distant now. Quiet. Warbling.

The sea of unconsciousness wobbles all around her. An open cavity yawning. Waiting.

She fights it. Blinks her eyes hard. Tries not to slip under the surface.

And then she stops. Holds her breath.

Listens.

The sounds of the woods form a barrier of white noise. The soft moan of the wind. Whispering leaves. Chirruping insects.

But then she hears it. Soft at first. Then growing more solid, more discernible.

Footfalls battering at the brush. A papery beat with a staggering rhythm. A thump falling in and out of time with itself.

She squints. Turns her left ear back the way she'd come. Closes her eyes and focuses on just the noises around her.

Shallow breaths suck in and out of her nostrils. Soundless. Not quite able to keep up with the gallop of her heart.

A lull in the breeze hits just then, confirming what she'd feared. The steps are close.

And getting closer.

CHAPTER 30

Light beams out of the cone of the desk lamp. A glowing cylinder aimed up at the glossy wall of the apartment. Makes the white paint shine.

Tobi sits on the floor beneath it. A cigarette in one hand and her phone in the other. She chain-smokes Parliaments and reads through the files. Eyes pinballing back and forth. Hand zooming and swiping and lifting her smoke to her lips.

Andre and Jade, too, smoke in their seats on the futon, though they watch TV instead of looking at the files. The volume so low it's almost inaudible.

Tanned bodies flicker on the screen. Some dating show where the girls all look artificial in a bland way. Big creepy smiles like child beauty pageant contestants. Bleached caps as big as Chiclets.

Smoke curls up and hovers along the ceiling. A cloud twirling around and around itself.

Tobi absorbs the text. Her brain downloading the information as much as anything. Eyes working like a broadband connection pulling in data packets.

Another part of her mind already works all the puzzle pieces. There's plenty on these pages to think about. Plenty to write about, too, when the time comes.

It seems the police take seriously the connection between the Campus Flasher, the Ski Mask Rapist, and the current killer, at this point at least. The FBI profile makes a compelling case that it's the same perpetrator, his crimes rapidly escalating as he goes unpunished. That's more than significant. It's damning.

Wind snuffles at the open window. Tries halfheartedly to suck all of the smoke out of the room. Slowly seeps a deep chill into the space, that icy feeling touching Tobi's flesh.

After dozens of police documents in a row, she swipes to something different. Something that stops her in her tracks.

She just stares at it at first. Blinks a few times.

It's a handwritten memo on university letterhead. Unsigned. Undated.

"Let's keep this out of the news if we can. Nothing good can come from this kind of story. Not for the students. Not for the community. Not for anybody."

Tobi reads it five times in a row. Eyes jumping back to the beginning each time she finishes.

An acrid smell makes her realize that her cigarette has burned down to the filter. She stubs it out in the ashtray and lights another.

Then she closes her eyes and thinks. Hits her cig and hears the cherry sizzle.

Finally she lets herself consider what this page on her phone really is.

A university memo giving the campus police orders about how to handle the case. Telling them, in fact, to hush it up.

It's a smoking gun, as far as she's concerned.

She wonders when it was written. When the guy was exposing himself at the library? When the serial rapes were happening?

She chews her bottom lip as she thinks. Feels how much the cold has crept into her face as she pulls the pink flesh into her mouth and grips it between her teeth.

I was right, she thinks.

Part of her knew, of course. But here's the proof. Actual

physical proof.

It has to be the university president who has written the memo, doesn't it? Who else would it be?

The woman's face flashes in Tobi's head. Diane Whitman. With her sleek pantsuits and her Hillary Clinton haircut.

Finally, she opens her eyes. Sees the blue ringlets of her hair out of the corners of her vision.

She's ready to write.

CHAPTER 31

Panic wells in Carrie's chest. Cinches her throat shut. Squeezes the skin of her scalp so tightly it feels like it might split further and peel away from her wound.

He's coming. He's running straight for her.

And though this awareness resonates dully in her head, the fear whittles her thoughts to a single word:

Run.

She opens her eyes. Squirms over the ground like an earthworm. Hips and shoulders bucking. Ribcage mashing into the soft earth. Arms continually trying to rip out of the twine and swim out in front of her.

The footsteps grow louder. Steadier. He's through the vines now and building speed.

Run.

Run.

Run.

She wrenches herself over onto her side. Blind panic moving her. Thrashing her against the ground. Getting her nowhere.

And now new words interrupt that monosyllabic mantra.

Stop.

Breathe.

Think.

Her chest loosens. Wind scrapes in. Big lungfuls. Cool against the clammy warmth of her chest cavity.

Frantic thoughts burble up from the depths of her mind now, racing along to match the speed of her fluttering heart, but she tamps them down. Needs to think.

Focus. Only focus.

Getting up and going with her hands behind her back will be slow. Awkward. If she rushes it, she'll only fall again. And if he sees that… it's over.

She wheels her head around. Swivels it again. Looks. Really looks.

Can't see him yet. But the plants surround her here. Shroud most of her.

Fern fronds tickle at her cheeks. Brush at the nape of her neck.

She flops back to her belly, falling out of the narrow sliver of moonlight she'd been in. Looks again.

The stalks of the ferns conceal her. The shadows thicker here just along the ground.

She pushes her face down into the dewy forest floor. Smells rich black soil in her nostrils. Lets the cold worm deeper into her, face and body both, like maybe that will help her hide, like maybe the earth can make her its own for just this next little while.

Take her. Swallow her. Cover her over in leaves and mulch. Conceal her.

Shallow breaths again. No sound.

The crash of his footsteps changes as he gets closer. That paper beat seems to get crunchier, thicker, as the details intensify. The sound of snapping stalks, crushed leaves, the thudding of his body weight bashing at the dirt.

He steps into the small opening just next to her. And he's right there. His shadow moving into her field of vision.

She closes her eyes. Some memory coming to her. Her uncle, a hunter, had told her that animals can feel eyes on them, be they predators or prey. Some ancient primordial sixth sense. Animal instinct.

Better to not look at him. Better to not look at all.

Suddenly he stops dead. Footfalls going silent. As though he senses her near. Smells her. Felt that little flash of her eyes on him, perhaps.

She squeezes her eyelids tighter. Holds her breath now.

The wind whispers again. A tree branch creaks. All the leaves hiss and rattle against each other.

When he moves again his gait has slowed. He pokes out a step. Pauses. Pokes out another step. Pauses again.

And still he draws closer, closer, closer. She can feel him.

Her heart hammers against the soft topsoil, the cold earth absorbing each blow. Ribcage seeming to bulge with each heartbeat.

He stops just next to her. Less than three feet away by the sound of it. He hesitates there. Grunts faintly.

And she knows that he has seen her. Is looking down on her now. Smiling that dead-eyed smile. Pouncing on her any second now.

Her ribcage throbs. Lungs on fire. Aching to breathe. But she squeezes her chest tight. Holds it still.

He sighs. Almost a snort. Angry puffs jetting from both nostrils.

And then he's moving away. Crunching footsteps steadier now. Trailing off to the right.

She waits what feels like a long time before she allows herself a silent breath. Then waits again before she takes another.

His footsteps fade to nothing.

Still, she waits. A full minute passes. Maybe more.

Finally, she picks herself up off the ground and runs toward the light.

CHAPTER 32

He stops again. Nostrils twitching. Head swiveling.

He squints his eyes and stares into the shadows. Looks for any movement.

Nothing. Nothing at all.

He stretches his mouth open until his jaw pops in the corners. Some aggressive habit he's had since he was young. A tic that comes out when he's annoyed.

She was there. Her silhouette twitching just in front of him. Crunching and bashing and flailing about.

He was closing on her. Almost there.

And just as quickly she was gone. No more shadow. No more noises.

He sniffs again. Doesn't smell her. For some reason just now he thinks he would if she were near. He'd smell the sharp ammonia scent of her fear, her adrenaline.

Her terror would reveal itself to him. Her dread and trembling would shimmer off her skin and draw her back to him like a tractor beam.

A trick.

Hiding behind a tree or a rock. He can picture her huddled down in a dark place, face probably mashed into the black dirt.

Yes. It's the only way she could have vanished so quickly.

He pops his jaw again. Shakes his head.

He was probably close before. Probably right on top of her.

He turns and trudges back the way he came.

Maybe it'll be better this way. She'll be awake when he takes his knife to her.

CHAPTER 33

She runs toward the rectangles of soft light. The houses in the distance. It's hard to tell how far away they are. Probably farther than they seem.

Uneven land still stands between her and them. Hills and swales choked with woods and ferns and shrubs and vines.

Shadowy tree branches block most of her view. Gnarled limbs of wood. Leaves shimmying in the wind. Looking through the foliage, she only gets glimpses of the gleaming windows, the vaguest silhouettes of the houses around them.

She breathes. Cold wind sucking into fiery lungs.

Spiky pain emanates from her right side now. A side stitch from the running. Feels like an ice pick spearing her liver in a steady throb.

Still, there's a relief in moving. Breathing. Knowing she's alive.

The land slopes down underfoot. Makes her legs go slightly floppy. Uneven. Feet chopping awkwardly at the soft earth, at the dead leaves. Balancing against the grade made all the more difficult with her arms lashed behind her.

The hill gives way to flat land, and all at once the woods thin out around her. Knee-high grass going crinkly and brown. A clearing.

She trudges over the shadowy borderline, part of her afraid to move into the open. Feels wrong. Exposed. Vulnerable. But this is the only way out.

The grass envelops her feet. Slows her stride.

She feels the dew soak through her pant legs up to her

shins. Calves and ankles going cold and wet, wrapped in tubes of soggy denim.

Breath steams out of her mouth and nose. Violent puffs dispersing in the cool night air. Ragged.

She picks her knees up higher to try to maintain some speed. Ripping free of the grass's raspy grip again and again.

The moon seems to drift out from behind the clouds just then. Glints its silvery glow across the ground. Blades of grass glistening everywhere.

And she can see again. Pick her way around the few obstacles in the field.

A fat tree stump going mushy and black.

A car tire lying on its side.

A pile of trash smashed almost flat to the ground — broken glass and twisted silver beer cans glittering amid the debris.

She keeps her eyes on the horizon. Where the field ends. The shadowy edge of things rushing closer. Watches the details there come clear in the moonlight.

Something dark lines the ground up ahead. Webbed-looking with what looks like posts strewn at odd angles. Some other dark strand spiraled around parts of the mesh.

It takes her a second to puzzle it out, eyes seeming to grasp it all at once.

A downed chain-link fence with barbed wire strung along the top. She runs for it, slowing as she draws near.

She spies a slashed line in one section of fence arched up off the ground — a hole somehow cut or otherwise split into the metal.

She ambles over to it, chest heaving, careful not to get tangled up in the barbed wire. Lowers herself into a squat. Turns her back to the fence.

A hand fumbles along the links until it finds the slit place.

Finger running over a sliced piece of thick steel wire. It feels sharp. One edge catches on her skin as though barbed.

This will work.

She squats lower. Lifts her wrists to the jagged spokes of metal and starts sawing the twine up and down against the sharp edge.

Her movements are awkward. Clumsy. She pokes her hands quite a few times. That pricking steel trying to penetrate the meaty heels of her palms.

But then she changes tactics. Realizes she should dig into the rope and rip at the fibers. Her makeshift blade, for lack of a better term, is too short for sawing. This works better. *It ain't like slicing bread*, some distant part of her thinks.

Dig and rip.

Dig and rip.

She thinks she can feel the twine wearing down, giving way. She can't see it to be sure.

Instead, her eyes scan over the edge of the woods behind her as she works. Waiting for him to come bounding out. Gun in his hand. Hate etched into the lines of his face.

When she finally braves a look the other way, the row of houses takes solid shape for the first time. She's closer to the residential slab than she thought.

Up close, the dull glow in the windows seems softer, hazier.

The twine pops. Still there. Still tied. But she's breaking it little by little, snapping the threads one by one.

She looks down at herself. Sees the top of her jeans still undone. Some flash of shadowy memories occurring to her. The orange flare of the muzzle flashes, those gunshots punching through the night.

She shivers. That wetness on her pant legs seeming colder now. A deep chill to it.

Silas is dead.

And she probably should be, too.

And she wonders what her mom will think of this. A sour taste creeping up from her throat at the thought.

Will she even tell her mom what happened? Can she? Will she conceal parts? Hide details?

She sucks in a wet breath. Whimpers once.

Heat flushes her face.

Embarrassment.

Embarrassment that in this life-and-death moment her thoughts would even go to such a childish place, such a pathetic place.

What will Mom say? Will I be in big trouble *for getting raped and shot in the fucking head?*

The heat in her cheeks intensifies. The embarrassment turning to anger. Old feelings rising up from the depths of her being, feelings she'd pushed down for so long now.

When do I get to be a fucking person like everyone else?

When does my life belong to me?

The suffocation never ends.

Her mom has always acted as though Carrie's life was happening to both of them. Needled it under both of their skin so deeply that even this dire moment doesn't feel like her own. Not entirely.

Even being raped and almost murdered, she worries how mom will react, how she can soften it for her, whether she can hide it from her. Is frightened of what harsh judgment will be coming her way.

And some part of her already feels guilty. Feels ashamed. Feels responsible. Already dreading having to explain this trauma for the sake of someone else's feelings. Reducing herself.

She breathes. Works at the twine.

But there is no one else here now. Just her.

Huddling in the dark.

Trying to slash through the rope around her wrists.

Trying to live through this nightmare.

The only feelings that matter now are her own.

The twine snaps. Falls. Disappears into the dark weeds.

She leans down a second. Lets her arms splay out before her, each hand touching down flat on the dew-slicked ground. Newly freed muscles twitching and popping in her arms and shoulders and back.

She stays like that. Forces breath into her throat. Feels the heat in her flushed face recede a bit.

Even squatted and breathing, she watches the edge of the woods the whole time. Eyes crawling over the borderline between the trees and the field. Her vision zooming in on the dark places, trying to knife through the shadows somehow.

She breathes. Feels her heart rate slow just a little.

Her skin responds before she even hears it. All the flesh on her forearms drawing taut, rippling with cold.

One last hiccup of breath enters her, and then she's quiet.

Listening.

Listening.

A stick cracks in the distance. Rings out over the wilderness. Sounds like a gunshot. Loud. Percussive.

She draws her arms up toward her chest. Skin crawling everywhere.

Every instinct tells her to turn and run. She can feel her legs twitching beneath her, carrying her over the uneven ground in a staggering sprint.

She waits a moment longer. Wants to be sure. Wants to know how best to proceed.

The thump of the footsteps slowly comes clear. Bashing. Advancing.

And frothy feelings swirl in her gut. She can hear the liquid lurching in there. Bubbling acid climbing stomach walls.

She stands. Starts backpedaling over the broken fence. Eyes still staring holes in the dark woods.

The ferns along the tree line shake around. Quivering fronds, shuddering in time with his footfalls, dancing in and out of the moonlight.

The foliage parts at last. A deeper shadow forming an opening in the thicket.

And then the shape comes crashing through.

CHAPTER 34

He crosses the thick plant barrier at the edge of the woods. Creeper coiling around knees and ankles. Leafy bits brushing at his collar.

He rips through the vines and prickers. Thrashing his arms and legs. And then he's free.

He steps into the opening. Leaving the woods and entering the field. Trudging through wet grass.

The clearing feels vast around him. A panorama of empty space. A vacancy stretching out to fill his field of vision.

The night opening herself to him again. Ready.

It takes a second for his eyes to adjust to the brighter light here. Everything washed out for a second. Shapeless and colorless and smeared with brightness.

Then the contours sharpen all around him.

The textured ground appears first. Droplets budding on the grass. Long blades of brownish-green tangled up like messy hair. Shimmering light reflecting off of it like frosted tips.

He lifts his gaze. Looks to the distant skyline.

And then he sees her there. In the distance. The moonlight shines on her white skin. Makes her glow a faint purple in the night.

Holy fuck.

A cruel laugh gibbers out of him as his eyes latch onto her. Something uneven evident in his own voice. Chaotic. Demented. A smile so big it pricks at the muscles in his cheeks.

He runs harder. Faster. Feels new strength in the beat of his heart. Urgency. Desire. His feelings, his internal world, channeled into that throb in his chest. Every muscle twitch expressing a lust for violence.

Release. That's all he wants. A way to get the aggressive feelings out. Like lancing a boil and letting the darkness drain like pus.

Release and relief. A kind of closure, even if it only lasts a short while.

And if it so happens he enjoys every depraved second of it, all the better.

Potholed spots in the ground jam his knees. Stumble and slow him. But he keeps going. Gaining on her.

He tromps over a busted-down fence. Watches her run through a line of scraggly pine trees.

Boughs wobbling from her touch. Brown needles carpeting the earth.

There's another barrier ahead. A wooden privacy fence beyond the pines. Faintly visible. Probably leads right into someone's backyard.

Damn. The houses are closer than he thought. Too close.

He eyeballs the lit windows. Tries to figure the distance. The yards must be big out here. The gap from the fence line to the nearest window looks considerable.

He can still catch her. Has to.

She takes a leap at the fence. Stabs one foot into the side of it and pushes herself up the wood in a scrabbling run. Looks like an outfielder climbing the wall to try to snag a homerun ball.

Her arms latch around the top of the fence. Elbows hooking over the lip of wood in a monkey movement.

She takes a breath and pulls herself up and over. Disappearing behind the boundary.

A faint pang ripples through him as soon as she's out of his line of sight. But he doesn't worry.

He's already right behind her.

CHAPTER 35

Her arms shake as she pulls her slack body up the wooden planks of the fence. Inching like a worm.

She kicks one leg up. Catches a toe on the lip of wood at the top.

Straining. Lifting.

And then she's tipping over the edge. Gravity ripping. Plummeting face-first.

She crashes into a leafy red shrub. Arms braced and then skidding out from under her.

Her belly pancakes the ground. Flops and slaps like a slab of meat tossed onto a cutting board. Breath woofs out of her.

She breathes. Smells that wet cedar smell. Blinks and sees the bed of wood chips her face is pressed into.

Two big breaths. Then she pushes herself up onto hands and knees. Brushes mulch from her cheek and looks at the sprawling backyard before her.

The house sits at the top of a big hill. Where she is, at the bottom of the slope, decorative ceramic tiles form a patio. Wrought iron furniture with puffy-looking pads draped over them. A glass table with an umbrella.

A flagstone path winds up to the house from there. A curving course choked with overgrown bushes. Shadows swelling to swallow much of it up. Neglected landscaping that forms a hedge maze in the dark.

She swivels her head. Expects to find him just behind her, already hopping the fence.

But there's nothing. Just that hard line where the wooden

planks cut off into the night. Empty space yawning above it.

She shudders at the emptiness. Feels a fresh jolt of adrenaline come over her.

She disentangles her limbs from the red shrub. Gets to her feet. Weaves through the furniture. Starts up the slope.

Her feet slap at the flagstone as she leaps from rock to rock. Clapping and echoing. A round of applause.

She realizes she can see strands of Christmas lights wound around some of the small pines along the path. They aren't on, but she doesn't like it.

About halfway up the hill she lets her eyes creep up to the home ahead, really looking at it for the first time. She winces a little at what she sees.

Dark window frames like closed eyes. No porch light. No bulb burning over the driveway. The house looks dead.

Shit.

Shit.

She thinks of the Christmas lights again. These people could be gone. This could be a vacation home or something.

She scans what she can see of the neighborhood from here. Everything cloaked in foliage and shadows. The hill itself blocking part of her view.

The houses on each side look just as dead as this one. Dark and still.

She blinks. Keeps looking.

Two houses down to the right there is a light. One glimmering square poking out through the dark branches blotting the way.

A pale glow in a downstairs window.

She swerves that way. Leaves the flagstone path.

Slick grass now skids underfoot with every step. Dewy and squishy.

She jumps another fence. This one shorter and easier. A chain-link barrier barely more than waist-high.

The next yard is better kept than the first. All the landscaping pruned and neat. No obstacles to weave around.

She runs across the grass to another of the big privacy fences. This time she's on the inside of the fence — the crossbeams are there to aid her climb.

She scurries up and over. Lets herself down on the other side more gently this time. Feet first.

She hits down in a crouch. Takes a breath.

Looks up at that glowing pane of glass. Can sort of make out a gauzy layer of curtain now. Something almost white, almost sheer, diffusing the light within.

She picks herself up. Runs for it.

And then she hears a thump behind her.

Her upper body goes rigid. Breath whistling between her teeth.

She turns.

Something knocks into the wooden planks just there a few feet behind her. The whole fence wobbling with the impact. Jolted.

And then he comes bounding over the top.

She blinks. Backpedals. Mind racing to try to process this.

Somehow he's right there. Right behind her. Stalking through the shadows.

She can see the shininess of his eyes in the dark. Two glossy black dots.

When he steps forward, she sees the same wetness lower. Bigger.

Glistening teeth. The big smile splitting the bottom half of his face.

She screams.

CHAPTER 36

The cell phone shrieked on the nightstand, the screen flaring in the dark.

Darger sat up in bed. Confused. Somehow aware she wasn't at home even though she couldn't see much more than the rectangular shaft of light rising from the phone like a tractor beam, glinting on the white ceiling above.

She took a breath. Chest heavy with sleep. Fragments of a dream still clinging to her awareness. Something involving Owen and a boat. Choppy blue waves stretching out to the horizon, glittering in the sunlight.

She rolled toward the nightstand. Eyes squinted to slits as she neared the bright glow of the screen. She realized where she was, what she was doing, as soon as she saw Loshak listed as the incoming caller.

Jesus. More victims?

"Hello," she croaked, pressing the plastic box to the side of her face.

Right away, his voice sounded more amused than alarmed.

"So, remember how it was decided to have the task force meetings in the campus police department?"

"Yeah."

"And you remember how we both thought that was maybe kind of weird?"

"Uh-huh."

Darger's mind raced, trying to decide how to process this information, her sleepy brain trying to leap ahead, figure out where Loshak was going with the Socratic method here.

"Well, someone broke in. Ransacked the conference room. They left the files, but they photographed everything. We've got surveillance footage of the perps sneaking in. Snapping pics."

Darger wondered if the killer might be bold enough to do something like that, but then she realized Loshak had used the word *perps*. As in more than one person.

"So it was multiple people?"

"Two. Dressed up in ski masks and tracksuits, so it'll be tough to ID them from the video footage alone."

"You think it could be someone from the press?" Darger asked.

"Not sure. But whoever it is, I figure they'll leak everything sooner than later."

Darger fell quiet for a second. She looked at the clock. 4:37 A.M.

She thought about the lilt in Loshak's voice, how funny he seemed to find all of this, and something about that irked her just now.

"So the DNA turned out to be garbage, and now someone compromised the task force in a major way. You wanna tell me what's so funny about all of that?"

Loshak snorted a little.

"I'll be the first to admit that civilians accessing case files is usually not that funny. Then again, it seems we're up against an agenda here that goes beyond the scope of solving the case, no? So the students find out the president of the university is meddling. Maybe that's not so bad. She must have had a hand in pushing for the task force to be housed on campus. Thought she could keep us under her thumb or something. Well… you reap what you sow sometimes."

Darger fell quiet again.

"See? Now when you say it like that, it does sound kind of

funny."

Loshak laughed hard. One of those loud surprised laughs that only lasts a second or two.

"Just wait until you see the video," he said. "They hide under the table at one point when a campus cop goes in for his Doritos. It's hilarious."

"So you're already down at the station?" Darger asked, rubbing her eyes.

"Yeah. I didn't wake you when the chief called, because I didn't find the scenario all that alarming. Honestly, this is something that could wait until morning as far as I'm concerned, but the Chief and Sheriff seem to think this whole situation requires immediate action. Fleming called an emergency meeting. Starts in twenty minutes. Figured you'd want to be here."

Darger closed her eyes and inhaled deeply.

"I'll be there in ten."

"OK. See you soon."

When the call ended, the quiet in the room got bigger. Darger blinked. Eyes going out of focus as the screen flickered to black. Staring into the nothing hung up around her without really looking at it.

She scooted to the edge of the bed, and the muscles in her legs and back protested. Begged her to lean back on the mattress again. Just for a few minutes.

Instead she threw back the blanket and slid off the bed. Feet coming down on cold carpet that felt like the texture of cauliflower. She just stood there for a few seconds, swaying faintly on tired legs, eyes drooping closed again.

Drifting. Drifting.

She wanted coffee. Sleep would be better, of course, but coffee would do. It usually did.

Yes. Hot coffee. Maybe one or two of Loshak's donuts. Or three or four of Loshak's donuts.

At last, she broke the inertia. Snapped open her eyes.

She staggered for the bathroom and set the shower to scalding.

CHAPTER 37

She shuffles backward. Picking up speed. Afraid to turn her back on him.

He seems content to walk for her. Stalking. Smiling.

His broad shoulders shimmy just a little with each step. The faintest hint of a rooster's strut to his movements now.

She looks lower. Eyes tracing down the length of his arm. Shoulder. Elbow. Wrist. She expects to see the gun in his hand, but it's not there.

She squints. Tries to make sense of the angular shape protruding from his fist. Long and pointy.

He tilts his hand, and then she sees it for what it is.

A knife. A butcher knife.

She screams again. Stumbles and almost loses her footing in a bed of gravel. Keeps screaming. Realizes it's her only chance now.

He creeps closer. Moving with some urgency again.

When he speaks his voice is quiet. Confident. Raspy and deep. A sandpaper whisper.

"Don't go making a fuss now. We need to get you peeled."

Her throat fights her. Tries to dry up. Tries to freeze.

She screeches through the tightness until her windpipe burns. Screaming bloody murder. A shrill sound torn from her throat. Piercing.

She can see him flinch at the volume of it. Lip snarling to expose clenched teeth.

He strides to within an arm's length. Hand coming up. Lifting the knife in front of him.

A spiked shadow jumping for her, lurching for her.

Her scream cuts off only as she darts back to evade him. A choked gasp spills out of her.

She stumbles again. Can't keep her footing with her wet shoes.

He lunges forward again. Knife arcing. Ripping through the shadows between them.

A clatter arises behind them.

Clicking and thudding.

A sound like an explosion of flapping dove wings.

Metallic screeching.

The telltale sound of a screen door squawking open and slamming shut.

Floodlights snap on. A series of audible clicks overhead that sound like snapped carrots.

Bright light angles down from the front and back of the yard. Spotlights assailing them. Gleaming cylinders.

Carrie scrunches her eyes shut. The light burns red blotches into her vision. Makes tears stream down from the corners of her eyelids.

Still she stumbles back, stumbles back. Arms flailing everywhere.

A man's voice booms somewhere behind her.

"What the *hail* is going on out here?"

He sounds gruff. Redneck accent.

Shimmying tendrils of hope leap up in her chest just at the sound of him. Wriggling there like sea serpents.

She moans a little. Turns. Pries her eyes open. Sees the shape of a man in a bathrobe, a shotgun angled in front of him.

"Jesus H., missy. You're bleedin' all over the *got*damn place. You OK?"

She doesn't know what to say. Still shuffling her feet. The

bed of gravel making sounds like tinkling ice cubes under the soles of her shoes.

When she turns back, the killer is gone.

CHAPTER 38

Walking into the campus police station almost felt like walking into a funeral. Law enforcement officers huddled around the lobby — the majority of them mustached men — looking bereft. Hard lines etched into foreheads and nasolabial folds creased as hard as pleated Dockers.

The one exception to the frown parade was Loshak. He couldn't quite keep the smile off his lips — one of those shaky smiles, twitching at the corners, like he was trying to reel it in and couldn't quite do it. He handed Darger a paper cup of coffee as soon as she reached him, then gestured at the box of donuts tucked back on the other side of the semicircle of sad cops.

Darger took a big slug of the coffee. Felt it sting all the way down, from the back of her throat into the curved pit of her stomach.

She eyed the donuts across the room. The flap of the cardboard box hung open, and the pastries within looked plump and promising. A mix of yeast and cake style, plus a few "specialties" — fritters, crullers, and long johns. Various glazes and ganaches adorned their tops, each one more tantalizing than the last.

She wanted to go right over and cram one of the lumps of fried dough down her gullet. Spike her blood sugar as a way of waking up.

She took a few steps toward the box. As she did, two of the cops turned to face her.

Dixon and Kirby stood practically shoulder to shoulder,

effectively blocking her way to the donuts.

"Can you fucking believe this?" Kirby asked, a half-eaten donut in one hand. Chocolate frosted with sprinkles. "The kids here, I'm telling you, they have no respect for the law. None at all."

Darger's first thought was that maybe they'd have a bit more if a certain cop hadn't bashed a student's teeth out, but she resisted the urge to say it out loud.

"You're sure it was students?" she said instead.

"We have no idea who did it, at this point," Dixon said, thumbing the screen of his phone. "Chief asked me to keep an eye on social media in case someone posts something there, but so far, there's nothing."

"I'm telling you guys, it's more frat initiation bullshit."

Kirby took a bite of donut and crumbs went everywhere. Then he gestured with the hunk of dough, thrusting it forward at the top of his forearm like a cobra's hooded head.

"You ask me, we should have shut all the fraternities down a long time ago. Bunch of little shit rich kids with their stupid rich kid club."

Beside him, Dixon took a bite of apple fritter and then let out a sputtering cough.

Kirby chuckled, slapping the other man on the back.

"Easy there, Dickskin. You gotta chew, *then* swallow."

Dixon shook his head.

"No. Look. It's one of the blogs."

He held out the phone.

Did SMU President Diane Whitman Allow a Serial Rapist to Roam Freely Amongst Us?

Darger scanned the first few lines.

An anonymous source at Southern Michigan University has uncovered damning evidence of attempts to cover up a series of rapes that occurred on and off campus. We have been presented with several official documents that show an overt effort by campus police to suppress public information regarding the Ski Mask Rapist, who investigators now believe is the same perpetrator of the Couple Killer murders.

"Anonymous source?" Dixon repeated. "Yeah, right."

Darger nodded, thinking it was a rather lame attempt by the author to distance themselves from the fact that a crime had been committed. But this person would no doubt end up the prime suspect in the break-in no matter how they tried to explain away the fact that they had the photographs.

Kirby pointed at the byline.

"What the fuck kind of name is Woodward Bernstein?" Kirby asked.

"It's the Watergate guys," Dixon explained.

"Who?"

"Never mind."

One of the documents that had been uploaded to the site was an excerpt of the profile she and Loshak presented, with the sections regarding the potential link between the Campus Flasher and Ski Mask Rapist highlighted. Oh boy. Darger could already imagine the reprimand they'd receive from Dr. Whitman over this.

That was, until she spotted the next leaked document. It was a memo on school letterhead.

Let's keep this out of the news if we can. Nothing good can come from this kind of story. Not for the students. Not for the community. Not for anybody.

Holy shit. Was that what she thought it was? A note from Whitman to Fleming, telling him to keep the case quiet? Of course, there were no details. No proof she'd been speaking about the Ski Mask Rapist case. And yet Darger wasn't sure that even mattered. People would draw assumptions, and none of them would be good.

As word went around the room and more and more of the men brought up the article on their phones and computer screens, Darger could sense the growing irritation. Cops were used to being in control — of information, of interactions. They hated feeling powerless.

Darger's eyes returned to the post, and she continued reading. Toward the end, there was a quote from a student named Tobi McCall.

"None of this is a surprise to the members of Students For Equality. We've been saying since the start of this that there was a link between the current crimes and the Ski Mask Rapist, but SMU wouldn't hear it. Now we know it's because Dr. Whitman attempted to cover up the fact that there was an active serial rapist on campus."

"Oh, I knew it!" Kirby threw a fist in the air. "I knew that uppity McCall bitch had something to do with this."

"I thought you said it was a frat thing," Dixon said.

"Yeah, but this was my second choice. I knew if it wasn't one of the frats, it'd be that little Feminazi."

"You know this person?" Darger asked.

Dixon pressed his lips together.

"Remember those students we ran into in the dorms earlier?"

Darger's eyes went wide when she remembered the group chanting.

Hey hey! Ho ho! Sexual assault has got to go!

"The blue-haired girl? The one with the fliers?"

Dixon nodded.

Darger considered whether the girl had seemed angry enough, vengeful enough, to actually break into the police station. The more she thought about it, the more she thought it seemed plausible.

Dixon glanced around the room.

"Has anyone let the Chief know?"

Darger spied Chief Fleming through the window of his office. The door was closed, and he appeared to be shuffling through the paperwork on his desk.

"I don't think so," she said.

Dixon looked at Kirby.

"Don't look at me, pal. You can deliver that bag of flaming shit to the Chief all on your own."

Dixon winced.

"I'll go with you," Darger offered.

She and Dixon proceeded to the Chief's office. When the young policeman hesitated in front of the door, Darger raised her fist and tapped her knuckles against the wood panel.

The Chief's voice was slightly muffled by the closed door.

"Come in."

Darger gave Dixon an encouraging nod. He grasped the knob, turned, and pushed it open.

He cleared his throat as he stepped over the threshold.

"I, uh… found something. Online. There's a… well, there's something you need to see."

He set his phone on the Chief's desk with the blog post open on the screen.

Darger watched the man's face as he read the article, his eyes zigging and zagging over the screen. His already grim expression went even more dour.

When he finished reading, Chief Fleming filled his cheeks with air and let out a slow puff of breath.

"Christ on a crutch," he said, wiping a hand over his eyes. "I'd better get Dr. Whitman on the horn. She is *not* going to be happy about this."

CHAPTER 39

A few minutes later, Darger found herself once more crammed into the small conference room of the campus police station. Again Dr. Whitman held court at the head of the table, though this time it was in person.

Despite the predawn hour, the university president was fully made-up, hair perfectly coifed, skirt suit neatly pressed. Still, her voice came out slightly husky, as if she'd only been awake a short time.

"And you believe it's an SMU student responsible for both the break-in and the blog post?"

"We don't have hard evidence to that effect, but we believe it's very likely."

Dr. Whitman's nostrils flared.

"I am absolutely disgusted to think one of our own students would do something so reckless and irresponsible. The arrogance."

Her voice caught in her throat a second, and she shook her head.

"Can we pull the website credentials? Find out who's behind this?"

"Yes, ma'am," Fleming said. "Officer Dixon is our resident cyber expert, and he's assured me that we'll be able to get the owner of the website."

He glanced over at Dixon, who suddenly sat up straighter in his seat.

"Uh yes… that's, uh… that's right," he stammered. "So far it seems that the domain registration is private, but there are other ways to find that information. Worst-case scenario, we might need to get a subpoena, but…"

"That shouldn't be a problem," Fleming said. "I'll get in touch with the DA's office once it's a reasonable hour."

Darger's leg started bouncing up and down, a subconscious sign of her growing impatience. She waited for the conversation to turn back to what they were really here for: to catch the Couple Killer.

Dr. Whitman laced her fingers together and leaned back in her chair. She pursed her lips.

"Good. I want these hooligans punished to the fullest extent of the law. That might sound harsh, but we need to send a clear message that this kind of behavior is completely unacceptable."

She leaned back in her seat as she went on.

"It will be a good lesson for the student body at large. They need to understand that actions have consequences."

Darger squirmed in her own seat. How much more time were they going to waste talking about the break-in?

The fact that important pieces of the case files had been leaked online wasn't exactly good news. There were many things in those files — their profile being one of them — that they'd rather hold back, for the investigation's sake. It wasn't uncommon for killers like this to try to change their M.O. just to throw investigators off.

There was speculation that the Zodiac Killer's final victim was a lone male cab driver simply because the police and press had made a big deal out of the fact that he "only" killed couples. It was as if, in murdering the cabbie, Zodiac had been saying, "You think you're so smart? You think you've figured me out? Then figure *this* out." He'd mailed a swatch of the cabbie's bloody shirt to the San Francisco Police Department as a sort of exclamation point on the subject.

So while the leak certainly wasn't ideal, there wasn't anything to be done about it now but figure out how to best move forward. Darger suspected the real fury here was over the fact that Dr. Whitman and Chief Fleming were still trying to do damage control over the botched investigation into the Ski Mask Rapist — all the talk so far seemed pointed that way.

"And what about the FBI?"

Darger's attention was suddenly drawn back to the meeting at the mention of the Bureau.

Whitman glanced from Darger to Loshak.

"What resources, if any, do you have available for this kind of thing?"

"For *what* kind of thing?" Loshak asked.

"This break-in… this… meddling with an investigation. Not to mention the posting of confidential police documents. I assume the FBI has a cybersecurity department? Would they be able to perhaps speed up the process in terms of finding the publisher of this blog and having the material removed?"

Before Loshak could answer, Darger raised her hand.

"I think we ought to set the whole break-in thing aside and discuss the next steps in the primary investigation. We were kind of pinning a lot of our hopes on those DNA results. Considering that didn't pan out, I think we need to start talking about what we do next. Both strategies and tactics."

"With all due respect, Agent Darger, my responsibilities are a great deal larger than this single investigation. It's my job to keep an entire university functioning — an undertaking much like running a small town. And so, while *you* may be able to afford to focus on the details, it is imperative that I consider the bigger picture. What happened here tonight threatens to undermine the entire foundation—"

Darger couldn't take it anymore. She'd tried to be patient,

but this was ridiculous.

She slammed both her hands onto the table.

"The 'bigger picture'? The bigger picture is that we have six bodies lying in the morgue and almost nothing to show for it. Some kids posted some files on the internet? Big fucking deal."

She shook her head.

"The cat is out of the bag. Those files are on the internet, and even if you do manage to find who did it and get the site to pull the article, it'll just be reposted a thousand other places. I'm sorry, but there's just no way you're going to unring that bell. If you think this is bad PR now, just wait until his kill count climbs to eight, ten, twelve victims."

The room was silent for several seconds. Darger braced herself for a fight. She didn't expect that someone in Dr. Whitman's position was used to people getting quite so real with her, and she waited for the fallout.

But it was Chief Fleming who spoke first, and to her surprise, he was nodding.

"Agent Darger is right," he said, licking his lips. "We're worried the public will lose faith when they see those files, but the truth is, they'll lose faith even faster if this guy is allowed to kill again."

Slowly releasing the tension she'd been holding in her shoulders, Darger closed her eyes. They were going to listen to reason. Thank Christ.

Dr. Whitman raised her carefully plucked eyebrows.

"Fair enough. Let's discuss this 'next step' then."

Darger felt several pairs of eyes on her and realized they were expecting her to have the answer.

"Considering that the DNA evidence from the most recent scene was a dead end, I think we should send the samples you have from the Ski Mask Rapist and those from the current cases to the University of Central Florida in hopes we can figure out what type of condom he's using."

"And exactly how long does something like that take?" Dr. Whitman asked, her eyes narrowed to slits.

"I'm not sure. I'd guess at least a week or two, at minimum."

Dr. Whitman made a small noise, which Darger interpreted as further disapproval of how "inefficient" she found the process of analyzing trace evidence.

"Is there something, well… more proactive we can do while we wait around for that? Imposing a curfew, for example?"

Loshak shook his head. From somewhere outside the conference room, Darger could hear one of the phones ringing.

"I'm still dubious about a curfew. If this was a community of families and retirees, it might work. But college kids? No way we'll get compliance."

"So then we enact strict punishments for anyone found in violation," Whitman said with a shrug.

Loshak sighed.

"We talked about this before. The problem is that then you end up wasting time enforcing the curfew instead of finding this guy."

"And your suggestion is what? Surely you don't propose we simply sit around and wait for him to strike again?"

Darger gritted her teeth at the condescension, even though it was aimed at Loshak and not her. Five minutes ago, Dr. Whitman had been so fixated on punishing whoever had broken into the station, she'd all but forgotten there was a killer on the loose. She had some balls to insinuate that Loshak was in any way passive or apathetic.

"I still think our best option is safety in numbers. A voluntary, citywide, community watch effort."

Dr. Whitman glanced at a fancy-looking gold watch encircling her wrist and gave a nod.

"Well, it's too late to put anything into action at this hour. I think we should all get whatever sleep we can and reconvene during daylight hours. Would 10 A.M. work for everyone?"

Before Chief Fleming could respond, one of his officers bolted into the room.

"I'm sorry to interrupt, Chief, but you're gonna wanna hear this."

Darger's gut clenched when she saw the look in his eyes. They were bulging with a manic intensity. Something had happened.

"What is it?" Fleming asked.

"There's been another attack. But the victim… well, she's alive."

CHAPTER 40

The killer drives. Rubs his hands along the smooth coldness of the steering wheel. Watches the dotted line flicker yellow in the middle of the road.

The night is fading. Fleeing. Leaving him alone again.

He wheels around a corner. Headlights sweeping over the still cityscape.

He wishes he could drive the night into staying. Like if he could drive fast enough to the west, he could stay ahead of the creeping dawn. Forever. Never see the sun crawl over the horizon again.

Permanent darkness. Endless night.

She got away. Ran from him. Clever girl.

But he won't dwell on it. Not tonight.

Let it go. Worry about it tomorrow. In the light of day.

A sharp smell invades his sinus cavity. The lingering odor of hand soap. A remnant from the gas station bathroom where he cleaned himself up.

He knows all the places where the cameras can't see. Knows the places where a person can walk a few paces from their car to the steel bathroom door cut into the side of the cinder block structure without being spotted.

So many times he's frequented these locales. Latched the door behind him. Washed red spirals down the drain. Stared at his reflection in a dirty mirror.

One witness to all he's done. The man in the mirror. Blinking when he blinks. Ugly the way he's ugly. Sad the way he's sad.

It's almost him.

Another turn. Another sweeping of the headlights over vinyl siding and brick and freshly mowed grass. All of it looking shiny and wet.

He's almost home now. Gets a queasy twinge in the belly at the thought. Some pit opening there. A black hole sucking, sucking.

Tonight's fun is over — sideways as it had gone. Back to real life.

The next turn lands him on a blacktop driveway. He thumbs the garage door opener on the visor. Waits for the panels to slowly climb up the metal tracks and curl out of the way.

The house looks strange in the dark. Swollen shadows plumping gloom around the bushes out front, adding sinister angles to the shutters. Wispy black lines elongating off the edges of things.

As the garage door sucks up toward the ceiling, yellow light spills out of the concrete chamber of the garage. Puddles on the matte gray paint on the floor.

He pulls in. Parks. Thumbs the button again to close the door.

He waits in the car as the garage door closes behind him. Seals him into this suburban home. His belly thrashing as he watches the door close off the night from him in the rearview.

The mechanical grind of the garage door chain cuts out. And he lets the quiet settle. Waits another full minute before he climbs out of the car.

Pushing through a steel door, he steps into a darkened foyer. Sets his keys in a wicker basket next to the door. Slips off his shoes.

A feminine scent wafts here. Vanilla and sandalwood

perpetually hanging in the air.

He strides through the gloomy house. Turns on no lights. Socked feet soundless on the carpet. Pausing only momentarily when a floorboard moans underfoot in the hall.

He glides past the kitchen. Moves into the back hallway where the bedrooms lie.

It's darker here. The contours fuzzy and soft. But he knows the building well. Almost doesn't need sight here at all.

He leans into the first doorway on the right. Waits a second for his eyes to adjust.

At first he sees only the dark. The trickle of light spilling in from the hall not quite enough. A shapeless void.

Slowly some of the objects take shape around the room. Toys on the floor coalescing. Some of the posters sharpening into a grayscale focus, SpongeBob and Dora suddenly there in black and white.

Finally, the small shape forms on the bed. Looks like a bean with arms and legs. Curled into the fetal position. Her small chest rising and falling, rippling the blanket.

He leans against the doorframe and watches for a while.

Then he moves down the hall. Enters the next door on the right. Edges over another carpeted floor, toes balling into fists.

He quietly disrobes. Takes a silent breath. Slips into the bed, careful not to jostle it hard enough to make the bedsprings creak.

He moves the bedspread and sheet in slow motion, not wanting even that whisper of fabric sliding over his skin to wake her.

The cool fabric settles over him slowly like a falling parachute. It feels good. Crisp just like the inside of the car. That bracing kind of cold that makes his skin contract.

Even as quiet as he's been, he's failed.

His wife stirs. The bed shifting. Her shape not quite discernible in the dark.

She rolls over to him. Her face finding his. Kissing him on the cheek.

Then she whirls back the other way, fiddling with the blankets a moment and then holding still.

The quiet stretches out again. Drifts into a settled position like the sheets and blanket.

Some of the lingering tension in his neck and shoulders releases.

His heartbeat can slow finally, though he knows that the process will be gradual. He stares up at the murky ceiling and waits for sleep to take him.

CHAPTER 41

A beat of stillness followed the announcement, and then everyone was up and jostling to get out of the conference room.

"Where's the victim now?" Chief Fleming asked.

"St. Vincent's," the officer said.

"How is it the EMTs already got her to the hospital, but we're only getting the call now?"

"It wasn't a 911 call. She was driven to the hospital. Good Samaritan, I guess. It was one of the emergency room nurses who called us."

"Do we know what state the victim is in?"

"She's stable, but they have her sedated."

"Did they get her name?"

"She had ID on her. Carrie Dockett."

The Chief opened his mouth to speak again, but every radio in the room suddenly let out a loud burst of static.

"All units, corner of West Monroe and Old Genesee Road, West Monroe and Old Genesee Road. Possible DB; EMS is requested. Unknown male subject in the trunk of a silver Volvo S40 parked at the eastern edge of the field there, off a small farm access road. Code 8-7 and 4-4, in RD1437."

"I think we just found the second victim from tonight's attack," Loshak said.

The Chief clapped his hands together.

"OK. Kirby and Harson, I want you down at St. Vincent's, guarding the victim. No one other than law enforcement and medical personnel gets into her room. Is that clear?"

The two men nodded and headed for the door.

"Dixon and Lewis, I want you two to get a statement from this Good Samaritan and canvas the area for other witnesses."

He glanced around the room.

"The rest of you will head over to the scene at West Monroe and Old Genesee Road."

Darger turned to Loshak.

"What do you think?"

"I'd like to talk to the surviving victim, of course, but… *sedated* makes it sound like she won't be able to answer questions for a while," he said. "So we might as well check out the newest crime scene in the meantime. That cool with you?"

"Yep."

With that, they joined the line of officers hustling out to the parking lot. Outside, they climbed into their rental and followed the caravan of SMU cruisers over to the scene.

The entire north end of Old Genesee Road had already been closed down by the time they arrived. A Sheriff's Deputy was in the midst of blocking access to the road with a line of sawhorse barriers, and a handful of neighbors loitered near the newly erected barricade, squinting and craning their necks to try to catch a glimpse of the scene.

Loshak let the car roll beyond the entrance to Old Genesee Road before parking on the shoulder with the rest of the first responders.

Darger spotted the EMTs standing listlessly near the ambulance, hands in pockets. She knew then that the "possible dead body" was an official one.

The first beams of real sunlight crept over the area as Darger stepped from the car. A yellow glimmer beating back the predawn gray.

The moisture left over from the rain last night had condensed into clouds of fog that hung in pockets over the field. The red and blue flashers on the tops of the cruisers seemed somehow more intense glinting through the haze.

Darger took in her surroundings. They were less than a mile outside of town, but the setting appeared about as rural as you could get. Old Genesee Road bisected a large rectangular cornfield, bordered on three sides by forest. From this vantage point, there wasn't a house in sight.

Chief Fleming was perhaps a hundred yards down the road, standing beside a tractor and talking to a man in a dingy pair of Carhartt overalls. As they approached, Darger caught the tail end of what the man was saying, and it became clear that he was the one who'd discovered the crime scene.

"… trying to get my cover crop planted by the end of the week, so I been comin' out before dawn most days. Anyway, that's when I seen the car. The dome light was on, so I could see it from a good distance as I brought the tractor up the road here. At first I thought it was dumped. I get a fair amount of that. People leaving household trash and whatnot. Usually it's smaller stuff. A little table or an office chair. But sometimes it's bigger. A sofa or a washing machine."

He said the two words as if they rhymed. *Washeen masheen.*

"Then when I got closer, I saw that the car was newer. Not a hunk o' junk like I first thought. When I seen that the door was open… Hell, I thought maybe someone pulled off to answer nature's call. Or some teenagers up to some mischief. Had my fair share of that, too. Sometimes I'll find a little cluster of beer cans and fireworks and whatnot out here. It wasn't until I actually got right up to the car that I saw…"

The farmer paused and wiped his sun-browned face. Hound dog eyes blinking hard.

"Jesus, at first I didn't even know what I was looking at. But then I seen the blood and… well, gosh. It's kind of a blur after that. And I know I probably wasn't 'sposed to, but I touched him."

"What's that?" the chief asked.

"The kid. I… I checked him for a pulse. I realize now that was probably stupid. He was dead, clear as day. But I just felt like… like I had to do something. Or try anyhow."

"That's OK, Mr. Reedy," Chief Fleming assured him. "You did everything exactly right."

While the man gave his statement, they'd been walking back to the narrow access lane, encircled by a clump of trees. The farmer stopped just shy of the dirt two-track.

"It's back thataway, through these trees," he said, pointing with a quivering finger. "I… hope it's OK if I stay back here? I really don't want to see all of that again."

"That's just fine, Mr. Reedy."

Relief shifted in the folds of those bloodhound eyes.

Fleming grasped a low-hanging branch from the nearest tree and lifted it high.

"After you, agents."

Darger ducked under the looming boughs and shuffled down the dirt path. Fallen buckeyes littered the ground, still in the shell, and their feet sent the spiky green orbs rolling and skittering.

"He must have followed them out here," Loshak said. "This spot is too secluded for him to just have come across them by chance."

"Yeah. Fits with the idea that at least some of the victims were stalked. He probably spotted them somewhere else and tailed them until they parked," Darger said, staring down the narrow lane.

Past the press of the apple trees, the sky opened up for

maybe a hundred yards before dead-ending at the snarl of trees at the edge of the field.

Photos of the three other scenes flashed in Darger's mind as they approached the inert Volvo. It was an almost exact carbon copy, with the male victim lying in the trunk, curled into a semi-fetal position. The only difference here was how fresh the scene was. She could tell just by looking at the blood that it hadn't gone tacky yet.

One other difference was that the driver's side door hung open, and the dome light cast its dim illumination over the interior of the car.

The chirp of crickets was the only sound in the field just now. The law enforcement officers stood and stared. A restlessness in the air as they waited for the evidence collection unit to arrive.

Darger had seen dozens of dead bodies by now, but she never got used to it. Everything about it always felt wrong. Wrong, wrong, wrong.

Here was this broken body. Bloody and eerily still. Perhaps lying here for less than two hours. If ever there were a time to leap to action, wasn't it now? And yet there was nothing for anyone to do.

It was like the farmer said, when he'd explained that he'd checked for a pulse even though he was certain the boy was dead.

I just felt like I had to do something.

It was such a human urge, to desperately cling to control in the face of death.

Even when it was too late.

CHAPTER 42

After several minutes of taking it all in, Darger became aware of a steady drip-drip-drip coming from the car. She slowly lowered herself to a crouch and saw something seeping from one corner of the trunk. Blood. A steady dribble falling from the floor of the trunk to the hard-packed dirt below.

She stood again, and it seemed that her movements had broken whatever spell had fallen over them. Fleming turned to one of his men.

"McCreary," he said, adjusting the hat on his head. "Run the plates on the Volvo, will you?"

"Yes, sir," the young officer said, jogging back down the path to the main road.

"We'll have to wait on the coroner to check his pockets for a license or what have you, but we might be able to get a head start on IDing this young man with the registry information," Fleming explained.

A few minutes later, McCreary returned, an official SMU PD tablet in his hands.

"Car's registered to a Silas Heemeyer. Twenty years old. Remington Hills address." He held out the tablet for the Chief to see. "I pulled his driver's license from the Secretary of State."

Everyone leaned a little closer to get a better look at the photo on the license. Silas Heemeyer stared out from the screen, a confident smile on his young face. Chief Fleming glanced from the screen to the body in the trunk and nodded.

"Close enough match that I think we can make a preliminary identification on our John Doe here." Fleming nodded to himself. "McCreary, I want you and Gunnerson to see if you can hunt down the family for Silas Heemeyer here and Carrie Dockett."

"On it, sir."

Fleming called over a second pair of officers.

"I want you to take an official statement from Mr. Reedy, our 911 caller. Then I want you to canvas the residents gathered up at the roadblock. So far we have four murder scenes and not a single eye-witness. Something's gotta give."

Darger heard the doubt in his voice and couldn't help considering the worst-case scenario. What if he kept on killing in the night, slipping unseen into the shadows once his evil deeds were done? How many more might die before they got even a scrap of something to go on?

But they did have a scrap. More than a scrap, even. The female victim had survived. Surely she'd be able to tell them *something*.

The techs had arrived by now, and Darger looked on as they photographed everything. The car, the body, the blood pooling near one of the rear tires. Once they'd thoroughly documented the exterior of the vehicle, they began on the interior.

To her right, Chief Fleming brought his radio to his mouth.

"Cass, call the coroner again and ask when we can expect him to grace us with his presence."

Darger checked the time on her phone, except she wasn't thinking about the coroner. She was wondering how long they'd have to wait before they could talk to Carrie Dockett. Beside her, she noticed that Loshak was also glancing at his watch. His eyes met hers, and he chuckled.

"The sit and wait game," he said.

Darger sighed.

"Yeah."

They were silent for a few moments. The morning was still quiet enough that Darger could hear the faint rustle of an evidence bag being opened.

"Well, I was wrong about one thing," Loshak said eventually.

Darger turned and squinted at him.

"What's that?"

"I said these guys rarely get sloppy. But he had a near escape last time and a definitive one this time."

"I don't know if that makes you wrong. Could be he just had a streak of bad luck," Darger said. "Which is good luck for us."

A little smile spread over Loshak's lips.

"You know, it's funny you should say that. I was just thinking about this detective who came through the National Academy. I think she was from Atlanta. Anyway, she had this theory she shared with me."

Loshak scratched at the stubble under his chin as he spoke.

"She said the most famous and prolific serial killers we know of often get credit for being super smart, super cunning. But she thinks that one of the big things that sets them apart is pure dumb luck. Said the unlucky ones get caught right off the bat, after a single murder. They go to prison, and so they never get the chance to kill more and become the next Gacy or Bundy."

Darger considered this.

"There's some logic to it," she said. "Gacy should have been caught way sooner. He killed people he knew. People he'd been seen with. There were practically paper trails leading straight back to him, in some cases."

Loshak nodded.

"And hell, Bundy was luring women into his car using his real first name, often in busy public places. He abducted two women from the same beach in broad daylight, four hours apart. Then he dumped them only two miles away. That's not exactly the picture we paint when we talk about an organized type, meticulously planning every step and making sure to cover their tracks."

"It's more brazen than smart," Darger said.

"Not to mention compulsive." Loshak let out a deep breath. "I guess I'll keep my fingers crossed that you're right, and this guy's luck is running out."

There was a triumphant whoop, and Darger whipped her head around, trying to find the source. It was one of the techs, a stout woman in a white bunny suit, squatting in a thicket a few yards from the car.

Darger and Loshak jogged over with the chief.

"What is it?" Fleming asked.

"Have a look."

The tech gestured at something crumpled on the ground. The white nub looked like a worm.

"There's another one over here," the tech said, gesturing with a penlight.

And that was when Darger realized what they were.

Two cigarette butts. One Marlboro, one Newport, both squashed a little as if they'd been ground under the toe of someone's shoe to put them out.

The techs seemed hopeful. Excited. Optimistic. But not Darger.

Different brands? Out here in a field?

She looked at Loshak and knew by the grim set of his mouth that he was thinking the same thing as her.

The killer had contaminated the scene again.

CHAPTER 43

Darger sensed a feeling of excitement and optimism ripple through the crowd of law enforcement officers on the scene. They'd found something. A piece of hard evidence.

But she tried to remind herself it was best to remain cautious. The gloves could lead to something. Or not. They'd need to wait and see.

The coroner arrived a few minutes later, assessing and recording the official time of death and performing a preliminary examination of the body. After that, Silas Heemeyer's limp body was bagged in white plastic and taken to the morgue to await the full autopsy, though Darger doubted there would be any surprises. It was obvious he'd died of two gunshot wounds to the head, just like the others.

Gravel crunched under Chief Fleming's boots as he turned to face the two agents.

"I'd like the two of you at the hospital to talk to Carrie Dockett when she wakes up," he said. "If you don't mind, that is."

"We don't mind at all." Loshak glanced at Darger, who nodded in agreement. "We'll head out right now."

"Excellent," Fleming said. "And I'll keep you posted on any developments here."

Darger and Loshak trudged back down the road to where they'd parked, ducking under a fluttering strand of crime scene tape. The media had arrived by now, a cluster of news vans and reporters waiting on the other side of the barricade.

Out of the corner of her eye, Darger watched one of the

reporters catch sight of them, her head swiveling around in an almost comical fashion.

"Heads up," Darger muttered to her partner. "We've been spotted."

Loshak's eyes moved slightly, so that he was looking at the reporter with his peripheral vision.

"Let's get to the car," he said. "But don't run. We don't want to trigger her chase instinct."

Darger snorted at that. She knew he'd meant it as a joke, and yet they really did resist the urge to run, as if they were truly being pursued by a predator. Instead, the two of them started an awkward speed-walk to the car, ignoring the reporter's attempts to get their attention.

By the time the woman reached them, Loshak already had the car in gear and was pulling away from the shoulder. The reporter waved her arms, still desperately trying to engage them. Loshak turned, smiled, and waved back, as if they were merely exchanging a polite greeting.

Darger chuckled.

A short drive delivered them to the St. Vincent's parking lot, less than five minutes away. Another forty seconds of walking moved them inside.

Coming from the grimy, blood-smeared scene, the bright white interior of the hospital was almost blinding. Darger's shoes squeaked over gleaming tile floors.

They found Kirby lounging in a chair outside of Carrie Dockett's room, guarding her as Chief Fleming had instructed. Leafing through a Sports Illustrated as he did.

"Is she awake yet?" Darger asked.

Kirby lowered the magazine, his face now peering over the top in a way that made Darger think of a Prairie Dog's head poking out of its burrow.

"Nah," he said, chomping on a piece of gum. "Doc says she might wake up within the next hour, but it's hard to say. They doped her up real good."

Darger leaned around the door and got her first look at the girl. She looked tiny in the baggy hospital gown. A small pale thing hooked up to numerous machines that beeped and whirred, white hospital blanket nestled up to her waist. Swelling contorted her features, dark bruising purpling one eye and a patch along her jawline. White gauze wound around the top of her skull, mummy tight about halfway up her forehead and above.

She was in rough shape, but Darger reminded herself that the doctors had said she'd make it. That was good.

Now they just had to hope she'd remember something about her attacker. Something they could use to hunt him down and put a stop to this.

Darger and Loshak moved down the hall to a small waiting area. Loshak coaxed a bottle of water from a vending machine and plopped into one of the chairs, but Darger couldn't seem to sit still, opting to remain standing.

Cable news flared on the flatscreen before them. The anchor's orange face hovering there, lips moving endlessly. Muted, thankfully. Darger had to keep forcing herself to not read the endless text crawling along the bottom of the screen. Too depressing.

Loshak's phone let out a blip, and he dug it from his pocket.

"Fleming just sent an update on Silas Heemeyer's background. He's a local kid. Went to high school over in Stonebridge, which is just north of Remington Hills. He was studying Information Science."

Darger paced the length of the room as he read the report.

"What about family?" she asked.

"His dad died earlier this year, but his mother is still alive. She lives in North Carolina now, with the victim's older sister."

They lapsed into silence as the full weight of the boy's death settled in. A son and a brother, gone forever.

Death crept up on everyone, took them all, sooner or later. It was a fact that everyone understood from a pretty young age. Something truly inevitable, truly universal.

And somehow it was still shocking to confront face-to-face.

Darger's phone vibrated. When she looked at the screen, she found a text from Owen.

I think I found it.

Darger frowned as she tapped out a response. *Found what?*

The smoking gun, he wrote back.

Right. Owen's wild quest to dig up dirt on his mother's husband-to-be. Darger smirked as she typed the next message.

Let me guess. Claude was the second gunman on the grassy knoll?

Cute. But no. I'll call you later with the details, but let's just say this guy has a LOT of explaining to do.

She rolled her eyes and typed out a noncommittal, *OK.* She'd been hoping Owen would chill out once he'd had some time with the idea of his mother getting married. But so far, that didn't seem to be happening.

And as much as she worried he was going to end up causing some major drama with his mother, ultimately it was his life. His choice. His consequences to face. She could only do so much to try to talk sense into him.

She thought she heard Loshak say something then, but when she turned, he was staring vacantly into his bottle of water, as if in a trance. She started to think she'd imagined the sound of him talking, until she observed him bring the bottle of water to his lips and take a drink. As he lowered the bottle, his lips clearly moved, and he muttered something under his breath.

"What's that?" she asked.

"Oh, just over here working on ingesting my weekly credit card."

The corners of Darger's eyes squinched in confusion.

"Your what?"

He waggled the bottle at her.

"The microplastics, Darger. Every sip, I'm just adding to my total. Watch."

He took a sip.

"Microplastics."

He moved the bottle away from his mouth, then raised it and drank again.

"Microplastics."

A third drink.

"Microplastics."

Darger shook her head, thinking of how paranoid Owen was behaving. Now her partner joining in, too?

"Is there something in the water or what?" she asked, talking more to herself than to Loshak.

"Yeah," Loshak said, incredulous. "I just said. *Microplastics.*"

Darger said nothing, continuing her pacing.

Loshak walked up and pressed a couple of the flat buttons along the bottom of the flatscreen.

A dramatic fragment of orchestral music blared from the TV. The morning news was beginning.

Naturally, they led with the latest murder, showing footage of the techs scuttling about the field with voiceover from the on-the-scene reporter.

They cut to a shot of Chief Fleming, a cluster of

microphones thrust in his face as he crossed the street.

"Is it him, Chief Fleming?" one of the reporters shouted. "Has the Couple Killer struck again?"

"Again, I'll repeat that there will be a news conference this afternoon. If you could please hold your questions until then."

He stalked off and the camera refocused on a dark-haired reporter. Darger recognized her as the same one that had tried to corner her and Loshak as they left the scene.

"And this wasn't the only new development related to the Couple Killer case, Andy. Last night, an anonymous blogger posted an article on the site *University Watchdog*, releasing what appears to be evidence that SMU officials covered up a serial rape case spanning the last two years."

A screenshot of the blog flashed on the screen. Then the camera zoomed in on a highlighted portion of text, scrolling over the words.

"When asked how the university responded to these allegations, Dr. Diane Whitman, SMU President, had this to say…"

A photo of Whitman appeared on the screen, accompanied by a text transcript of her recorded statement.

"The safety of our student body has always been and will always be the primary concern of Southern Michigan University."

Her voice was clipped and professional, utterly devoid of emotion.

"Frankly, I find it quite tasteless — not to mention irresponsible — to be discussing these tabloid rumors when the investigation is still running its course. Furthermore, I feel it's an injustice to the memory of the victims."

Darger turned her back on the television. She wanted to say she was stunned that Whitman was still trying to do damage control, but she wasn't really surprised. Once a bureaucrat, always a bureaucrat.

"I'm gonna go try to find some coffee," she told Loshak. "You want one?"

Loshak glared at the bottled water in his hands and chucked it in a nearby waste bin.

"Yeah. Hospital coffee usually isn't great, but at least they probably use tap water."

"Since when do you care what kind of water is in the—" Darger stopped herself when Loshak turned his fierce gaze on her. "Right. Microplastics."

Foot traffic bustled in the halls now, and Darger had to flatten herself against a wall to make room for a worker pushing a trolley loaded with breakfast trays. Around the next corner, she dodged a nurse organizing meds into small paper cups and a nursing assistant carrying a stack of bath towels.

A small kiosk at the far end of the floor offered snacks, coffee, and other beverages. Darger bought two large coffees and two bagels with cream cheese.

As she trudged back to the waiting area, Dr. Whitman's quoted sound bite from the news echoed in her head.

The safety of our student body has always been and will always be the primary concern of Southern Michigan University.

President Whitman sure had a funny way of showing it.

Darger sipped the hot brew and wrinkled her nose. Loshak had been right. The coffee was mediocre at best. Weak and burned-tasting — the best of both worlds.

When she returned to the waiting area, Loshak had his phone pressed to his ear. She could tell by the look on his face that whatever he was hearing wasn't good.

"I'm not sure how many different ways I can say I think this is a bad idea," he said, and then there was a pause. "Right. And when is she going to announce it?"

Darger ground her molars together. Why did she have a strong suspicion that the "she" in this scenario was none other than Dr. Whitman?

"Alright. Thanks for the heads up," Loshak said before ending the call.

He closed his eyes and sighed.

"So what's Whitman up to now?" she asked, handing over his coffee and bagel and steeling herself for bad news.

"She's going ahead with the curfew. There'll be a press conference in twenty minutes where she plans to announce it."

"She's panicking," Darger said. "She thinks she can still control what's happening here."

Loshak nodded.

Darger's eyes slid over to Carrie's room. Now Kirby was flipping through an issue of *Rolling Stone*.

"Well, Kirby has orders to let everyone know when the girl wakes up. Shall we go down there and watch the dumpster fire live and in real time?"

"Might as well," Loshak said, pushing up to his feet. "No point waiting around here doing nothing."

CHAPTER 44

He dips the razor into the sink. Sloshes it back and forth across the top of the water pooled there. Lets the surface tension push the tiny clumps of hair out.

Then he brings the Gillette back to the top of his skull. Scrapes all five blades in the disposable head over his scalp. Watches the line where the hair disappears. Reminds him of a lawnmower shearing down one row of grass at a time.

The razor grinds out a tiny sandpaper sound as it glides over his rounded skull, but the feel is totally smooth. Totally painless.

He looks at that other in the mirror. The broad-jawed one with half of his head still coated in a thin layer of shave butter.

When the girl gives a description to the police, she'll say *short dark hair*.

Not anymore, sweetheart.

He smiles a little as he cleans the blades again. Easiest disguise in the world, just about.

Steam coils over the water in the sink. Hot and moist like breath on his knuckles.

Tiny hairs fan out into the pool as he swishes the razor around. Some floating. Some sinking.

He thought he'd still be more upset about the events of the night prior, about the girl who got away. Went to bed thinking he'd wake panicked, disturbed.

In the light of morning, he finds he doesn't care much.

The police will either come after him now or they won't. He'll die in a blaze of glory, or he'll live on indefinitely.

What's the difference, really?

He knows that death is baked into this experience for everybody. A constant companion. The end of every story.

Oblivion comes for everyone eventually.

Some now. Some later.

Some young. Some old.

Some lucky. Some unlucky.

He's made his peace with impermanence. Something he knows most people can't or won't do.

The top of his head is clean. Almost done. He moves the razor to the back. Pulls up from the neck with quick strokes. Cutting against the grain.

Going to prison is the one thing he doesn't see happening for him. Locked up in a little cage? Yeah, no thanks. He'll live free or die trying.

What's that saying?

Better to die on your feet than live on your knees.

A pinprick of pain flickers to life on the back of his head. A tiny cut in the folded bit of flesh along his brain stem.

He stops the razor. Pulls it away. Turns his head in the mirror until he can see the wound.

The red spot glimmers there, catching the light. Miniature. About the size of a fruit fly.

He holds still. Watches the blood bulge from the tiny wound. Spilling over the rim. Slowly draining toward his neck.

He lets the pain bloom. Lets it swell.

Feels opened up. The air somehow sharp against the tiny gash. Brighter and brighter.

It makes him grin in a way that looks more like a grimace on that other's face in the mirror.

This, too, is an experience on the edge.

Pain. Pleasure. Somehow they wind around each other.

Intertwine. Every human body, every single nerve ending, a paradox equally capable of heavenly bliss and nightmarish suffering.

Sometimes both at once, maybe.

Pain expresses the limits of human experience better than anything else he knows — his own pain or someone else's. Experiencing it. Inflicting it. Either way, he gets a striking sense of the horizons, of how far you can push this meat vessel you're trapped inside.

The boundaries are ultimately far-reaching, he's found. Vast. Appalling. The suffering he can cause. The pleasure he can feel. Unthinkable.

There are levels of pain and pleasure that reach almost beyond the scope of one's imagination. Almost.

The water tinkles over itself as he runs the Gillette through it again. Bathtub sounds echoing off the tile.

Maybe death, he thinks. Maybe death expresses the limits of the human experience even more completely than pain. Hammers home that finality.

But death is just pain's logical conclusion, he thinks.

And it's different.

You can put it on someone else, death. Cause their death. Vacate them from their body, from this realm.

But you don't get to experience it yourself the same way.

Once your own death arrives, you are no more. The two — you and death — can never coexist, not in the same body. This is what he believes.

Still, death holds its own fascination. Guards its own frontier.

At some point, you push the blade far enough, thrust it past the point of oblivion. And now you've crossed the final borderline, the final taboo. Stepped out of the bounds of this life, this body, and into nothingness.

And after that?

Who fucking knows?

He rips off a tiny piece of toilet paper. Adheres it to the red spot on the back of his head.

Dips the razor in the steaming water. Swishes it back and forth.

And a faint pink swirl ripples through the pool.

CHAPTER 45

The Liebert Administration Office sat smack-dab in the middle of campus, a brick Colonial Revival-style building surrounded by another lush green lawn peppered with oak trees. A raven-shaped weathervane perched on the cupola on top of the building, gently swaying in the morning breeze.

Word must have already started to spread among the students about Whitman's press conference, because a group of several dozen people milled about on the steps that led up to a set of four marble columns at the building's entrance.

Some of the students carried signs, many of them clearly referencing the blog post and the Ski Mask Rapist cover-up.

Welcome to Rapington Hills.

SMU = rape culture.

Fuck the patriarchy.

I shouldn't have to be afraid to walk alone.

Whitman is NOT an ally.

Darger studied the faces as she passed. She saw fear. She saw curiosity. But mostly she saw anger. And she had a growing sense that the president's curfew was going to go over like a lead balloon.

A chant started up in one section of the crowd.

"What do we want?"

"Justice!"

"When do we want it?"

"Now!"

"What do we want?"

"Safe streets!"

"When do we want it?"

"Now!"

"Shatter the silence! End the violence!"

Darger searched the group for the blue-haired girl but didn't find her. If Kirby was right, and she played a part in the break-in at the campus police station, Darger supposed she could be lying low.

There were two policemen erecting sawhorse barriers at the top of the steps to hold the crowd back.

"We have a right to be in there! This is our school, and we pay thousands in tuition to be here," one girl shouted.

One officer held his hands up.

"There's limited seating in the press room. If you have the proper credentials, you can enter, simple as that. Otherwise, you'll have to watch the president's address on TV like everyone else."

Darger and Loshak elbowed their way through the huddle of bodies on the steps, showing their badges when they reached the barricade. The officer waved them through.

The press room was at the very center of the building, a grand space with a domed ceiling. One section of the wall at the front of the room was patterned all over with the SMU logo. In front of that stood a podium surrounded by lights and cameras. It looked like the kind of place a football coach would give his postgame remarks. Darger realized that was probably exactly what it was.

The rows of folding chairs facing the podium were filled with press, mostly local news people, but also someone else Darger recognized. The blue-haired girl. Darger remembered then that she'd mentioned the student newspaper before. Not lying low, after all.

Darger spotted Whitman up front, going over pages of

notes with a group of assistants.

By now, the rant in Darger's head had built to a crescendo. She couldn't believe the gall this woman had to insinuate herself into this investigation and then to make a call like this in direct opposition to their recommendation. It was one thing for the local police force to make their own decisions. It was their jurisdiction after all. But this woman wasn't law enforcement. She had no idea the chaos she was about to unleash by announcing, to use Loshak's words, an unenforceable curfew.

Darger was tempted to scream all of that in Whitman's face. To just tear her to shreds.

She was still staring daggers when the other woman's head flicked up and met Darger's eyes. Surprisingly, Whitman's face seemed to brighten when she saw the two agents standing there. She waved them over.

Darger followed Loshak down a center aisle between the cluster of chairs. When they reached her, Whitman was scribbling something in her notes.

"And change this line here to read 'horrifying and incomprehensible.' We've already used 'tragic' and 'tragedy' too many times."

The underling scuttled off with the sheaf of papers, and Whitman turned, clapping her hands together.

"Agent Loshak, Agent Darger, I'm so pleased you've come. I was wondering if you'd speak after my announcement?"

She was looking at Darger when she said it.

Darger blinked.

"You want one of us to speak?"

"Just a quick statement to give a sense of scope to this thing. I think having an authority such as yourself would give proper weight to what's happening here. Not only as a way to reinforce the curfew, but I also think it would reassure the students and the general public to know the FBI, the federal government, is taking an active role in this."

Darger's mouth hung open as she tried to formulate an appropriate way to say *no fucking way.*

"And I know this is very last minute, but we do have a statement prepared for you, so it wouldn't have to be off the cuff."

The word *propaganda* echoed in Darger's head, and she let out a little breath. Not quite a scoff, but almost.

"Uhhh… no. Definitely not."

Unperturbed, Whitman's gaze turned to Loshak.

"Unfortunately, it's against Bureau policy for us to give unauthorized comments to the press," Loshak said. "Our hands are tied."

"Well, that's a shame." Whitman sighed. "I do think you could lend a certain gravitas to this whole matter, but rules are rules, I suppose."

That rekindled the anger in Darger's chest. They weren't here to *lend gravitas* or *reinforce curfews* or even to *reassure the public.* They were here to catch a monster who'd killed seven people, something that seemed entirely secondary to Whitman's agenda. Did this woman actually think that she or Loshak gave a single fuck about the school's public relation maneuvers?

Darger opened her mouth to let it out, but Whitman abruptly turned on her heel and stalked over to one of the student aides.

"Joshua, did you manage to find my blue scarf?"

When the man held up a length of azure silk, Whitman clicked her tongue.

"Wonderful! You're a treasure."

A loud voice suddenly boomed from Darger's left.

"If I could just have everyone vacate the stage area, please? We're going live in less than a minute, and we need this area cleared."

The man literally shooed them away with the clipboard in his hands, forcing them back among the rows of chairs. Instead of taking a seat, she and Loshak moved off to the side of the room.

Darger was still fuming but forced herself to admit that nothing she might have said would make a difference here. Whitman was going to go ahead with the press conference and the curfew with or without them. The university could impose a curfew on campus as they pleased.

Still, she was glad to be standing instead of sitting. Sitting somehow felt… complicit. As if they were doing their part as a dutiful audience member. Standing felt a touch rebellious.

Whitman took her place behind the podium, tugging at the blue silk scarf around her neck. An aide with a makeup brush stepped forward and dabbed a bit of powder on her cheeks, nose, and forehead. And then the man who'd shooed them held up a hand.

"We're live in 3… 2…" He didn't say one, but held up his first finger instead.

And then he gave Whitman the signal to begin.

CHAPTER 46

A hush fell over the room, and then the live broadcast began.

"It is with great shock and sadness that I announce yet another senseless murder of an SMU student," Dr. Whitman began. "This morning, police discovered a body in a field on the outskirts of town. A second victim, also an SMU student, was found alive and is now receiving medical attention at St. Vincent's. At this time, I am unable to release the name of the two students or any details until the families have been notified."

Darger studied the president's face as she spoke, noting her expression. Eyes soft. Brow line slightly furrowed. Chin held aloft. And the barest hint of a frown touching the corners of her mouth. It was just the right mix of grave and stoic. Darger imagined Whitman practicing it in the mirror.

"My heart breaks that another bright and talented member of our community has been taken from us. As the SMU family mourns the loss of one of our own, I want to encourage you to reach out for support. Free counseling services are available for students at the Student Resources Building from 9 A.M. to 7 P.M. daily. Counseling services for staff and faculty are available through the TruMed Employee Program."

Darger considered the use of the word "us." Reframing the victims as a loss that affected the community at large, as if the school itself were a victim. It wasn't the first time Darger had encountered this phenomenon, and she wondered if there was a PR handbook or something perpetuating this approach. One way or another, manipulative messages had a way of breaking down into "us and them."

"I don't think I have to tell you that this is a challenging time for our community. These recent tragic events have touched each and every one of us, and I know many of you are left with a sense of unresolved anxiety," Whitman continued. "But I want to assure you that law enforcement is working around the clock on identifying, locating, and apprehending the perpetrator of this horrifying and incomprehensible crime. I am receiving continuous updates from both campus police and the sheriff's office, and I vow to continue doing the same for you, staying in touch to pass on pertinent information as I have it."

Darger had been waiting for some sort of reminder that it wasn't the university's responsibility to apprehend the killer, and there it was. Whitman was indirectly telling the public that the onus for stopping this lay squarely at the feet of law enforcement, which it did, except that the school had interfered from the beginning.

"Our students come here with an expectation to live and learn in safety, and I doubt any of them anticipated being confronted with such tragedy and brutality. As president, I take my duty as an advocate and guardian of our family very seriously. The extra police patrols I requested last week are ongoing, but after speaking with campus public safety leaders, I have determined the increased patrols simply aren't enough. Therefore, I have no choice but to take immediate action. This morning I'm announcing a mandatory curfew to begin immediately."

There was an audible response from the students in the crowd, gasps and murmuring. Some of the heads in the room turned toward the source of the noise.

Whitman lifted her arms, demanding everyone's attention

return to her.

"While this may seem like a severe response, I assure you that this minor inconvenience will be worth the lives saved. The curfew will begin tonight at 8 P.M. and will extend through 6 A.M. After consulting with Sheriff Kittle, the curfew will apply not only to the SMU campus, but also the municipal city of Remington Hills, and it will stay in effect until further notice."

There was more muttering among the students, and then one voice rose above the rest. It was Tobi Bluehair.

"What about the Take Back the Night march?"

Whitman blinked slowly.

"That will have to be rescheduled."

"Bullshit! We specifically planned the march to coincide with Homecoming. We have the permits and everything! You're sabotaging us on purpose. You're trying to silence us. Again!"

Another voice broke in. A male student this time.

"Who cares about some stupid march? What about the Homecoming game?"

Whitman raised her arms in the air.

"If you could hold your questions until the end, I'm nearly finished. Naturally, the Homecoming game itself will continue, with additional security measures in place. I know that many of you have private celebrations planned to coincide with the game, but obviously any off-campus parties will have to be canceled."

The whispering intensified again, and if Darger wasn't mistaken, she thought she could hear the group outside booing.

"In lieu of the usual off-campus get-togethers, we will be setting up on-campus 'watch parties' for the game, with refreshments, in addition to a Homecoming Mixer in the

Student Mall. There will be shuttle services available to and from these festivities as well as to the game so that students can safely get home."

Whitman fluttered her eyelids before she went on.

"While I know everyone will be disappointed to have some of the usual Homecoming celebrations curtailed, there will still be an opportunity to keep the tradition alive, while keeping everyone safe. This school will do the right thing, no matter what price there is to be paid."

Darger let out a bitter, silent laugh. If only the school had done the "right thing" when the Ski Mask Rapist was on the prowl.

"Now, before I take your questions, I want to say one final thing. And that is, as we begin to grasp the magnitude of this tragedy, let us put forth a united effort to support one another and to create a stronger, safer, more harmonious community."

Whitman nodded once to the group sitting in the press area, and a dozen hands shot up in unison. She pointed at one of the reporters.

"The implication is that this is another attack by the so-called Couple Killer. Is that correct?" the man asked.

"I'll remind you again that I cannot speak to any specific details of the crime, lest I inadvertently compromise the ongoing investigation. Any questions about the homicides themselves should be directed at Chief Fleming and Sheriff Kittle at the joint press conference they have planned later today. If you have questions about the university's response or the specifics of the curfew and so forth, those I can answer."

Darger's attention was drawn to a buzzing in her pocket. As she pulled her phone out, she heard Loshak's phone blurting out a notification as well. They each read the text message from their respective screens and then looked at one another.

Carrie Dockett was awake.

CHAPTER 47

The muffled sound of the crowd outside intensified as she and Loshak left the conference room. In the front hall of the administration office, the dissonant voices became more clear. What had been a dull roaring noise crystallized into more distinct booing and jeering.

They pushed through the doors, and Darger saw that the number of students had increased noticeably. There had to be close to a hundred people on the front steps now. And instead of milling about, they were packed together tightly, straining against the sawhorse barricades.

"Why are we being punished? We didn't do anything wrong!" a red-faced student shouted from the upper steps. "This is bullshit!"

The last word seemed to ring in the air, and the mob seized on it.

"Bullshit! Bullshit! Bullshit!"

Within seconds, the entire group was chanting in unison. Darger wondered if they could hear it from inside.

Loshak put his hands on his hips and stared at the throng of people.

"How the hell are we going to get out of here?" he asked, gesturing at the way the horde surrounded the entire entryway.

Darger shrugged.

The "bullshit" chant was still going, and then a company of voices from somewhere in the back broke off. The words were almost entirely drowned out at first, but slowly the mass of voices shifted until the new set of repeated phrases was clearly audible.

"Whose streets?"

"Our streets!"

"Whose streets?"

"Our streets!"

Chief Fleming came out from the building then, a megaphone clutched in one hand.

"OK, listen up," he said, his amplified voice booming over the noise of the crowd. "If you want to hold a peaceful demonstration, no one will deny your right to protest. But standing out here, doing all this hooting and hollering? That won't do. This is neither the time nor the place. I need all of you to step away from the building."

Instead of moving back, the mob pressed closer, nudging the sawhorse barriers. The voices devolved into a random babble. After a few moments, Darger again heard a group of voices in the back unite.

"Riot! Don't diet! Get up, get out, and try it!"

The horde made a brief attempt to join in, but Darger thought the chant was a bit too long, a bit too detailed to last. Instead, someone decided to truncate it, and soon the entire mass was screaming a single word.

"Riot! Riot! Riot!"

"I am asking you to disperse now," Chief Fleming started again. "This is not safe. This is not peaceful."

The students at the front grabbed the sawhorse barriers and began rocking them back and forth.

"Riot! Riot!"

Darger instinctively took a step backward, and Fleming turned to face her.

"You two should get back inside. This might get ugly."

He lifted his radio to his mouth and shouted into it.

"Cooper, where the hell are you? I need all of you out here *now*. This is starting to get out of hand."

Something struck Darger's cheek, and then there was a strange rattling sound. The first thing that popped into Darger's head was someone dropping a handful of Skittles on the ground. She put a hand to her stinging face, staring at the jagged pieces of gravel on the ground, but it was still several seconds before she put it all together. Someone had thrown a handful of small rocks, and one of them had grazed her face.

Loshak grabbed her by the elbow.

"Let's go," he said, tugging her toward the door.

He paused when he noticed she was touching her cheek.

"Did they get you?"

"I'm OK," she said, staring at the faint streak of blood on her fingers. "It's just a scratch."

Just as Loshak reached for the door handle, it swung open, and their way was suddenly blocked by a dozen police officers decked out in riot gear. Shields, helmets, batons.

Darger and Loshak had no choice but to step back from the doors to let them pass.

Fleming lifted the megaphone once more.

"This is your final warning. Disperse now."

From her new vantage point, Darger could see that the crowd wasn't dispersing at all. In fact, it was still growing. Students were pressed along the sides of the building now, beating their fists against the windows.

Darger couldn't help but remember the insurrection at the capitol. All those angry faces. All that camo gear. It was a fresh reminder of what happened when the mindless fervor of the mob took over. Nothing good.

Another handful of gravel rained down. Darger wasn't hit

this time, but she could hear it pinging against the riot shields.

"Alright, boys," Fleming said. "Let 'er rip."

There was a low whumfing sound followed by something metallic clickity-clacking over the concrete steps. A few seconds later, three distinct clouds of smoke rose from the canisters on the ground. Two of the plumes were green, one was whitish gray. Darger felt a stinging sensation in her nose, and her eyes began to water.

"Goddamn it!" Fleming growled. "I said smoke canisters! Who launched tear gas?"

"Must have been a mix-up, sir," one of the men said, barely containing a smirk. "Looks like it's doing the trick, though."

And he was right. As the billowing clouds of gas curled up and into the air, the singular mass of bodies began to break up. Darger heard shrieks and saw students rubbing their eyes and coughing.

An exodus of students spilled down the steps, moving into the grass beyond. Running for the dorms in the distance. The crowd was already dwindling.

Two of the men in riot gear turned and high-fived.

"Fucking hilarious. These kids act all tough, like they're revolutionaries or some shit, but they quit in two seconds if you actually challenge 'em."

"Right?" the other cop said. "One little canister of tear gas sends them running for the hills. Pussies."

Darger couldn't help but think their celebrating was a bit premature. They might have won the battle, but they were looking at a much longer war of maintaining this curfew the president had just announced.

Worse, instead of solely focusing on finding the killer, the police would inevitably be distracted with putting out countless fires like this over the next few days.

Loshak was already being proven right.

CHAPTER 48

Some of the early morning bustle had waned by the time they returned to St. Vincent's. Compared to the scene they'd just come from, the inside of the hospital felt as hushed as a church.

Darger couldn't stop herself from internally scoffing at Whitman's doomed curfew plan again. Was there anyone in academia that wasn't a pompous idiot? She was certain there was, but she'd yet to meet them.

Darger's internal rant went on until she spotted the doorway to Carrie Dockett's hospital room, and she reminded herself to put all the frustration surrounding the curfew and Dr. Whitman aside. She needed to focus now.

Kirby still stood sentry outside the room, fiddling with his phone.

"How is she?" Loshak asked.

"Still a little groggy, but the nurse said it was OK to talk to her for a few minutes."

The door stood slightly ajar, but Darger knocked anyway. She peeked inside as the girl's eyes blinked open.

"Carrie?" Darger said, taking one step into the room. "My name is Violet Darger. This is my partner, Victor Loshak. We were wondering if you were up to answering a few questions?"

The girl seemed to consider it for a moment before nodding her head once.

Darger and Loshak entered the room, each taking a chair at the side of the bed.

"How are you feeling?" Darger asked.

Again there was a pause before the girl answered. She

blinked hard in a way that reminded Darger of a cat.

"I'm not sure what they gave me, but right now I mostly just feel kind of foggy and dumb."

Carrie reached up and touched the bandage awkwardly taped to the top of her head where the bullet had grazed her scalp.

"And my head feels too big."

Looking at the bandage, Darger got a flash of pain along her own scalp and remembered more clearly than she had in months what it felt like to be shot.

"I've been there," Darger said, running her fingers over the scarred place concealed by her hair.

"You were shot?" Carrie asked.

Darger nodded.

"Your head will probably feel funny for a few days, but it'll fade. You'll feel normal eventually," Darger said, though she wondered how true that was.

Did a survivor of this kind of attack ever feel truly "normal" again?

Carrie bunched and unbunched the blanket in her fingers.

"I guess you probably want to talk about what happened, but... I'm having a hard time remembering. I don't know if it's the drugs or what, but it's all mixed up in my head, and I think there are pieces missing. All of it feels more like a dream than something real."

She shrugged a little. Did that cat blink again.

"I don't know if I'll be very good at answering your questions."

"That's OK," Darger said. "Just do your best. Let's start with what you do remember."

"I remember being at the movies with Silas. And then we drove around for a bit. Silas liked to do that. He was from around here, so he knew every nook and cranny. Like this spot where you can pull to the side of the road and pet the alpacas in this farmer's field. Or this really pretty lake that's way at the end of this narrow road through the woods."

Something between a smile and a wince passed over the girl's lips as she spoke.

"Anyway, he said he knew this little hidden place we could go."

Carrie paused and her breath came in little gasps.

"Silas heard it first. A car door, I think. I thought he was teasing me. He'd been kind of making little jokes about the killer all night, and I didn't like it, so I thought he was playing a prank. But then I saw something a little later — a shape outside the window — and I could tell Silas didn't believe me. He thought I was jumpy from watching the movie earlier. That I was imagining things."

She paused for a few breaths. Her eyes piercing empty space up and to the left. When she spoke again, it was just above a whisper.

"But then he was right there. Right outside the door. And he had a gun."

Trembling, Carrie shook her head.

"I just remember thinking that Silas should just give him the keys and his wallet… like that'd help. That I'd give up my purse, my phone, whatever the guy wanted. But then Silas tried to grab the gun, and the guy must have hit him in the face with it because Silas was suddenly in my lap, bleeding everywhere."

Carrie stared down at her lap, as if expecting to find bloodstains there even now.

"And then he took Silas. To the trunk. But even then part of me didn't really believe it was him. Still thought it was a mugger or something. It seemed too… dramatic. Like I felt like

I was being silly and that if anyone knew that I thought it was the Couple Killer, they'd laugh at me."

Carrie let out the faintest scoff.

"And then when he came back, I knew. I knew who it was and what was going to happen. Because he was naked."

Another cat blink.

"That's when things get really… fractured. I remember his weight pressing on me. And the pain. But I think I sort of went… somewhere else."

"Did you see his face?" Darger asked.

Carrie's head swayed from side to side, and she started to shiver.

"It was so dark. His face was just a gray smear with wet black spots for eyes."

The girl's entire body was shaking now, and her breath came in short gasps. She was panicking.

Darger put a hand on hers.

"Carrie, you're starting to hyperventilate, but you're OK. Take a breath in and then let it out like you're trying to blow out birthday candles."

Carrie's eyes locked on Darger's, the terrified look of a hunted rabbit in her eyes. One of the hospital monitors began to beep out an alarm.

Darger squeezed the girl's hand.

"Breathe in. You can do it."

Darger wasn't sure her words were getting through. But finally, after several long seconds, the girl's ribcage quivered with an inhale.

"Good. Now let it out slowly."

Carrie pursed her lips and exhaled.

After a few rounds of this, Carrie's breathing returned to normal.

"Sorry," the girl said, her eyes wet with tears.

"You don't need to apologize," Darger said.

"Maybe we should leave it there for now," Loshak suggested. "We can come back later."

"No." Carrie shook her head. "No, I need to do this. And I was wrong before. I did see his face."

Darger held absolutely still, waiting for her to go on.

"It was only for a second."

"Do you think you could describe him to a sketch artist?"

"I could try. I'm not very good at describing faces, though."

"That's OK. The artist will help you through it. But for now, just give us the basic details. Age. Race. Hair color."

Carrie nodded and studied Darger for a moment.

"He was… maybe thirty?" she said and then shifted her gaze to Loshak. "He was white, and he had dark hair. Short. Almost black."

"Could you tell if he was tall or short?"

"Maybe a little tall… and in good shape, I think. Like not bulky but toned. Kind of muscular."

"What about identifying marks? Moles or scars or tattoos?"

Carrie frowned.

"Mostly I was surprised how normal he looked. He could have been one of my professors or the guy who sold us our movie tickets, and I wouldn't have thought anything of him."

The look in Carrie's eyes softened, and she blinked twice, staring off into space again. They waited for her to continue, but eventually it became clear that she was in some sort of a daze.

"Carrie?" Darger said quietly.

Carrie flinched and shook her head.

"What? Oh. Sorry… the drugs…"

"No need to apologize," Loshak said. "Just one more

question, and then we'll let you rest."

The girl didn't say anything, but Darger thought she sensed relief in her body language.

"Can you tell us how you escaped?"

Carrie's eyes scrunched in concentration.

"That's where things start getting really hazy. I saw the gun pointed at me. And there was this bright flash of orange light, and it was so loud. And I felt it. The pain and the burning."

Darger's scalp itched.

"I closed my eyes. Played dead, basically."

Carrie's teeth chattered as the shaking started up again. This time, she took a deep breath, calming herself before continuing.

"I realized when I heard more gunshots that it must be him shooting Silas. So I ran. There was blood all over me. That's the part I remember least. There were woods, and I could see lights up ahead. And I could hear him behind me. I kind of remember climbing a fence, maybe. And screaming.

"And then bright lights clicked on. And a man's voice. The man who brought me here. I don't even remember his face… or his name. I think I passed out before he even got me in the car."

A doctor and a nurse bustled into the room then, and Darger took that as their cue to end the interview.

"I wish I could remember more," Carrie said.

"You did great, Carrie," Darger assured her. "Really great. If you're up to it, we can send a sketch artist over here this afternoon, but for now, just focus on getting some rest."

Back in the hallway, Loshak got out his phone and dialed Chief Fleming to fill him in on what they'd learned. When he got to the part about a sketch artist, Fleming's voice grew excited.

"Oh, that's fantastic news. Dr. Whitman will be delighted to hear about this."

Darger made eye contact with her partner and smirked.

As Loshak finished up the call, Darger started running through what Carrie had said again. About how normal her attacker looked.

He could have been one of my professors or the guy who sold us our movie tickets.

Darger's scalp tingled, only this time it wasn't sympathy pain.

She got out her phone, brought up a map of Remington Hills, and used her thumb and forefinger to zoom in on part of the city. When Loshak ended the call, Darger glanced up at him.

"I have an idea."

CHAPTER 49

He sits behind the wheel again. The captain of this small ship. The prow of the Camaro slicing into the empty space of the street. Catapulting forward.

After work he drives around town. Knifes through the back streets and alleyways. Looks at the college town from the reverse angles of what the university photographers shoot in their bullshit brochures and magazines.

Here's the real thing. Ugly. Decaying. Crumbling like rotten teeth.

He sees the cracks in the brickwork. The craters pocking the streets.

The homeless faces sleeping on slabs of cardboard. Tucked out of sight where the campus police flush them. Better to push them to the edge of town by the bus station. Secluded. Far, far away from campus. Away from the image they're trying to construct and sell.

He sees the ripped places in the dream. All the scabs and scars they try to hide.

He wheels along the main strip of Remington Hills. Sidewalk bustling with afternoon pedestrians.

He zooms past it all. The touristy businesses going seedier the further away from campus he gets.

Strip clubs. Bars. Neon lights already gleaming.

Part of him craves a beer. The logos triggering a thirst. A frosty mug. A bitter drink. Crisp.

But he pushes the feeling down.

Doesn't like drinking much or often. Doesn't like to feel out of control of his faculties.

Fears very much, in fact, his senses dulling. Dreads, too, the sad feeling that alcohol sometimes brings over him, his aggression receding like a warm blanket sliding away from him.

And what might he find underneath, if he stares too long under those covers? He doesn't want to know.

In some ways, he thinks it's like the split between his family life and his personal life.

With his wife, he has a comfortable setup. They coexist. Get along. There's a kind of love to it, maybe, but not much in the way of passion. He has to go outside the marriage to sate most of his appetites.

Women, he thinks, are somewhat like spiders. Wanting to catch a man in their web. Wanting to wind their silky strands around him. Tie him down in that suspended state. Paralyze him with their venom. Keep him. A domestic trap. Forever.

And much of the time, he thinks their desire doesn't go far beyond that. The trap is the goal. The keeping. Something primordial in them craves that. There is little joy in any part of the relationship beyond the tying down.

He thinks that's why romance novels so revolve around courtship. Around a proposal. A ring. A wedding. The capture of the man is the fantasy. Rarely does fiction stray into the ongoing marriage — the joyless part of the equation that stretches on and on. That part goes beyond the bounds of the fantasy.

Just like a spider doesn't fantasize about the dried-out husks it's already suckled. It dreams only of the ritual of the trap itself — the tug of the strand shaking it awake, the tumbling of the prey in its legs, the winding of the silk, the sinking in of the fangs. All of its behavior serves that ritual, that fantasy.

Always hungry. That's nature.

Even so, he loves his wife. Tries always to understand her, even if sometimes it's a struggle. That's natural, too, he thinks. Just as she would struggle to understand his dark longings, his fantasies, the violence he inflicts.

He can taste the beer on his tongue, he wants it so bad. He doesn't know what that's about. Some ache for release, maybe. Booze does sometimes seem to flush the mounting frustration, like hitting a reset button.

Well, tonight he will get release.

Aggression written in someone else's skin, arcing down his arm into his blade. Flickering voltage.

Darkness drained from his heart, from his soul. The longings sated.

He will get a moment's relief from the gnawing tension that fills him most of the time. Desires that almost never sleep will be laid to rest for a time.

And all the things inside that push and pull and scream and thrash, they'll all hold still. Motionless. Peaceful.

Total satisfaction. Total reprieve. Just beautiful yawning emptiness in his head.

And then, just a few minutes later, the dark feelings will come back. Fresh lust. Renewed cravings.

Always hungry.

That's nature.

CHAPTER 50

It was late afternoon by the time the task force regrouped around the conference table again. Darger and Loshak stood at the front of the room, going over the plan.

Carrie's mention of the movie theater had jogged something in Darger's memory. Layla Perlman and Kyle Herbert, victims five and six, were shot outside of Macbeth's Pub. But before that, they'd been at the bowling alley, which happened to be right across the street from the movie theater.

Coincidence? Maybe.

But then Darger had checked the files for the previous attacks, and a pattern began to emerge. Each couple had visited somewhere on the outer edge of the SMU campus the same night they'd been murdered.

Of course, they were working with limited data. Darger couldn't deny that. But if her suspicions were right, the killer operated in a fairly small area of town when he was out hunting for victims.

"You'll be in pairs, one male and one female. If you're in a male-male group, one of you is playing the 'female.'" Darger put air quotes around the word. "Plainclothes, unmarked cars."

"Maybe I should ask my wife if I can borrow one of her dresses," one of the officers joked.

"To go with your panties?"

"I told you. They're not panties. They're bikini briefs. There's a difference."

When they were finished, Darger continued.

"Some of you have never been on a stakeout detail before.

So let me just put this out there now: it's boring. More boring than you can possibly imagine. Ninety percent of the time, you'll be sitting, doing nothing. Bring snacks. Bring drinks. Listen to the radio. Do whatever you need to do to say alert."

She held up a walkie-talkie.

"Each team will have one of these so the various teams can communicate with one another. We've designated channel 4 for the stakeout detail. With the number of people we've got on this assignment, it's important we keep the chatter to a minimum. We need the line open for critical communication.

"Based on the profile, we'll be looking for any kind of macho car. Mustangs. Corvettes. Dodge Chargers. And so on. If you see one, get on the radio, and we'll collectively keep an eye on it."

Loshak lifted a piece of paper from the table featuring the sketch they'd just received from the artist sent to talk to Carrie Dockett.

"This is a sketch of our killer. We've emailed a copy to everyone so you can study it before tonight. You'll note he's a clean-shaven white male, age 25 to 40, with dark brown or black hair. Since he knows we have an eyewitness, he may have changed his appearance. He may dye his hair, wear glasses, or even put on a fake mustache. So take the sketch into consideration, but don't underestimate this guy's craftiness."

Chief Fleming paced the back of the room, phone pressed to his ear. He raised one hand in the air to get Darger's attention.

"Bellington PD has agreed to send over a dozen officers to assist."

"Excellent. That's six more 'couples,'" Darger said, glancing at the map stuck to the wall.

Red X's mark the four spots where the victims had been just

hours prior to being attacked. They spent a few minutes deciding where to place the additional six vehicles.

"We've got the stadium area and the movie theater pretty well covered," Loshak said, dragging his finger over the map. "Maybe we put a few cars over here."

"OK."

Darger added the thumbtacks.

She took a step back, studying the blue tacks that radiated outward from each red X epicenter. She was confident that this plan was the right course. But in this kind of manhunt, the right course didn't always work.

And even if it did, it might not happen quickly.

Darger swallowed.

"I hope this isn't a colossal waste of time."

Loshak pursed his lips.

"It's what they did in the Son of Sam case."

"And then they ended up stumbling across his car instead."

Loshak clapped her on the shoulder.

"You can only work the case to the best of your ability. This is a good plan. It's proactive. It employs what we know about the guy. And it puts a lot of eyeballs where we know he likes to go."

Officer Dixon cleared his throat.

"Hey Chief?" He held up a tablet. "We got another post on the *University Watchdog*."

Fleming went and stood behind Dixon.

"What do the miscreants have to say for themselves this time?"

Dixon licked his lips.

"They're uh… they're essentially calling for the student body to intentionally violate the curfew."

The mustache over Chief Fleming's lips quivered.

"Now that's sedition if I've ever heard it. Who wrote it?"

"It's another anonymous post."

One of the other officers in the room scoffed.

"Oh come on, we all know who it is. It's that blue-haired strumpet. Tobi McCall."

"Strumpet?" another officer chuckled. "What the hell century are you from?"

"That's enough," Fleming barked. "What else does she say?"

"Well, she's pretty critical of the curfew in general," Dixon went on. "Says the university willingly and overtly failed to keep the student body safe and is now passing the buck to them. They are being told to stay inside. They are being told they can't attend any of the Homecoming festivities."

Darger tried to imagine the blue-haired girl rooting for the football team and couldn't do it. She doubted the girl cared about sports at all.

"She says the school's response to the murders is classic victim-blaming."

Dixon cleared his throat and began to read aloud.

"'Why are we the ones being punished? Why are we the ones paying the price? We aren't the ones guilty of rape and murder. We aren't the ones guilty of a mass cover-up.'"

The Adam's apple in the center of Dixon's neck bobbed once and then he went on.

"Uh, then she goes on to talk about how there was a Take Back the Night march scheduled, which is a school tradition every bit as important as Homecoming. And that it would be an embarrassment to everything Take Back the Night stands for to obey the curfew. 'The whole point is to show the world that we aren't scared. That we refuse to be blamed for the actions of the predators among us. That the night belongs to *us*. That as a group united, we are a force to be reckoned with.'"

Kirby barged into the room then, his hands weighed down with four bulging Spirit Halloween bags.

"You guys shoulda seen the cashier's face when I walked up with my cart jammed full of this stuff."

He dropped the bags on the table and thrust his hands into one of them.

"Check this one out."

He bent over and affixed a long blond wig to his head. The thick blonde strands made it look a little like a plate of al dente spaghetti had been spilled on his head. When he straightened again, he flicked one of the blonde locks over his shoulder dramatically and batted his eyelashes.

Everyone laughed.

"OK, everyone," Darger said. "Partner up. Those of you who need a wig, pick one out. We don't know exactly when he starts stalking. For all we know, he's already out there. But he seems to prefer attacking after dark, so I want everyone in place before sunset."

CHAPTER 51

Darger fiddled with her phone. Eyes shifting from the screen to the mirrors and back again, finding only the dark street reflected in the glass. No cars in over fifteen minutes.

She chewed the inside of her cheek. Impatient.

From the corner of her eye, she caught a glimpse of Loshak's silhouette, altered by the insane wig atop his head. Short and spiky and a bleach blonde shade that reminded her of uncooked ramen. She'd come to think of the wig as "The Guy Fieri." It didn't look remotely natural in daylight, but in the dark, it would read younger than Loshak's real hair. And that was important.

She wore her own hair loose, something she rarely did on the job. It was annoying to constantly have to brush the strands out of her face, but she wanted her silhouette to come across as overtly feminine to anyone passing by.

"Pretty dead tonight," Loshak said, echoing her earlier thoughts. "Seems like people are actually abiding by the curfew. For now, at least."

Darger grunted something that might have been assent.

"I'm really going to have to eat my own words if the curfew ends up helping us in the long run."

"God forbid you be wrong every now and again," Darger said.

"It's not that. I have no problem admitting when I'm wrong. I just don't want to have to admit it to Dr. Whitman."

"Well, don't count your chickens. We've still got the Take Back the Night group advocating a willful disregard of the curfew."

Loshak waved it away.

"Don't mistake loudness for popularity."

"What does that mean?"

"Just because she's got her blog and makes a lot of noise on campus doesn't mean the student body as a whole agrees with her. Or will do what she says." Loshak ran a hand through his fake locks. "You know Meghan and Harry?"

Darger turned to face him, eyebrows raised in disbelief.

"Prince Harry and Meghan Markle," he clarified. "The Duke and Duchess of Sussex?"

Darger blinked.

"I know who they are. I'm surprised that *you* do. Have you suddenly become a *People* magazine buff or something?"

Loshak shrugged.

"I don't really know anything about them. But I read an article about how there's all this social media criticism of them, especially on Twitter. If the average person scrolled through Twitter, they'd think these were two of the most hated celebrities on the face of the planet. As it turns out, all this hostility is actually originating from a tiny group of accounts. Like fifty or so accounts are responsible for seventy percent of the tweets they analyzed. And they evaluated something like a hundred thousand tweets, so we're talking a decent sample size here. Then there's a secondary level of about thirty accounts used to boost the messages from the first group. All in all, they have a potential reach in the millions. So they've managed to take what are essentially the fringe opinions of a couple dozen weirdos and amplified them to make it look like it's an opinion shared by the masses."

"That's kind of disturbing," Darger said.

"I know."

Loshak's bespiked head bobbed up and down.

"And we're only talking about a pair of celebrities. Like, who cares? But imagine if this same scheme was utilized in politics."

"I mean, it probably is."

"Exactly. Anyway, my point is, perception is not always reality. We've got a small group of students with a very loud figurehead making a lot of fuss, but that's not necessarily representative of the student population."

Darger thought about the blue-haired girl. All that righteousness. All that anger. Maybe it was preferable to apathy, but Darger sensed so much rage in the girl simmering just beneath the surface.

"What'll she do once we catch this guy?" Darger wondered out loud. "Will all that outrage just fizzle out once she loses her cause?"

"Nah. She'll just come up with something else to be pissed off about. It's what keeps her going," Loshak said. "And it's not just her, either. It's everyone. Seems to happen every few decades. Culture changes, and anger erupts. Probably'll get worse before it gets better."

"That's a cheery thought."

A few minutes later, a voice came over the radio, and Darger sat a little straighter in her seat.

"Anyone else seeing this latest announcement from President Whitman?"

"No," another voice answered. "What is it?"

"She just canceled all in-person attendance to the Homecoming game."

"I mean, it kinda makes sense. The game wouldn't be over until after curfew, and those kids are gonna spend two or three hours guzzling beer from the concession stand. It's dumb to think you're gonna be able to keep them from doing whatever the hell they want once the game lets out."

"I don't get why they don't just cancel the game outright."

"Because it's on ESPN, and the athletic department gets a giant check out of the deal. I think it's like half the yearly budget comes from this one game."

"Of course. It's always about the money."

The most cynical part of Darger's mind thought of another reason Whitman would cancel in-person attendance. She could frame it as yet another sacrifice. Another piece of evidence that the school was making safety their top priority.

The radio chatter died out, and silence settled over them once again. Darger returned to checking the mirrors every few seconds. Her gaze flicked from one side mirror to the other, hoping for something. Anything. But the streets remained motionless.

She shifted this way and that in her seat, suddenly restless. What if this plan didn't work? It was something of a long shot, she knew. This kind of stakeout always was.

Then again, it was better than doing nothing.

CHAPTER 52

The angry mob from the morning press conference slowly re-forms in the quad as the morning bleeds into afternoon. A horde of restless students. Ever growing as the time passes.

It meanders as the evening hits. An amoeba slowly adding to its size as it glides down Michigan Ave. The shape of it morphing, morphing with every step.

Tony cracks a Red Bull. That metallic snap sounding out among the troubled throng. He tilts his head back and chugs most of the amber elixir, effervescence tingling in his nose.

With no particular place to go, the mob stops and starts around him. Piles up on itself like a flock of confused birds. Then it smooths out and keeps moving. Always moving roughly toward its destination, even if it doesn't know where that is just yet.

Soon they're fully off campus. Away from the brick dorms, the glass facades, the smooth concrete walkways leading to various lecture halls.

Tony tosses his empty can. Watches it get kicked around by random tennis shoes before he loses sight of it.

The parade keeps moving. Now they drift into a residential neighborhood. Houses clad in vinyl siding. Sod lawns cropped tight. Adorned with decorative landscaping — fiery-looking bushes, neat beds of wood chips and gravel, well-groomed trees still clinging to most of their leaves for now.

The many feet tromp at the concrete, at the curb, at the asphalt. Too wide for a normal sidewalk, the outer edge of the flock mashes grass flat, beats a path into the front yards.

The footsteps fall into a loose rhythm. Pounding down in something close to unison. Something vaguely aggressive in the sound. Like orcs marching on Helm's Deep.

Chatter rolls out of the cluster of bodies. An endless babble of voices tangling over each other. A many-throated thing venting irritation, anger, hostility.

A stoplight blinks on the corner. Red light. Green light.

They move for it. Picking up just a little speed.

Tony feels himself swept up in something here. Alert but not really thinking. Eager but unsure what for.

Some collective instinct must already know where they're going. Must have known all along where they'd end up, what would happen here.

It's not until they reach the corner and wheel hard to the right that this inevitability dawns on most of their conscious minds, Tony among them.

Stadium Avenue lies open before them. The concrete structure rising in the distance, decorative arches of gunmetal gray garnished with the bright colors of the school banners hanging from them. The scoreboard rises up and over the grandstand, an oval loop of seating that holds just less than 55,000 bodies at maximum capacity.

Heads turn around Tony. Slowly but surely all eyes focus on the stadium some two blocks ahead. And their speed picks up even more. The plodding slog of earlier now turning to a speed walk.

Fresh excitement spirals energy into the many bodies of this morphing amoeba. The collective posture goes taller, goes rigid. A bounce finds its way into their shared gait. Ugly smiles cut open the faces. Hungry smiles.

The horde reaches the concrete steps that lead down into the parking lot. Two flights. Some forty feet of stairs.

They pound their way down. Bumping shoulders now. Electricity sparking wherever they touch.

Fields of asphalt stand between them and the stadium — blacktop sliced into countless pieces by lines of yellow paint. Heat radiates up from the dark lot, a day's worth of sunlight collected by the bitumen, reflected up into their ankles and shins.

The lot looks weird this empty, Tony thinks. A barren tundra of asphalt.

Normally the place would be swarming with cars. A jam-packed parking lot throbbing with life, with movement, with sound, right up until the game kicked off and even sometime after.

Tony pictures it how it would normally be:

Cracking cans of Miller Lite ringing their metallic clicks over the expanse.

Smoke coiling up from hibachi grills — burgers and brats slowly browning, wafting their savory smells everywhere.

All varieties of bad music blaring out of boom box speakers, some fifty years' worth of one-hit wonders resurrected to compete with each other here for dominance of sheer volume. Vanilla Ice going toe-to-toe with Gary Glitter and the band that sang "Eye of the Tiger."

"Achy Breaky Heart."

"99 Luftballoons."

"Who Let the Dogs Out?"

"Jump Around."

All of the greats.

The tailgating masses should be jabbering at each other, stuffing meat into their faces, drinking, throwing footballs around, playing cornhole. Everyone dressed head to toe in purple and green, or whatever the opposing team's colors were this week. Strutting about each other like riled-up roosters.

Instead, a few ESPN vehicles sit in the mostly empty lot. A long antenna extends out of the top of a van, a wire coiling around the telescoping column, leading up to a curved dish at the top. The satellite feed for tonight's broadcast.

The mutating mob shoots straight for the TV vehicles. Drawn to them. Really moving now. Passing over the blazing asphalt like they're floating.

The bodies swarm around the van. Necks craning to point their heads at the dish some twenty-five feet above. Arms stretching out to touch the glossy white enamel, to run fingers over the red letters emblazoned there.

And the chatter dies back. Something almost religious in the moment. Something sacred.

But then, what could be more sacred than being on TV?

Tony brushes his fingertips against the E in the logo. Feels some spark of something there, he thinks.

Slowly, most of the heads turn to the gates into the stadium. An arched place in the concrete where the turnstiles squat. Just on the other side of a chain-link fence from the van.

It looks gray there, under that domed place where the stadium lies open. The fading light of dusk no longer able to light it so well.

No one is out here now that they can see. No security. No players or coaches. No one at all. The game doesn't kick off for another ninety minutes or so.

They run for the fence. Taking off all at once as though a starter pistol has been fired in the air. Rushing up on the wiry grid of steel.

They fling their bodies at the links. Start climbing the twelve-foot barricade. All up and down the line, they jump onto the fence, loop their fingers into the metal mesh, haul themselves upward, inch-worming at the waist.

Small metallic pings ring out every time another body hits the fence. The chain links rattling against the posts.

A few frat-looking guys spill over the top first. Thudding down to the sod on the other side. Smiles curl their mouths, but their eyes look dead.

The sense of progress only seems to stoke the fire burning inside the mob. They fling themselves harder and faster. More and more human bodies stuck to the side of the fence, dangling there like monkeys, reaching out arms, hooking fingers.

Tony reaches through the mess of limbs. Grasps the metal loops. Hefts himself up toward the top.

The fence starts to wobble. Their cumulative weight turning it flimsy.

"Oh, shit. She's going down," one voice says, rising above the rest.

Like there's blood in the water, the mob's frenzy grows stronger still.

They fight to get closer. Elbowing through the swells. Jockeying for position. They flock up to the fence and start kicking at it.

The sheet of chain link slaps harder at the steel posts now. Piercing. Percussive. Metallic chimes shrieking and shearing off abruptly.

Clink.

Clink.

The fence leans forward. Bending. Buckling. Giving way to what they want. Ready now to rip a post out of the ground.

Clink.

Clink.

Something snaps. The fence topples forward. Broken. Trampled.

Tony flops down and pops right back up.

And the rush of humanity pours over the fallen barrier. Stomping over the meshwork. Picking up speed now.

Jogging and running. Excited kids jumping up and down among the group.

Set loose.

They jump the turnstiles. Rubber soles battering at the sidewalk. Clapping and echoing in the hollow of this arch.

Then they hurtle through the shadowed place. Move into the actual stadium.

The yawning space opens up before them. Rows and rows of stadium seats mounted in the concrete. Bleacher benches forming the cheap seats in each end zone. All of the oblong structure's seating looking down on the field.

The last of the sunlight glints on that green grass on the far side of the field, dappling orange spots on the ground like camera flares. And the stadium's shadow falls on their side. Colder and darker.

A few TV workers take shape in the distance, manning large cameras on the sidelines. And silhouettes become visible up in the press box. Blurry torsos standing there behind the glass.

It all happens quickly from there.

The mob rushes down the stadium steps. Hops another rail. And then they're spilling out onto the field. Running into the light. Feet swishing through green grass. Breaking into the open.

Joy. Bliss. Jubilance.

They whoop and yell and prance as much as they run now. Unchained. Set off.

Freedom. Rebellion. Euphoria.

The mob congregates in the center of the field. Jumps up

and down on the logo. Stomping it. Stomping their own school logo. Pogoing up and down in loose unison. Feet clomping at the painted grass.

The TV cameras swivel to get their shot. Maybe this will air on TV later, but maybe not.

Tony feels a smile pinching at his cheeks as he jumps up and down. The ecstasy of victory coursing through him. Unblocked. Finally.

He looks over to his left, sees his friend from the dorms. Josh. It takes a second for Tony to process what he's seeing.

In the midst of the stomping cluster of some 200 bodies, Josh stands still. His head leaned forward. Looking down at his feet.

Dick out, Josh pisses on the SMU logo. The stream of yellow puddling just before the toes of his shoes, frothy bubbles spiraling out from the point where the current hits the pool.

"What the fuck?" Tony says, his jumping falling in and out of time with the others. He bats Josh on the shoulder as he says it.

The pissing kid's head snaps around to face Tony, and he hisses out a crazy laugh, more spitty sounds than vocal ones.

"Couldn't think of what else to do, I guess," he says, his voice coming out breathy and strange to match the laughter. Almost like he was whisper-screaming the words.

Crazy as it sounds, there's some kernel of truth in the reasoning, Tony thinks.

What are they supposed to do now?

The release feels good, but it's somehow incomplete. Not enough. Jumping up and down on the logo? Not even close to enough.

Even before they've finished besmirching the school's symbol, that restless clawing already seems ready to return to his gut, the increasingly trapped feeling he gets on this campus. A place where all he can do is clench his jaw, furrow his brow, grit his teeth.

A place where he is powerless and under attack. Where they all are.

And a place where no one cares what happens to him or any of his peers. Where they only care how it looks.

A voice calls out from the edge of the field, and all the heads in the mob twirl that way. Many of the logo jumpers stopping right then and there.

One of the frat guys who was among the first to jump the fence now stands on the crossbar of the goalpost. Tony remembers his red t-shirt with a cartoon crab screen-printed on it in wispy white lines.

"We're done here, yeah? We've made our point," Red Shirt yells, his voice sounding thick and a little gravelly. "Now we hit the town."

He jumps the ten feet down from the crossbar. Landing in something akin to a Spiderman pose in the end zone. Then he hops up and jogs toward the tunnel leading out of the stadium.

And the mob follows.

CHAPTER 53

Loshak flipped his sun visor down, and the little light next to the mirror lit up. He turned his head back and forth. Prodded the tips of his fingers at the spikes of his wig.

"You think this wig makes me look younger?" he said, his voice kind of thoughtful.

"Why? You thinking about wearing it full time now?"

"No… unless it makes me look younger. Then yeah."

Darger snorted.

"Well, it looks like you're wearing a helmet of horse hair or something. So I don't know about younger… But at least you didn't get stuck with the Hitler wig."

One of the local officers had gotten a dark side part that somehow strongly resembled the coif of the late Fuhrer.

"I know. Jesus. I thought he was going to start screaming in German as soon as he put that thing on. *Sturm und Drang* this and *blitzkrieg* that. Mustache twitching. Spit flying."

Darger chuckled a little.

One strand of the coarse blonde hair hung over Loshak's forehead, and she had the urge to flick it out of the way for him. Her own scalp itched just looking at it. But the wig didn't seem to have much give — the strands appeared to be shellacked in place — so she doubted it would do any good.

Headlights flared in the rearview, and Darger's body went tense as she watched the car zip closer. A sedan — something made by General Motors based on the shape of the headlights. Her eyes tried to pierce the glare on the windshield, see into the gloom in the driver's seat behind it.

The car juddered over a pothole. Crept closer. And the shape behind the wheel came clear.

Bony shoulders and a ponytail. Narrow jaw with a pointy chin. A scrawny girl was driving. Probably college-aged, maybe younger.

Darger let out a sigh. She tried to release the frustration along with her breath, as though she could vent the agitation through her mouth like some smokestack on a factory.

And still the tension welled up in her body again, pulling muscles and tendons into taut rubber bands, making her heart knock harder and faster than it should. The pressure constricted inside her like a python until it got so tight that she wanted to scream.

A voice crackled on the radio for the first time in what felt like a long while. The quiet rumble of chatter quivering out of the tiny speaker. Loshak turned it up, and they listened.

"Well… Just checking the chatter on the other channels, we've got word of a, uh, disturbance on campus. Or just off campus, I guess. The stadium, you know. A couple hundred kids ran out onto the football field, and now it seems like they're heading into town."

Another voice responded to the first.

"They do any damage? Trash the concession stands or tear down the goalposts or anything like that?"

"Negative. Aside from knocking over a section of chain-link fence, the stadium is fine. Even then, it seems like they were climbing it, and it just kind of went over more so than they intentionally, uh, you know, trampled the fence there."

"Well, well… Seems like our rabble-rousers are of the gentle sort. So far, anyway. Man, back when I was a kid, we would have savaged that stadium like rock stars tearing up a suite at the Hilton. The kids these days can't even riot right.

Gen Z or whatever the hell they are now. Too sensitive or something, you know?"

More voices joined the conversation. Amused.

"Hey, even a riot needs to be a safe space, right? Hopefully there were trigger warnings."

"Oh sure. We wouldn't want this civil unrest to upset anyone."

"That would be deeply problematic. A lot of riots are, you know?"

"That's enough chatter," Fleming cut in. "The curfew unit is handling the, uh, gathering by now, I'm sure. Let's all just concentrate on the task at hand, alright? We've got a long night ahead of us."

Darger felt intense relief that the Chief was keeping his eye on the prize and not allowing the stakeout detail to get distracted with whatever else was happening in town.

She settled into her seat. If they could stay focused through the night, their plan just might work.

A dispatcher came over the line then. The woman's voice sounding tinnier than the other radio chatter.

"All units be on the lookout for a muscle car reported in the stadium area. Possibly a Camaro or Dodge Charger. Driving with its headlights off."

Darger's scalp tingled.

A muscle car with the headlights off. This is him. It has to be.

"Dispatch. Whereabouts exactly on our muscle car?" the Chief said over the line, his voice eager.

"Just south of the stadium, heading west on Miller Road. Caller says it's been a few minutes now, so… He could be blocks or even miles from there."

"Roger. Well… thanks for the update. We'll keep our eyes peeled."

CHAPTER 54

Jay feels a body buzz in the center of his torso as he tromps among the mob moving down University Ave. Electric tingles throbbing in his belly, bolts of it shooting up into his chest.

Holy shit. Is this, like, bloodlust or something? Jesus.

The mob clusters around a corner. That flexing amoeba of humanity hanging a crooked left onto Dartmouth Road.

The mob seems to have already grown since the football field, perhaps doubled. As though it's multiplying. Rapid asexual reproduction like the single-celled creature it somehow is.

And more kids pour out of the sprawling apartment complex nearby even now. Racing across the street and spilling into the crowd. Making the edges of it grow like a puddle.

Expanding. Engulfing.

Maybe it's the weed, but for Jay, a strange current flickers off of this teeming mass of humanity. Like arcs of high voltage popping and lurching and sparking between them. Chain lightning shooting through all of them. Spreading the… the… bloodlust or whatever the hell it is.

An appetite for destruction.

The prickling in his belly crawls up higher. Winds around and around in his chest like a water moccasin thrashing around in haphazard figure eights. Somehow excited and terribly anxious at the same time. Heart pounding not fast but hard. Slamming like an unaccompanied kick drum keeping the beat.

The body buzz reminds him of the time he took pure DXM in powder form — dextromethorphan, a dissociative often found in cough syrup. In small doses, it essentially shuts off the part of the brain that triggers the cough reflex to provide some relief. In higher doses, it works as a profound dissociative along the lines of ketamine or PCP. Repeated use literally wears holes in the brain, according to numerous studies.

He'd snorted it out of the grooved spot along the spine of one of his textbooks. Harsh powder that felt like glitter filtering through his nasal passage and dripping down his throat.

The first wave had been overwhelming. Nauseating. He vomited in the kitchen sink. And after that, the world started to feel more and more distant. Like he was just floating through it, dreaming, neither the external world nor his internal world all the way real. Watching a movie and somehow in it at the same time.

Isolated. Apart. Detaching entirely.

This walk with the mob feels like that. Exciting but numb. Dramatic but distant. Engrossing but not quite all the way real.

The mob wheels up to the liquor store on the next corner. A pink neon sign flares from the storefront, cursive script spelling out the shop's name in gleaming letters — *On the Rocks.* Its glow tints the fissured white paint over the brick, looks like cracked mud along a riverbank.

The windows are covered over entirely by sun-bleached beer posters that all look strangely dated to about 1996. Weird smiling faces blanched pasty by the UV rays. Ghostly. Dead.

The whole group sort of balls up there on the sidewalk in front of the place. Piling into each other. Packing tighter together like they did by the ESPN van. Like here's something exciting again, here's something worth stopping for, worth reaching out and touching. The pink light seems to dye the hair of those nearest a pale bubble gum shade.

Jay pushes closer. Feels the same draw they must all feel. A magnetic force that makes him ache to be close to the place.

"Front door is locked."

This murmur reverberates through the mob. Unsettles them.

Someone tries the door again. The glass thing shakes in its frame. Doesn't budge.

Had they seen the mob coming and locked up? Decided to close up early because of the curfew? Neither option makes a lot of sense to Jay.

He doesn't see the rock rise out of the crowd. Not really. Just sees a blur shoot over his head, gets the sense of something moving there like a swooping bat.

And then he hears the window crack.

The golf ball-sized rock chinks into the glass plane. Lodges itself there in the middle of a Milwaukee's Best poster.

Another rock flies. Slams.

There's a thick sound like a snapped femur. Lines running up and down from the first rock like cracking ice on a lake. Spreading in all directions.

The rock falls.

And the liquor store glass shatters and drops all at once, all together. Tumbling. Cascading. Not safety glass. Older. Brittle.

Big pointed shards of it come loose from the frame like fangs falling out of a mouth. Drop to the sidewalk with shrill cymbal crashes screaming out over everything.

The glass explodes again and again as pieces fall and hit. Raining down in strange waves. Bursting on the sill, on the concrete. Splintering into smaller and smaller bits.

The glassy sounds ring out. Echo in the hollow of the empty street. Shivering in the air. A piercing vibrato like a struck tuning fork.

And then it's quiet. Still.

Everyone watching. Everyone waiting.

Flaps of a tattered Bud Light poster float down among the debris. Scuff at the ground.

It feels good. Breaking the glass. Watching it fall. It feels good.

Jay swallows. Surprised to hear that juicy saliva sound in his throat in the stillness. Too loud. Makes goosebumps plump on the backs of his arms.

The fratty looking guys at the front of the line step forward. Feet gritting over the bits of glass, grinding it into the cement.

They enter the vacancy where the window used to be. Legs lifting over the exposed wood of the windowsill. Carrying them over the threshold. Their figures turn right and disappear into the fluorescent glow of the liquor store.

A few more members of the crowd stream in after them, but most wait. Expectant.

Jay holds still. Stares into the empty window frame. Only able to see a section of a wine aisle and part of a cardboard Jägermeister display.

Soon some of the first kids return. Leaning out the window. Handing out bottles of booze into the crowd.

Armloads of Grey Goose and Jim Beam are distributed. Swigs taken. Bottles passed.

Once those hanging out of the window have distributed their booze, they head back for more.

It keeps coming. Cases of Coors and Corona. Fifths of Johnny Walker and Old Crow.

Cheap and expensive. It doesn't matter now. This is fuel. This is life.

Something clicks and scrapes off to the left of the windows. A bell dings.

A red-faced clerk vaults through the door and rushes away.

Stumbles a little as he sees the mob up close. Wincing and jerking. Eyes as wide as something in a cartoon. Scared shitless.

He races away from them. Rockets down the sidewalk and into the dark. Arms and legs strangely sharp in their motions like he's a fleeing gazelle.

The crowd is quiet for a few seconds. Watching him sprint away. Perhaps a touch disturbed. They squint and tip bottles to their faces.

Then a mocking voice rises up from the mob.

"Abandon ship!"

And there's laughter among the ranks. A release of some tension. Jay can feel it.

As the clerk vanishes around a corner in the distance, some new reality sinks in. Jay licks his lips as he contemplates it.

The liquor store is unguarded now. They can plunder and move on. Safe in the crowd.

Roving on from here. Fueled up. Ready for the night's next adventure.

Truly free. Disentangled. Striking back at a world that doesn't care what happens to them.

Jay finds a forty of King Cobra thrust into his hands. Sweaty glass cold against his fingers.

He shrugs. Cracks the top and drinks deeply, that malt liquor smell swelling around him. Sweet and pungent.

This is life.

CHAPTER 55

Headlights swept past the rearview mirror. Rounded the corner and pushed down the street next to the rental car. Two beams spearing the darkness, sliding over the asphalt.

Darger sat forward in her seat. She blew a lock of hair out of her eyes and tucked it behind her ear.

The car slowed as it neared them, the engine's growl lowering in pitch, and she felt her heart creep up into her throat. Pattering there like moth wings.

"Can you see what kind of car it is?" Loshak asked, his voice low.

He held utterly rigid in his seat, as though any sudden movement might scare the killer off.

Darger waited before she answered. Watched the mirror where the car seemed to grow as it crept closer.

"I can't tell yet."

"He's moving awfully slow," Loshak murmured.

The car practically stopped next to them. Inching forward in something akin to slow motion, like someone rolling through a stop sign. The front end roughly in line with their rear bumper. Headlights gleamed in the mirrors, flooding the rental car with light.

Darger chewed her bottom lip, wondering if this was it? Was it happening?

She resisted the urge to crank her head back and glare at the vehicle. Not wanting to spook him... *if* it was him.

"Could be someone messing with their phone. Texting. Changing their music."

She said it as much to try to temper her own soaring expectations as she did to communicate with Loshak. Either way, he said nothing.

Her slitted eyes stared at the mirror, though she couldn't see anything there now. The glare of the headlights washed everything out. Left a glinting halo glimmering from the edges of the rounded glass, rainbowed along the perimeter like a hologram.

She pictured the killer perched in the driver's seat, shrouded in shadow. Head craned hard to the right. Eyeballing the car. Agitated. Hungry. Snuffling around for fresh meat.

Loshak smoothed down his shirt, though it had no rumples that Darger could see. A nervous tic. Some nonchalant gesture moving his limbs.

The car's engine growled louder as it crept forward inch by inch. The vibration rumbled through the rental. Made Darger's bucket seat tremble against her lower back like a massage chair.

"Looks like a muscle car, right?" Loshak said. "A Dodge Charger or Camaro is what the dispatcher said."

Darger tried to read the lines of the front end, the shape of the headlights, everything bleached into a soft focus by the glow of the headlights.

"Yeah," she said after a few seconds. "A Charger, I think. Newer. But the headlights are on."

"Fits the profile still. Macho, almost overly masculine in outward appearance."

Darger swallowed hard again. Thought of what she'd said in her profile.

Above all, he wants to identify with strength. He wants to see himself as powerful.

She nodded.

The dark shape of the car slid forward in the rearview.

Indistinct. It looked like a close up special effects shot from a horror movie playing in the glass — the creature so close to the camera that its slithering body filled the frame, texture visible, but the bigger picture details were left indiscernible. It was frustrating.

The Charger suddenly jerked. Lunging over the next section of the asphalt.

Both Loshak and Darger flinched at the abrupt movement.

The engine's pitch whined into something higher pitched. The rumble giving way to a screech.

The Charger sped off. Fled like a bolting rabbit.

After a few seconds, the taillights were glowing red eyes in the windshield of the rental car. Mocking them. The crimson dots shrinking as the car rolled down the street. Then the Charger wheeled around a corner and disappeared.

Darger gripped the wheel so hard that the rubbery plastic coating squeaked against her palms, against her fingers.

She wanted to tear off after him. Chase him down. See where the hell he was going.

But she couldn't. She knew that.

There was no guarantee it was him, first of all.

And she couldn't risk compromising the operation. Even now, the whole area was swathed with undercover law enforcement. If that was him — *if* — he'd still fall into the trap. She believed that. Had to.

Just maybe not here with her and Loshak. So be it.

She turned her head. Looked out at the dark hung up all around the rental car.

He was out there tonight. Darger could feel it.

CHAPTER 56

Finished with the liquor store, the mob heads into the student ghetto — a collection of shabby older homes that serve as off-campus rentals. They march right down the middle of the street now, perhaps emboldened by the booze. The glass bottles clink where they've been stuffed in pockets or stowed in fabric tote bags. Some members of the mob hug cases of beer to their chests, handing out cans left and right as they walk.

Jay can feel the King Cobra swirling in his bloodstream, killing brain cells most pleasantly. He has moved on to a pint bottle of cheap brandy that tastes like vomit already, which seems funny to him. Usually the alcohol doesn't taste like puke until much later in the evening. This brandy has decided to cut out the middle man. Smart.

Kids are still streaming out of apartments and houses and join the congregation. The original group was male-heavy — something of a sausage party, to be honest — but now there seems to be a strong female contingent joining the fun. Maybe that makes sense, Jay thinks. The college had been covering up crimes against women long before there were male victims. Maybe they're just as angry. Just as hungry.

As they get to the next block, Jay sees activity in the street. Two guys drag a couch out into the middle of an intersection. Waddling funny as they lug the thing. Then slamming it down.

A jet of lighter fluid snakes onto the upholstery — a brown and orange plaid pattern that looks older than most of the students gathered around it.

The kid juicing up the couch is a scrawny long hair in a

blue flannel shirt. Jay has seen him around campus, usually looking pretty baked. Hair always dirty. Greasy light brown strands draped on both sides of his face. Blue flannel shirt always present, either worn or tied around his waist. Always laughing at something that's not there.

A Zippo flicks open in his bony hand. Grits and snaps. And then a triangle of flame flutters atop the hunk of metal, hissing, almost whistling a little as the wind touches it like someone blowing across the top of an empty bottle.

A cheer goes up from the crowd. Wordlessly egging him on.

The kid hums some song Jay doesn't know as he takes the flame to the couch cushion. Some rap chorus turned war hymn. He dances in place as the flame touches down. Feet sliding everywhere, sliding everywhere.

Flames shoot to life. Rise from the cushions. Peeling back the upholstery in slow motion, melting it away from the middle out. The foam inside is basically just oil turned to a semisolid form. Fabric bags of fuel ready and waiting their whole lives long for this.

The mob draws up on the burning couch. Fanning out to circle around it.

It reminds Jay of a video he watched on YouTube or something. A flock of turkeys circling a dead cat. Winding around and around the crumpled creature. A perfect circle. Some strange death ritual seeming to take place among the birds. Crazy what meaning animal behavior can seem to have sometimes, how instinct seems to know things that reach beyond the here and now.

A few houses down, someone has placed a keg of beer out in their front yard. The metal cylinder tucked down in a large ceramic plant potter full of ice. A jolly-looking fat guy mans the tap, handing out Dixie cups filled to the brim with Pabst Blue Ribbon.

Jay hands off the remnants of his pint of puke brandy to someone and walks over to the keg. Feels the hard asphalt give way to grass underfoot.

He gets a cup of beer. Tips the flimsy plastic to his lips and lets foam and brew drain down his neck. It tastes good. Cold. Bitter in a familiar way. Washes away the lukewarm puke taste of the brandy.

A second couch is burning now. Raging flames reaching up some fifteen feet. Orange cracking and dancing and licking everywhere.

And it feels good. Burning. Fire. It feels right. Seems in tune, somehow, with how they all feel.

Fire. Destruction. Aggression rendered physically in some chemical form. Consuming.

You could call it anger or fear, this feeling that has spread over campus. But Jay doesn't think either is quite right.

It's a burning, gnawing… something. Maybe something there is no word for. Something that wants to destroy, wants to combust, wants to detonate. And maybe tonight it is.

He moves closer to the bigger of the fires. Wanting to be near it. Wanting to feel it on his skin.

One of the frat-looking guys from outside the liquor store lurches forward and jump-kicks one of the burning couches. His foot hammering one of the arms with a downward stroke and then pushing him off.

A bunch of sparks shoot out of the burned-out hollow where the springs are exposed. An explosion of tiny orange flecks rising into the heavens. Twisting in the air.

Jay stands right next to it. Feels the heat on his face to match the heat inside. He chugs his beer.

And for this moment, the mob is one. Together. Not as a collection of students with disparate backgrounds, but as one entity.

Hungry together. Hurting together. Lashing out together. Shoulders and hands just barely touching now and again.

The flames reach higher and higher.

CHAPTER 57

"I still don't get why we're doing this," Andre says, his voice tremoring again like a toddler about to start bawling.

Tobi roosts behind the steering wheel like a hawk up on high. Upper back locked upright. An acrylic knit cap hides her blue hair. Head tilting just slightly to look at the rearview mirror. Furtive glances. Not wanting it to look obvious to anyone outside the car.

Andre slouches in the passenger's seat. Looks like he wants to melt into the upholstery and disappear.

"When Son of Sam was terrorizing parked couples in New York City, the police set up a massive sting operation," Tobi says, her voice low and even. A little dead. "Cops sat in parked cars, posing as young couples, and they tried to lure the shooter in."

She hits her Parliament. Blows out a cloud of smoke. Continues her deadpan spiel.

"I figured it was only a matter of time before the task force started treating this case the same way. You saw all those cars heading out. A flood of them rolling out of the Campus Police Department lot. Parking in strategic spots around town. Tonight's the night."

Andre lights a cigarette of his own. Lighter rasping and clicking. Smoke coiling.

"Yeah, I understand that part, Einstein. Why are *we* doing it?"

Tobi doesn't blink.

"Because we are going to catch him."

She doesn't speak the second part of her thought out loud — *and I'm going to write about it.*

Music plays softly from the car's speakers. Turned down so low as to seem tinny. But it fills some of the emptiness in the car, eases just a touch of the tension.

They're parked right on the line where the city gives way to patchy woods and cornfields. Homes line the left side of the wide street, a few windows glowing in the living rooms set back from the asphalt. And tree trunks jut from the ground on the opposite side, some of the leaves already going wispy and brown.

A panel of light shines on one section of asphalt, the limited glow of the one streetlight operational here.

Yeah, it's the perfect spot. She imagines couples end up parking here not infrequently. Exactly the kind of place he would go hunting in.

Good.

With her cig perching between her lips, Tobi rubs her hands together. Cold fingers poking out of fingerless gloves, knit material that extends into her sleeves, rumples around her wrists, trails halfway up her forearms.

She plucks her thermos from the cupholder. Takes a drink and then holds onto the warm metal canister. Lets its heat leech into those icy mitts.

No matter what she does, her hands can't seem to get warm. It's the adrenaline, she knows.

Andre sucks his cigarette too hard and makes a little high-pitched sound that Tobi reads as a whimper. He always sounds like a cartoon toddler.

"Don't piss your pants, Andre. You have the taser, don't you?"

He prods a finger at the dark bulk resting on his lap. Jade's dad — a prepper with a full-blown bunker stocked to the gills — had bought her a top-of-the-line taser as a high school graduation present. The black and yellow thing looks kind of like a price gun at a supermarket. He fingers it like he's trying to find its g-spot, pointer finger nudging and jabbing all over the thing.

He takes a breath. Then he nods his head.

"Well, you don't even have to be that close. The wires extend up to thirty-five feet."

"Are you kidding? He's going to come up to the car door, your side or mine. That's pretty fucking close. Jesus."

Tobi exhales. Frustration venting from her nostrils.

"It's not hard. You just aim and fire. It's truly idiot-proof, Jade's dad made sure of that. Line the laser sight up on him, center mass if you can. Squeeze the trigger. The probes will fire out of there and do the rest. 50,000 volts. This thing would knock an elephant on its ass."

He prods the taser again. This time his breath sounds slightly less bewildered.

"Yeah. I guess you're right."

"You'll have the element of surprise on your side. He'll never see it coming. Shit, you could probably take out an entire linebacking corps with this thing, let alone one guy."

Tobi looks at herself in the rearview mirror. Sees the ribbed acrylic of her hat reach down to just above her brow, hiding all of her hair. And she smiles at the image.

The cops will all wear gaudy wigs. Ridiculous blond things that glow like bleached teeth from a mile away.

They're so hung up on the surface details — seeming young, seeming like a helpless college kid — that none of them will do what a real girl would do on a chilly Michigan night. Put on a winter hat.

She chuckles at the thought: *I look like a real girl. For once.*

Glancing over at the taser sitting on Andre's lap, she thinks about her own weapon. A hunting knife tucked inside the cuff of her pantleg, taped to the side of her boot. A hulking thing. Serrated on one side. So big it looks like Rambo and Crocodile Dundee would fight over who gets to fashion it into a spear and harpoon a whale with it. Another of Jade's father's little gifts.

She's glad to have the ridiculous action movie knife, but it's a *just in case* kind of thing. She hopes like hell she doesn't have to use it.

Tobi takes another big drink of coffee. Stubs out her cigarette in the ashtray and waits about ten seconds before she lights another. The Parliaments don't taste good anymore, and they make her throat feel filmy with ash and nicotine and tar, but she's too antsy to just sit here idly.

The lighter's flame flickers just beyond the tip of her nose. A blaze that burns incandescent within the sedan's cabin.

But the dark outside remains untouched.

CHAPTER 58

The mob plods back toward campus. The smell of burnt polyester still clings to their clothes, to their hair. A stench both acrid and chemical. Like burnt almonds or spices mixed with plastic, Jay thinks.

The couches had burned out within twenty minutes. Turned to blackened husks abandoned in the street. The metal wire skeletons laid bare. Coiled springs with clumps of ash and melted shit all stuck to them. Looked like oversmoked ribs or something.

The mob quickly moved on as soon as the second fire guttered out. Vaguely disappointed, Jay thought. Irritated.

Still hungry. Their blood still up. No release for the lust that has built up inside of them.

At least they're still one step ahead of the cops. For now.

Slouching toward campus. Groping after something.

Some kind of release. Some kind of satisfaction.

Something here and now that Jay can feel in his heart. Something he suspects they all can.

They walk up a ramped sidewalk and toward a decorative glass skyway connecting two lecture halls — an arched gateway that leads onto campus proper.

Jay cranes his head to look up at the glass veined with steel above them. A transparent section of building bisected with dark lines. Something about it reminds him of a fly's wings.

He keeps looking up as they walk underneath the skyway. Everything going darker for a second as the structure blots out the streetlights. Feels like walking through some short tunnel, crossing some crucial threshold.

Their footsteps stab the concrete. Heavy-footed. Some of the kids staggering and bumping into each other. Drunk.

And the campus opens up before them. Trees jutting up from the hills. Smooth concrete contours cutting pale ribbons in the grass, drawing lines to the various buildings.

It's full dark. Full night. The moon and stars hung up above seem brighter now that they've crossed the line onto campus. Shimmering in the heavens.

They file past a parking garage and a couple of brick residence halls. All of the structures lit in a mix of yellow streetlamps and silvery moonlight, textures varying from sharp and hard to that soft focus like a movie dream sequence. Feathery. A little smeared.

Jay swallows. Still tastes yeasty beer on his tongue, though he's been out for a while.

He wonders what they'll do next. What will feel right. Some fresh boredom settling over him. Restlessness.

Like *here we are. Here we are. So what?*

He feels his jaw flex in rapid bursts. Feels his eyes skittering over the manicured landscaping that forms a median between two sidewalks. Campus seems dead, at least what he can see of it. A still life of some administrator's ideal.

What does he even want to happen here? How does he want this to end?

Is this it? Is this all there is?

A shiny new placard outside of Wilson Hall brags about various academic honors, the text blurry to Jay's eyes now, but he reads enough to get the gist. Something about how the school has had the second most Rhodes Scholars among Michigan universities or some bullshit. Some reference to research endowments.

His teeth grit harder. Molars quivering. Thoughts pounding in his head like a hammer divoting brass.

Yeah?

So what?

Who cares?

Too busy worshiping big endowments to give a fuck what happens to the real live human beings at your bullshit school.

Abused. Raped. Killed.

They don't give a shit.

No one fucking cares.

A few rocks fly out of the mob. Crack against the brick facade. One plinks at a window, maybe chipping it.

But the mob keeps moving. Still restless. Still searching. Broken windows don't seem like enough anymore.

When they round the next bend, Jay sees it. Like fate brought them right here, right now. Delivered them to this moment.

Pines form a small wall to the left. A copse of landscaping that almost serves as a divider between buildings, blocking their view.

As they come up to the corner, the pine trees seem to slide out of the way. And parked in front of the next building, they see what they've been seeking, even if they didn't know it to be so.

A campus police car wedges into a diagonal parking spot. Looks glossy in the dark. Streetlights glinting off the windows, spreading puddles of light over the hood and roof.

"Yes," Jay whispers to himself in an exhale, his voice sounding almost sexually aroused. "Yes. Yes."

The mob rushes for the car. Heavy breathing and giggles rippling through the masses.

The kids fan out. Encircle the vehicle. Reach out their

hands.

Fingers curl around the lip where the car door butts up against the frame, sets of palms hugging around the fenders. Gripping. Pushing.

Jay feels the cool of the thing against his skin. A little moisture as the evening's chill has brought about a thin layer of condensation.

He pushes. Gets low to put his legs into it.

The cop car rocks back and forth, back and forth. Wobbling at first. Then swaying. Harder and faster.

A rhythm takes over the arms and hands of those surrounding the vehicle. A trance-like groove. All of them catching it. Muscles twitching in time. Working together. Something empowering in the feeling of it, Jay thinks. Like they're all pulling the same direction for once in their lives.

The vehicle finally reaches its tipping point. Rocks up onto two tires. Seems to hover there a long time. Set at an angle.

Weightless.

Everyone takes a big step back.

And then it crashes down onto its side. Cracking and crunching. The weight settling lower and lower as it crumples one side of the body toward flatness.

A big cheer erupts from the crowd. Dancing. Whooping.

A couple of the frat guys kick at the windshield. The safety glass spider webs. But it holds together in a big shattered sheet. A layer of frozen damage.

They kick and kick. Dent the plasticy glass into the cabin.

Finally a foot plunges through the barrier. Punches out an empty space in the glass. Leaves a hole about the size of a bowling ball.

That gets another cheer. Voices chittering everywhere, chittering everywhere.

And now more bodies cluster to the vehicle, and Jay falls back. Euphoria crushing through his skull. Makes his eyes open wider.

Smiling. Breathing deep. Waiting for the next disaster. Looking forward to it.

Within minutes, the car is on fire.

CHAPTER 59

Plastic crinkled as Loshak tore open a bag of potato chips. A vaguely food-like odor filled the car.

"Good God, those are potent," Darger said. "What the hell are they?"

"Dill pickle cheddar chips."

"They smell like dill pickle farts," Darger said, fingering the window control.

Fresh air seeped in through the cracked window, and she waved a hand in front of her nose.

"I take it you don't want any?" Loshak asked.

"No, thank you."

He smiled and popped a chip into his mouth.

"More for me," he said, crunching away.

Darger's phone buzzed. She pulled it from her pocket and winced at the name on the screen.

"Who is it?"

"Owen."

Loshak shrugged.

"Answer it."

"Are you sure?" Darger asked. "We're kind of busy."

"Yeah, busy sitting here for potentially hours on end."

Loshak held a chip in the air as though to emphasize.

"Besides, we're supposed to be incognito as a couple of college students. They're on their phones all day. It'll add some authenticity to the situation."

"But they don't actually talk on the phone, from what I've observed. They text. They voice chat. But regular old phone calls? Lamesauce."

Loshak frowned.

"Lamesauce?"

"It's what the kids are saying these days."

"Really?"

"I have no idea," Darger admitted. "Probably not."

"Just answer it."

Darger thumbed the green phone icon.

"Hey," she said.

"Hey," Owen said back. "Are you on your stakeout detail?"

"Yeah."

"Anything happen yet?"

"Nope."

"I know that game," Owen said with a sigh. "So do you have time to hear what I found out about ol' Claude?"

Darger stared up at the ceiling of the car. She didn't actually want to hear it, but that wasn't what he'd asked. And she was trying to be supportive. That's what girlfriends were supposed to do, right?

"Sure."

"He's got a daughter," Owen said, his tone suggestive.

"OK."

"He says he doesn't have kids."

"I see."

"I mean, this is huge."

Darger was beginning to hear the tinge of mania to Owen's voice again.

"I guess," she said.

"You guess? Come on, this proves he's a liar. Not to mention a deadbeat dad. And who knows what else? I bet this is just the tip of the iceberg. If he's gonna lie about not having kids, who knows what other nasty secrets he has. Anyway, I'm thinking I should see if I can find her and have a little chat."

Darger's grip tightened on the phone.

"You want to talk to the daughter?"

"Yeah."

"Uh… I think that's a bad idea."

"Why?"

"Because dragging a third party into this isn't cool," Darger said. "You have no idea what you might be unleashing. If you want to talk to your mother and Claude about it, fine. But it's totally unfair to drop this on someone else's doorstep."

"Seriously? I thought if anyone would understand, it would be you. You know what it's like."

"To be abandoned by a parent? Yeah, I do know what it's like, and I can tell you right now that I wouldn't be happy if some P.I. came around asking me for dirt on my dad."

Darger used her free hand to press her fingers into the space between her eyebrows.

"But it's not about what I would want anyway. This is someone else's life. Tell your mom whatever you want, but leave his estranged daughter out of it."

"Wouldn't you want a chance to tell the person what kind of man your father really is?" Owen asked. "Doesn't my mom have a right to know that before marrying the guy?"

Darger ground her molars together.

"If I were this guy's daughter, and your mother came to me asking, then I'd probably tell her. But this isn't your mom asking, Owen. It's *you.* And I really don't think your mother would want you to be doing this."

"Well, you don't know her like I do. Believe me, she'd want to know she was marrying a deadbeat."

Owen let out a breath, and Darger could hear the irritation in it.

"You know, I'm kind of annoyed that you're not on my side with this whole thing."

"I *am* on your side. That's why I'm telling you not to do this."

"Right." He clicked his tongue. "I should let you go."

"Owen—"

"You're busy. I'll talk to you later," he said, and then the call disconnected.

Darger groaned and tucked the phone back into her pocket.

Loshak crunched loudly beside her, and after a few moments, she realized he was staring at her, waiting for an explanation.

"What was that all about?" he asked finally.

Darger let the back of her skull fall against the headrest of her seat.

"Owen's mother just got engaged."

"Ahh," Loshak said knowingly. "I'm guessing Owen is none too happy about that?"

"He's gone slightly insane, I think. He's dead set on finding dirt on this guy, I guess in hopes that his mother will call the whole thing off. But I've seen how this kind of family drama plays out. The phrase 'don't shoot the messenger' exists for a reason."

Loshak dusted cheese powder from his fingers and reached for the bottle of water he'd rested in one of the cup holders.

"He'll probably cool off eventually."

"That's what I thought," Darger said, shaking her head. "But if anything, I think he's gotten more invested."

Unscrewing the lid of his drink, Loshak raised an eyebrow.

"Well, his mother is his only family at this point, right?"

"Pretty much."

Loshak nodded and brought the bottle to his lips. Just then, the radio buzzed with excited voices again. Clear fluid jumped out of the mouth hole of Loshak's bottle and slapped onto his lap.

"Aw, crap," he said.

Darger laughed.

"Yeah, laugh it up. Real funny when a guy has to sit in a car indefinitely with a wet crotch."

Darger laughed harder.

"Hang on. What are they saying now?"

He turned up the volume on the radio.

"—got a situation at On the Rocks on Merganser Street. The windows are all smashed out."

"Is there looting in progress?" another voice asked. "Do you need backup?"

"No, everyone had moved on by the time we got here, but they cleaned the place out pretty good."

Suddenly Chief Fleming's voice came over the channel.

"I need all of my people in the student ghetto ASAP. That includes those of you on the stakeout detail. I just got off the horn with the fire department, and they're dealing with multiple fires in the Elm Neighborhood."

"Structure fires?"

"Negative. Sounds like the kids pulled some couches into the street and lit 'em up. Nothing too dangerous from what Captain Diaz told me, but we've got multiple groups of students on the move now. Hundreds of 'em. Some on campus. Some not. It might not be fully out of control yet, but it's teetering. We've got State boys coming in as reinforcements now, but I need all of my units on crowd control in the meantime. So gear up and get over here. McCray, how many smoke canisters do we have left?"

"Should be nine or ten, I think."

"Bring them all. The tear gas, too. Just in case. I'll get on the horn with Sheriff Kittle and see what he's got on hand."

Loshak turned the radio down again and swiveled to face her.

"Should we call it off? That's more than half of the detail gone to deal with… whatever it is."

Darger chewed the inside of her cheek and stared into the darkness beyond her window.

She imagined the killer looking out at the confusion and disorder from his car. And she sensed somehow that he wouldn't be able to resist it.

"No. He'll be drawn to this. The chaos. The violence. He'll love it. Be stimulated by it. And he'll see it as an opportunity. With the police focused elsewhere, he'll think he's safe in the shadows. Free to operate unchained."

Darger got out the map they'd used to arrange the stakeout detail again.

"We've got… what? A dozen or so cars left, if you tally up the out-of-towners, plus us?"

"That's right," Loshak said.

"I think we have enough to make this work," Darger said, nodding. "If anything, this whole thing might increase our chances of catching him. If he thinks the police are distracted, he might let his guard down. Do something careless."

"Let's get on the radio and make sure the remaining detail knows to sit tight."

Loshak reached for the walkie-talkie and brought it to his lips.

CHAPTER 60

Kelly breathes. Smells the gasoline. Feels its sting inside her nostrils. Even tastes the acrid sharpness of it a second before she hears the whoomp.

The mob jostles around her. The whole group taking a stutter-step backward. All those warm bodies cinching around her shoulders, squeezing tight, picking Kelly up and carrying her one-and-a-half steps back involuntarily. Then a sag ripples through the group and releases her.

Reminds her of the time she got trapped in a mosh pit at Warped Tour. Bodies getting trampled on the asphalt. Tumbling over each other. Piling up. A memory so strong it tightens goosebumps into her skin.

But this is different. Somehow she feels safe in this crowd. Empowered. Not thinking about how she's scared to sleep in her own dorm room alone. Not thinking about how she set up crystals along the windowsill as a sort of moat. Among her peers, among the destruction they've caused, she feels free.

She swivels her head in time to see the flames go up.

The cop car is on fire.

Thrashing orange spikes reach out of the broken windows of the vehicle. Climbing high from the driver's side.

Some jubilant touchdown cheer spreading through the crowd.

Kelly's mouth drops open. Eyes wide. Staring at those dancing flickers as they reach higher and higher. Enraptured like this is some magic trick. Some impossibility unfolding before her.

And some detached voice in her head explains what she's seeing. Walks her through it.

Someone dumped gas inside the car. Lit it up.

She closes her mouth. Smears her sleeve at the bit of saliva collecting on her lip.

Frantic motion near the car brings her back to the present.

A guy in a blue flannel shirt takes something to the exposed underbelly of the vehicle. Something long. Something that looks like a spear or a pole from a pole vault. He rushes forward and thrusts. Jams his makeshift javelin into the folds of metal that make up the undercarriage. The metal shrieking.

She squints. Focuses on the angular shape in his hands.

It's a street sign post, she realizes. Green metal ripped out of the ground and turned into a weapon set to puncture.

He backs up a couple steps. Runs at the car again. Jabs it with the street sign lance. Looks like he's trying to harpoon a beached whale.

The post connects with the gas tank. Stabs at it with a squawk of metal on metal.

The impact jolts the kid. Buckles him. Jerks him off his feet like he stubbed all of his toes at once. The jouster de-horsed.

He skids on the pavement. Asphalt grinding at his knees. Then he kicks forward onto his hands. Heaving there in a crawl position.

But a moan of ecstasy swells through the crowd nevertheless.

The spear has punched home. Penetrated the dimpled steel. Plunged into the gas tank. Still stuck there like a planted flagpole.

Liquid weeps out around the green metal of the post, seeps from the new hole. Sluicing to the ground. Leaving a gas trail all over the bottom of the cop car. The smell spreading everywhere.

Holy shit. Holy shit. When the flames reach that...

Kelly steps back. Realizes the whole crowd does the same around her. A collective wincing.

Blue Flannel Shirt scrabbles back in a crab walk. Giggling maniacally like a coked-up chimp. Swallowed up by the slowly retreating crowd.

They all wait. Chests heaving in unison. Rising and falling. Eyes flitting over the flames raging out of the driver's side window, over the black shiny places where the fuel from the gas tank puddles.

Dozens of phones film the car. Glittering screens in the dark. All waiting to get the money shot, the big explosion to cap this dazzling special effects sequence. Any second now.

Nothing happens.

Not at first.

The car's interior keeps burning, brilliant orange flaring in the night, but the trail of wetness leading to the gas tank remains untouched. A slowly spreading pool. Nothing more.

A couple of beer cans crack open as the crowd begins to lose interest. Some of the phones get put away. That restlessness swelling in the ranks again. Smiles fading. Weight shifting from foot to foot.

No satisfaction. No attention span. They want more, and they want it now.

Heads start to swivel again. Ready to move on. Ready to see what other trouble they can find tonight.

A bright flash blinds Kelly for a moment. Blazing light piercing her pupils. Overtaking her entire field of vision.

And then there's another *woof* of flame taking to the air. A crack like thunder right on top of them. Hot wind blowing hard in their faces. Pushing them all back another step with rough hands.

The vapor rising up from the asphalt has caught. Lighting all at once in a small explosion. Banging loud. It flings some of the loose bits of glass around.

"Holy fuck!" a voice in the crowd says.

And now a bunch of them do that homicidal chimp laugh. Ready to rip off faces. Ready to burn the campus to the ground.

The flames reach higher than ever now. Seething. Fevered. Lurching and jumping and spitting. Heat rolling off. Its distortion visible as a billowing shimmer in the night, warping everything near the car.

And the power lines sizzle overhead where the fire licks at them. Crackling like bacon dropped onto a cast-iron skillet.

The phones point up at the lines now. Filming as black rubbery stuff melts and drips down into the fire. The searing goo popping as the fire takes it.

Watch it cook.

Watch it char.

Watch it all melt.

The fire burns so brightly that it swallows the glow of those glittering screens. Kelly can only see the phones in grayscale in the foreground. Her squinting eyes stinging as the blaze dominates everything now, its heat saturating her cheeks, plumping beads of sweat along her hairline.

And the flames reach higher. Thrash harder. Angrier than ever. Exuberant.

No satisfaction.

No satisfaction.

The power lines snap. One and then another. Splitting. Fluttering to the ground like limp snakes.

The streetlights wink off. The windows go dark in all directions.

The power is out.

The mob goes quiet. Motionless. Staring into the black nothing all around the orange glow of the burning car.

Gaping. Empty.

The night has gone vast. A cavernous expanse of nothing all around them.

Some primordial sense of smallness occurs to Kelly as she stares into that black hole.

Shrinking. Insignificant.

This angry group. This angry generation. Turned away again and again.

Lesser than. Lower than.

Like all they can ever do is limited. Trivial. Meaningless.

Like it can't last no matter what. Up against the black seas of infinity, nothing can last.

Maybe it's already gone.

The yawning void contorts above the toppled cop car. The dark itself buckling and curving like bent spoons. Deformed where the heat distortion touches it.

Only the dark and the fire are real in this moment.

The universe reduced to the fury and the abyss.

And now the night will take a darker turn.

CHAPTER 61

Tobi stares down at the glowing screen of her phone. Sees the flames close around the cop car there like an orange fist. Sees the glow reflecting on the shiny smiling faces in the crowd. As soon as the video ends, she touches the circling arrow to replay it.

Good.

Good.

"They're going apeshit," Andre says in the passenger seat. He watches the video over and over on his own phone.

"Finally," Tobi says. "They're finally doing something. *We're* finally doing something."

Andre grimaces a little. The whole bottom half of his face puckering like he just chugged an IPA that tasted like bitter shoe leather.

"You think it'll accomplish anything? I mean, setting a cop car on fire? Won't they just lock down campus even harder?"

Tobi doesn't look up. She watches the orange thrashing on the car. Whoomping as the fumes from the gas tank catch and the flare washes out the camera lens for a second, makes the phone shake in the filmer's hand.

"The first step is not feeling powerless. Feeling like you actually have agency. Feeling like you can do something. Change something."

She taps the screen again to keep the video rolling.

"So do I think this car fire is some strategic masterstroke? No. But I think we're telling them that we're not just objects for them to move around the chessboard in whatever way suits them. We're not just the victims of their reality. We're here. We're alive. We have a hand in shaping the world, in shaping society, a responsibility to do so just like them. And we're angry. You know? The way you treat us has consequences, and the consequences are real. And permanent."

She shrugs a little before she goes on.

"You fuck with us, you get a rock in the face. You get your car set on fuckin' fire. That's the first step. Right? That's empowerment. It's kind of all we have. For now."

They sit in the quiet for a few seconds. Watching the video play.

"It's like that Mario Savio quote from Berkeley," Tobi says. "'And you've got to put your bodies upon the gears and upon the wheels... upon the levers, upon all the apparatus, and you've got to make it stop! And you've got to indicate to the people who run it, to the people who own it, that unless you're free, the machine will be prevented from working at all!'"

CHAPTER 62

Officer Chip Anderson pokes his head down another empty hallway. A few candy and Coke machines glow at the far end. Dark glass on the doors to the left and right speak to the emptiness of the game rooms. The glowing fluorescent tubes above buzz like insects, the only sound here.

"Nothing this a-way," he says over his shoulder. "Surprise, surprise."

He and Officer Adam Trask are on the dorm beat tonight. It doesn't involve much.

After dark, they walk through the lobbies of a few dorms and the student union. Weave through a mess of hallways to take in the full ground floor. Sometimes, once or twice a month, they'll walk up the steps and meander down a floor or two of the dormitories. *Just to keep the freshmen on their toes*, Trask always says.

Some study a few years back had found that just having the police presence visible in these locations at night reduced incidents on campus by about twenty percent. Well worth the department's investment.

From Anderson's perspective, walking the dorm beat is boring work, but he doesn't mind. Better than being somewhere dangerous. He also likes the idea of the cops simply walking through and making the kids all piss themselves. Dumping beers. Flushing bags of dope. Sphincters clenching tighter than oyster shells.

Yeah. It's a good feeling. There is a saying around the precinct — the only real problem with campus is the students.

Quite true in Anderson's experience.

Anyway, he's glad to have Trask along with him tonight. Always is.

Officer Trask is older than most of the other campus cops. One of those brawny 50-or-60-something men with thick silvery body hair that coats not just his arms, but the backs of his hands all the way up onto the knuckles. Akin to Robin Williams or Alec Baldwin in that way. If he lets his stubble grow out for more than a day, it looks like he's turning into a werewolf. Thick hair all the way up to his cheekbones. A grizzled lion.

Trask worked on a real force for decades. The State Police, mostly. Saw some shit. Moved over to the campus cop shop to wind down his career in a more peaceful setting.

Anderson can't help but see himself as the complete opposite of the old bear. Scrawny. Young. Inexperienced. Can't even grow a legit beard, though he has a 14-year-old-esque mustache coating his top lip. Blond whiskers. Something just a little denser than peach fuzz.

"Not bad," Kirby had told him when he first grew the 'stache. "Not quite as thick as Rosie O'Donnell's mustache, but not bad."

Anyway, that had been months ago. It's much thicker than that now. Fuller. He's pretty sure of that.

They walk down another vacant hallway. Not a soul around. The student union is always dead this late on a Friday. Kids have better things to do than play foosball. Like drugs, probably. Unprotected sex.

They keep going. Move toward the back of the building where the Chick-fil-A and Subway sit dark and closed. Almost done. Thank Christ.

He always feels safer when he does these shifts with Trask.

Feels like there's a real cop here with him. Someone who has actually fired his gun in the line of duty — Anderson has never even unbuttoned his holster in his eighteen months on the job, let alone drawn his weapon.

He knows he should feel lucky for that, thankful for it, but he doesn't. He feels useless. Powerless. A phony. Like a little kid putting on a uniform. A faker playing cop for pay.

"Quiet night. Here, at least," Trask says. "I guess there's a bit of a ruckus off campus. Chatter on the radio about it. Football team must have won, right? The student ghetto always gets rowdy when they do."

Anderson checks his watch. He thinks about telling Trask that the game wouldn't be over yet. He doesn't like correcting the old man, though. It somehow feels wrong. Deeply wrong.

"Anyway, that's the end of the line. No major crimes going down in the student center tonight," Trask continues, smiling a little. "Shall we head back?"

Before Anderson can answer, the lights snap off above them. All those fluorescent cylinders going dark, going quiet. Plunging the hall into darkness.

Anderson swallows. Hears Trask digging out his flashlight. Remembers to grab along his belt for his own.

Their beams click on. One and then the other. Both lights swing up toward the dark bulbs above, as though visually confirming that they're off is necessary.

Then the glowing shafts sweep around the room. Glinting on glossy drywall, decorative ferns, another pair of Pepsi machines, both gone dim.

"Power's out," Trask says to himself.

They swish their lights around for another few seconds. Highlighting the same few features. Perhaps not sure what else to do.

Anderson has a tiny LED flashlight no bigger than a cigar. Bright as hell for its size. Trask brandishes one of those big Maglites that Anderson has always thought looks like a big black dildo. Old-school like the man himself, sure, but ridiculous. Totally ridiculous. Or maybe it just makes Anderson self-conscious about the size of his.

"Well, we may as well head back nevertheless," Trask says with a semi-shrug.

"Yeah. Typically only goes down for a few minutes. Maybe half an hour."

As Anderson speaks, he considers that he's talking about the usual scenario. The power going out in a thunderstorm. Maybe a windstorm. This is something else. Something *un*usual. Something unknown. It makes him uncomfortable, and he falls quiet.

They plod back down the hall. Everything they just passed now looking strange in the shadows. Plants and seating and candy machines seeming to have grown deeper dimensions from the dark lines blooming around them. Eerie. Vaguely sinister.

"I tell you about my wife's latest nag-fest?" Trask says.

Anderson snorts a little puff of laughter. This is one of Trask's recurring jokes. Complaining about his wife, the ball-breaking battle axe. It has the exaggerated feel of a bit, and the younger cop can never decide if any of it is true. For all he knows, Trask isn't even married.

"She's on the warpath again, my friend. All over my ass, 'cause I keep forgetting to pick up milk on my way home on Wednesdays. This is some royal decree she handed down at some point, you see. Wednesday is milk day now. Like I can keep track of that crap."

Anderson snorts another laugh-puff.

"With no milk, she can't have her Special K, you know? And let's just say you don't want to cross her when her Special K levels are low, OK? Like, dangerously low K levels? Uh-uh. No sir. That's when she's at her boldest. Without the cereal, she's like a wolverine, man. She's small, but she's so damn aggressive that she has no natural enemies. She'll come right at ya. Claws out. Rip your goddamn face off."

Trask did a wolverine claw motion in the air with his free hand, and Anderson laughed.

"She can really lay it on when she wants. Hollers at me. Points one stubby little finger right in my grill. Gets all red-faced like her damn head might just pop one of these times. Fountain of blood just geysering out of her neck.

"Hey. I love her with all my heart, though. She's a complicated lady. You understand."

Trask's battle axe talk cuts out abruptly, and they both fall silent as they work their way down the final straightaway to the front door.

Going slower now. Unsure.

It's so quiet in the empty hallway of the Student Union. Utterly still.

Tension. Anderson knows they both feel it, even if they don't understand it yet.

They creep forward. The dark encroaching everywhere around the beams of their flashlights. Thick shadows.

Finally they see the front door. Glowing panes of glass letting at least a faint light in. Maybe the streetlights are still on.

Anderson breathes easier as they walk toward the door. It's almost over.

A screeching wail from outside makes them both jump.

They stop some thirty feet from the glowing glass that leads outside.

The high-pitched wail is unmistakable. Raspy. Shredded vocal cords. Electrifying.

A man.

But not the sound of someone in pain.

The sound of aggression. Fury. A battle cry.

It makes the hair on the back of Anderson's neck prick up hard. Sends the icy touch of alarm over his shoulders, down his back.

He swallows hard. Feels something click deep in his throat.

He glances at Trask. Their eyes meet. A look passing between them.

Something glints in the old man's face that Anderson doesn't like. Something soft. Something indecisive.

Maybe Trask is scared, too. Jesus.

This can't be real.

The old cop shakes his head. Says nothing.

They wait another three breaths, and then they inch forward again. Slow steps. Heel to toe. Soundless. Wary.

They glide up to the front door. Peer out through the glass.

Anderson can't tell what he's seeing at first. It comes to him in stages.

Dark silhouettes dance everywhere in the street. Black shapes flitting in front of the orange glow of… a fire.

Something is on fire out there. Flames reaching high. Shapeless orange thrashing like liquid.

The kids don't seem disturbed by this. Not running away.

They seem to be celebrating it.

Worshiping it.

Trask seems to be one step ahead of him.

"The car," he whispers.

Anderson looks again. The burning object is indeed a car. A sedan.

And then it dawns on him.

Not just *a* car. *Their* car. The cruiser has been flipped onto its side and set ablaze.

Holy fuck.

"It's a… a riot," Anderson whispers as much to himself as to Trask.

That bloodthirsty scream rings out over everything again. Makes Anderson wince. Muscles all up and down his back flinching, twitching in rapid pulses.

And for just a second he pictures those dancing, screaming kids coming toward them. Closing on them. A surging wave of humanity pouring through the glass doors to flood into the building. Sweeping them up in the undertow.

His hand fishes along his belt, and he unbuttons his holster. For the first time in his career, he thinks it necessary.

Once again he finds himself thankful to be out with Trask tonight. At least there's one real cop here. Someone he can defer to.

Not a child playing cop. A man. A policeman. The real thing.

His heart hammers harder when he thinks those words.

The real thing.

Trask groans next to him. A defeated sound rising through what sounds like a clenched throat. The syllable choking off at the end.

Anderson looks over just as the old man topples to the tile floor. The image playing in slow motion in the younger cop's perception.

The old cop tipping. Leaning like a listing ship, like the world has tilted hard under his feet. Falling over sideways.

Upper body stiff and strangely upright. One hand clutching at his ribs.

Trask makes no attempt to catch himself. Just slaps down onto the floor like a big sack of potatoes.

The thud somehow sickening. Wrong. Heavy.

In his shock, Anderson can't block the words from entering his mind.

Dead weight.

The body goes motionless the second it hits the ground. Not stirring. Not twitching.

Inert.

"Trask!" Anderson says in an involuntary falsetto.

He kneels next to the fallen officer. Hands running over the old man's hairy wrist. Two fingers searching for the place between the bone and tendon. Feeling for a pulse.

Nothing.

No flutter. No twitch. No thready weak beat.

Nothing at all.

Jesus fucking Christ.

He holds his breath. Waits to feel any sign of life thrumming through the old man's veins.

Waits.

Waits.

He blinks over and over. His brain seems to work at the edges of the thought for a while before the words will finally come:

Trask is dead.

Anderson can't move. Can't breathe.

He just clutches that hairy wrist between two fingers and a thumb. Pinches it there as the body slowly goes cool, as the kids scream and dance and burn the campus outside.

He stares hard at nothing. Eyes spearing emptiness. Unblinking.

His own skin is frigid. Shock surging adrenaline through

him so hard that his field of vision has gone blurry around the edges.

And the movie of Trask falling replays in Anderson's head.

Tipping. Falling. Grabbing his ribs. Slamming down on the floor.

Gone. Just like that.

Except he wasn't grabbing his ribs, Anderson realizes. He was grasping his chest.

Heart attack.

Massive coronary.

Probably dead before he even hit the floor.

The chaotic sounds outside get louder. Closer.

Officer Anderson reaches down for his holster. Fingers probing along the edges of the gun's grip, along the leather encasing it.

He finds the button and snaps it shut again.

Then he reaches for the other side of his belt and switches off his radio.

He rises slowly. Backs away from the body. Backs away from the glass. Lets the shadows close around him as he gets deeper into the lightless hallway.

He can find a place here in the building. An office or utility room with a heavy steel door he can lock from the inside.

Until the students move on. Until the riot is over.

He will hide. He will cower.

Not like a cop. Not like a man.

Like the boy that he is.

CHAPTER 63

He drives down a darkened street. Camaro purring like a kitten. Chilly inside, just the way he likes it.

The area surrounding campus has gone dark. Wild. Scary.

Kids running everywhere.

Fires crackling in the distance.

He's getting a steady dose of adrenaline just watching it. A little awed by what he's seeing.

Activity off to his right catches his eye. Dark figures stirring there. Agitated.

He creeps closer, and the image sharpens.

Kids cracking open the windows of a Dairy Mart. One of them banging what looks like a tee ball bat at the glass. The webbed lines all silvery in the moonlight.

He goes slow to watch it. Fascinated. Licking his lips over and over.

The aluminum bat pings. The glass shrieks and tumbles.

The kids climb into the ruined holes where the glass had been. Disappear into the dark structure.

He waits. Watches.

The figures reappear. Fling gallons of milk out the busted windows.

The plastic jugs collapse on impact with the parking lot. Seas of opaque white flowing over the asphalt.

He keeps driving. Watching. More pedestrians ahead.

At the corner a few kids try to surround his car. Five of them cinching around the front end.

They thump on the hood of the Camaro. Snarling faces

yelling words that he can't understand.

He jams the accelerator. Pulls away from them. Watches their arms ripped away from his car like praying mantis limbs. Their shoulders brushing along the windows.

And then he's passed. Moving. Plunging deeper into the night. Head swiveling to take it all in.

The chaos is everywhere. Sprawling in all directions.

Cars and couches on fire in the streets. Windows smashed with rocks and boards. Kids fighting, drinking, breaking shit.

No sirens. No twirling lights. The police are nowhere to be seen.

Yes.

This is perfect.

Tonight is just perfect.

He smiles in the dark.

All the animals in the zoo are loose. Running amok. Flinging shit.

No rules tonight.

He grips the wheel tighter. Presses the accelerator down and feels the car surge with power.

Time to swing by his usual hunting grounds.

CHAPTER 64

Andre groans a little. One hand clutching his belly.

Tobi watches him out of the corner of her eye, still mostly staring at the side mirror, waiting for twin lights to prick to life there. All dark. It's been twenty-two minutes since they've seen a car come down this way. The last was a beat-up minivan with an older woman behind the wheel.

Andre groans again. Shifts in his seat. Fingers still clawing into his stomach.

She waits for him to say something, but he doesn't.

"What?" she says, after a second, careful to keep any trace of a sharp edge out of her voice.

"Nothing."

She waits again.

"I'm hungry, that's all," Andre says finally. "Too much coffee, maybe. My gut is churning butter or some shit."

He shifts in his seat. His eyes angling vaguely toward Tobi in the driver's seat but not quite looking at her.

"Hang on. I think there's something…"

She leans over. Opens up the middle console. Digs around inside. Hand knifing through napkins. Kleenex. A bag of loose coins.

Finally she finds what she was looking for. Pulls a Ziploc baggie free of the pile.

"Trail mix," she says. "Not the best, but…"

Andre takes the bag. Holds it into a bright spot in the patchwork of moonlight glinting through the passenger side window.

"Peanuts… raisins… peanut M&M's," he says, poking at the bag's contents. "Not bad. I was expecting a bunch of pumpkin seeds and almonds and shit. Hippie stuff."

A single puff of laughter vents through Tobi's nostrils.

"You think I'm a hippie?"

"Uh, yeah," Andre says through pursed lips, a lilt of incredulity in his voice.

Then he seems to realize what he's walked himself into and stops in the middle of eating another bite of trail mix.

"Er… I mean, no. Not really."

Tobi just stares at him. Not letting herself bust out laughing like she wants to.

Andre stammers.

"It's just… I mean, you're a teensy bit like one of those crunchy granola girls, you know?"

"Crunchy… granola?"

"Like once you have your degree, you're probably going to drive a Jeep and go hiking all the time and shit. Live in the mountains somewhere. Eat bowls of Grape-Nuts without adding any sugar. Dress like a lumberjack. Flannel everything right down to the undergarments. Plaid."

"What are you talking about? I don't dress like a lumberjack, Andre."

"Hey, you have a Carhartt coat, right? You're like halfway there already."

Tobi blinks. Hard. She shakes her head, not quite able to get words out right away.

"It's just a warm coat."

"Hey, tell it to the other girls who watch NASCAR or whatever else you do. Like compete in rodeos. How should I know?"

"I feel like this has veered away from crunchy granola. I

mean, NASCAR? Really?"

Andre chews on a few raisins and swallows before he answers. Shrugs one shoulder.

"I mean, sorta. The crunchy granola thing covers a lot of ground. Look, there's a wide range of people who *do their own research.* And don't believe in vaccinations. And eat granola. And probably forage food or something. It takes all kinds, even under the crunchy granola umbrella. You're one of 'em is the point."

Tobi nods sarcastically. Then she shakes her head again and digs a couple of peanut M&M's out of the bag. Crunches through the candy shells.

Neither she nor Andre notices the car that has parked about half a block behind them. The one with the headlights off.

CHAPTER 65

Runny egg yolk drips down Officer Kirby's chin just as the diner goes dark. He feels the sludge wicking into his mustache like yellow snot. Senses it dripping down onto his chest, soiling his uniform with unborn chicken goo.

Christ.

He sighs. Crunches down on the toast and bit of yolk that actually made it into his mouth.

His hands fumble around on the table. Silverware clinking. He finds a napkin. Dabs it at his 'stache. Folds it in half. Uses the clean side to kind of swipe at his shirt the best he can in the damn near pitch-black booth.

As he tries to clean up, a murmur spreads through the few customers at the other end of the diner, sitting along the snack bar.

Power's out. Big whoop. These idiots will probably panic right up until it kicks back on in thirty seconds.

"It's that riot," a voice whisper yells. "I'm telling you. It's that goddamn hooligan riot. I heard about it on the radio."

Kirby squints. Tries to make his eyes use the little bit of moonlight angling in through the windows. But he sees contours more than objects.

Riot? The kids storming the football field? Big fuckin' whoop.

He'd flipped off his radio as soon as he went off duty. Truth be told, he'd flipped it off about ten minutes early. Maybe fifteen. Hates getting suckered into responding to a call just as his shift is ending. Getting roped into mind-numbing paperwork during what should be his time. Total bullshit.

Fine. Twenty minutes early. Or twenty-five. Whatever.

His fingers pat around on the Formica table again. Find the edge of his plate. Follow the rounded rim until they find the crispy slab of bacon protruding there.

He crunches through the last two slices. Wipes his mouth again with the now-twice-folded napkin. Takes out a few bills to cover the meal, plus a buck for the tip. And then he stands.

The shadows shift around him as he rises. The dark morphing and then clearing just a little as he gets out of the booth and into the open.

He plucks the radio from his belt. Flips it on, keeping the volume low and holding it near his ear so as to not rouse the gossiping jackals at the counter.

Chatter spews rapid-fire from the tiny speaker. Urgent voices. He struggles to keep up, only making out every other word or so at first.

But he gets "fire," and "power lines snapped," and something about there being at least three separate groups of looters and rioters now. Growing. At least two car fires.

He tries to look out the window as he takes this in. He's just able to differentiate the sheen of the asphalt from the more matte texture of the sidewalk. All else is covered over in gloom.

He looks over at the gossips huddling at the snack bar again. Can really only see the curved backs of the elderly men perched there like gargoyles. He thinks about talking to them, asking what they know, but for what? What value could they add?

Instead he pushes through the heavy front door of the place. Bells jingling. And he steps onto the sidewalk.

Gauzy shadows cover everything in black lace. But out here, he can kind of make sense of the contours. Can see the brick apartment buildings across the street, at least in silhouette. Can discern the lampposts jutting up here and there, spindly things usually not far from the thicker telephone poles.

He strides forward a few paces. Stands on the curb. Looks up and down the street.

No light in any direction. Stupid kids probably fucked the grid, blew a transformer or something. He doesn't know shit about how any of the electrical shit works, and why should he?

He stares into the dark and listens.

It's all quiet, all still. Makes the sound of his own breath seem loud. Huffing and puffing like the borderline fat fuck that he has let himself become. Too much beer. Too much deep-fried shit.

But he thinks he can hear something in the distance. A muffled roar. Many-voiced. Like hearing the football stadium a few blocks off during a game.

He walks toward the sound. Grows more and more certain that it must be one of the groups they mentioned on the radio. Looters. Jesus. An actual riot.

He smiles to himself. Touches the heel of his hand to the gun snugged down in his holster.

Bringing a loaded gun to a fist fight.

Ready and fucking able to defend myself, too. Quite eager, you could say.

When he gets to within a block or so of the action, the crowd sound becomes clearer. Reminds him of coyotes going nuts in the dead of night. Packs of them howling and moaning and cackling to celebrate a kill — sounds like they're laughing, but it sounds cruel. Hateful and gleeful at the same time, blood and saliva dripping from their jaws.

He checks along the other side of his belt. Finds the canister of pepper spray dangling there.

Good. Start with the spray, mow a few down that way, and

if push comes to shove, don't hesitate to get out the Glock.

Shoot first. Sort 'em out after.

Light shimmers off to the right, probably around the next corner from the looks of it. Orange thrashing. Another fire. He can only see the flashes of it rising up above the trees and buildings. Can't lay eyes on the actual flames from here.

Perfect. Dumbfuck students burning their own campus is one thing. Burning the town, though? His town? Fucking ungrateful shits, the lot of 'em. Spoiled as a finely aged milk.

But he could teach 'em all a lesson that ain't in the curriculum at their bullshit school. A lesson that leaves marks. Draws a line between life and death that won't be soon forgotten. Shit heels.

Spoon-fed every luxury by Mom and Dad from the cradle on. Not tonight, by God. Tonight they'd get foot-fed his boot in their ass. Heaping helpings of ass foot, delivered with gusto over and over.

Maybe worse, if he thinks he can get away with it, if it feels right.

He chews his lip as the violent fantasies montage on the movie screen inside his head. Breath going a little fluttery. Orgasmic.

No rules tonight. No rules.

God, he wishes he had his nightstick. He could crack some skulls. Shove that big black stick up a rectum or two. Have a fucking blast.

He grits his teeth. Slows his pace as he comes up on the corner near the noise, near the fire.

Readies the pepper spray in one hand. Unclasps the button on his holster with the other.

It's go time, you punk motherfuckers.

Time to bring the pain.

He creeps up beside the brick facade that shears off at the corner. Licks his lips. Watches the fire's glow flutter wavery light over everything in the street ahead. Still not sure what's burning there. Smells like shit, whatever it is.

He runs the last couple steps. Wheels around the corner. Pepper spray lifted, aimed, ready.

The street slides into view. Comes clear at last.

He sees just a hint of a burning pile of mannequins. Ripped out of a department store window. Plastic arms and legs melting in the street. Flames lapping at them like many hungry tongues.

The mob hits him like they were waiting for him. Surrounding him. Walls of humanity.

Grabbing. Shaking. Swallowing him up.

A gang tackle.

He takes an elbow in the nose and tears flood his eyes. It blurs the dark shapes all over him into shimmering smears.

Shit.

The pepper spray gets raked out of his hand. Ripped from his fingers. Gone.

Shit. Shit. Shit.

The mosh pit flexes around him. Cinches tighter. Wild limbs knocking into his chest, into his chin.

But it's not just flailing limbs. Not just a mosh pit. Some part of him knows it's not so haphazard as that.

Fists.

Feet.

Aiming for him with bad intentions. Wanting to do permanent damage.

They're beating him. Kicking the shit out of him.

Animals now. Not the students he's known.

These are wild animals. Completely unhinged.

He reaches for his gun. Fingers sinking into the nylon shell of the holster. Empty.

Jesus fuck.

Gone.

Gone.

I'm dead.

He gets glimpses of faces screaming in the dark. Furrowed brows. Knobby cheekbones. Gnashed teeth.

He tries to shuffle back. Pistons his legs. Leans his torso and trucks his weight backward. Nowhere to go.

The rioters surround him. Cage him in like the ropes penning in a boxing ring.

They're all around. Spiraling. Circling like hyenas.

A big right hand reaches out of the shadows and cracks him in the jaw. Cranks his head around hard.

And the dark gets bigger, gets deeper. Discharges numbness down the lengths of his limbs.

He staggers backward. Retreating endlessly on wobbly legs. Pushing into the crowd. Making his way backward little by little.

Only the walls of the mob keep him on his feet now. Holding him up for more abuse.

But the part of his mind still thinking knows that's good, that that's the key to this now.

Stay up.

He needs to stay up, needs to keep his feet. If he goes down, they'll stomp him, and if they stomp him, he's dead. Actually dead. Right here and right now. Head broken like an egg on the blacktop, cracked and recracked by the soles of their shoes.

Stay up. Defend yourself. Survive.

That's it. That's all.

He tucks his chin. Locks his arms in a cage in front of

himself and shields his head and torso behind them the best he can.

Fists batter at his forearms to little effect. Feet try to chop his knees out from under him.

He backpedals. Circles away from the kicks. Waits for his opening.

Looks out between his fists. Watches the mindless violent world through that narrow tunnel.

At last he lurches. Clenches one of the nearest bodies. Arms hugging around a stocky guy soaked in sour sweat.

That slows some of the punching. Softens some of the blows headed his way. He hears them landing against the guy's pudgy back with sounds like someone hammering a chicken breast flat on a cutting board. Friendly fire doing him some good for now.

He presses his head down into the top of the human shield's shoulder. Grips two handfuls of the sopping blue t-shirt draped over the torso. Closes his eyes and breathes.

Ribcage aching with every inhale. A sharp feeling on the left side like maybe they cracked a rib or two somewhere in there.

But he can feel some of the strength coming back in his legs. A steadiness. A solidness. Doesn't feel like he's wobbling around on the deck of a listing ship anymore.

When he opens his eyes again, the mob has thinned around him some. Moving on. Restless always. Seeking something more entertaining than two clenched fighters staggering about in the street like dancing bears.

He lets go of the t-shirt. Gives the kid a shove and stumbles away.

Feels the strange cold of the night where that body had been pressed into him.

A roiling emptiness pressing its chill against him. Swirling iciness into his soggy torso.

The open air makes him feel naked. Wrong. Vulnerable.

He moves. Weaves through the sparse crowd still around. Feet quicker than they've ever been. Darting through the darkness.

He ducks down between two cars parked on the side of the street. Wedges himself between the bumpers. Gets as low as he can. A shadowy spot.

He sucks breath. Cold wind. Dry inside his throat.

Watches the animals weave everywhere, weave everywhere. Close. All around still. But they don't seem to see him now.

Throwing rocks at shops and houses. Circling back toward the burning mannequins like moths.

More breath. So dry. Harsh. Makes him want to gag, want to cough, but he stays quiet. Stays still.

Hidden. Probably safe for now.

Christ. Jesus.

He thinks he's through the worst of it. Thinks he'll be OK if he keeps his head down for a while.

And then the gunshot rings out.

CHAPTER 66

The shadow creeps up the street. Drifting closer to the car, to the two figures huddled in the front seat.

The night's chill drifts in through the open window on the driver's side. The icy air makes Andre wriggle in his seat. He eyes the open window.

"You and the cold," he says, hugging his arms around his chest. "You say it keeps the windows from fogging up, but I'm pretty sure you just like being cold as hell. Like a succubus or something."

"I thought I was a crunchy granola girl. Now I'm a succubus?"

"Nah. You're definitely on the granola spectrum. All the way up in *the very crunchy* range."

"Well, if I'm a crunchy granola girl, what the hell are you?"

Andre drops another quarter handful of trail mix into his maw. Crunches. It's stale, but somehow still kind of good.

"I don't know. You tell me."

Tobi chews and swallows. Eyes flitting. Mind whirring like some turbine deep in the bowels of a power plant.

"See, I think above all you're kind of a pussy," she says. "A scaredy-cat. Insecure. Frightened of everything in life. Almost comically so. Bordering on one of those… in Japan they have these people who just totally withdraw from society and literally stay home and play video games and shit all the time. I forget what they call that, but you're like that."

Andre digs out another load of trail mix. Eats a few seconds and shrugs one shoulder before he responds.

"I have no problem with that."

Tobi guffaws.

"Yeah. I guess you wouldn't."

"You think you're going to say something that digs all deep and shit. Something that gets under my skin, peels me open. Something that hurts me. Like I don't already fucking know it all. Like I don't already beat myself up for being a fucking useless pussy. That's the difference between us maybe—"

And then there's a shape outside the driver's side window. A shadow leaning over the car.

Tobi and Andre both jump. Andre moans, arms shrinking back toward his chest.

The car door pulls open. Makes a sound like smacking lips when the rubber seal detaches from the frame.

The dome light clicks on.

And Andre fumbles for the taser in his lap. Feels it squirm away from him like a trout.

He squints down at the thing. Sees its lines gone blurry under the bright light that attacks his eyes.

He finally gets a hold of it. Feels his fingers slide into the grip. Flexing around it.

Trigger snugged beneath his index finger.

He lifts the taser. Sweeps it to the left.

Sees the laser site line up on the silhouette's chest. The little red dot shaking along with the tremor in his arm.

He squeezes his trigger.

But his arm jerks just as he does. Shoulder contracting and ragdolling his whole arm upward. Limp like one of those dancing tube men outside of a car dealership.

The probes fling out of the taser. Twin metal tubes like silver bullets.

The barbed metal darts embed themselves in the curved

spot just above the door. Sink into the soft upholstery lining the car's ceiling. Cling there like swollen ticks jutting from a dog's neck, hanging from matte blue fabric that looks almost like crushed velvet.

The probes crackle. Surging electrical current snapping and popping.

An acrid stench hits Andre's nostrils. And then he sees two little puffs of smoke roll out from where the probes butt into the padding. Gray coils glinting yellow under the dome light.

I missed.

I fucking missed.

The weapon shakes at the end of his outstretched arms. Limbs quivering like a newborn horse's.

He swallows, and a racquetball-sized lump sticks in his throat. He blinks hard.

His eyes trace the squiggly cables that lead from the taser to the ceiling. The wires form spaghetti strands hung over most of the front seat. Slack lines that arc in front of Tobi's face. Squiggly.

And Andre realizes that the guy is gone. The dark shape no longer framed in the open door.

He sucks in a big breath. Lungs jittery in his chest. A whole mess of heaving meat inside of him.

Then he rips the spent taser cartridge free from the muzzle of the gun. Tosses it to the floor. Those spaghetti strands pulling downward as the cartridge sinks.

He stabs his free hand into his jacket pocket. Feels for one of the backup cartridges. Finds the angular thing and rips it free. Jams it into the front of the gun.

Jesus. Can't fuck up again.

The passenger door tears open. The shape is there. Right there. Broad chest filling the open gap in the doorway.

Andre swings the taser. Watches the red dot of the laser sweeping toward the broad-shouldered silhouette.

Something dark leaps for him. Something hard ripping downward. Striking his knuckles. Wrenching both his arms and the weapon toward the floor.

The taser rakes out of his hand just as he squeezes the trigger.

The probes fling outward.

Too late.

This time the mini-harpoons at the end of the probes jam into the floor. Zapping the nappy carpet and smoking there.

The taser clatters down alongside them. The wires snaking down around all of it.

Andre doesn't see the butt of the gun coming for his head. Just sees the faint dark blur streaking like an inky comet in the corner of his eye.

And then everything goes black.

CHAPTER 67

The gunshot splits the night. Cracks the darkness into shards. Loud and close.

Too close.

A little whimper escapes Officer Kirby's lips. Some mousy sound. Involuntary.

He sinks lower. Tries to disappear fully into the shadows between these two parked cars. Love handles sandwiched between the bumpers. Top half bent low.

He wishes he could slither down beneath this sedan. Worm his way under. Pinch his big body between the undercarriage and the street. Hug himself flat to the cold asphalt. Change colors there like a chameleon.

His eyes scan everywhere, scan everything.

He'd seen the muzzle flash — an orange burst lighting up shapes in the dark. Bony figments illuminated by fire. Eerie.

But he couldn't place the source of the light. Couldn't find the gun. The glow there and gone too fast.

He squints. Searches.

The dark lurches all around him. Hard shapes moving in the gloom.

Angular contours. Details smeared.

His breath catches in his throat over and over. Little sucking sounds. Like he's choking on the air.

Needs to calm down. Needs to be quiet. Now more than ever before in his life, he needs to be quiet.

Sweat leaks from his skin. Pores opened wide to let the juices flow. Beads of it snaking down his face, down his body.

Icy tendrils. The cold reaching right through his clothes. Gripping and squeezing his soft middle like the fish white belly of the Pillsbury Dough Boy.

A silhouette emerges from the murk.

Broad shoulders. Upright posture. A cockiness evident in the bouncing stride. Something strange — wrong — in the shape of the head. Too round. Too smooth.

The shape moves closer. Inhuman. Aggressive.

And the gun becomes clear at the end of his arm. The hard shape dangling there.

He's walking straight for Kirby's spot between the cars.

The cop holds his breath. Silence now. Total silence. Even his heartbeat hammering in his chest seems too loud now.

He might not see me. Might wander on if I keep still. If I don't show him I'm prey.

As the silhouette creeps closer, Kirby sees why the head's shape looks strange. The kid is wearing a ski mask. Red and white stripes forming bands around the eyes. Dark ribbed acrylic coating the rest of the face like a neat coat of fur.

Still. Frozen. Totally still.

Hissing sounds grow louder with each step the gunman takes. Sounds like a leaking tire.

He's laughing. The kid with the gun is laughing between his clenched teeth, spitty sounds pulsing out of him.

Kirby swallows. Closes his eyes and tucks his head toward the ground. Feels the skin on his back contract. Fights the urge to run. Each heartbeat like a gong blast in his chest, its impact reverberating throughout the walls of his upper body.

Shit.

"That you, Officer Kirby?"

He laughs a little as he says it. Voice somehow strung high and tight and giddy, like someone who just got dosed with laughing gas at the dentist.

"Why don't you come on out into the moonlight, where I can see you?"

Kirby opens his eyes. Sees the outstretched arm. Sees the barrel of the gun pointing at him. That black hole somehow looking eternal in the dark.

He blinks a few times. Can only look away from the weapon long enough to see the smiling mouth and eyes poking out of the holes in the ski mask, and then his own eyes snap back to the open mouth in the barrel of the gun.

"Come on out, now, big boy. We've got affairs to discuss."

Kirby doesn't move. Doesn't breathe. Just stares at the gun.

The masked student points the Glock into the air and squeezes the trigger. Pops off two shots. Metallic explosions. The gun bucking and flaring in his hand. Then he points the weapon at the cop again.

His voice goes harder now. Flatter. The gravel of it audible even over the shrill tone filling Kirby's ears.

"I ain't gonna ask you again. Come out into the open. Now."

Kirby gulps. Crawls out from between the cars. Feeling naked in the open again. The cool night swirling around him. Brushing his sweaty neck and cheeks with icy fingers.

He starts to get to his feet. Hands pushing him up. Shoes scuffing under him, grinding grains of dirt into the street.

"Ah-ah-ah. On your knees, big boy."

Kirby settles his knees onto the asphalt. Cold and gritty.

"Piggies can't walk upright on two legs. Everyone knows that."

Kirby feels his lips flapping against his gums as he sucks in big wet breaths, snuffling and blubbering, and he thinks he might be crying.

He doesn't look at the gun anymore. He doesn't look at anything. Just stares into the darkness, into the emptiness.

The silhouette drifts closer. Light on his feet.

He presses the muzzle of the gun into Kirby's forehead. The polymer colder than the ground, deader than the dirt.

Kirby closes his eyes. Can't look. Can't think.

Can just feel that angular hardness prodding at the thin swath of flesh above his brow.

When the ski-masked figure speaks again, it's in a whisper. Close. Cooing right in Kirby's ear.

"Any final words, you fat fuck?"

No images flicker in the cop's head. No montage of childhood memories. No thoughts of his mom or dad or siblings.

Only fear.

Fear and emptiness.

A black expanse stretching in all directions inside his skull.

The big nothing. No meaning.

Darkness. Gaping and sucking and ready to take him under.

Its arms open wide. Waiting.

He hears the laughter first. That hissing, sick laugh pulling him back into the present moment, back into the real world. Puffing its breath right in his ear.

Then he feels the warmth spreading over him. A shocking heat against his skin. Feels its prickle all over at first.

Is this death?

Is this some miracle rippling over his earthly body?

Then the heat seems to localize. Sharpens into a tighter focus. And it's not all over anymore.

The warmth centralizes in his lower body. Spreading outward from his crotch.

He opens his eyes to verify it. Looks down at himself.

A dark splotch puddles outward over the fabric of his pants. The darkness overtaking his thighs in an uneven expansion, conquering more territory on the right pant leg.

He is pissing his pants.

His bladder the source of the miracle warmth.

He and the ski-masked rioter watch the spreading piss puddle together. The liquid reaches the asphalt and pools around Kirby's knees. Glossy and dark.

The gunman laughs maniacally. Wild eyes. Toothy maw glistening in the moonlight.

He makes eye contact with Kirby and laughs harder. Cruel laughter. Hateful. Psychotic.

And the swirling cool touches the cop's wet legs now. The night's chill saturates his flesh quickly. Sinks deep into the meat of his quads. Makes him shiver a little. Frigid.

I'm going to die on my knees in a pool of my own piss. A coward.

"Bruce Kirby. The pissing piggie. Fucking legendary."

The gunman lifts the gun again.

Closes one eye as he lines the barrel up with Kirby's forehead again.

Kirby tries to force words to his throat, to his lips. Tries to beg and plead and appeal to whatever thread of empathy this person might have left.

But he can't speak. Can't make his mouth work.

Instead he blinks and shivers and hunches his shoulders. A frozen lamb in the kill chute.

The gunman makes a little gun noise with his mouth.

"Ka-blow."

He rocks the Glock back as though the recoil of it has bucked against his hand.

Then he whirls and takes off. Running down the street. Yelling about how big bad Officer Kirby pissed himself.

CHAPTER 68

Andre's legs slide over the lip of the car's body. And then the car door slams.

From the backseat, Tobi can hear her friend's feet scuffing over the asphalt as he's pulled toward the trunk.

Itchy feelings spin behind her eyes. Heart galloping in her chest. Sweat beading between her shoulder blades. Drawing snail trails down the length of her spine.

She hiccups for breath. Waits until she hears the pneumatic cylinder sound of the trunk door rising, that little exhale.

Then she leans down. Rips the knife free from the side of her boot. Lifts the spiky thing into the moonlight for just a second.

He's tied her hands in front instead of the back. Frazzled by the taser, maybe. Rushing. She needs to make him pay for that.

She looks out the window. Sees the street gone dark out there. Realizes that the streetlight has gone out.

She should run. She should try to get away. Bolt like a rabbit.

She knows she should run.

But she doesn't.

Can't.

Can't leave Andre.

That's what he'd said. His voice deep from outside the car. *Try to leave and your friend is dead right here and now.*

That's his trick.

Because survival for either of them is unlikely. Almost impossible.

But it'd be better to die here than to leave Andre behind.

How could she ever live with that?

She tests the heft of the blade in her hand. Holds it low in the shadows. Arcs the tip toward the side of the seat back in front of her in slow motion.

She'll do something. She has to.

Jam it into his guts and rip as soon as he gets back. Punch it home into the middle of him.

She tries to picture it. The blade puncturing his abdominals. Slitting. Slashing. Ripping. Tearing him open from the middle out.

She grits her teeth. Tries to cast a spell of hatred in her heart. Tries to conjure aggressive feelings when she mostly feels afraid. Tries to squeeze the hilt tighter, but her hand is numb. She can barely feel the knife clutched there. Feels like she can't grip it fully. Like she can't really squeeze either of her hands into fists anymore.

Everything icy. Numb. Weak. Like she's been out in the cold for hours and her motor skills are breaking down.

The car shifts beneath her. A single tremor rippling through the shocks as Andre's bulk is loaded in. Wobbling the vehicle.

The trunk door slams.

And he's there. Opening the door. Climbing in the passenger seat.

Tobi freezes. Breath hitching in her throat. Little choking sounds pouring out.

He's naked. Looks greasy in the half-light. Filmy. Like oil floating on top of a mud puddle.

She lifts the blade between them. Holds it up as if to ward him off.

His eyes flick to it. He doesn't flinch. Doesn't slow.

When he speaks, his voice is gravelly. Some strange trace of humor in it.

"You brought your own little toy, huh? Guess you came ready to play."

She swings the blade at him. Shaking. Feeble. Her arm weak like this is all a bad dream.

He catches her by the wrist. Closes his big fist around her tiny one.

And he takes the knife from her. Nothing violent in the act. He just plucks it from her hand like she's handing it to him. Throws it out onto the curb behind him.

Then he closes the door. Slithers closer to her.

"See, I already got one, hon. Got my own blade I been itching to test out."

If he's holding the knife up, she can't see it. Can only stare at the oily skin of his face. Tan and angular. Dark around the eyes. Pocked along the cheeks. Only vaguely aware of his shocking nakedness beneath that.

He pulls her hat off. Tilts his head when her blue crinkles spill free.

"Aw. I know you. And you know me, don't ya? Writing all about me, yeah? Not a fan. I get it."

Tiny gasps roll out of her. One after another. Lips spluttering like she's trying to talk.

He grabs her. Fingers sinking into her upper arms. A grip like steel.

He manhandles her against the backseat. Lifts her by the shoulders and thrusts her downward.

She tumbles. Shoulder blades striking down on the flat of the seat cushion. Legs folding up on top of her. Her own knees driving into her chest, woofing out a breath.

He starts to climb after her. Naked body straddling the back of the driver's seat.

And as his shadow creeps over her, she comes alive. Finally.

She squirms into an upright position. Leaps for the door opposite him.

He dives for her. Torsos colliding.

His weight pinches her into the upholstery. Chest pressing her deep into the padding of the backseat.

Then he pulls back. Punches her in the face three times.

Fist banging. Hips torquing into the blows.

Her cheek clapping with the impact.

And the world gets dark.

CHAPTER 69

He hovers over the unconscious girl. Kneeling in the backseat. Her body laid out before him as though presented on a sacrificial altar.

He leans closer and watches his shadow split her down the middle. A hard line of darkness drifting over her torso. Engulfing her in slow motion.

A little laugh gutters out of him. A spitty whisper sizzling between his teeth.

Excited.

Pleased with himself.

He rubs his free hand on the top of his freshly shaved head. Feels smooth skin there. The faintest trace of prickly stubble. Whole head tingling now.

His grip shifts on the hilt of the knife in the other hand.

Blade first tonight. No fucking around. No hesitation.

Slice and dice up front. Then we can do the other.

The dome light clicks off overhead. Plunges the car's interior into darker shades. Cuts them off from the rest of the world that little bit further.

And now his shadow strengthens. Thickens. Black nothing where it touches her skin. Blotting her out.

He scoots up onto her torso. Bare thighs clenching around her middle like a cello. Hugging just beneath her ribcage. Balling up her shirt a little around her hips.

He lifts his legs. One then the other. Pins her arms under each shin. Kneecaps pinching into her upper arms. Just in case she comes to a little early.

Sweat begins to weep from his pores. Beading on his forehead and top lip. Slicking the muscular slab of his chest.

Anticipation.

He licks his lips. Tastes the salt. Holds the knife into the sliver of moonlight glinting in through the window.

Wants to see it. Wants to see the silvery glitter of the light touching the blade before he does this.

Knife first. Knife to her dome. To cut away something to keep.

Her bringing that gargantuan Rambo knife is a sign. A portent.

The riot, too. Everything falling into place.

Tonight.

He knows what he's supposed to do. What he was always meant to do.

It's his destiny.

So let it guide you. Let it show you. Let it show the world.

And he will draw his legacy into her skin inch by inch. The tip of his blade slicing. Carving.

Leaving a permanent mark in a world where so little can stand the test of time, where so little can matter.

All will know he was here — *is* here — soon.

The angular spike glides back into the shadows. Drifts closer to her face.

Part of him expects her to stir. To wake. To try to fight him off now that the moment is near. Some animal instinct flaring to life in her chest, in her heart.

She remains motionless. Heavy breath pouring in and out of her nostrils.

A sleeping baby.

The knife touches down. Metal contacting the layer of skin like soft cheese.

He presses the tip of the blade along one edge of her hairline. Feels the skin slowly give. Parting.

The knife jabs all the way to bone. Scraping there like he's touched the metal to porcelain, to crockery, something ornate, something delicate. Which she is.

Now he breathes heavy too. Both of them panting. Excited.

All the way real. All the way together.

He slides the knife to the side. Slices straight through. A straight line. Right along the borderline where her blue hair sprouts like rows of crinkled crops.

Slow. Steady.

He carves his lines. Feels like etching letters into her flesh. But there's no message in the lines themselves. Nothing alphabetical or numerical.

His message lies in what's left. In what will be taken away. Like an artist using negative space.

And the world will see. Will be struck dumb by what he's doing here.

Shockwaves rippling outward from this time and place. Cast like a dark spell from the tip of his blade. Maybe violence has always been a kind of sorcery.

And for perhaps just a moment, the whole world will feel how he feels. Understand what he understands.

Anything is possible if you will it. If you have the strength to will it and carry it through.

Anything.

No rules can bind you. No taboos. No simple meaning.

He slides the knife farther back on her head. Cuts through the thicker flesh just above her ear. Then moves to the other side to do the same.

Society tries to stack order onto chaos. They write rules. Try to reduce the human experience to thoughts. Boundaries.

Limitations. Words.

Words are fucking wind.

Words miss the point. The whole world misses the point.

Life isn't a thought. It doesn't happen in words.

It's an experience. You live it. You feel it.

Now he turns her head. Traces the metal edge over the curved bit behind the ear that slopes down to her neck.

And what does society get for reducing life's experience to words? Mass misery. Quiet despair.

A bunch of schoolmarms scolding everyone. Shunning and shaming and emasculating. Like they're punishing a dog.

A joyless existence. Ghastly.

And you all line up and try to be good dogs. Grovel. Roll over and beg. Conforming to the nth degree.

For fear of the pack abandoning you. For fear of society's love falling away from you.

Living in fear.

The knife snicks as it passes through a sinew of elastic skin.

He closes his eyes. Heart hammering. Almost done now.

But it's not real. Society's love is not real. The favor of the pack is meaningless. Empty. Worthless.

One's experience is all that's real. What happens in one's internal world — a limitless universe in your head through which all you encounter is filtered. That is real.

What is lived. What is felt.

Boundless joy is possible if you unlock the door.

Drop the world. Dismiss society. Discard the rules.

Don't live like a dog trying to please its masters.

Live like a man. By your own rules. To please only yourself.

He leans back to admire his work. Eyes following that wet red line just beneath her hair.

The flesh parting wider now. A seam in her skin that he's

unstitched.

Pins and needles bristle everywhere on his body now. His skin buzzing with the excitement of this.

And it strikes him that he pities the masses. Cucks by choice, all of them.

So few will ever experience the freedom he feels in this moment, the power he feels in this moment. Unchained. Invincible.

Whole body throbbing with ecstasy.

Because the only rules here are the ones he writes with his blade. Chiseled into her body.

Nothing else is real.

The girl twists a little beneath him. Head turning. Arms straining. Eyelids fluttering, not quite opening.

She's awake.

He giggles again through clenched teeth. Saliva sibilant in the gaps.

He watches her wriggle. Helpless beneath his bodyweight.

Little birdy. Gentle and small.

She opens her eyes. Blinks a few times.

He smiles at her. A tame animal trapped in a petting zoo built just for him.

Can't even fight for your life, can you? Just kind of squirm a little like a newborn kitten.

Her head jerks on her neck. Recoils from him.

Blood trickles from that line etched across the top of her forehead. Red beading and dripping from the crease he's made.

He leans forward again. Reaches out his hand.

Time to finish this.

CHAPTER 70

Officer Dixon weaves through the mob. In plainclothes, he can walk among them. Undetected.

He needs to find a safe way out of this mess. Let the Riot Unit handle it. The National Guard troops, too, if it comes to that. He knows they're on their way now, though his walkie-talkie is flipped off at the moment.

What he sees on the streets makes him physically ill. Acid lurching up the sides of his belly, its sting climbing his throat, coating his tongue with a rotten spaghetti sauce taste. Pungent.

The students rage through the streets. Running without direction. Wild animals turned loose. No longer thinking. Wanting only to destroy.

Horrors unfold in all directions. Fires lighting the scene in red and orange flickers. Broken glass glittering on the sidewalk, on the street. Overturned cars everywhere — at least fifteen or twenty that he's seen so far, windows kicked out or left as dented safety glass all spiderwebbed and misshapen.

The kids look so natural breaking everything around them. Their body language jubilant. Standing up straight. Shoulders back. Arms flared in some perpetually aggressive pose.

Fighting breaks out over and over — more like beatings from what he's seen, usually three or more on one. Punching. Kicking. Pushing. Always trying to get the unlucky victim onto the ground so they can do some real damage.

He turns down a darker street. Residential. Just needs to make it out of the fray. Get home or get to the station. Anything. He'd left his car on campus, back when he didn't know what he was getting into, and he wasn't going back through that to get to it. Not a chance.

He keeps one arm inside his jacket as he walks. Sweaty palm like a clam pressed up against the butt of his gun. It strikes him that pulling the weapon here and now could only lead to more violence, more injury, whether his own or someone else's. Still, it makes him feel more secure to touch it, to have it ready.

He swallows in a dry throat. Tries to focus on the positive.

He knows the Riot Unit is probably on the ground somewhere within a five-or-ten block-radius. Doesn't do him much good at the moment, but soon. Soon.

Dark shapes swoop everywhere like bats. Kids running in the shadows. Looks kind of like Halloween, trick-or-treaters out in droves. But tonight is all trick and no treat.

His eyes adjust to the moonlight as he moves, and some of the details start to fill in around him. He recognizes the neighborhood. A rich enclave of large houses where a bunch of university administrators live. He shudders to think what the students have gotten up to here, what they might be thinking.

A hissing erupts a few houses ahead. Then a metallic pinging. Right away he places it as a spray paint can. Rattling and sizzling out something.

Dark shapes flee from the front porch ahead before he gets there. Laughing and practically skipping away.

He draws up on the scene of the graffiti, only placing the building as he gets there.

Jagged red letters have been sprayed on the front of the university president's house, covering a huge patch of the Tudor-style siding. Two words. One punctuation mark.

Who cares?

The words give him chills, though he isn't sure why at first.

He stops, plants his feet on the concrete, and stares at the red message, eyes tracing over the spiky lettering.

Then he turns and looks back the way he's come. Sees the fires flickering on the cross street. Sees the dark outlines of the flipped vehicles. Sees the savage shapes swooping everywhere, looking for more.

And the spray-painted words echo in his head as he takes it all in again.

Who cares?

Fighting. Breaking. Burning your own campus to the ground.

Who cares?

Binding. Raping. Killing. The Couple Killer out there somewhere even now.

Who cares?

What the hell is going on in this town, in this world? How has it come to this?

He shuffles forward again. Needs to get the hell out of here while he can.

Some of the silhouettes across the street veer his way. Coming in fast.

He panics. Squeezes the gun. Hesitates. Doesn't want to draw it. Not here.

They run for him. Three of them. Feet heavy on the asphalt. Thudding and slapping.

His heart punches. He scrabbles back a few steps. Thinks about running into one of the backyards, turns and looks that way, but he doesn't want to end up cornered in the dark somewhere. Needs to leave himself a way out no matter what happens.

He turns back and they're on him. They're there.

Something sprays in the lead kid's hands, and at first Dixon thinks they're spray-painting again. Squirting red paint into his face. Another Halloween prank.

But when the smell hits, he knows.

Pepper spray.

The sting hits. Grows worse.

Searing pain in his nose and eyes. Burning. Impossible.

He bends over at the waist as though he can lean out of the pain. Pulls the gun out of the holster, not quite able to make himself draw it out of his jacket yet.

"Uh-oh! Spicy!" a voice yells in his face, flecking his cheek with spittle.

The kids laugh like hyenas. Screaming. Hysterical.

And then their feet are pounding on the sidewalk again. Moving away. Hustling on to their next victim.

He stumbles forward. Staggering. Mostly blind.

Shit.

He turns. Tries to see through the tears flooding his eyes, smearing everything around.

The dark curves twitch everywhere. Frolicking in bursts as if yanked along on puppet strings.

All he can see is the light in the distance. Flickering firelight illuminating swaths of the street behind him. The moonlight, too, clearer back there.

He walks up into the yard next to him. Wants to stay near the shadows of the houses. Stay off the sidewalk.

Then he trudges back the way he came, a pit opening in his stomach as he moves back toward the fire, toward the thicker action. He needs to find a place to hide. But it has to be somewhere he can actually see, somewhere he can actually know that he's concealed, even with his vision compromised.

Water pours from his eyes. Drains over his cheeks. The pain impossibly growing worse, or so it seems. Burning brighter and hotter. Like a griddle so fevered that droplets of water dance over the surface before they flash to steam.

He smears a sleeve at the faucets of his nose and eyes, only managing to slop the mucus around his face. A film of snot coating his lips and chin and brow.

Nothing helps.

It feels like acid dissolving his eyes and nose. Melting new holes in his head to let all the goo drain out. Or maybe just one big hole.

He pictures it as a runny gel jetting out of a fist-sized cavity where his face used to be, gore sluicing out as though shot down a water slide.

A burning couch crackles in the middle of the intersection ahead. He can see the rough weave of its upholstery, divots running across the back edge of the thing in silhouette.

Was that there before?

He swivels his head. Disoriented. The street looks foreign around him. Gloom swallowing up huge patches and rendering them in a hazy focus.

The dark makes everything unknowable, unfathomable. Fills him with dread that makes his stomach churn harder, with doubt that makes him want to stop his feet beneath him.

And do what? Stand here and cower in this front yard?

He keeps moving. Wading through landscaping — dry plants crackling around his ankles for now. Maybe decorative grass of some kind, though he can't tell.

He keeps his eyes trained on the street ahead. Scanning the buildings and trees on the horizon. Trying to read something useful in the murk.

A shape in the distance starts to look familiar. A skeletal structure forming a freestanding awning of some kind. Posts and a roof.

When the yellow slowly seeps into the bollards in front of the awning, he knows what he's looking at for certain. The bank drive-thru — the one that sits kitty-corner from the Dairy Mart.

Yes. He can picture it.

The brick facade. The cracked asphalt lot going pale and gray, seamed with ribbons of dark tar here and there. The system of pneumatic tubes that shuttle checks and cash in and out of the building in cylindrical containers.

There are thick bushes along the edges of the lot. Evergreens standing about five feet tall with densely needled branches packed tight. Shadows thick around them. He can hide here.

He breathes. Deeper. Easier. Cold rushing into his lungs.

He walks faster. Crossing a couple more front yards.

In the last yard before the fiery street, he trips on what he thinks is a wood beam forming a plant bed underfoot, but he keeps his feet. Stomps over some taller plant life, unperturbed.

He hesitates before the open of the street. Snot and tears still weeping down from his throttled mucus membranes. The agony pulsing hard in his eyes, in his nostrils.

The bushes are there, some twenty or thirty yards across the narrow strip of asphalt, the foliage forming a perimeter around the bank just as thick and dark as he's remembered it.

OK.

OK. That's good.

He squints. Looks both ways.

Some of those bat-like shapes swoop down the street farther down. Dark blots flitting around one of the fires. Dancing and laughing. They look like ancient beings celebrating some blood sacrifice.

But there's no one too close that he can see. This is his

chance.

He steps into the open. Leaves the partial cover of the house that has been hugging along his left, immediately feeling vulnerable as he leaves the deeper shadows behind.

He edges up to the curb in a semi-crouch. Squats at that row of cement on hands and knees. Holds perfectly still like a hunched statue.

He counts to three.

One.

Chest and back shaking. Hands tingling against the cement of the curb.

Two.

Nose still spigoting snot. Eyes gushing.

Three.

He shoves himself to his feet. Sprints. Stiff legs like stilts propelling across the street. Clunking out choppy footsteps.

He steps up onto the opposite curb. Zips over another slab of sidewalk.

And dives into the dark roughage of the bushes.

CHAPTER 71

Andre blinks. Waking. Rubs at his eyes.

Confused. Groggy.

Smells something familiar. Earthy. Motor oil?

His eyes are open.

But the dark remains. Black draped all around him. No light at all.

He tries to sit up. Bangs his head on the trunk lid. Sees a bright flash. Motes bursting everywhere in his field of vision.

It all comes back then.

The feel of squeezing the taser trigger in his hands. Missing the target. Twice.

I'm locked in the trunk.

Waiting to die.

Like all the rest.

He pats at the walls of his enclosure. Feels the rough fabric lining this space.

Breath going ragged, going heavy. Breathing hard. Spit sizzling between his teeth. Sucking and sucking and unable to get enough oxygen.

Shit. I'm hyperventilating.

The world starts to turn pink like bubble gum along the edges. Blots of the gum detaching and floating around. Drifting smudges of neon.

He makes himself stop gasping for breath. Makes himself slow down. Deep breaths.

In-two-three-four. And hold it.

He listens.

Can't hear anything at first. Wonders how long it's been, how long he has left.

Wonders how the hell he missed with the taser. Both times.

Useless pussy.

Lips peeling back to bare his teeth. Grimacing in the dark.

Stupid shit.

Tears swell in his eyes. Hot water spilling over the rims. Draining down his cheeks.

The nothing is big now. Bigger than it's ever been.

Nothing is everything.

Nowhere is everywhere.

Just the black emptiness and the quiet. A pit opening around him. Waiting for him to fall in.

A sound interrupts the void.

A moan. Feminine. Sounds like it's just on the other side of the backseat.

He feels the car shift beneath him. Weight adjusting, swaying on the shocks a little.

Tobi screams.

CHAPTER 72

She screams. Her eyes open wider for a second and then quickly thin to slits.

He shudders at the piercing sound. Surprised. Shaking in place.

He's still floating over her. His free hand rising toward her face. Stopping there. Unsure.

She screams harder. Louder.

He cringes. The tone spearing his eardrums. Strident.

He feels her core tense between his thighs. The yell catapulting from her belly. Hurling from her throat.

And the scream just keeps going. Endless. Somehow louder as she goes.

The words *screaming bloody murder* spring into his head.

Jesus Christ.

He swivels his head to the open window on the driver's side. Gapes at the empty air between the glass and the frame. A spike of adrenaline turns his blood to icy rivulets in his arms and legs.

Fuck. Too loud.

Didn't think she had it in her.

She bucks underneath him as he's turned away. Hips ripping upward. Tossing him off balance.

Stronger than she looks, too.

He rocks back. Flails his arms for balance. Flapping two bird wings behind himself.

The butt of the knife catches on the headrest and bounces his arm back. Sends a shock up through the limb. Wobbles him anew.

Elbow banging on the back of the seat again. Knife tumbling from his hands. The blade disappearing to the murky floor.

Now he pitches forward. Fights for balance.

She sits up partway. Props herself on her elbows. Aims her head toward the open window and screams harder still.

Piercing. Impossibly loud.

He leaps for her. Needs to clamp his hands over her maw.

Needs to cut off her wind.

Needs to shut that bitchy mouth for good.

CHAPTER 73

Deep voices gurgled on the radio. Agitated. Tangling over each other.

Darger and Loshak still sat in their car, swathed in darkness now, listening to the riot unfold in real time over the radio. The orders had been to keep the channel open for stakeout detail communication only, but that had flown out the window once it was evident the "minor disturbance" had become more of an actual riot situation. Everyone wanted to know what was happening on the ground.

"We're getting reports of fatalities. Unconfirmed so far, but… it seems inevitable at this point. Some people are gonna die tonight. Some probably already have."

The chatter waned for a few seconds. The silence hanging in the air.

"What a clusterfuck," someone finally said.

"Whole thing got out of control so damn quick. Like a wildfire or something, you know? Like they were swarming there on the football field, no big deal, and within half an hour there were cars and couches on fire. Windows busted out. Stores looted. It just happened so fast."

"National Guard is en route from Lansing now. Riot squads are headed out with shields and tear gas as we speak."

"What a shitshow. Just… a mess."

"When will the troops hit the ground?"

"Not sure about an ETA right now. Things are a little hectic on the comm lines as you can imagine, but—"

A voice Darger recognized cut through then.

"This is Dixon. I'm right in the middle of it. It's unbelievable. Multiple cars on fire on this block. Fighting and looting. They bashed out all the glass on the Dairy Mart, and they're throwing two-liters out into the street to burst. Every few seconds there's another Faygo bomb jetting pop everywhere. The kids are running around in the spray like sprinklers."

He sounded like he was keeping his voice low. Probably hiding. Wet lips pressed right to the mouthpiece of the walkie.

"What's your position now, Dixon?"

"I'm sort of hunkered down in some bushes outside the bank drive-thru here. We were ordered to stand down once they called in the Riot Unit, and I tried to get out, but it's like being trapped in a war zone. I, uh, heard gunshots earlier. Six shots. They were close. Probably within two blocks, if not closer."

"Damn, man. Hang in there. You just keep your head down until there's a clear path outta there. The cavalry is on the way now."

"That's why I flipped over to the stakeout channel. I was wondering if you guys had heard where the Riot Unit is at. It's hard to communicate with dispatch right now. They've got a metric shit ton of irons in the fire, I guess."

There was a lull after he asked his question. Another pregnant pause that seemed to fill the air.

"All I know is they're on the ground now, Dixon. Heading toward you, I figure, but I don't know where or how fast they're moving. We're not too clued into the tactics or anything, man. Sorry to say."

"Yeah. Well, I didn't figure… Just thought it was worth a shot. You know… just in case."

"It won't be long. Once they come marching through,

banging their batons on their shields and firing off canisters of tear gas, the kids will scatter with their tails so far up between their legs they'll be shittin' tail for a week."

Some laughter chittered over the line, but Dixon didn't seem to hear this.

"Oh, shit…" he said, his voice flat. "They're beating him. Some kid just outside the Dairy Mart."

Everyone fell silent. Waited for Dixon to go on in that whispery tone.

"They've got him down on the ground, and they're clubbing him with boards. Two-by-fours."

The silence stretched out over the line before one of the people on the stakeout finally replied.

"Jesus."

"I think they're killing him. Blood everywhere. Should I… go over there?"

"You've got orders to stand down, right? You go poking your nose in that hornet's nest, it's just going to be you getting beat to death."

"I'm gonna fire a shot into the air. See if that breaks it up."

"Wait. Don't draw any attent—"

The gunshot cracked over the radio. Sounded fizzy and clicky through the tiny speaker.

Darger could hear her heartbeat in her ears as she waited for Dixon to come back on the line. Blood squishing and pounding through her flesh.

"It worked. All their heads snapped around, and then they took off running."

"Is the guy on the ground gonna be OK?"

"I'm not sure. He's not moving. Just lying there with a puddle of blood around his head."

Another beat of quiet.

"Wait. He's stirring now. Getting up. Looks a little wobbly, but… he's alive."

"Well damn. Good call, Dixon. I wouldn't have done that. Not worth the risk."

"Oh no," Dixon said. His voice seemed so small now. "A group of them are dragging a girl into the alley behind the Dairy Mart."

"Fuck."

"I've got to do something. I've got to go stop it."

A bunch of voices broke in then. Yelling over each other. Begging him not to put himself in danger.

Then the line went quiet. Still. Eerie.

Loshak pinched one of the knobs between his thumb and index finger and twisted. Turned up the volume.

Nothing.

Silence screaming out of the speaker. The emptiness opening there in the car between Darger and Loshak, as though the abyss were being broadcast into their sedan.

The line clicked once as though someone had pressed down their button and let it go without saying anything. Then it fell to quiet again.

Loshak swallowed beside her.

A scream broke up the stillness, and Darger jumped in her seat. Skin drawing taut. Hair pricking up over the top of her scalp.

At first she thought the girl's voice was on the radio, part of the unfolding drama pouring out of the speaker, but then she remembered her window was cracked.

The scream was coming from outside.

CHAPTER 74

Tobi screams and screams.

Cold hands cup her mouth. Try to stifle her.

But she wrenches free. Screams harder.

Pain draws a cold border along her hairline. Searing agony in a hard crease. Chiseled. Chilly where the air touches the flayed open flesh.

The hurt slopes down from the forehead to part the thicker flesh just above her ears. Stretches all the way to the back of her skull.

She sees him now through slitted eyes. That dark mass hovering above her. Shoulders tapering to the waist. The hard contours of his arm reaching for her.

Rough hands clasping at her sodden cheeks. Trying to find her mouth again, squelch her scream again.

She jerks her neck once more. Pulls a fraction of the way free of his stony fingers.

His hands glide lower. The callused ridges of the palms tracing down past her chin. Finding the soft flesh of her throat.

She tries to get her hands up. Tries to hook under his stranglehold.

His grip tightens. Cinches her windpipe closed.

She can see his whole body go rigid. The tautness seeming to spread up his arms into his chest. His abs clenching. His neck setting into something elongated and hard.

His whole body working as one to squeeze her throat shut. Like a boa constrictor squishing the life out of something little by little, the flex spreading through the thing.

She feels water bleed from the corners of her eyes. Feels her tongue loll out of her mouth.

Her chest spasms. Muscles jittering. Lungs lurching. Trying to draw wind.

Can't.

Face going hot. Tiny prickles of electricity strobing in her vision.

She pries at his grip. Tries to knife a finger between his hands and her neck.

Can't.

But it's no use. He's too strong.

He leans forward. Chokes her harder. Arms shaking over her.

And those lightning bolts streaking her vision start to fade. The black of the night seeping into the car around her and him. Growing thicker, darker.

The gloom winning. Pulling on her. Wanting only to take her under for keeps.

Harder to keep her eyes open now.

I can't.

She closes them. Lets the darkness fill her field of vision. Black seas of nothing.

And now her hands seek lower. Away from his grip. Sliding over the quivering tautness of his contracted belly muscles.

Lower.

Lower.

She finds the soft flesh she seeks. Cold to the touch. She wraps her right hand around the bulge.

Her fist clenches around the looseness. Compressing.

And now she squeezes back.

She crushes his scrotum. Forearm shaking. Fingernails digging into the dimpled skin.

Piercing.

Squashing.

He bucks back. His grip around her neck loosening though still clamping her windpipe.

Harder.

She squeezes harder. Feels her own body drawing taut little by little just the way his did.

All of her will, all of her being projected into this. Every muscle. Every fiber.

She pulls on his sack. Jerks her arms in unison like she's swinging a baseball bat.

Tries to rip it off.

He screams.

Shakes.

Winces.

Topples backward off her.

She sucks in a big scraping breath. Opens her eyes.

Watches his shadow crumple ass first into the space between the front and backseat. Hips wedging there.

He folds up. Clutches uselessly at his crotch. Teeth exposed in a snarl. Eyes pinched shut in agony.

She scrabbles.

Dives into the front seat. Sliding on her stomach. Fingers finding the door handle. Opposite forearm shoving it open.

Cold air blooms into the stuffy car. Whooshing.

She crawls for the opening. Wriggles her shoulders over the threshold. Feels the chilly air surround her wet face, her aching neck.

And then he's there. Arm looping out of the back seat. Hand clambering at her back, at her neck.

She pushes off with hands and legs. Lunges forward.

His hand finds the top of her head. Gripping like he's

palming a basketball. He pulls on her hair.

And she feels just a little resistance along that searing fissure of her wounded hairline. A tackiness as the flesh fully parts. Peels.

And then her scalp slides away from her skull.

The momentum jerks her upright. Pulls her fully into the glow of the dome light.

And she sees the horror reflected in the rearview mirror.

The rumpled scalp bunching at the back of her head. Crinkled blue hair balled up there like a small pelt.

The exposed dome of her skull gaping above her forehead. Bloody bone. Glistening. Perfectly rounded.

Impossible.

And the cold is all over her. All over her. Reaching into her. Somehow under the skin.

But there is no skin.

She screams again.

Tears blur her eyes.

She dives forward. Snakes between his outstretched limbs. Flops onto the street on elbows and torso. The cold asphalt pushing the air out of her.

Headlights swing around the corner. Glinting in the water in her eyes.

Engine revving hard along with them. Going too fast.

The lights grow brighter, bigger. Coming this way. Pushing over the blacktop to reach her.

The car slams on its brakes.

She stands up into the light.

CHAPTER 75

Dixon shoves the radio down toward his waistband. Tucks the clip into his belt.

No sounds of protest come from the tiny speaker now. He's turned it off.

The wails continue across the street. A girl thrashing and screeching in the arms of five college guys, all of their faces dark, eyes dead and pitted with shadows.

They have her tipped horizontal to the ground, and they surround her as though they're pallbearers toting a casket. Each man holding a piece of her — a limb, a hip, an armpit, a handful of hair.

They shuffle funny as they carry her toward the mouth of the dark alley behind the Dairy Mart. Shoes scuffing the asphalt, gritting at flecks of gravel. All of them taking short choppy steps, sliding their feet as much as anything. Knees bouncing. Toes tripping on cracks or plunging up to the ankle into craggy potholes. Awkward.

Dixon swallows. Rises from the bushes.

Crooked branches and needles snag at his clothing. Beg him to stay put.

But he strides forward. Into the open. Pulls his gun from his holster. Lets it dangle at his side.

The pain in the hollow of his face is still there. Same for his eyes. But the pulsing bright agony of the burn has died back to a steady flame of hurt. An ache now instead of bolts of torment.

The group totters into the darkness behind the Dairy Mart, and the shadows swallow them. The white facade blocking his view now like a curtain.

The girl's screams grow louder. Harder. The feathery shrill sounds of earlier going solid and full-throated as the dark surrounds her, as fresh panic courses through her.

Dixon adjusts his grip on the gun. Squeezes it a little. Palm moist against the textured grip like a starfish adhering itself there.

He swallows. Picks up the pace. Feet clapping against the street. Eyes locked on that strip of asphalt that shears off into gloom where they've taken the girl.

His heart batters at the cage of ribs around it. Angry and scared and trying to jab its way free.

Will he yell when gets there? Tell them to freeze?

He swallows again. Doesn't know. Can't think. Doesn't know what the hell to do here.

The barrier of the white facade seems to rush toward him. Cinder blocks painted white. Whatever will happen next existing just beyond that line where the edge of the building meets the alley.

He's supposed to be serving tickets to drunken college kids. Breaking up parties. Maybe handing out the occasional noise violation for the keggers that get a bit too rowdy.

Not this. Not all of this.

He tries to swallow once more, and this time his throat hitches. That tunnel of muscle clenching like a fist. Disobeying him so he gags a little on the saliva.

He can hear another chunk of the mob headed toward him. Screaming and yelling and laughing like jackals. They're close. Maybe flushed this way by the Riot Unit. But he can't worry about that now.

He steps up onto the curb on the opposite side of the street. Moves into the alley. Lifts the gun so it bobs along before him, black barrel pointing the way like a divining rod.

He wants to run away. Wants to vomit. Wants to explode into a bloody mist.

Wants to be anywhere but here and now.

But he keeps going.

He crosses that line at the back corner of the Dairy Mart. Strides into the murk. Slowing as the shadows consume him.

He squints. Can't see. Needs to let his eyes adjust.

Shit.

There's motion. More struggling.

He can only see the flutter of it in the dark, some rippling sense of movement to the blackness, like the disturbed surface of a lake after rocks have been thrown in. Eddies and concentric circles. Undulating smoke.

He fires the gun into the air. The weapon jerking into the web of his hand. The crack like thunder rushing down the alley.

The bright muzzle flash lights up the ghouls surrounding the girl in orangey hues. They've got her on the ground by a navy blue dumpster. Huddling over her like wolves swarming a kill. Some of them work to hold her arms down while others rip at her pants.

They flinch at the sound of the gun. Lurch into motion.

But the light is gone too fast. That blanket of darkness hung up everywhere again.

His heart slams harder. Sends tremors through his whole body. Arms shaking. Neck quivering. Blood clubbing through his veins.

His mouth opens. He doesn't know what words will come out until he hears them.

"Leave her the fuck alone!"

His voice is hard. Aggressive. Sounds much more confident than he feels.

He stumbles forward toward where he thinks he can see the dumpster's outline. Feet clumsy in the dark. Distrustful of the pocked asphalt here.

They're moving. Bolting into action. He hears the lurching footsteps.

But are they fighting or fleeing?

He braces himself. Listens over that encroaching crowd noise somewhere behind him. Teeth clenched. Hackles bristling as hard as they can.

The footsteps are moving away. Running away.

A shaky breath sucks into his lungs. Cool and thick.

Jesus. It worked.

Maybe.

He fires another shot into the air. Wants them to think he's shooting after them. Also wants to get another look at what's going on here.

He sees the girl first. She runs. Hops a small chain-link fence on one side of the alley. Rushes through someone's backyard.

She'll get away. Good.

Then he sees that some of the others have fled straight down the length of the alley. Arms and legs pumping like Usain Bolt.

He sees the board last.

One of the other males stands closer. Off to his left.

He swings a two-by-four toward Dixon's head in that momentary orange flash of the muzzle flare. Looks like stop-motion animation somehow. The rectangular slab of lumber growing huge as it gets close.

The flash dies to black.

The wood bashes him in the side of the head. Slams him in the ear. Hits before he can even think about ducking.

The thud of the impact sounds dull. A solid thump that rings a muted tone inside his head like a fucked up xylophone.

The wood cranks his neck. Swings his skull to the side hard.

And then his head gets lighter. Loopy.

The ringing moves from his head into the ear that was struck, its pitch going higher like a buzzing mosquito as it flies into the beam of the zapper.

His eyes droop. His shoulders sag. That dark deeper now, fuller now.

He bumbles backward on dead legs. No real thoughts in his head. Just scoot back, scoot back, keep scooting back until you fall off the edge of the world.

Rocks grit under the soles of his shoes. Ankles soft like bread dough. Flexing and rolling and slowing him down.

He hears footsteps closing in. Coming toward him.

He lifts the gun and fires into the dark. Twice.

CRACK.

CRACK.

Aims high. Over the perp's head. Even now, he doesn't shoot to kill. Knows he probably should, but he doesn't.

Can't.

He backpedals beyond the edge of the Dairy Mart. Moves into the moonlight.

He keeps expecting the board carrier to emerge, wielding his weapon once more, but he's not there. That onyx wall holds still. Empty.

He's gone.

The warning shots worked after all.

When he reaches the curb, he stops. Breathes. Keeps the gun up just in case.

And the night wobbles around him. The sky flexes and sucks like the dark is breathing, living. The fires in the distance all warped around the edges, morphing and strobing. His brain still not right from taking that lumber shot to the dome.

Ragged breaths heave in and out. Shot through his throat. Roiling a second in his chest and then released.

It feels like his eyes are crossing. Feels like now that his adrenaline is ebbing, he might go under. Might pass out.

Shit. No.

He leans over and breathes. Tries to will his mind to sharpen, his eyes to focus. Like he can just snap out of it. Push through it.

He stares at the line where the curb and grass butt up against each other. Watches it drift in and out of blurriness, softness.

And then the mob is there. Behind him. Oozing up the street. Fire lighting up the edges of the horde. Bodies thrusting back and forth among the amoeba-like mass. A mobile mosh pit closing on him.

Yes. He remembers thinking this might happen. If the Riot Unit flushed the others this way, he knew there'd be more. A mass exodus surging right for him.

He pushes himself upright. Stumbles backward again.

And he picks out a voice in the crowd. A strident tone rising above all the rest.

"Hey! That's a fucking cop! I seen him riding around with Kirby."

He turns to run, but they're already there. Already here.

The mob. The single-celled creature ready to absorb him like it has so many others. Its walls opening like many hungry mouths.

"Don't worry," a voice full of humor says right in his ear as the students close around him. "We're all friends now."

The crashing wave of humanity surrounds him fully.

Quickly. Sucks him into its deeper shadows.

Confusion. All those bodies cinching tight around him. Pressing into him.

He pushes back. Tries to finagle through. Nowhere to go.

When he falls down, the dark mob crushes out all of the light.

CHAPTER 76

Darger wheeled around a corner. Watched the dark of the street ahead give way to the glow of her headlights.

Trees lined one side of a wide street. A dense-looking patch of woods. Homes far apart. Everything separated by landscaping boundaries — bushes and pine trees. The land itself cut into neat portions.

Quiet here. Still. Dark behind every window.

"This would have been a good place to park," Loshak said. "Still close to town, but… private, you know. A peaceful neighborhood."

Darger nodded. Her pulse thrummed in her neck. Body taut. Electricity going crispy behind her eyes.

They rolled past a few vacant sedans and low-end sports cars parked in the driveways on the left. Darger tried to stare into the spaces beyond the dimmed glass of each. Making sure there was nothing stirring inside any of them.

Everything held still.

And then movement drew her eyes back to the road ahead. Something fluttering in the street in the distance.

Even before she could tell what she was seeing, the scene made Darger's skin crawl.

Her eyes scanned the moving shapes, the glint of light surrounding them. The pieces coming into focus one by one.

An opened car door clogged with human bodies.

Skin. Blood. Moving too fast to discern.

Torsos. Limbs. Thrashing and shuddering and jiggling.

Yellow light gleaming on the mess of body parts. A dome

light shining down.

Darger blinked. Tried to make the image sharpen into some kind of clarity, make some kind of sense.

Another piercing scream ruffled her hackles. Shrugged her shoulders up into the side of her neck.

This was it. The scream was coming from the car she was looking at.

This is him. Here and now. It has to be.

And finally she could see what she was looking at.

A girl struggling to crawl out of the driver's side door of a Volkswagen Jetta. Screaming and trembling.

A man's arms trying to stop her. His shirtless back draped over the back of the driver's seat. Hands reaching for her, swinging for her.

The girl lurched out of the car. Landed on hands and knees in the street. Stood up into the beams of Darger's headlights.

Darger wheezed. A gasp sucking in-between clenched teeth.

Loshak groaned. Braced one hand on the dashboard. Said nothing.

The bloody dome of the girl's head stood exposed. Naked.

Skin peeled away from bone.

Syrupy red coating most of the white arc above her forehead. Glittering in the headlights' glow. Wet.

One bleach-white patch laid bare where the blood had been smeared away. Pale. Stark against the red. About the size of a pack of gum.

Wild eyes swiveled everywhere beneath that gleaming red arch. Crazy eyes. Rotating in her face like marbles.

Mouth open. Breath heaving. Teeth exposed. Tongue pulsing in the gap. Like a frightened possum.

What the fuck?

The girl's hair was gone. She'd been *scalped.*

And then Darger eye's drifted lower. Saw that her hair wasn't gone. Not entirely.

The scalp bunched at the back of her head. Wadded up against her neck where some of the skin was still connected. Scrunched blue hair like ramen noodles all smooshed together there.

The girl's shoulders jerked. A cough, maybe.

And the flap of scalp swung. Floppy like a slice of American cheese with hair on it.

Shocking.

Wrong.

And Darger was out of the car. Glock drawn and raised. Sprinting toward the scene.

Moving. Charging in.

Before her mind could even catch up. Before she could even process what was happening here.

She drew up alongside the girl. And Loshak was there. Swooping for the motionless figure on the asphalt. Being the caretaker already. Saying things to Tobi but not getting any response.

Darger turned toward the car. Toward the open door.

The Glock pointed into the interior. Yellow light shining down on pale gray upholstery. Splotches of blood glossy in the backseat. A few smears in the front. Some kind of cordage hanging in the front seat like naked strands of Christmas lights.

Taser wires?

Fractured thoughts throbbed in her head.

Struggle.

Backseat.

If he's still here.

Ducked down behind the barrier.

About to bolt.

She took a step closer. Whole body shuddering like a struck wind chime. Blood whooshing in her head like helicopter rotors.

Chuff.

Chuff.

Chuff.

Chuff.

She leaned her top half into the car. Glock first.

Then she saw him. Naked. Squatted in the shadowy spot in the passenger floorboard in the back. Reaching out for the knife on the floor behind the driver's seat.

She stepped forward and squeezed the trigger.

The Glock blazed and popped. Bucked in her hand.

He jumped back.

Plastic bits of the door splintered just beneath the window. The pocked place appearing there as if by magic instead of by bullet. Right where his head had been a fraction of a second earlier.

Missed.

He gave up on the knife. Scrambled the opposite way.

The backdoor snapped open. Swung into the dark.

Darger fired again.

Too late.

His naked body blurred through the opening. Greasy skin. Shiny. Tan everywhere. Blood smeared on his hands and chest.

Twisting. Moving away from her. Scrabbling. Getting to his feet.

He loped into the dark woods like an antelope.

And Darger followed.

CHAPTER 77

Officer Kirby ducks behind a leafy bush. Peeks out to watch the rioting mob drift down the street.

He follows the biggest group at a distance. Finds it safer to stay behind them. Better than wandering off and getting caught out in the open again.

He swivels his head in all directions. Looks for any signs of movement. Hoping, above all, to see the twirling lights of patrol cars.

Somewhere. Anywhere.

The empty night gapes back at him. Nothing so far.

He licks his lips.

The riot squad has to be near. He just has to find them. Fall into the safety of their strength, their authority. Hell, he might hang around a while and watch them crack a few skulls. After the night he's had, he deserves that, at the very least. Watching some snot-nosed student's brains leak out onto the concrete like a runny egg yolk would really take the edge off about now.

He scans the area again. Makes sure he's alone.

Then he darts out from his covered spot behind the bush. Runs out toward the road and ducks behind the front fender of a minivan parked along the curb this time.

He squints to make sure he's seeing right.

The roving riot has stopped advancing up Walnut Street. Instead, the mob thrashes in place at the top of the hill before him. Their yells louder. Their body language more violent.

Looks like the pack found something.

A chill tingles along Kirby's back. His scrotum clenches.

Shrinks into a plum pit.

The kids look like sharks knifing through the waves of humanity. Predators. Beasts of prey. Thinking only *kill, kill, kill.*

The mob flails and howls and jitters and heaves for what feels like a long time. Churning in place. The migrating mosh pit turned stationary. Heat rolling off them in a visible shimmer of heat distortion just above all their heads, warping the night.

Kirby has to remind himself to breathe as he stares at the spectacle. Some kind of awe keeps freezing his chest in place. Rendering him cold and still.

He gets a whiff of his own piss every time he takes a big breath — smells strongly of coffee — and he remembers the dark stain on his crotch. The version of shame that he can feel stirs at that thought, at being faced with that reality. Something undeniable in it. Something he wants to conceal.

So maybe he won't hang around once he gets to the Riot Unit. Maybe he'll just get the hell out of here, once and for all. Shit, a hot shower and a few silver bullets will take the edge off just as well as watching a little skull-cracking. He has an 18-pack of Coors Light waiting in the fridge even now, the Rocky Mountains on the cans gone dark blue to indicate their full chill level.

He can feel the crisp brew on his tongue. All those tiny bubbles bursting. Effervescent.

Goddamn, that sounds good. Sounds real, real good.

The amoeba flexes and jerks forward again. The ever-morphing mob advancing. Sliding over the rim of the hill and slowly moving out of sight. That march across Remington Hills resumed, like Sherman marching to the sea — bent on destruction, on scorching the earth.

Kirby mops sweat from his brow. The back of his wrist swiping, sleeve coming away soggy.

When the last of the stragglers creeps behind the hilltop, he moves again. Sprints on heavy feet another half a block. Ankles aching faintly with every step.

He glances down at himself. Stupid beer belly flopping. Slamming down every other step to put that much more strain on his joints. He really needs to melt that thing down some. Get back in shape, like when he was young and damn near all muscle. Not very toned but a side of beef nevertheless. Then he could really bust some heads.

He veers off the street, off the sidewalk. Ducks behind the rear end of an SUV tucked in the shadows of a gravel driveway.

Waits. Sucks in a few breaths. Watches the pink blotches drift around in his eyeballs, four of them, all shaped like cutouts of the moon above, floating and darting wherever he looks.

Finally he dares a peek. Sticks his head out from behind the back bumper of the RAV4. Scans the dark horizon.

The top of the hill remains barren. No more moshing college kids. Nothing.

He stares into that blank space where the hill cleaves off into emptiness. Makes sure there's no movement there at all.

Then he lets his eyes drop to the foreground, to the space between him and the hill. Vision skimming over the tops of vehicles, over the muted contours of driveways leading up to houses.

No movement. Nothing of note.

The mob still howls and screams and carries on in the distance. But not here. Not close. They're moving on. Slowly growing quieter.

He breathes a little easier. Chest shaky as it inhales. Skin cold there. Entire torso drenched with sweat.

Then his eyes snap back to something in the street. Something left behind.

A crumpled shape sprawls on the ground at the top of the hill. Dark and small.

A body.

It's right where they stopped and moshed for a while, he realizes. But they weren't moshing. They were stomping someone. Killing someone.

He thinks back to his own brush with the mob, how reality whittled down until all that mattered was keeping his feet. Kirby had done it. Stayed up. Fought them off long enough to survive.

Get stripped of his weapons? Yes.

Get punched, kicked, spit on, humiliated? Yes.

Pissed his pants? Yes.

But none of that mattered in the end. He'd fucking survived. Period. End of story.

The poor bastard lying up there now hadn't been so lucky.

Kirby ducks back behind the SUV for another couple breaths. Dreads what will happen next. But he wants to know. Has to know.

Finally he leaves his cover and approaches. Jogging. Body squatted low. Lighter on his feet now, like he's coming up on something sacred and wrong all at once.

He keeps his eyes down, and the street slides by underneath him. Textured asphalt rolling past. Silvery in the moonlight.

And then the body is there. And his feet stop. And he doesn't breathe anymore. Doesn't think anymore.

Because he knows who it is. Even with the face obscured, he knows.

Dixon lies facedown on the asphalt. When Kirby finally

leans over and rolls him, he finds his partner's nose basically smashed flat to his head. Forehead caved in.

Instincts slide Kirby's fingers to the neck, though some part of him knows it's useless. He searches the curved flesh just under the jaw. Finds the spot just next to the windpipe.

No pulse.

Dead.

And Kirby's eyes close. And his teeth clench. And he wants to open fire on the fucking mob.

He pictures it. Dreams it. Just him sweeping an AK-47 across all of them. Hot nails puncturing flesh. Tearing red holes in faces and bellies. Firing until all the bodies stop twitching, and then firing some more. To be sure.

He doesn't know he's crying until the tang of salt hits the corners of his mouth. And then a single choked sob scrapes somewhere deep in his throat.

CHAPTER 78

Darger crashed through the foliage at the edge of the woods. Crossed the border from light into darkness. A snaggle of plants gripping her for a second and then releasing her.

She jogged through the thick stuff. Glock pointing the way in front of her.

The plant life thinned as soon as she got about five feet into the woods. Trees jutting up from the landscape — the black tendrils of the trunks and branches darker than the rest. Panels of moonlight shining down here and there where the gaps had begun to form as autumn threatened.

She picked up speed in the clearing. Gave the branches a wide berth. Moved toward the empty space.

A bed of dead leaves and pine needles carpeted the ground. A few ferns here and there.

She heard his footfalls ahead. Crunching leaves. Thrashing shrubs. Snapping twigs. Balls of his feet pounding into the soft earth, a thudding sound like someone slapping wet clay against a table.

She pumped her limbs harder. Gun now swinging at her side instead of pointing the way, throbbing along with her gait, a black flicker in the corner of her eye.

She was gaining on him. She could hear it. His footsteps louder, closer. Growing more frantic.

That made sense.

She pictured him as she'd last seen him. Greasy and tan. Leaping from the backseat and darting for the woods.

He was barefoot. Naked. Unarmed.

She pictured him reaching out for the knife on the floor of the car. Unable to grab it.

Tried to bring a knife to gunfight.

He was certainly still dangerous, though. She knew that.

She had the upper hand. No doubt about it.

But if he moved for her, she would fire. No hesitation.

The gun pulsed there beside her at the end of her pumping arm. Her trusty Glock. Ready and waiting.

And then she realized that the papery thump of his footsteps had cut out. That rhythm cleaving off into silence a few seconds before. Its absence ringing out over the wilderness. Striking and wrong in Darger's ears.

She stopped. Listened.

Nothing.

Her eyes drilled into the empty space around her. They'd adjusted to the lack of light as she ran. Details sharpening everywhere. The texture of bark and crushed leaves and mossy patches on the ground appearing where once only an indistinct texture had been.

She took a few steps forward. Light on her toes. Breathing muted. Ears still sharp.

She stopped again. Froze in place.

Her hackles slowly pricked up. Every follicle turned electric.

He was near. Hiding. She could feel it.

Is he watching me now? Waiting for me?

She thought about what she'd heard about mountain lion attacks. How the 200-pound cats watch a human being's eyes as they creep up on them. Wait until their back is turned before they pounce.

Her own eyes swiveled in her head. Scanning everywhere. Looking for any minuscule sign of movement. She turned and tried to stare into the shadows behind her.

But the woods held steady. Cryptic. Not ready to give up any secrets just yet.

Darger took a shaky breath and crept forward.

CHAPTER 79

The riot squad marches down Park Street. Soldiers marching in a rigid formation. Faces tucked behind Plexiglas and gas masks. Batons banging against the sides of their riot shields in a thumping rhythm in time with their march.

Jay watches them coming up the street. Wants to do something. Wants to… He doesn't know what.

A cluster of kids stands in the center of the street, a couple dozen, Jay among them. Many more loiter near the brick storefronts along the sidewalk. All heads turned. All eyes watching the rows of the black-clad men encroaching.

An alarm bell rings endlessly from one of the gaping windows behind them. A hardware store that got busted up. Mannequins and camping gear and weed whackers piled up in the street and set ablaze.

A couple of the mannequins still smolder in the intersection between the police and the students. Orange coals glowing among the mess of plastic limbs.

Jay stares unblinking as the police come to a stop across the street. That thumping march hitting a final rat-tat and cutting out all at once.

The face-off begins. Rioters starting to fan out. Spreading across their side of the street in a neat row as if to mock the soldiers. Some forty or fifty feet of asphalt standing between the two sides.

A bullhorn comes on. Some voice bellowing something about dispersing. Crackling and distorted.

Jay is too jacked up to even understand the words.

Adrenaline slamming through his veins. Heart knocking too hard in his chest.

It's about who has the stronger will. Who wants it more.

This whole display, the pageantry of the marching and banging on the shields. The ritual. It's about trying to break our wills. Make it seem like they want it more.

Like all that shock and awe shit.

A triumph of the will.

Jay's eyes scan along the ground. He finds a rock in the street. Stoops to pick it up.

He stands and hefts it in his hand. A jagged thing a little smaller than a golf ball. That drone of words still buzzing through the bullhorn. A babble in his ears.

Should I throw it?

Who wants it more? We have to show them. We have to.

Before he can decide, the lisping crack of gas canisters being fired rings out over everything.

SHUNK.

SHUNK.

SHUNK.

The smoking cans skip across the street like stones. Skitter into the crowd. Gas coiling out of them. Fogging up everything to make it hard to see.

A bunch of the kids run. Ceding ground. A stampede fleeing the confrontation.

Jay pulls the collar of his shirt up over his mouth and nose. Eyes burning now. He staggers forward through the exodus, into the murk of the gas. Moving toward the police.

He rushes for one of the canisters on the ground. Picks up the hissing thing.

Hurls it right back into the hive of riot police. An arcing throw that rainbows down among them. Bounces on the ground, spinning like a top.

He watches the tight formation of soldiers break up. Even with gas masks they scatter. Scampering out of the way. Elephants afraid of a mouse.

Jay sees another of the canisters fling out of the crowd. Flying into the haphazard riot squad.

And his heart thunders. And his eyes sting. And his throat aches.

See?

See?

We fucking want it more.

CHAPTER 80

Darger glided forward on light feet. The foliage thicker here. Fern fronds flapping around her ankles. Prickly stuff gripping at the arms of her jacket.

She didn't run now. Needed to stay quiet. Needed to listen.

Still, she knifed forward at a decent pace. Brisk. Not wanting to let him get out of earshot, either.

The Glock pointed up into the canopy above. Nestled in the crook of her right hand. Ready to point and shoot when the time came.

If it came.

She still couldn't hear him, near or far. She could only let instinct pull her forward, let intuition guide her where it would.

The ground sloped upward underfoot. A game trail slashing a shadowy line into the thicket, lit in that lacework of moonlight filtering through the branches.

She climbed the hill. Followed the beaten way. Feet sliding around a little in the muddy path.

Panic swirled somewhere in the back of her head, chaos whipping just beyond the realm of her conscious mind — tried to tell her he was long gone, that she'd failed.

But she didn't let the fear in, didn't let it take over. She observed its whirlwind from a distance. Somehow staying steady in the midst of it. Perhaps because she had to.

At the top of the rise, the horizon once more came into view. She could see the lights of the city ahead. The line where this copse of woods gave way. Streetlights dotting the skyline. Gleaming through the branches. A meshwork of light and shadow angling to the ground before her.

The power must still be up on this side of town, at least partially. Looking closer, she saw that it was just a handful or so of streetlights glowing, darkness shrouding everything beyond them. Most of the city still dark.

And yelling broke through from what sounded like a few blocks away. The roar of an angry crowd. Excited. Glass exploding shrill into the night.

The riot.

She was closer to it now. Jesus.

She plodded forward a few more steps. Stopped and listened.

Nothing but the distant yelling and crashing of the students running amok. The din of the anarchy drowning out the hushed sound of the forest around her, somehow pulling her farther away.

She didn't feel him here anymore. Didn't like it.

She poked a couple more steps forward, and a gas station sign glowing red and yellow peeked out through the branches. Really close now.

The edge of the woods was right there. No more than twenty or thirty feet before her, it transitioned into someone's backyard, the silhouette of a picnic table vaguely discernible in the patchy light.

She could smell the smoke of the distant fires. The acrid stench of burning rubber. Probably tires.

She swallowed hard. Something didn't feel right.

She stopped again. Some part of her mind trying to reach out for him, trying to feel his presence.

She breathed. Closed her eyes. Flushed all her thoughts away. Ignored the distant sounds of the riot and let stillness fill her head.

Drifting.

Lighter now. Calmer now.

Wind hitching in and blowing out. The empty space of the sky somehow growing bigger in her awareness, so much bigger than the trees around her, bigger than the riot, bigger even than the distant buildings. All those stars some millions of miles away, tiny dots in all that hollow black.

And after a long peaceful moment, words arose from the stillness.

He's close. He's close. Still hiding.

The intuitive leap popped fresh insight into her head, logical deductions rolling forth like an unspooling coil of gauze.

He couldn't leave the cover of the woods so quickly. Couldn't risk exposure. Even the riot offered him no safety. Being naked and bloody, he couldn't really blend in. Not on a campus full of people terrified of him and his crimes, haunted by him day and night, constantly vigilant, angry.

She opened her eyes.

Yes.

Yes.

If she could just keep him pinned down until backup got here, they could corner him. Outnumber him and overwhelm him.

Just can't let him slip away.

Her gut told her to drift a little to the left. Not to move toward the lights ahead.

She obeyed the hunch. Left the picnic table behind. Walked back into the dark. Drifted part of the way back down the hill. Pressed into new territory.

The land leveled out, and she stumbled on some knobby tree roots jutting out of the ground. Stopped under a hulking oak tree and listened again.

Silence surrounded her, even the sounds of the riot somehow shielded from this spot. Probably muffled by the hill more than anything — a wall of dirt between her and the mayhem.

She held still. Scanned the darkness in all directions. Listened to her pulse drum in her ears.

Something creaked above her. A tree branch shifting in the wind. That subtle groan of wood that always reminded her that the trees were alive.

Then something snapped. A branch cracking.

She looked up just as he dove out of the branches and crashed into her.

CHAPTER 81

Loshak hooks his hands under the girl's shoulders. Carries her to the car. Her feet dragging along behind them.

A bloody sphere of bone stares up at him. Shockingly white like bleached teeth underneath the glaze of red.

And she's a small thing in his arms. Cold and bony. Birdlike.

She goes slack as soon as he sets hands on her. Limp as a wet rag.

She must have been out on her feet. In shock, probably. Not fully unconscious, but not really conscious, either.

He veers toward the passenger side.

The exposed skull cap glitters red as they move into the beams of light spearing out of the rental car. That floppy skin dangling behind the wound.

For a second he thinks about trying to pull her scalp up, drape it over her dome. Like that might help somehow.

He swallows. Decides it'd be better to not touch anything. Let the ER handle it. Get her there as fast as possible.

He rips open the passenger door. Shuffles back on heavy feet to get at the opening. Hefting her along with him.

He thrusts from the hips. Flops her down into the seat.

She bounces once and curls into a semi-fetal position. Limbs and neck loose. Every muscle gone flimsy.

Loshak rushes around the front of the car. Legs churning right through the bright barrels of the headlights. Sees the dark splotches of her blood on his coat, on his pants.

He lurches for the driver's seat. Sits down, his legs all folded up, knees knocking against the bottom of the steering wheel. Back twinging against the rigid lumbar support.

He snakes a hand under the seat. Finds the jutting knob there. Shoves the seat backward from Darger's upright position. Feels it settle back and sink under him, jolting his back again as it locks in place.

And then he gets moving.

The car lurches forward. Zipping down the street. Flying through a stop sign. Building speed.

He looks over at her as soon as he's confident that they're on their way to the hospital.

She's bleeding all over the rental car. Red drips weeping from the edges of the open wound. Drizzling onto the upholstery in viscid puddles of dark.

Her eyelids flutter endlessly. Her eyes two screens trying to come on, to open.

But they stay shut.

Maybe that's better.

To not be awake for this, aware of this.

Better.

If she lives long enough to get help.

He takes a hard left at speed. The car slides a little. Rear end fishtailing, straining over the white line into the bike lane, leaning toward the curb.

He wrestles with the wheel. The tires scream. Four warbling screeches forming a discordant harmony.

He lifts his butt up off the seat. Jams all of his weight onto the accelerator. Guns it harder.

And the rubber catches again beneath them. Straightens them out. Hurtles them forward.

The hospital is away from the riot. The opposite side of town from the campus.

That's good. He can avoid that fiery mess entirely. Be there in just a few minutes.

She moans softly. Those eyelids still flitting like her eyes are rolling endlessly behind them. Two broken TV screens endlessly scrolling up.

Light shines ahead of them. The flare of traffic lights and a Walgreens sign looming up from the darkness. A couple sets of taillights like glowing red eyes just before the bigger lights.

The hospital is there. Not far. Up on a hill a half a block or so beyond the pharmacy. Mostly shrouded by trees for now.

Loshak sets his jaw. Muscles flexing in his face and neck.

They race toward the illumination. Faster, faster.

He jerks the wheel again. Veers around a small cluster of cars at an intersection. Jerky motions. Something about the speed pulling him back into his seat now.

A red light flits past above them. There and gone in a blink.

Loshak isn't stopping for anything.

CHAPTER 82

The naked man leapt directly onto her. Latched onto Darger's back like a monkey. Arms coiling around her shoulders. Tugging.

The brunt of his body weight hit a fraction of a second later. Chest bashing into her neck and back. Hammering down on her like her spinal column was a nail.

The force drove her straight down, buckling her legs beneath her.

Folding her up. Smashing her into the ground.

Her knees tucked up into her chest as she hit down. One kneecap clubbing at her chin. The sudden compression squeezing the wind from her lungs. Chest rhythm going choppy.

He groaned on top of her. Rocked up for a beat. One hand clutching at his middle with knuckles curved like claws.

And she realized that she'd jabbed her spiky elbow into his solar plexus upon impact with the ground. An accidental blow that had done some damage.

Fucking good.

His weight came back down right away. He writhed on her back. Slithered on her. Adjusting his position over and over. Arms contracting in that hold around her collarbone.

She swore she could feel his oiliness even through her clothes.

She tried to unball her limbs, but the angles were wrong. Joints all smashed between his bulk and the leaf-strewn dirt. Arms and legs pinned there underneath her.

The gun was there. Somewhere. She could feel its hard lines digging into her chest.

His face pressed down into the back of her neck. Wet lips smearing the hairline. Juicy.

The pressure pushed her face into the black soil. Scoured dead leaves against her cheek.

And then his hands moved up. Fled the collarbone. Fingers crawling for the softer flesh. Callused palms seeking after her throat.

She shuddered. Levered an elbow between her ribcage and the ground. Pitched. Rolled herself to the side as hard as she could.

His legs shuffled. Little kicking motions rotating his angle along with her movement. He tried to beat her to the spot. Stay fully on top. Like Royce Gracie grappling for superior position in the Octagon.

Darger twisted hard. Managed to break his hold partially. Wrenching away from those rough fingers.

She got up onto her left hip. Tried to swing her right arm up. Point the gun at him. Again, the angle made it awkward.

He grabbed the limb with both hands while it was still bent. One hand on the wrist. The other clutching the meat of her upper arm. He locked it there in a chicken wing position.

The gun still useless. For now.

But she'd stop his advancing chokehold. Now she needed to get out from under him.

She tried jerking forward. Hoping to free her arm from his clutches.

His grip held fast. His weight came down on her harder. Mashed her into the ground again.

Lungs imploding inside. Burning. Screaming.

Darger felt her ribcage sort of bounce up from its touch

down, and then his torso was there. Crushing it right back down. Squeezing her flat like a chicken fried steak.

And he was hitting her.

Right hand releasing her upper arm.

Fist banging into her temple over and over.

Thunder rolling in her head.

Darkness creeping in around the perimeter of her vision.

He leaned back farther to try to get more leverage into his shots.

Darger thrashed. Pistoned arms and legs in unison to try to throw herself forward.

He lowered himself again. Pressed his chest tightly to her back.

Grinding her into the dirt.

Shallow breaths fluttered in and out of Darger's open mouth. Hot wind on wet teeth.

The gun was pinned underneath her again. Sharp edge of the barrel trying to burrow into her sternum.

He drove a forearm across her shoulder blades. Jammed her harder into the ground.

And he held his head down close. Lips brushing at her neck again. Sliding to the right. Mouth right next to her ear.

And he giggled. A little gurgle of laughter rippling out of him. Lurching. Uneven.

The mouth retreated. Lifted once more. Weight relenting just a touch as he adjusted his position again.

She brought her skull straight back as hard as she could.

Pounded that hard dome of bone into his face. Felt his front teeth shatter at her touch. Soft flesh pulped against the broken bits. Total collapse.

Thick runnels of blood jetted onto her neck. Shockingly hot against her skin.

And his weight was gone from her shoulders all at once. His whole body shuffling back from her.

He screamed. Scrabbling back into the thicker undergrowth. Kicking up leaves and dirt.

Darger heaved in a big breath. Jolted into an upright position. Spun to face him.

The shadows had taken him. Swathed him in gloom once more.

She swung her Glock toward where the shrubs jostled. Aimed at the murky center of the disturbed plant life.

And squeezed the trigger.

CHAPTER 83

Loshak peels the girl out of the passenger seat. Tacky blood adhering her to the upholstery somewhat. Skin and bone prying free from the soft fabric with a faint zipping sound.

He drapes her against his chest for a second. Adjusts his grip. Starts backpedaling.

Her feet drag along behind them again, scuffing over the blacktop, jostling when they hit stray flecks of gravel.

The open car door glares at Loshak as he shuffles backward, the narrow slice of light from the dome light shrinking in slow motion as he moves away from it.

He drags her over a curb. Over a bed of woodchips surrounding an immature tree about as thick as a cigar.

The lamps over the parking lot burn bright. Shiny on her slimy red skull. The illumination strange after driving so long in the dark.

They reach the sidewalk leading up to the loading bay at the back of the hospital. The final straightaway. The glass doors here lead directly into the emergency room.

A harsh glow spreads out from the glass doors. An elongated puddle of fluorescent light. Loshak pulls the girl to within the rim of the brilliance. Squints his eyes and keeps going.

Back twinging. Wrist throbbing where it loops under one of her arms. Eyes stinging as white light spears them.

Almost there.

Almost there.

Almost there.

And there are workers clad in scrubs there as soon as he hits the doors. Surrounding him. Helping him. Reaching out purple nitrile gloved hands and taking her from him.

Whisking her away into a cordoned-off area beyond the receptionist's desk. Careening off to the left and out of sight.

Gone. Just like that.

He takes a shaky breath. Eyes and lips jittering. Feels like he might cry.

It feels wrong letting her go.

A hollow opening in his chest.

As empty as he's ever felt.

But he made it. He'd gotten her here. Hopefully in time.

He stands in the gleaming lobby and breathes for a second. Hands cupping his hips. Chest puffing and shrinking. Light reflecting from the pale tile floor. Too bright.

He shambles back to the car on legs gone numb. The night feeling chilly around him. Cold and vacant.

He closes the passenger door. Fumbles at the opposite door handle for a second. Fingers atwitter with pins and needles.

Plops down in the driver's seat. Head still buzzing. Full of black noise.

He radios in the plate number from the car he'd spotted a little less than a block behind the Jetta. A red Camaro that he knows is the perp's car. The only other car parked on that side of the street within two blocks, and the macho make and model fits the profile.

He's surprised by how normal his voice sounds speaking into the walkie-talkie. Calmer and saner than he feels inside. Even if he's breathing a little heavy.

Still, he has a hard time concentrating on the words coming through from the dispatcher. A quavering babble like Charlie Brown's teacher.

But he picks out a name.
Thomas Lee Walker.

CHAPTER 84

The muzzle flash flared and dimmed at the end of Darger's arm. The tiny fire flitting orange light, casting strange shadows everywhere.

Two shots.

Two cracks splitting the quiet night.

Two rounds of orange strobing over the tree branches.

Then the light was gone and the darkness plunged to something blacker around her. Thicker. Impenetrable.

Darger stared into the nothingness. Tried to listen over the shrill tones still ringing in her ears.

Nothing stirred. Not that she could hear.

She stepped forward. Heart thrumming.

Her eyes readjusted to the dark as she crept onward. Contours congealing in the void.

The camera in her head seemed to zoom in on that cleft in the thickest of the ferns. The curved opening in the plants that had thrashed just seconds before.

The place where he'd been.

The place she'd aimed the Glock and fired.

It held still now. Stagnant and eerie.

Each step inched her closer. Gun still pointing the way. Finger resting on the trigger guard. Ready to move that fraction of an inch again if need be.

She swallowed as she drew to within an arm's length of the shadowy spot. Steps going slower now. Stride shortening some, too.

Still nothing stirred among the fronds. No sound

discernible over that buzzing aftereffect of the gunshots like cotton shoved into her ears.

Is he there?

Hiding close by?

She took a big, shaky breath. Held it for a second. Let it go. Then she stepped into the shadows.

CHAPTER 85

Andre sucks in a wavering breath. Listens through the walls of the trunk.

After a bunch of commotion, all has gone quiet around the Jetta. Eerie.

The silence rings in his ears. Screaming emptiness blaring there like a siren.

The sounds jumble in his memory, replay themselves out of order. Everything dull. Muffled by the metal encasing him.

He remembers car doors slamming nearby.

Two gunshots.

Voices.

Tobi screaming like a banshee.

And then a car's engine ripping away. Fast.

After that, the quiet bloomed until it was everything. The only thing. A vast abyss stretching outward from the dark cell of this trunk.

Did someone else intervene?

Or did the Couple Killer shoot Tobi and leave him here? Forgotten. Trapped in the trunk with his arms bound behind his back.

Andre licks his lips. Sets his jaw. Tries to force words to his throat.

He tongues the roof of his mouth. The tip of the muscle tapping at the hard palate like a warm snail antenna. His teeth part.

But no sound comes out of him. Just a little puff of breath.

He closes his eyes. Feels beads of sweat leak down his face

as his muscles shift.

His shoulders ache. Pulled funny by his weight smashing his arms behind his back.

Another shaky breath heaves into him. He tries to push the panic down. Tries to focus.

Just needs to yell "Hello?" and see if anyone's there. For better or worse.

His tongue starts tapping again. His lips pop as they open. His diaphragm flexes to shove the words out.

Something rumbles beyond the trunk. A diesel engine drawing up near the Jetta and stopping.

A door slams.

Footsteps clap over the pavement. Rush toward the car.

Andre screams.

CHAPTER 86

Pink blotches still float in front of him where the two tongues of flame had burst from the barrel of the gun. Their memory temporarily scorched into his retinas. Misshapen cylinders gliding around his eyeballs.

He scuttles backward like a crab. Tries to be quiet, almost robotic in his motions. Arms staying a little rigid. Slow and steady. Picking out each backward step. Avoiding the animal scrabbling that must have told her where he was before.

Leafy shit brushes over his arms and chest. He holds his torso low. Limboing under the fronds.

Clods of dirt and moss had kicked up from the ground when the bullets hit just shy of his feet. Divots torn out of the earth like a bad golf shot. Explosions of black and green, everything tinged orange in the muzzle's glow.

Now he watches the woman's silhouette behind him as he scoots backward, what he can see of her shape among the gloom and the pink blotches. She stands motionless for a moment, the gun still raised.

Then she presses forward. Coming at him. Careful steps. Still too fast for his liking.

He gets to the edge of the thicker foliage. A breath shuddering into him as the plants cut off beside him.

He stands up in the clear. Runs. Keeping on the balls of his feet. Quieter this way. Those ridges behind his toes softly pattering at the mushy clay, pressing their shape into the yielding earth.

He scans the horizon to his left. A couple of streetlights

glowing over there. The roar of the rioting kids audible in the distance. He runs parallel to it for a while. Tries to think.

He looks back over his shoulder. Can't see the woman's silhouette anymore. But he knows she's there. Coming closer.

And he knows now what to do.

CHAPTER 87

Strobing lights twirl over everything when Loshak returns to the crime scene. Glinting slices of red and blue that elongate over the asphalt and flicker against the tree branches.

He parks the rental not far behind the mess of law enforcement vehicles clogging the street. Gets out and heads for the sedan at the center of all the commotion.

A couple of techs flutter over the scene already. Photographing, mostly, from what he can see. Others pull on bunny suits off to the side. Ready to join in on the frenzy.

Loshak sidles up to Sheriff Kittle and a couple of his men, standing back behind the thin yellow barrier of the police tape next to an ambulance.

"Any word from Darger?" Loshak says, though he figures not.

Kittle shakes his head.

"Got a live one in the trunk, though," one of the deputies says. He's chewing a wad of gum and smiling as he speaks.

Loshak takes a second to process his words, eyes watching those chawing lips as he replays them in his head:

Got a live one in the trunk.

Another victim. The male. Of course.

"You're sure he's alive?"

Kittle and the deputy nod in unison.

The deputy's pink gum waddles in his mouth like a second tongue as he speaks.

"We could hear him thumping and yelling when we first got here, but the trunk is locked. Techs will hopefully find the car keys here in a second."

"Don't the rear seats fold down?" Loshak asks.

"They're supposed to, but the latch is busted." The deputy shrugs. "Figure if they don't find the keys in the next few minutes, we'll have the fire department cut the trunk open."

"The girl," Kittle says, his voice deep. "She going to be OK?"

Loshak swallows and feels a tremor in his Adam's apple. Tries to tell him that he doesn't know.

But yelling near the car turns all heads that way before he gets a chance.

"Got the keys!"

The tech holds up the keyring in the air. Shakes it back and forth and the metal bits jangle out over the quiet.

Then he hustles toward the back of the car. Thrusts the key into the little hole in the center of the trunk. Cranks his hand hard to the right.

The trunk lid glides up with a faint pneumatic hiss.

And then everything is still. All eyes watching that shadowy cell in the back of the Volkswagen.

The tech leans forward. Tips his top half into the breach. Then he stutter-steps back.

A frightened face drifts up into the light. Hovering and blinking there. Eyes swiveling everywhere. The boy in the trunk sitting up.

"You all right?" Loshak calls out from a few feet away.

The kid's head bobs funny. An uneven nod that reminds Loshak of a child.

The tech steps forward. Hooks a hand under an elbow to help the kid out of the back of the trunk. Another tech grabs the opposite arm.

His hands are tied, Loshak realizes.

They all watch as the kid rotates around until he's sitting on the lip of the trunk, and then he's stepping down onto flat ground.

The pair of techs hustle him over to the back of the ambulance.

"What's your name, son?" the Sheriff says, walking alongside now. He's already got a utility tool out, ready to cut the twine around the student's wrists.

The kid just stares at him for a second. Some catatonic blankness adorning his features. Then he blinks and seems to wake up.

"I'm Andre."

CHAPTER 88

Darger darted forward. Gun swinging around. Heart thudding.

She'd heard him. Just for a second.

Somewhere up ahead.

She paused briefly when she saw the craggy spot where her bullets had torn out clods of dirt. The rounds had angled into the ground. Left pockmarks.

Missed.

Probably.

No blood spilled here, anyway.

She beat her way through the thicket. Reached the edge where the ferns died back again to that clear forest floor of pine needles and crushed leaves.

Nothing.

Shit.

He'd slipped away somehow. Gotten clear of the brush and made a run for it.

But he can't be far.

She lifted her gaze from the ground. Scanned the woods in all directions. Breath pinched to silence at the back of her throat. Concentration on the woods around her total.

Her eyes crawled over everything. Touching every line and curve in the darkness. Ears sharp.

The riot sounds had grown tiny here. Like a TV turned almost all the way down in the next room — the muffled crowd noise from a football game sounding about flea-sized. Something in the landscape must be muffling the din again. She was thankful for that.

Now she just needed him to make some noise.

When she'd done a full circle, she stopped. Waited. Listened.

As if on cue, his footsteps burst to life somewhere ahead of her. Crashing through the brush. Louder than before. Something wild in them.

She listened for another second to try to place the direction, pointing her arm that way. Somewhat ahead and to her right. That surprised her.

He's running for the city after all?

She jogged that way. Trying to stay quiet enough to follow the sound.

And before long he appeared there. A running shadow. Speeding toward that line where the trees gave way to the glow of the few city lights still burning.

Darger lifted the gun. Tried to line up a shot.

But he kept veering to avoid the trees. Surprisingly agile for a naked man. Changing directions. Juking this way and that.

She picked up speed. Tried to close the distance.

He seemed to sense her then. Upper back tightening. Neck craning his head back for a quick look.

His shoulder clipped a tree trunk, and he went down. Shoulders kind of bulldozing into the mossy ground. Collarbone plowing into the earth.

Darger clenched her teeth. Tried to press the advantage.

But he was up again and going right away. Like his legs had never stopped churning as he went down. Just kept rolling. Kept twitching. Pushing him upward and onward.

He broke through the edge of the woods and ran into the light.

CHAPTER 89

Kelly's phone rumbles in her pocket. Draws her eyes away from the burning pile of mannequins and wicker lawn furniture — the bonfire that dominates the center of Walnut Street.

She takes out her phone. Fingers the screen.

She notices others on the street doing the same out of the corner of her eye.

All those phones lifting from pockets. All those glowing screens glinting in the dark. Brightness flaring from every set of hands, or so it seems.

Something is happening here.

She refocuses on the screen. Eyes scanning the words there. Trying to absorb them.

Red text blares at the head of the emergency message.

SMU EMERGENCY ALERT — Suspect identified in the Campus Killer case. Thomas Lee Walker. 29-year-old white male. 5'11", 180 pounds. Shaved head. Wanted by police for multiple felonies. Considered dangerous. Last seen fleeing active crime scene in state of undress. Bloody. Possibly injured. On foot near campus now — in the Park Woods neighborhood moving toward the school. Do not approach or attempt to apprehend. Call 911 immediately to report suspect's location. If you are safe, stay where you are until authorities arrive. Otherwise, try to get to a safe location. Click link for photo.

Kelly moves her thumb to the blue bit of text at the tail end of the message. Presses it.

A wheel turns in the center of the screen. Loading. Her mind whirs, the two-second wait stretching out.

Holy shit. They've identified him.

The faceless creeper I've imagined crawling into my window, over my crystals, so many times…

They, like, actually know who he is.

And then his face appears on that rectangle in her hand. Filling the screen almost all at once.

The top of the photo emerges right away, revealing his visage from the mouth up. His chin and neck filling in a fraction of a second later.

A driver's license photo from the look of it. Something stiff about it.

She studies the features. Hands going icy around the phone.

Dark hair just longer than a buzz cut.

Hollow cheeks.

Thin lips.

Straight nose.

One of those chiseled faces. Every little curve of muscle visible through the flesh. Everything taut. Angular. Severe. Almost unhealthy-looking, like he might be veering toward emaciation if he skipped a single meal.

The dark eyes draw in her gaze. Two black pits in his face. Something dead in them. Something predatory.

But then that cold feeling in her hands relents. Dies back. She feels the heat of the fire again.

She blinks. Looks at him again.

He's just a man, isn't he?

Just like any other person she'd pass on the street. Another face in the crowd. Another ant in the hill.

And now that he's been drawn out into the light, maybe he's not so scary.

CHAPTER 90

He sprints through a backyard. Picking up speed.

Crosses a flagstone patio. Hops a bed of flowers. Hits the open space leading up to the house.

Anger pulses in his head. The aggression that fuels him. Courses through him. Drives him onward. A restless thing perpetually knifing forward like a shark.

Moonlight glints on his pumping arms. Slicked with sweat. Shiny and purple in the partial light.

He smears one hand at his mouth. Sees his fingers come away smeared with thick red.

Even beaten and bloodied, they can't sap the fight out of him. Can't drain the fire from his belly, the hatred from his heart. Never ever.

He'll run and hide. Survive the night.

And he'll be back. Again and again, he'll be back.

Unstoppable.

He rushes into the shadows along the house, and that violet glow on his skin is vanquished. The dark swallowing him again. Obscuring him to murky grayscale.

His feet thump over another slab of patio and then a bed of rugged gravel. The details of the building coming clear now that he's up close.

Vinyl siding shoots up the side of the house. Parallel lines of textured cladding reaching for the peaked roof.

A grid of brickwork occupies the bottom three or four feet. Windows cut into the mortar.

A suburban home indistinguishable from any other.

For just a second he imagines himself plunking a rock through the panes of glass. Crawling in.

He could hide. Check on the homeowners snug in their beds.

He pictures his naked body standing in their bedroom doorway. A faceless shadow lit from behind. Blood smeared on his face and hands and chest.

Guess who just popped in for a late-night visit?

But with that FBI bitch not so far behind him, he can't risk it. Keeps running.

He rounds a back corner. Hurtles along the side of the house.

His feet mash at sod now. Grass squishing between his toes. A row of tall bushes brushing at one shoulder.

He spills out into the front yard. Moves toward the street. Out of the shade of the houses and the trees surrounding them.

And the land opens up before him. He can see now in all directions. View unblocked.

He stops for just a second in the middle of the street. Turns his head and takes it all in. Breath dry and harsh in his throat.

He stands in a small island of light. Four streetlights and the gleaming red of a gas station sign touching this small swath of land.

But the dark gapes back in all directions. An ebon wall hung up along the edges of the lit space. Looks like black fog creeping closer and closer.

Good.

Dark is good.

When you're naked and running from a federal agent, dark is very good.

He jolts forward again. Runs toward the dark end of the street. Wants to put some distance between himself and the woman before he cuts through some more yards and maybe finds a place to hunker down and catch his breath.

Has to keep moving, though. Can never rest for long.

This whole place will be crawling with police soon. Some for the riot and some for him.

A bunch of goons done up in riot gear. Faces hidden behind Plexiglas shields like the cowards they are. Batons clenched in their tiny fists.

His jaw flexes as he pictures them. New heat flooding in his head.

His feet chew up the asphalt. The street sliding by beneath him. Houses scrolling by on each side. Faster, faster.

He reaches an intersection just past the last of the streetlights. The spot where the electricity shears off to black nothing.

And he leans forward. Pushes himself harder. Crosses the line.

He plunges into the darkness. Rolls down the hollow of the shadowy street like a bowling ball thrust down the pale wood of the lane.

The start of a smile twitches in the corners of his mouth. Threatening. Not quite overtaking his lips.

Something interrupts the grin before it can fully form.

Something moving in the distance. Brightness rising from the street. Coruscating above the asphalt.

And then his vantage point adjusts. Buildings sliding out of the way as he runs. And there are more of them.

Dots of light piercing the night. Orange thrashing. A charred smell strong in his nostrils.

Fire.

Multiple fires.

Not just couches and cars anymore.

The campus is burning.

CHAPTER 91

Darger's eyes scanned everywhere as she ran. Crawling over the knobby shape of a tarp-draped grill and the skeletal meshwork silhouettes of wrought iron patio furniture in the dark.

No outline of a shaved head over broad shoulders. No pale caterpillar glow of his naked skin in the moonlight.

He wasn't there. Already gone. Pulled out in front of her as she got bogged down in the thick stuff at the edge of the woods.

Shit.

She bit down hard on her bottom lip. Thin skin pinched between incisors. Then she made her teeth let go.

But it's OK. It's OK.

He can't run forever.

Darger's mind worked at the algebra of what he'd be thinking. Fitting together shards of his profile with the varying demands of the situation like knobby jigsaw puzzle pieces.

He'll want to get out into the open of the street. Pick up speed. Put as much distance between us as possible.

And then he'll want to find his way into the dark. Disappear into the cityscape.

Probably find his way inside a building eventually. Get dressed if he can. Once his location is obscured enough.

Next he would want to get a vehicle. But he won't be getting that far.

She sprinted out into the light in front of the house as her mind whirred. Head swiveling to something flitting off to her right. Feet stopping beneath her.

It was him. Running. Naked flesh looking glossy.

He crossed into the dark place where the glow of the streetlights cut out.

She lifted her gun. Lined up a shot.

But she lowered the weapon again right away.

He was too far away. A moving target shrouded in murk.

She needed to get closer.

CHAPTER 92

He hears the bitch's footsteps behind him. Heavy fed boots clobbering the street. Clopping like horse hooves that echo over the empty neighborhood.

Shit.

He looks back to confirm it.

Sees her bounding over the asphalt. Sprinting for him. That gun still clasped in her right hand.

Shit. Shit. Shit.

He'd hoped to dive off the roadway before she could catch up. Retreat into the shadows. Worm into a hidey-hole for a bit. Maybe find something to cover his nuts. Pants, preferably.

Now he needs to lose her again before he hides. Create some space between them. A diversion. Something.

He runs toward one of the fires in the street. A pile of furniture engulfed in flames. Sofa. Loveseat. Recliner. A couple of beanbag chairs melting in the middle of it all.

He wonders if the owners consented to the blaze. Were all the pieces from the same living room set? Or had the mob broken into multiple houses and looted some home furnishings for fuel?

Something bony moves near the edge of the fire. Then another. Makes his eyes stretch wider.

There are people there, he realizes. Maybe a dozen or two — could be more beyond them but he can't see anything past the fire yet.

They surround the blistering furniture. Standing around the flames.

No.

Not standing.

They mill around. Walking this way and that like zombies.

Something restless in their body language. Something pointless in it, too.

He chews his lip.

Maybe... just maybe...

He can get swept up in the rioters. Get himself lost among them. Break away from the fed on his tail.

Safe in the angry mob. Just another snarling hateful face in their midst. Worshiping dirt and fire and destruction, for tonight at least.

Ironic.

Moving among them will be a risk. His initial instinct is to avoid them.

But he's up against it now. Crushed between the mob and the FBI agent.

He licks his lips. Asks himself again about the wisdom of this move.

These kids are angry. Somehow changed. Hardly the tame creatures he has preyed upon over the years.

They are something else now. Something lean and hard. And if they sense him, they will turn on him...

But no.

He sees a few glowing screens among those roving zombies around the fire. And he knows.

Knows that they're still the same under the surface. Still buttery soft in the underbelly.

House cats.

Tame.

Tonight is just another party to them. A celebration of destruction. They're drunk on it.

But soon they'll grow bored and go back to their memes, their video games, their Instas and whatever-the-fucks. They'll go back to behaving like the world exists to entertain them.

He takes a breath and runs into the crowd circling the fire.

CHAPTER 93

The naked man hit the crowd along the fire and morphed into another shadow there. A silhouette tucked among so many others.

Darger blinked. Scanned for the telltale bald head. Scoured for any sign of his gait. Anyone running. Anything.

Nothing.

She'd lost him.

A lump bobbed upward in her throat. Made it hard to swallow.

She ran for the flames. Eyes still swiveling everywhere. Trying to make his shape form there among the sets of shoulders.

Filmy orange light danced over everything. Flickered on all those faces. Painted thick shadows under chins and brows and erased them just as quickly.

Up close, Darger could see that the crowd extended beyond the bonfire, stretching far past what she could first see.

A smattering of kids lined the street in haphazard chunks from here to the next fire some block or two on. A meandering mob veiled in shadow. Bits of it roving here. Other parts loafing there. It looked like a collection of outdoor festivalgoers slowly making their way toward one of the stages.

Human bodies everywhere. Standing. Walking. Ribbons of them stretching as far as the eye could see.

Too many people.

He could be anywhere.

And then she had her badge out, unfolded and raised, and

she was yelling into the mob.

"FBI! The killer is here among you. Naked and bloody and trying to hide."

The words kept rolling out of her. Repeating the same concept in different phrasing. Explaining that she'd chased him into the crowd. That he was here.

Right here. Right now.

A murmur began to spread through the ranks. A buzz like a beehive swelling among them as the message spread.

And all the heads began to turn.

CHAPTER 94

He runs through the throng of students. Smells ash and beer and melted plastic and vodka here. Something sharp and biting on top of it all that he thinks might be pepper spray or tear gas clinging to the clothes of those exposed to it. A swirl of uprising odors.

He slices right through the first mob around the fire. Slows as he gets a few rows in.

And he sees that the mob stretches on from here. A partially broken line of kids reaching out for the horizon. More fires dotting the way.

A huge gathering to get lost in. It's perfect.

He strides among them. Part of them. Anonymous. Free.

Laughing inside but keeping his face stern. This protest is serious business, after all.

He works his way another twenty-five or so feet in. Veering toward one side of the street and then the other. A serpentine path he hopes will throw off any sense the fed back there might have of his gliding away from her.

The chatter seems to get louder around him as he advances. Excitement spreading among the ranks.

And then the heads around him start turning. Confused swiveling at first. Looking around. Finally locking onto him one by one.

And it's like a switch flips among the herd.

The crowd turns on him. Staggers for him. Swarms over him.

All of them at once. No warning.

Kicking and punching. No hesitation.

He backpedals up over the curb. Onto the sidewalk. Tries to fend them off.

But there are too many. Way too many.

All those torsos closing around him. Hands ripping at him like crab claws. Clutching and pulling and scratching. Trying to hold on.

Trying to pull me apart.

Faces dark. All their faces dark gray smears. Ashen cavities where their features should be.

He dodges backward. Bounces off the bodies behind him.

Fingernails gash his chest. Slash red lines there. Claw marks. Clumps of his skin balled up under someone's nails.

He sets his feet wide. Tries to punch back. Throws a wild haymaker into the encroaching darkness. Somehow hits nothing.

Off balance. Pushed backward.

A cold set of hands reaches out and grabs him. Bigger and stronger than the rest. Clasping him by the upper arms. Managing to hold on.

They lift him up onto his tiptoes. Tip him and throw him down toward the concrete. Dumping him to the ground.

He careens. Twists and falls backward. Slams into the cold cement.

Something pops in his lower back as he hits down. A flash of heat flaring in his spinal column and going frigid all at once.

Cold and numb radiating outward. Thrumming like electricity.

He grimaces. Feels one whimper leave his lips and nose. Quiets himself just as quickly.

And then the feet start grinding down. Rubber soles pounding into his chest, belly, arms, legs. Clubbing him like hammerheads.

Pain detonating everywhere at once.

The sounds of the impact drumming through him. Vibrating in his bones, in his teeth.

He stares up into the dark. Into the lacework of light shining down through all those pistoning limbs. Only able to see the faintest shadow of his attacker. All of them jelling into one being now.

He's small and powerless. At the mercy of the crowd.

The many-legged creature stomps him into the ground. Hateful. Powerful.

They're like me now.

Ribs crunch. Something in his breastbone pops and gives.

They're breaking me.

I'm falling apart.

He holds up his hand as though to block the feet from raining down on him. Fingers splayed. A glimmer of light filtering through them.

A hand grabs his wrist. A boot comes ripping.

His forearm splinters in front of him. Shatters.

Snaps in the middle. Bends the wrong way.

Spiky bones protruding from the flesh like two spears.

Blood weeping. Spurting. Jetting onto his chest and neck.

He breathes hard. Ribcage shuddering. Hot blood spreading over all of him.

The feet keep coming. Pelting. Flattening. Smashing his body into the ground.

His flesh and bone grinding against the gritty cement of the sidewalk.

Skin grated away. Granulating. Pulverized little by little.

And it's OK in a way. It's OK.

Because they're like me, and I am like them. Their strength is my strength.

In a way.

In a way.

This is what he thinks as the boot treads crush his face into the grainy texture of the concrete.

Smashing his skull like a cantaloupe.

Collapsing.

Caving in.

And the world will cower.

Whimper.

Tremble.

The world will tremble when they see how strong we are.

Bright redness gleams in both of his eyes. Filling the scope of his vision.

Flashing like ruddy lightning every time one of the shoes comes down on his broken head.

Peeling the shards of cranium farther and farther apart. Red jelly oozing through the cracks.

Tremble.

Tremble before the mighty.

And then it all goes black.

Finally.

CHAPTER 95

Darger saw the mob flex around the fallen figure of the killer. Caught just a flash of his sheening scalp reflecting the firelight, and then an angry thrashing mass of limbs closed over him like a fist.

She staggered closer. Pressed into the crowd. Breath hot and dry in her throat.

She briefly considered firing her gun into the air, the way Dixon had done to scare off the hooligans outside the Dairy Mart. But the streets had been nearly empty then. Firing a gun in a tightly packed mob could only cause more harm, she thought. The stampede would trample many.

More bodies piled on the man, and they were still coming. Still flocking to this one spot on the pavement. Angling toward the fallen killer. Crushing together. Desperate to reach the center.

Darger got swept up in the wave.

The press of bodies contracted and relaxed against her like a muscle. Inhaling and exhaling. And each time she was squeezed tighter. Found less room to maneuver. Less room to breathe.

The mob moaned around her. Some sick ecstasy plain in the voices. Wailing and mewling. Eyes open all the way.

She had to get out. Couldn't risk getting crushed or trampled now.

She timed it. Waited for the release of breath. Waited for that momentary respite.

And then she probed for the soft spot in the crush. Levered

her arm between torsos. Turned herself sideways. Slipped into gap after gap. Knifed her way through the bulldozing horde.

She spilled out into the open on the second such contraction and release. Stumbling over asphalt and sucking breath. Chest quivering on the inhales.

Free of the mob, she turned back. Saw the knot of bodies as one organism. One thrashing beast. Full of fury.

The Couple Killer was somewhere in there. Naked and bleeding. At the mercy of the angry creature squatting over him. No longer hidden in the shadows.

Darger pulled her phone out and called for backup, knowing they'd be too late.

EPILOGUE

By the time the Riot Unit rolled through town, assisted by the National Guard, five people were dead, Thomas Lee Walker included. Dozens more were seriously injured. Between the Sheriff's Department and SMU Campus Police, nearly two hundred arrests were made. The damage to physical property was estimated at over a million dollars.

Darger watched the footage replay on the TV as she packed her suitcase, struck again by the amount of destruction done in a single night. Shot after shot of streets lit only by the strobing glow of fires: a car here, a recliner there. The next clip was from the following morning, the burning car now a smoking, blackened husk. Broken glass in the street glittered in the sunlight like shards from a disco ball.

It was frightening to think of the thin veneer that kept this from happening all the time. The way all the rules simply vanished once people felt like a faceless part of the crowd.

And bits of the riot still burst to life now and then in Darger's head. She could still smell the tang of the tear gas mixing with the acrid smoke of burning plastic and rubber. Could still hear the echoes of blaring car alarms and shattering glass. But over all of that, she heard the sounds of fists striking flesh. Of boot heels shattering bone. Of those voices moaning in rapture as Thomas Lee Walker's head came apart.

She knew they hadn't been thinking, the people who'd killed Walker. They'd been operating on animal instinct. A nameless urge for violence that came from deep inside. Swept up in the manic bloodlust of the mob. A wounded creature wanted to strike back, lash out, wreak havoc and destruction.

Men like Thomas Lee Walker embraced that kind of violence outright. Lived to inflict pain.

In a sense his end was a fitting one — a brutal man struck down in brutal fashion. Somehow, that didn't make her feel any better.

The local news ended, and Darger couldn't help but feel relieved. She wouldn't mind a break from the nonstop rehashing of the riot and of Walker's death. That loop of images on the screen only fed the one inside her head.

An orchestral jingle swelled, and then a booming male voice blared out from the TV.

"This is a Newsline Special Report."

The fancy animated news logo was replaced by a familiar face. Jillian Barrow walked slowly toward the camera as she delivered her lines.

"Good evening. I'm Jillian Barrow, and tonight we'll be delving into the case of Thomas Lee Walker. A man described by those who knew him as a doting father, a devoted husband, a trusted friend. But police say he was also something else." Barrow stopped walking and perched on top of a desk. "A serial killer."

The next segment was overlaid with drone footage of the SMU campus. A sweeping shot that flew past the trees and brick buildings. Students meandered below, probably unaware they were being filmed.

"Our story takes us to Remington Hills, a sleepy college town in southern Michigan, nestled in a lazy bend of the Muktypoke River. The residents of this peaceful suburban haven are relative strangers to violent crime. They have their share of drunk driving and misdemeanor drug offenses, but the streets are considered safe. Or so they thought. For all that provincial tranquility was about to be shattered by a string of gruesome and shocking murders."

Photos of the first two victims appeared on the screen.

"August 19th. Shannon Kole and Mark Terry, both 22 years old, have just returned from an outing with friends. Parked in a secluded area on the edge of town, they have no idea they are about to become the first two victims of the man dubbed 'The Couple Killer.' Mark is forced into the trunk at gunpoint, forced to listen to the brutal assault of Shannon just inches away. Powerless to stop it. After raping Shannon, the killer shoots both victims in the head."

Still resting on the edge of the desk, Barrow steepled her fingers together.

"Over the coming months, there are four more attacks, each more brutal than the last. The town is left reeling. Investigators, mystified. Very few had any hope The Couple Killer would be caught."

Barrow paused, turned to face a different camera.

"And then, last night, a bombshell announcement out of Remington Hills. In what appears to be a bizarre twist of fate, the man police now believe to be responsible for these heinous crimes is dead."

Now they cut to footage from the press conference where Chief Fleming ran through the circumstances of Walker's death.

"Two task force members participating in a strategic stakeout detail heard screams and proceeded to investigate. On the scene, they discovered Walker, in a state of undress and covered in blood, in the midst of attacking a female victim. Walker fled the scene on foot, and one task force member pursued while the other secured medical attention for the victim. As the chase proceeded, Walker ended up in the Elm

Neighborhood, which was one of the central points of the rioting. It is believed that the citizens in the area recognized Walker from an alert sent out over the university's emergency SMS system, and an attempt was made by these civilians to apprehend him. A violent struggle ensued, and Thomas Lee Walker was killed."

The screen switched back to Barrow, her face a mask of solemnity.

"An extraordinary story that only gets stranger still. To most people, the stereotypical serial killer is a loner. A social outcast on the fringes of society, stalking his victims like a lone wolf. But Thomas Lee Walker, the man alleged to be the infamous 'Couple Killer' is proving those theories wrong, " Barrow said. "We asked Dr. Margaret Prescott, one of the nation's leading criminologists, how Walker fits into the standard serial killer paradigm."

Darger rolled her eyes the moment her former boss's face appeared on-screen. How had they gotten her so fast? Did the news channels all have her on speed dial?

Or perhaps, knowing Prescott, it was the other way around.

"It's a grand oversimplification to assume all serial killers are these outsider types," Prescott said. "In fact, it's not all that uncommon for them to have a family. A wife and kids. To have friends. We've seen this with Dennis Rader, the BTK Killer. With Joseph DeAngelo Jr., the Golden State Killer. With Peter Sutcliffe, the Yorkshire Ripper. There are countless examples of this type of perpetrator being capable of living quite an ordinary life. They can be very adept at hiding their darker side from pretty much everyone. Except their victims, of course."

"How is that possible?" Barrow asked. "How can someone hide something like that from the people who are closest to them?"

"I think these are men who are very skilled at compartmentalizing. They are fathers and husbands and coworkers during the day. And creeping terror at night. They are living embodiments of Dr. Jekyll and Mr. Hyde."

A photograph of Walker filled the screen now. A gym selfie from one of his social media accounts, by the looks of it.

Darger studied the face, thinking about how Carrie Dockett had described him.

He could have been one of my professors or the guy who sold us our movie tickets.

And it was true. He was, above all, a normal-looking man. Or had been, before the mob had their way with his features.

Darger shivered then, remembering the sight of the broken body left behind once the Riot Unit had cleared the streets. He'd barely looked human in the end, all smashed and bloody. Like a giant hole puncher had divoted his face. Turned him to roadkill.

Barrow's special report was focusing on Walker's background now. Showing photographs of the home he'd grown up in, on the edges of Coldwater, Michigan. Another photo lifted from social media, Darger guessed, which showed Walker holding a little girl. Her face was blurred out.

Now the screen transitioned to a picture of Karen Walker, Thomas's wife, followed by footage of her exiting her house, shielding her face from the cameras as she tried to make her way to her car.

Darger's stomach clenched.

The press was going to put that woman through the wringer, perhaps even more so since her husband was dead. His story was over. So they'd flock to the living other half. Demand answers where there probably were none.

"Call me naive, but I'd like to imagine that if my husband

were a vicious sexual sadist, that I'd have at least an inkling," Barrow was saying.

Prescott chuckled.

"I'm sure we'd all like to believe that."

Darger squeezed her fists. It was already starting. Outcry that Walker's wife "should have known" who her husband was. That she was somehow complicit. But Darger didn't think that was so. Didn't think it was fair to make an innocent woman pay for the crimes of her husband.

Darger's phone rang, and she glanced at the screen, making sure it was someone she knew and not one of the media vultures scrounging around for a quote. It was a video call from Owen, and Darger was glad to have an excuse to turn the trash on the TV off.

She pressed the "Answer" icon and held the phone up. Owen's face appeared on the screen, smiling with some note of concern present in the wrinkles around his eyes.

"Hey."

"OK, so I'm just going to get this out of the way," Owen said, skipping right past the formalities. "I'm an idiot. You were right. I was wrong. Now how about them Cowboys?"

Darger laughed.

"What are you talking about?"

Owen tipped his head back and heaved out a breath.

"Well, even though I thought you were way off base, I took your advice anyway. Talked to my mom and tried to gently float the idea of Claude having things in his past that she didn't know about."

"Uh-huh."

"And she's no dummy. She knows me. She asked me right off if I'd been poking around in Claude's life." Owen paused and ran his fingers through his hair. "So I admitted that I had *maybe* looked into one or two things and *possibly* uncovered some stuff I thought she should know. She got kinda mad then. Told me I was out of line, crossing boundaries I had no business crossing. I interrupted and asked if she knew Claude was a deadbeat dad."

Darger winced.

"What happened?"

"She got real quiet. And then she said I didn't know what I was talking about. So I showed her what I'd found. She wouldn't even look at it. She just said that she'd appreciate if I didn't bring this up to Claude, because it would only upset him. And I realized that she knew. She already knew. I couldn't believe it. So I asked how she could marry a man who'd abandoned his only child."

"Oof."

"Yeah. Well, like I said. I'm an idiot," Owen said, scratching at his stubble. "If I hadn't had my head stuck so far up my own ass, I would have read the signs. Considered the broader range of possibilities. Known that my mother wouldn't overlook such a thing without good reason. So she told me how it was. That Claude had only been seventeen when he got his high school girlfriend pregnant. How their parents forced them to give the baby up for adoption. That he regrets it still to this day. Feels like he should have done more to fight it."

"Oh," Darger said. "Wow."

Owen nodded.

"So anyway, I owe you one."

"What for?"

"For talking sense into me. Or trying to. And I'm sorry for accusing you of not being on my side." Owen closed his eyes and shook his head. "I mean, if it weren't for you, I probably would have gone in with guns a-blazin', only to find out both barrels were loaded with blanks. And just imagine if I had tried to make contact with his daughter. Then I really would have made a mess."

"So does this mean you're cool with Claude?"

"I wouldn't go that far…"

Darger snorted.

"But I'm willing to give him a chance," Owen said, shrugging. "I'm not unreasonable."

There was a knock at the door, and Darger glanced at the time.

"Well listen, I'm about to head to the airport. See you in a few hours?"

"OK. Have a good flight. I love you."

"Love you, too."

Darger hung up as she opened the door. Loshak shuffled in, dragging his suitcase behind him.

"You ready to go?"

"Just about." Darger went to the bed, tossed the rest of her belongings into the suitcase, and zipped it shut. "How's Tobi? Did you get to see her?"

Loshak nodded.

"The doctors were able to reattach her scalp. She'll probably have some numbness and maybe even paralysis. They were able to reattach the four main arteries there, but sometimes they don't function right after this kind of trauma. There might be more surgeries down the line. Skin grafts, if the arteries aren't providing proper blood flow to support the tissue. Still, she's lucky and she knows it."

They fell quiet. The wall clock ticked out a few seconds between them.

More of those images burst inside Darger's head. Flashes of the riot. Fire and violence. Dead faces in the crime scene photos. Waxy skin. Purpled flesh around the eyes.

Loshak blinked hard and looked at the floor. Maybe he was thinking the same thing.

"She'll live," he said, his voice going gravelly. "Can't say that for all of 'em."

☾

Tobi sits up straight in her hospital bed. Adjusts the hand mirror to look at her scalp again.

The blue crinkles reflecting back at her look withered. Saggy. Wilted like a plant that hasn't been watered in a month.

The doctors have told her that some of the hair might go thin and wispy in time, like a balding patch on a lawn, depending on to what degree the blood flow recovered, that there could be more surgeries to try to fix that.

She keeps checking it in the mirror every time she's alone, as though she might be able to catch it in real time, her hair dying back. Like she could do anything about it.

The mirror slides lower. The wound flashes there — the mottled line where the stitches run over the angry red gap in her skin — and then she puts the mirror face down on the bed.

She pinches her eyes tightly shut. Breathes. In through her lips, out through her nostrils.

The room has gone quiet. Still. The closed door deadening the light bustle of doctors and nurses out in the hall.

She can't feel her scalp. Not really. Just a tight line where the stitches pull everything taut and gaping numbness above. An impossible sensation. Wrong.

But she's still here. Still alive.

She'd fought him off. She'd clawed and fought and screamed.

And she'd lived.

She smiles a little to herself.

Maybe that's what she'll call the book she's going to write about it all.

The Girl Who Lived.

COME PARTY WITH US

We're loners. Rebels. But much to our surprise, the most kickass part of writing has been connecting with our readers. From time to time, we send out newsletters with giveaways, special offers, and juicy details on new releases.

Sign up for our mailing list at:
http://ltvargus.com/mailing-list

SPREAD THE WORD

Thank you for reading! We'd be very grateful if you could take a few minutes to review it on Amazon.com.

How grateful? Eternally. Even when we are old and dead and have turned into ghosts, we will be thinking fondly of you and your kind words. The most powerful way to bring our books to the attention of other people is through the honest reviews from readers like you.

ABOUT THE AUTHORS

Tim McBain writes because life is short, and he wants to make something awesome before he dies. Additionally, he likes to move it, move it.

You can connect with Tim via email at tim@timmcbain.com.

L.T. Vargus grew up in Hell, Michigan, which is a lot smaller, quieter, and less fiery than one might imagine. When not click-clacking away at the keyboard, she can be found sewing, fantasizing about food, and rotting her brain in front of the TV.

If you want to wax poetic about pizza or cats, you can contact L.T. (the L is for Lex) at ltvargus9@gmail.com or on Twitter @ltvargus.

LTVargus.com

www.ingramcontent.com/pod-product-compliance
Lightning Source LLC
Chambersburg PA
CBHW021958040826
48979CB00045B/2295/J

* 9 7 8 1 9 5 4 2 0 3 0 9 9 *